SNOWFALL IN BURRACOMBE

It's December 1953. As the village prepares for the festivities, for many people a happy Christmas is by no means certain. For Stella Simmons, recovering from a car crash, the winter wedding that she and her sweetheart had planned seems impossible. Elsewhere in the village, Jackie Tozer is dreaming of America and Hilary Napier, who thought the war had robbed her of her chance of happiness, has to ask herself if she could ever imagine leaving her life at the big house for the sake of love and adventure. The darkest time of the year finds everyone asking questions with no easy answer.

SNOWFALL IN BURRACOMBE

SNOWFALL IN BURRACOMBE

by

Lilian Harry

Magna Large Print Books
Long Preston, North Yorkshire,
BD23 4ND, England.

British Library Cataloguing in Publication Data.

Harry, Lilian
    Snowfall in Burracombe.

    A catalogue record of this book is
    available from the British Library

    ISBN   978-0-7505-3739-1

First published in Great Britain in 2012 by Orion Books,
an imprint of The Orion Publishing Group Ltd.

Copyright © Lilian Harry 2012

Cover illustration © Marcus Garrett by arrangement with
Arcangel Images

The moral right of Lilian Harry to be identified as the author of this
work has been asserted in accordance with the Copyright, Designs
and Patents Act, 1988

Published in Large Print 2013 by arrangement with
Orion Publishing Group

Magna Large Print is an imprint of Library Magna Books Ltd.

Printed and bound in Great Britain by
T.J. (International) Ltd., Cornwall, PL28 8RW

For Jackie Beavon,
a friend for nearly thirty years.

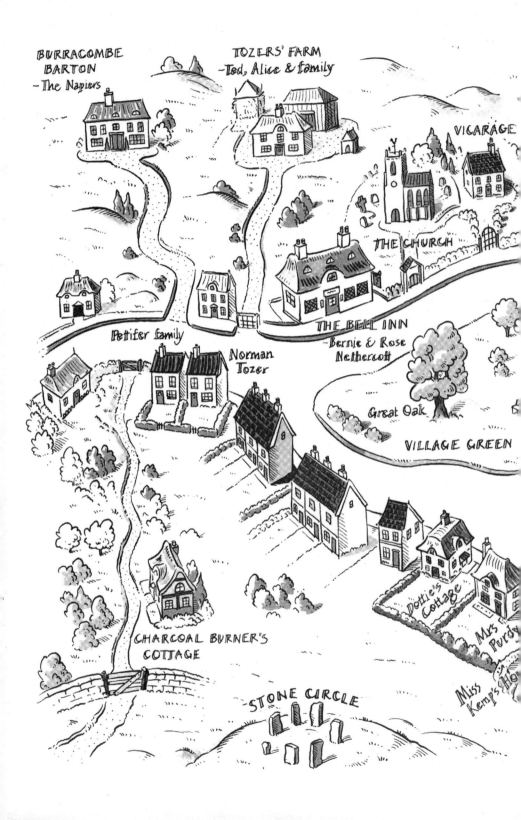

Chapter One

Burracombe, Thursday 3 December 1953

Never, Hilary Napier thought, never in all my life, would I have believed myself capable of this kind of behaviour. A web of deceit, growing more tangled by the minute; that was what it was. If anyone had told her a few weeks ago ... a *month* ago... But she'd learned that you could never be sure how other people would behave in certain situations – look at her brother Stephen, with their sister-in-law Marianne. Unless she had seen the evidence with her own eyes, Hilary would never have believed that the Frenchwoman would seduce him – and in the family home, too!

And now it seemed that you couldn't know much more about yourself. When emotions took you over, really strong, powerful emotions such as those that had so suddenly invaded both her body and her heart, your mind itself and all the beliefs and codes you had grown up with seemed to change. You found yourself doing things you had never dreamed possible. Things like her recent trip to London, for example – and look where that had led. To disaster. Possibly even to tragedy.

The memory of the terrible accident on that December evening was still all too fresh in her mind. Felix Copley, the young vicar of Little Burracombe, over the river, and his fiancée Stella

13

Simmons had gone to Exeter to collect Hilary's half-French nephew Robert after his attempt to run away from school and return to France. It was on their return journey, on an icy, fogbound road on Dartmoor, that Felix's little sports car, Mirabelle, had crashed into a herd of wild ponies, leaving Mirabelle wrecked and Stella so badly injured that they had feared for her life.

Hilary still blamed herself for the accident. If she had not gone to London that weekend to be with David ... if she had been at home to see just how unhappy Rob was, to comfort and help him ... if she had been there when her father had had his second heart attack ... if she had been able to go to Exeter herself...

But *ifs* never achieved anything. All she could do now was deal with the situation as it was. And to do that, she needed all her strength.

I need David, too, she thought with a sudden surge of desperation. I need to hear his voice, even if I can't see him. And he must be wondering what's happening, after he rescued Rob in London and put him on the train home. I have to ring him.

She waited until her father had gone to bed, and then slipped into his study to use the telephone. Her hand was trembling and her heart thumping as she picked up the receiver and asked the operator for the number. As she heard David's deep voice, the thumping stopped and her heart leaped instead.

'David! You're still there. Is it all right to talk?'

'Yes,' he said. 'I've stayed late at the surgery every night, hoping you'd manage to call. Darling,

14

how are you? How's that poor girl? And young Rob?'

'I'm all right – nothing wrong with me, after all.' Nothing that being with you wouldn't cure, she thought longingly. 'And there's been better news about Stella – she's opened her eyes. Felix was with her, and he's sure she knew him.'

'That's a good sign. And Rob?'

'Very quiet, but then he always is. I'm afraid he feels terribly guilty, though nobody could say it was his fault. But Father's agreed that he should go back to France after Christmas and return to his old school. I'm sure it will be better for him. He's too young to be uprooted from everything he knows and thrown into English public school education. His mother and brother and sister are coming over for Christmas, and I think that'll be good for him too. And–'

'But how are *you*, Hilary?' he broke in quietly. 'That's what I really want to know.'

She felt tears sting her eyes. 'I told you – I'm all right.' But her voice cracked a little on the last word and she stopped abruptly. As she took a deep breath, David continued.

'I don't think you are, darling. It sounds to me as if you have all the troubles of the world on your shoulders. I wish there were something I could do to help.'

'Just talking to you helps,' she whispered. 'And I don't really have all the troubles of the world. I'm not the one lying in a hospital bed fighting for my life.'

'Thank God for that,' he said sincerely. 'All the same, you're bearing a lot. And you've got

Christmas to plan as well. Did you say Rob's whole family are coming over?'

'Some of them. His two grandmothers are staying in France and his aunt will stay to look after them. And I'm sure the patisserie will be too busy to spare Marianne for long. I don't suppose they'll be here more than a few days.'

'There'll be a lot for you to do, even so.'

'Mrs Ellis will be here – our housekeeper and cook. We'll share most of it, although of course she does have her own family to think of as well. If only Stephen would come too.'

'Your brother? He's still not agreed, then?'

'No. I really don't think he will. It's – oh, it's all so *complicated.*' Her voice wavered again as she said, 'It's so good to hear you, David.'

'It's good to hear you too. But it's not enough.' His voice deepened again. 'I want to be in the same room with you. I want to be able to *see* you – touch you. Hilary, this being apart isn't good. We're going to have to do something about it.'

Hilary was silent. She was fighting the tears now, longing to be back with him in the hotel room in London, or walking round the Serpentine – anywhere, just as long as they were together. But he was in Derbyshire, and she was here in Devon, and hundreds of miles lay between them.

And not just hundreds of miles. The real distance was far greater than that.

'There's nothing we can do,' she said shakily. 'We shouldn't even be talking like this.'

'We have to talk, Hilary. We have to talk seriously.'

'But there's nothing more to say,' she wailed.

16

'Please, David – there's nothing we can *do*. We ought to stop. Now. This very minute.'

There was a moment of silence. Then he said, very quietly, 'We can't do that. You know we can't.'

Hilary leaned her head against the receiver, feeling hopeless. 'I know.'

'I want to see you again.'

'David...'

'Soon.'

'Not before Christmas,' she whispered. 'It's impossible. You know it is.'

'Afterwards, then. As soon as you've got rid of all your visitors.'

She sighed, longing to say yes. 'I can't make any plans now. Please, David – you know how difficult it is. It must be as bad for you as for me.'

'Not quite as bad,' he said bleakly. 'I don't have a family clamouring around me. Only Sybil, giving parties and dragging me to others, just for the look of it.'

'After Christmas,' she said, with a sudden flash of insight as to how his life must be, with a wife who cared nothing for him but only for her position in the community. David had told her so much about the life they led that Hilary had never once doubted him. 'After Christmas, as soon as we can.'

'But we'll talk again before that,' he said with sudden urgency. 'We must talk. I can't get through without hearing your voice.'

'Whenever we can manage it,' she promised. 'But it won't be easy. I can't always talk privately.'

'Write as well, then. We'll both write.'

'Yes,' she said quietly. 'We'll write.' She heard a

footstep on the stairs and her heart jumped. 'I'll have to go now – Father's coming. Good night.'

'Hilary...' he said, anguished. 'Oh, my darling... Good night. Good night, my sweet.'

'Good night,' she whispered, and then, on no more than a breath, 'Good night ... my love.'

The door opened just as she replaced the receiver. She looked up at her father's face and felt her cheeks flame, but his eyes were searching the room and he didn't seem to notice her expression. He moved about, lifting up papers and replacing them in a fretful fashion.

'Left my reading glasses down here somewhere. Wanted to read for a while. Have you moved them?'

'No,' she said, struggling to regain her composure. 'I don't think they're in here at all, Father. Didn't you have them in the dining room when we were having dinner?'

'Hmm? Oh – well, perhaps I did. I'll go and look. No – you stay there,' as she began to rise to her feet. 'They're probably on the sideboard. What are you doing in here anyway? Working on those papers?' She opened her mouth to reply, but he was halfway out of the door and turned back before she could speak. 'Leave them for now, girl. Let Travis have a look at them in the morning. You've got enough on your plate – don't want you cracking up as well.'

Hilary sat quite still. She watched as he closed the door behind him and listened as he went into the dining room and then came out. He opened the door, said, 'Found them!' and closed it again. She heard him go up the stairs, and once more she leaned her head on her hand and drew in a deep, shuddering breath.

Oh, David, she thought, David. Whatever is going to happen to us?

'And a tree with coloured lights outside,' Rose Nethercott said firmly as she stood on the green outside the Bell Inn, looking up at the sign. 'It's easy enough to run a wire out from one of the sockets, and it'll make the village look a real picture. We want to give poor young Stella Simmons a proper welcome when she comes home from that hospital.'

Her husband, Bernie, and Dottie Friend looked at each other doubtfully. Bernie said, 'I don't know it's as easy as you think, Rose. Electricity can be a bit risky outside. Suppose it gets wet. It's bound to rain sometime over Christmas.'

Dottie's concerns were different. 'I don't know as Stella will be home in time to see it anyway. She only opened her eyes for a minute or two, from what Maddy told me, and the doctors themselves don't know what damage has been done. 'Tis only just over two weeks to Christmas – I can't see her being let out in that time, not the way she's been.'

'Yes, but it's another twelve days after that until the decorations come down,' Rose argued. 'That's near enough a month. Surely to goodness she'll be out in that time. Why, the wedding's fixed for the ninth of January – they won't want to put that off. And I tell you what – we'll keep the tree up till then anyway.'

Dottie pursed her lips. After a moment or two

she said, 'That's asking for bad luck, that is. I don't reckon Stella and Felix need any more of that. They'll be glad enough for her to come home, never mind whether there's Christmas decorations up or not.'

There was a short, awkward silence. Then Bernie cleared his throat and said, 'I'll see if I can get some waterproof lights like they use round the shops in Tavvi. I reckon I could get young Bob Pettifer to run a proper cable out and we'll make a show anyway, for the village. Us might even get Jessie Friend to put some up round the shop. The place needs a bit of cheering up, with all that's been going on.'

'You'm right there,' Dottie agreed soberly. She turned to Rose. 'I didn't mean to say 'twasn't a good idea – just that I didn't reckon young Stella would be out of hospital that quick. But you never know – they can do wonderful things these days in hospitals, and maybe now she've started to take a bit of notice she'll buck up in no time. It might not be anywhere near as bad as it looked at first.'

'That's right,' Rose said, smiling at her. She and Bernie had been worried about their friend and barmaid ever since the village had heard about the accident. Stella had been living at Dottie's cottage since she had first come to Burracombe to teach in the village school, and the two had become more like mother and daughter than landlady and lodger; even more so when it had been discovered that Stella's younger sister, Maddy, had actually been fostered by Dottie during the war. The news that Stella had been badly injured when her fiancé

Felix's car had run into a herd of ponies on the Princetown road had hit Dottie very hard; although, being Dottie, she had responded immediately by sorting out Stella's favourite nightdress to take to the hospital, putting a casserole in the oven to simmer gently until it might be needed, even making sandwiches and baking cakes to sustain Felix and the others while they waited for news. If she had given way at all to her own fear and distress, Rose thought she had probably done it when nobody else could see.

Rose turned to lead the way back inside the inn. She and Bernie had already festooned the ancient beams with paper chains and hung up some glistening gold foil globes and bells that they'd bought in Woolworth's in Tavistock the previous week, and with the big log fire burning in the inglenook, the pub looked cheery and welcoming. A Christmas tree outside would lure people in, Rose thought, and set the tone for the whole festive period.

'Not that Burracombe folk need a Christmas tree to lure them in,' Bernie commented when she told him this. 'The ale does that. But you'm right, my dear, it do look proper seasonal and jolly. The hard part will be getting 'em to leave, I reckon.'

Christmas preparations were going on all over the village. Most people didn't put their own decorations up until the week before Christmas, but there were already a few trees set in front windows, their coloured lights twinkling, and Jean and Jessie Friend had got paper chains all over the ceiling of their shop. George Sweet had several

21

Christmas cakes in his window, mostly iced with snow scenes, and Bert Foster, the butcher, was taking orders for turkeys, which would be supplied by a big turkey farm near Okehampton. Alice Tozer, who kept her own geese, had fattened up quite a few and would soon be busy plucking them ready to be collected or sent out to her customers, and a lot of the village people kept chickens and had already decided which ones would grace their tables on Christmas Day.

In the school, where Stella would have been overseeing the making of Christmas cards and paper chains to hang in the classroom, Miss Kemp had let the children make get-well cards for their young teacher instead. As for the Nativity Play, which Stella had just begun to rehearse with the younger children, the headmistress was in a quandary as to whether it should go ahead. The children looked forward to it so much, but on the other hand, they were all so upset about their teacher that it seemed callous to carry on as if nothing had happened.

'I think we have to do it,' Basil Harvey, the Burracombe vicar, advised when she consulted him. 'It does the children no good to brood about Stella, and when she's feeling better she'll want to know all that they've been doing. How can we tell her we cancelled the Nativity Play?'

'No, of course we can't.' Miss Kemp's eyes met his and she knew that they were both aware that Stella might not get better, although neither would voice the thought. 'I'll call the first rehearsal this afternoon.' She sighed. 'It's just that there's so much to do in these last weeks before

Christmas, and Stella took so much on her own shoulders. It being her last term before getting married, she wanted it to be the best she could make it.'

'You need help,' Basil told her. As a governor of the village school, it was one of his duties to see that the teaching was carried out as it should be, and although it was by no means Miss Kemp's fault, the situation now was far from desirable. 'If only we could get someone in to help you.'

'I don't think there's any chance of that, so near Christmas. I did wonder if there might be a parent or two who could give a hand, but I don't think we've any in the village who have experience of teaching.'

'Are you sure about that? I have a feeling Mrs Warren told me once that she'd trained as a teacher.'

'Mrs Warren?' Miss Kemp echoed. 'Oh, I don't think so! She doesn't seem at all the type.'

'No?' To Basil's mind, although he would not have dreamed of saying so to Miss Kemp, Joyce Warren seemed exactly one type of teacher – organising to the point of being bossy, and certainly not likely to tolerate bad behaviour from the children. Even the Crocker twins might stand in awe of her. 'She has run the village amateur dramatic society quite successfully in the past,' he pointed out. 'If she were just to take over the Nativity Play...'

Miss Kemp thought about it and nodded rather reluctantly, not relishing the dominating presence of the solicitor's wife in her school. 'She did help quite a lot with the excerpt we put on from *A*

Midsummer Night's Dream. But I don't suppose she'd have the time...'

'Why not ask her?' he enquired, and pulled the last rug from under her feet by adding, 'I'll do it on my way home, if you like. You really do need the help, Miss Kemp.'

'Very well,' she agreed with a small sigh, and smiled as she caught the twinkle in his eye. 'You're quite right. I mustn't look a gift horse in the mouth.'

'Not that you don't need other help as well,' he went on firmly, 'and I've another suggestion to make. One that you might find more to your taste. I think you already knew that my wife taught, many years ago.'

'Yes, of course. We've had many a chat about it. But you're not suggesting...'

'I certainly am. In fact, Grace suggested it herself. She's willing to come along for two or three afternoons a week until the end of term. What a good thing we've got Stella's replacement coming in January, when she was going to leave us anyway.' He paused. 'Although I can't really think that she'll be well enough for the wedding. In fact...' He hesitated, and the headmistress put his thought into her own words.

'Someone ought to be thinking about whether to cancel it – or at least postpone it. There's so much already arranged – the guests, the reception in Tavistock, the service itself. But how can we suggest that to poor Felix? How can anyone tell him that Stella may never recover enough to be his wife?'

Chapter Two

Even knowing that one of your dearest friends was lying in a hospital bed hovering between life and death didn't stop Christmas preparations going ahead, Dottie Friend reflected as she slid a tray of mince pies into the oven that afternoon.

It was one of those things that came around with the seasons, and even if you felt no more like doing it than flying to the moon, you still went through the motions – finding the box of decorations, seeing if the fairy lights still worked, getting Jacob Prout to bring along the little tree you always stood in the window, making a cake and pudding and these mince pies. It was as if you were wound up and couldn't stop. And dear knows who's going to eat them, she thought, getting a dishcloth to wipe flour from the pastry board she'd put on the scrubbed wooden table, because I don't suppose Maddy will want them, and even Felix has lost his appetite now – and no wonder, poor young man, sitting hour after hour in that hospital ward beside his sweetheart, and wondering if her life was slipping away before his very eyes.

Dottie put away her tins of flour and sugar, and took the butter back to the outside meat safe in the back porch, where it was kept cool with cheese and meat or fish. There was a shepherd's pie in there, made yesterday but not eaten because nobody had the heart, and she took it back indoors with her. It had better be eaten now, she thought, even if she had to give half to her cat, Alfred. He'd be pleased enough and it would last him two days.

She sat for a few minutes in her rocking chair by the range, holding her hands out absently to the fire and thinking about Stella and the horrific road accident that had landed her in hospital in Plymouth.

It had been no one's fault, by all accounts, and Felix and the young French boy, Robert Aucoin – or Napier, as the Squire would like him to be known – had been scarcely hurt at all. It was Stella who had borne the brunt of it and Dottie, along with a terrified Maddy, had gone to the hospital as soon as they'd heard the news, with Joe Tozer and his son Russ, who had hired a car to go about in while they were over here from America. Hilary Napier had gone too, but as soon as Robert had been discharged, she'd taken him back to the Barton, where, to make matters even worse, the Squire had had another turn with his heart. It seemed as if Fate was determined to throw everything it could find at them, just to see how much they could stand.

Well, if Dottie had learned anything through her life, it was that if you were the right sort of person, you'd stand up to anything at all. She was pretty sure Felix could, although it would hit him very hard if anything worse happened to Stella, and Hilary too was made of tough stuff. But Maddy ... Dottie was not so sure about Maddy. She'd lost so many people in her short life – her parents, her baby brother and, less than a year ago, her own fiancé, Sammy – and she was still only twenty-three years old. She'd just begun, falteringly, to get over that, but if she lost her sister as well, Dottie was afraid she'd collapse completely. She was such a fragile little thing, and she'd tried so hard.

Russell Tozer had taken Maddy to the hospital again an hour or so ago. Dottie doubted they'd be allowed to see Stella, or if they were it would be for only a few minutes, but Maddy was fretful and anxious all the time she wasn't there, and Russ had agreed to take her this morning and again in the evening. Dottie would go this afternoon on the train and stay for about half an hour. It was as much to comfort Felix as to see Stella that they were keeping up this rota. He needed someone with him, and the poor man wasn't going to be able to continue to stay all the time anyway – he had his parishioners in Little Burracombe to think of, over the river, and all the preparations for his first Christmas as vicar. How he would have the heart for it all, Dottie couldn't begin to imagine, but she'd grown very fond of Felix while he'd been curate in Burracombe and begun to court Stella, and she knew that there was a hidden strength beneath his often rather flippant exterior.

And them supposed to be getting married in a month's time! She thought now, opening the oven door. The pies had turned a rich golden brown, and she took them out and set the tray on a folded teacloth on the kitchen table to let them cool a little before she turned them out on to the wire rack. Well, there would be no wedding that soon, that was certain. There was a long way to travel before Stella Simmons would be able to walk down the aisle on Frank Budd's arm, to be given in marriage to Felix Copley.

A knock sounded on the back door, and she turned to see Val Ferris come in, with her baby Christopher in her arms. She smiled at Dottie, but her eyes were red, and Dottie felt her own throat ache at the sight of the young woman's distress. The whole village is at sixes and sevens over this, she thought, and no wonder.

'Sit you down, Val,' she said, clearing one of the kitchen chairs of that day's *Tavistock Gazette*. 'And how be little Christopher, then?' She parted his shawl and looked down at the tiny face. 'My stars, he'm growing into a fine young man.'

Val smiled a little wearily. 'He certainly has a fine pair of lungs. Kept us awake half the night again. Mum thinks it's hunger – she says I ought to start putting him on to a few solids. Three months, or twelve pounds in weight, they say, so I'm going to get him weighed at the chemist's shop in Tavistock and get a packet of Farex.'

'Can't do no harm,' Dottie agreed. 'He'll soon tell you if he don't like it. Mind you, they all spits it out to start with. It's because their tongues don't curl the right way, so I've been told. Got used to sucking, see.'

'I didn't know that. It makes sense, though. But I really came in to see if there was any news of Stella.'

Dottie shook her head. 'None since this morning. I suppose us must consider it good news – at

28

least the poor maid seems to be in her senses. But it's early days to know more. I'm going in myself this afternoon, so when I come back I'll pop in and let you know.' She moved the kettle on the range and fetched the big brown teapot. 'You'll have a cup of tea while you're here, won't you? And one of my mince pies – I've just this minute taken them out of the oven.'

'They look lovely.' Dottie gave her a plate and Val took a pie and bit into it. 'Nobody makes mince pies like you do, Dottie, only don't let Mum hear you say that. It's my first this Christmas.'

'You ought to make a wish, then,' Dottie said, and picked one up for herself. 'I will, too. And I don't reckon it will be hard to guess what either of us wishes for.'

'No,' Val said soberly, 'it won't.'

Their eyes met over the golden crusts, and although for luck neither spoke her wish aloud, each could read it in the other's face. Like the rest of Burracombe that day, they were wishing that Stella Simmons would get well; that she would recover from her injuries and, at some time in the not too distant future, walk up the aisle to marry Felix Copley and live happily ever after.

If only, Val thought sadly as Dottie made the tea and poured it out. If only life could be like that.

'Stephen – *please*,' Hilary Napier said into the phone. '*Please* come home for Christmas. I need you here. We all do.'

She could feel her brother's reluctance over the miles that lay between Burracombe, on the western edge of Dartmoor, and the RAF station

29

in Hampshire where he was doing his National Service. She gripped the receiver a little more tightly and added, aware of the beseeching note in her voice: 'Please don't say no.'

She heard his sigh. 'You know what the problem is, Hil. If Marianne's going to be there...'

'Steve, you can't let that stop you! What happened between you and Marianne – that's in the past. We've got other things to consider now. There's Dad – you *know* he's had another heart attack–'

'I did come to see him,' he cut in quickly.

'For one night, yes.'

'It was all I could get leave for.'

'And we understood that. But he wants you home for longer than one night. He wants you home for Christmas. And so do I.' She took another breath. 'There's Rob, too. He's been through a difficult time. He needs a friend.'

'He'll have his mother. And his brother and sister – what are their names again?'

'Philippe and Ginette. Yes, they'll be here and of course he'll want to spend time with them. But he's feeling very alone just at present, and he feels responsible for the accident. He needs someone like you – one of us – who'll give him some reassurance and not blame him. A *man*.'

'How *is* Stella?' he asked. 'The last time we spoke, you said she'd recovered consciousness.'

'Yes, she came round yesterday, when Felix was with her. But she's not out of the woods yet, not by a long way. She's not talking at all, and she seems to be in a lot of pain when she is awake. Apart from some broken bones – her leg and a

30

couple of ribs, I think – they still don't know how much harm was done.' Hilary thought again of the bitterly cold winter's night when Felix's sports car had run into the group of ponies on the Princetown road. 'They think there may be some damage to her spine – she may be paralysed and never walk again,' she went on a little shakily. 'Poor Felix is distraught. He wants to be with her all the time, but he's still having to cope with all the Christmas preparations in the church at Little Burracombe. He's got people there to help him, of course, and I've been doing as much as I can here, but – oh, Stephen, this is no good. We can't talk properly on the phone. We need you here. *I* need you. Dad needs you. And Rob... He's so upset, and I just haven't got time to give him the attention he needs.'

'What about Travis?' Stephen asked, but she could sense a wavering in his tone. 'He gets on with him, doesn't he? And Jennifer. Didn't you say he's been going to see them at the estate manager's house?'

'Wood Cottage, they're calling it. Yes, and it does him good to go there, but they're not family, are they? And Travis is very busy just now, with the shoot and everything. We just seem to have so much on our plates at the moment.'

'Yes,' he said with a sigh. 'Yes, I can see that.' He paused, and she waited, hardly daring to breathe. 'All right, Hilary, I'll come. I'll keep out of Marianne's way as much as possible, and I'll do whatever I can for Rob, and I'll try not to annoy Dad too much, and I'll bring in holly and fetch whatever you need, and be a willing slave all

31

round.' He paused. 'There's one person you haven't mentioned.'

'Maddy,' Hilary said, nodding although she knew he couldn't see her. 'Well, of course, she's terribly upset. She and Stella were separated for so long, and when she thought Stella might not live, she was just beside herself. But she seems to be coping quite well now, all things considered.' She paused in her own turn, debating whether to tell him more, than decided that it was better for him to know now, before he arrived, and added as casually as possible, 'I think Ted Tozer's nephew, Russell, has been quite a help to her. You know, the American one, who's been staying with the Tozers with his father for the past few weeks.'

'I see,' Stephen said in a flat tone. 'Well, that's all right then, isn't it? That's one person who won't be needing me.'

'Stephen, don't talk like that! You know Maddy will be pleased to see you. She thinks the world of you.'

'Not quite the whole world,' he said drily. 'But let's not go into all that. I'll come home and do whatever I can. I'll do my best to make it a happy Christmas for the whole family – even the French side of it. I can't promise more than that.'

'I'm not asking you to,' she said, smiling. 'Thank you, Stephen. Thank you very, very much.'

She put down the phone and leaned her head against the wall for a moment. Now there would be at least one person she could turn to over what promised to be a very difficult Christmas. One person she could share her thoughts and feelings with.

Not all of them, though. Even her brother – who had his own difficulties to contend with, not least a French sister-in-law who had been determined to seduce him during his summer leave – knew nothing of the most recent development in Hilary's life. And she was still not sure if she would tell him. It was still too new, too unexpected, too overwhelming to share with anyone just yet.

There was nobody she could tell about David.

In the Tozers' farmhouse, Alice was rolling out pastry for her own mince pies while her mother-in-law Minnie sat in her chair by the range, making a few final adjustments to some harmonies for the handbells. She had added two new carols to the repertoire this year and was determined that the notes should chime musically together when the carol singers began their rounds of the village.

''Tis no good you thumping that pastry as if it had done you an injury,' she remarked as Alice turned it over for the third time. 'It won't do Stella no good, and you'll only make it heavy.'

Alice paused and rested her rolling pin on the wooden table, sighing. 'I know, Mother. It's just that when I start thinking about her, lying in that hospital bed ... I'd have thought Russell would be back by now, with some news.'

'He'll be back as soon as he can be. He'd have taken young Maddy back to Dottie's first, and maybe he've stopped for a cup of tea.'

'Coffee, more like,' Alice said. 'You know him

and Joe haven't really got the hang of tea. It comes of them being Americans, though I'd have thought Joe would still have a taste for it, being Burracombe born and bred, even if he did go off and emigrate when he was a young man.'

'Well, whatever he's drinking, I dare say he's stopped at Dottie's for it. She'll be wanting the news, too, after all. Get those pies in the oven and they'll be ready for him to have one as soon as he gets in.'

Alice nodded and began to cut out rounds with a glass tumbler. She put them into the baking tin, filled them with mincemeat she'd made a month earlier, and then cut out smaller lids with an eggcup. She brushed the pies with beaten egg and slid the tray into the oven.

'Talking of cups of tea,' Minnie said, 'I could do with one myself, if you'm not too busy.'

'I was just thinking the same.' Alice moved the kettle over, poured some hot water into the brown teapot and took two cups and saucers down from the dresser while the water came to the boil. She tipped the hot water out of the pot and put in three spoonfuls of tea from the old tin caddy on the shelf before pouring on the boiling water, then turned back to the table. 'Now that I'm doing pastry anyway, I'll make a meat pie for dinner. We'll have it with boiled potatoes and winter greens, and bottled plums for afters. How are those harmonies coming along, Mother?'

'I think they'll do. We'll get Ted to bring the other ringers in for a bit of a practice before they starts out tonight. I've put in "Oh Little Town of Bethlehem" and "In the Bleak Midwinter". They

34

both got nice tunes and the singers have got all the words, so it ought to sound proper handsome.'

Alice nodded and poured two cups of tea, handing one to her mother-in-law before sitting down in the chair opposite her. 'I'll just have five minutes before I start again. Mother, what do you think about Russ and young Maddy? D'you reckon he's a bit sweet on her?'

'I don't doubt it for a minute,' Minnie replied, lifting her cup to her lips. 'And why not? She'm as pretty a maid as you'd find in any long day's march. I'm not so sure what she thinks of him, though. 'Tis still barely a year since her lost her sweetheart.'

'I know. But hearts can mend quick at her age. It would be good to see her settled with a nice young chap. I don't know that Stella would like to see her go off to America, though.' She stopped abruptly as her words reminded them both of the young woman lying so ill in her hospital bed, and after a short silence, she shook her head, put her cup back in its saucer with a small clatter and got quickly to her feet. 'Well, this won't buy the baby a new bonnet! I'd better get on with the dinner if 'tis to be ready when the men come in.'

The men – Ted, his son Tom and brother Joe – all arrived together, in time for dinner, stamping the mud from their boots outside before taking them off and hooking them over the set of short poles that Ted had fixed in the stone porch. They came into the kitchen in their socks, sniffing in appreciation of the smells of meat, pastry and vegetables that drifted from the range, and had barely closed the door when it opened again and Russell entered. All eyes turned to him at once and he began to tell them the news even before he had his coat off.

'Well, she's opened her eyes again and Felix is certain she knows him. She hasn't been able to say anything yet – just a few whispered words, but nobody can make out what they are. She's very drowsy, but I think that's partly to do with the medication they're giving her. Apparently they're going to try giving her a bit less, so that she can think and talk a bit, but they're not sure how much pain she'll be in if they do... It's a bad situation, I'm afraid. She's still in a very critical condition.'

'The poor maid,' Minnie said softly, and Alice asked, 'What about Maddy? How's she bearing up?'

Russ shook his head. 'She hardly knows what to do with herself. She wanted to stay there but I persuaded her to come home, for a while at least. They won't let anyone stay by the bed for very long at a time, and Felix can't bear to leave. I said I'd take Maddy back this evening, when she's had a decent meal and some rest, and I'll bring Felix back then. He's worrying about his parish as well – it's his first Christmas there, isn't it?'

Alice nodded. 'He've got all sorts of things to do over there. But he's got a good churchwarden and there's plenty of folk ready to help, in both villages. Times like this, us all pulls together.' She handed him a steaming cup of tea. 'You drink that down – you need something hot inside you.

But if you bring him back tonight, Russ, who'll fetch Maddy home? She can't stop in the hospital all night.'

'Oh, I'll go back.' He wrapped his hands around the cup and took a sip. 'Oh my, that's good. I'm beginning to see why you English all like tea so much.'

'Go back? But you'll have driven to Plymouth and back three times by then! Our Tom'll go – won't you, Tom?'

Tom opened his mouth but Russ shook his head firmly. 'No, Aunt Alice, I'll go. It's the least I can do – I'm not much use otherwise. And I think Maddy's getting used to me. We're kind of sharing what's been happening, if you understand me.'

Alice took a look at his face and thought she understood very well. She said no more, but turned to the range and began to transfer large dishes of food to the table. Joanna and Robin came downstairs then, and the family gathered round and began to eat. At least their appetites weren't affected, Alice thought, and hoped that Dottie was managing to coax Maddy into eating an equally good meal.

Chapter Three

'Come on now, my pretty,' Dottie urged. 'It'll just slip down, and it'll do you good. Little and often, that's what you want to eat at times like this. You got to keep up your strength if you're going to go back to the hospital later on. 'Twon't do no one any good if you make yourself ill as well.'

'I know.' Maddy leaned her elbow on the table and rested her head on her hand, staring at the scrambled eggs on toast that Dottie had placed before her. She picked up her fork and moved it about uninterestedly in the pile of golden fluff before taking some in her mouth. 'I just don't seem able to swallow it.'

'Try again, lovey. Just a little bit at a time. One bite'll give you strength to take another, and before you know it, you'll have eaten it all.' Dottie watched anxiously as Maddy heaved a sigh and took her second mouthful. 'And just another one, for luck.'

'It doesn't taste of anything,' Maddy said drearily, swallowing with obvious difficulty. 'I'm sorry, Dottie. I think I've cried so much my throat's all swollen up. I'll have one more – will that do?'

'It's better than nothing.' Dottie took away the plate and produced a glass dish, one of her best, with fluted edges. 'I'm sure you can manage a nice junket, though. That hardly needs any swal-

38

lowing at all.'

Maddy smiled faintly but she did manage the whole dish, and Dottie gave a little nod of satisfaction.

'That was good fresh milk, with plenty of cream in it – it'll do you good. And I'll make you something else in a little while. You've got to keep your strength up for visiting your poor dear sister, you know.'

'I know. Thank you, Dottie.' Maddy rested her head on her hand again. 'I feel so worn out – I think I'll go and lie down for a while.'

'That's right, my bird, you try to get some sleep. When's young Russell coming to collect you again?'

'About six, I think. Visiting hours are between seven and eight, and I want to see Felix again, of course. Russell's going to bring him back while I'm with Stella. But when he collects me as well, it means nobody will be with her all night. I'm not sure I can leave her.'

'The nurses will look after her,' Dottie began, but Maddy shook her head.

'It's not the same. Suppose she wakes up and wants one of us? She'll feel so alone.' Her eyes filled with tears again, and Dottie made up her mind.

'I'll go for the night. Russell can take me in when he goes to fetch you, and I'll stop in the waiting room all night if I have to. Then if the poor maid wakes up, I'll be at hand.'

'Dottie, you can't! There's nowhere to sleep. You'll be so uncomfortable.'

'I'll take a couple of blankets and a pillow.

There's chairs there, I can make up a sort of a bed. I'll take a Thermos of cocoa as well, and a bite to eat. I'll be as right as rain. You'm right, Maddy, one of us has got to be there, and you and Felix both need a night's rest. Now, you go up and have a lay-down now, and I'll run over to the pub and tell Bernie and Rose. They won't mind, I know. They can get young Sally in to help at the bar.' She took off her apron with an air of determination, and Maddy hesitated for a moment, then gave her a wavering smile and turned to go up the narrow staircase.

Dottie watched her go and sighed. Yet despite her unhappiness, Maddy was bearing up better than Dottie could have hoped. Fragile as she was, she was keeping herself going by thinking of others before herself, and that was an encouraging sign. It wasn't so long ago that she was acting like a spoilt child over the news that Ruth Hodges was having a baby. She'd come on a lot since then.

As Dottie started to wash up the tea things, her thoughts turned to Ruth and Dan Hodges in Bridge End, near Southampton, and to the Budd family in April Grove, Portsmouth. They'd have to be told about Stella. Maureen Budd was set to be a bridesmaid in only a few weeks' time, and there were all the other wedding guests to be notified as well, if the wedding were to be postponed, as Dottie felt sure it must. But nothing of that sort could be dealt with until Felix was back and able to make decisions, and he wasn't likely to do that until he was absolutely sure that Stella was going to recover.

Poor young man, she thought. All this, and his

40

first Christmas as vicar of Little Burracombe too. And him and Stella both so happy. It wasn't fair. It just wasn't fair.

'Stephen's said he'll come home for Christmas,' Hilary told her father as they finished their evening meal. Dr Latimer had said he could come downstairs, but was not to do anything at all active. Gilbert had growled at that and said sarcastically that he supposed it would be all right to sit at a table to eat, like a Christian, and Charles had laughed and said yes, as long as he didn't load his fork too heavily.

'Was there ever any doubt of it?' Gilbert enquired, and she remembered that she hadn't discussed her worries with him. Neither had either she or Stephen ever given any hint about what had happened with Marianne in the summer. She let it pass and, instead, began to talk about the arrangements for Christmas.

'We can put Marianne off if you're not feeling up to a houseful,' she suggested, thinking longingly of a quiet family Christmas with just the three of them. 'Rob could go back to France, as we've arranged, and–'

'Put her off! Of course we won't,' he snorted. 'Been looking forward to it – show them what a proper English Christmas is like. Rob needs to be here, too. Give him a bit of fun after the past few weeks.'

Hilary looked at him thoughtfully. Until a few days ago, he'd refused to accept that his French grandson could be anything but happy at the nearby public school he'd been sent to. Robert's desperate escapade in running away, causing Felix and Stella to go to Exeter to bring him home and leading directly to the accident on the moor and Stella's injuries, seemed to have changed his view. Possibly, in his heart of hearts, he even blamed himself, although that would be unlike him. But it certainly sounded as though he wanted to make up to Rob now for what had happened to him.

Probably, she thought wryly, it was the only good thing to have come out of the whole sorry affair.

Her thoughts turned to David, who had come to their rescue by meeting Rob as he got off the train at Paddington and returning him to Devon. Sooner or later, questions would be asked about this friend of Hilary, of whom nobody had ever heard before but who was apparently the kind of friend who could be turned to in an emergency. Gilbert was bound to ask, and Stephen would be full of brotherly curiosity. She sighed, knowing that the relationship that had begun so recently was likely to be subjected to unwelcome scrutiny, and wondering just where it would lead. I didn't want them to know, she thought, and I certainly didn't want them to know yet.

'This friend of yours in London,' Gilbert said, breaking into her thoughts as though he had been reading them. 'You were going to give me his address. Ought to thank him myself. Heaven knows what would have happened to young Rob if he hadn't been on hand to scoop him up and put him back on the train.' He paused to eat his last mouthful. 'How d'you come to know him, anyway? Thought it was just women friends you

42

went up to London to see.'

Hilary felt her heart sink. She had known from the start that she would find herself telling lies to her father, and she had still not found a way to do it without feeling she was betraying all his ideas of family and what it stood for. Truth, integrity, honest dealings with each other – that was what had always been drummed into both herself and Stephen. Baden too, of course – the eldest son, of whom so much had been expected before he was killed at Dunkirk. They were the foundation of what Napiers stood for.

'There were men as well as women at the reunion,' she said carefully. 'I knew David when we were in Egypt.'

'But the last time you went wasn't the reunion,' he objected. 'That was back in November. What was he doing there this time? Husband of one of your friends, I suppose.'

She considered saying yes, if only to stave off the conversation until another, less fraught time, but dismissed the idea. Leave the lies until there was no alternative, she thought, and then she would probably tell the truth anyway.

'No, he's not a husband – not of one of my friends, anyway. I don't know his wife. They live in Derbyshire. But it doesn't matter now, surely. The important thing is that he helped us.'

'And I want to thank him. Myself.' Gilbert narrowed his eyes. 'There's no reason why I shouldn't, is there?'

'No, Father, no reason at all. I'll give you his address.' And with any luck, David's wife will never see the letter, she thought with a sense of doom. 'I'm sure he doesn't want thanks, but of course you want to do it. I'll get it for you now.'

She escaped from the room, feeling that it was only a temporary respite, and went upstairs. Sometimes she wondered if it had been a good thing that she'd gone to London only a few weeks before, to attend the reunion of the women and men she'd met in Egypt during the war. She had been an ATS driver and it was there that she had met David, a doctor who had been called up at the beginning of the war. The affair they'd been swept into, dazzled by the hot nights, the brilliance of the stars and the sense of being so far away from everything that was familiar, had come to an end when both acknowledged their existing loyalties, Hilary's to her fiancé Henry and David's to Sybil. They had parted with both reluctance and relief, and never contacted each other again. It wasn't until they had met again in London that their old feelings had surged to the surface, and this time, like a dormant volcano suddenly woken into life, they would not be suppressed.

Henry had been killed soon after their parting, but David had gone home to marry Sybil. It was not a happy marriage, he told Hilary, and Sybil had begun to take lovers long ago. All the same, his position as a doctor made it impossible for him to divorce her without her consent. She would fight him all the way, and leave him with neither home nor livelihood. And it would be all the worse if she found out about Hilary.

I never meant it to go this far, she thought, writing his address down on a slip of paper. I should have refused to spend the day with him, that very first time. I should have refused to go back to his hotel. I should definitely have refused to go to London the second time, pretending I was meeting some of my old friends, simply to be with him. But I just didn't have the strength. I wanted so much to be with him. I still do...

And if I hadn't, where would Rob be now? Back in France with his mother? And in that case, wouldn't Stella still be fit and well and looking forward to her wedding?

How could you ever know where your actions might lead?

She snatched up the scrap of paper and ran downstairs to give it to her father. Whatever was going to happen next, it was out of her hands. She might as well just give up trying to control events and wait for the next disaster to come upon her, as, in her present gloomy mood, she felt sure it would.

In the schoolhouse, Miss Kemp was thinking over the changes she was having to make with Stella in hospital. She had already held a short meeting earlier that day with her two new assistants. Joyce Warren had fallen with glee upon the task of producing the Nativity Play and had already mapped out several ideas, while Grace Harvey had promised to take the infants' class on three afternoons. The rest of the time, the partition between the two rooms would be folded back and they would have to join Miss Kemp's class of older children.

'They can get on with drawing and threading

beads and that sort of thing, and some of the lessons – the Bible stories and so on – will be suitable for the whole school. But if you can keep their reading and writing and sums going, Mrs Harvey, it will be a tremendous help.'

'And I can rehearse them on the other two afternoons,' Joyce Warren said eagerly. 'There are several nice little carols and songs they could learn as well, if we could have the piano in there.'

'I didn't realise you could play, Mrs Warren,' Miss Kemp said in surprise.

'Oh, yes. I learned as a child – we all did, at my school. Either that or the flute or violin. I can play simple tunes on all of them, but the piano was my *forte* – if you'll forgive the pun,' she added with a roguish smile.

'Well, that would certainly be helpful. Perhaps you could play for the school carol service as well. Stella was going to do that. And there's the Christmas party – musical chairs and so on.' Miss Kemp became aware that she was piling more tasks on willing shoulders than perhaps she should. 'But only if you have time,' she added hastily.

'Oh, I'll squeeze it in, never fear,' Mrs Warren said robustly. 'We must all pull together at times like this. So sad for the poor vicar.'

The other two gazed at her for a moment before realising that she was referring to Felix, until recently Basil Harvey's curate. The thought reminded Miss Kemp of another question, and she asked Grace if there were any chance of another curate being appointed.

'Goodness knows. Basil's hoping for one soon, but there seems to be a shortage at the moment.

46

It's such a pity, because if we'd had one, we could have sent him over to Little Burracombe to help poor Felix out. Basil will do the best he can, of course, but with Christmas coming... There's always so much for him to do, with extra services and so on, not to mention all the Christmas parties he's expected to attend.'

'I would have thought in the circumstances he might be let off some of them,' Joyce Warren remarked. 'The Mothers' Union and Women's Institute get along very well without him for the rest of the year, after all.'

Feeling that this was a little tactless, Miss Kemp said hurriedly, 'Well, I'm certainly very glad of both your help here. I'll only need to have the babies in with my class for the mornings. And you can have the older children for the Nativity Play rehearsals as well, of course. Stella and I had already decided who would play the main parts. The little ones are usually angels or sheep.'

'Tomorrow's Tuesday, so I'll start then,' Joyce promised. 'I've got a nice little play that I wrote myself a few years ago – we can use that.'

Miss Kemp opened her mouth to say that they already had a script for a Nativity Play, which they had used for years, but she thought better of it. After all, Mrs Warren was well aware of the nativity story – it couldn't be so very different – and she had helped with the production of the excerpt from *A Midsummer Night's Dream* and even put on pantomimes in the past, before Felix had taken over.

'I'll start this afternoon, then,' Grace Harvey said. 'You'd better let me know what you want

47

me to do.'

Relieved to have at least one assistant prepared to take direction, Miss Kemp led them both into the infants' classroom. There were a dozen children in this class, between the ages of five and seven, and they sat around small wooden tables, much stained with the painting efforts of infants long grown up, and threaded beads or painted wobbly houses, invariably foursquare and with chimneys in the centre of the roof – even though there were no such houses in the village. With tongues sticking out from the corners of their mouths, they learned to write their names and words such as 'cat', 'mat' or 'dog', and, before progressing to the other side of the partition to join Miss Kemp's class, to read quite creditably from their reading books.

Grace stood by the blackboard and surveyed the room. Christmas preparations had already begun, with a pile of freshly made paper chains in one corner and a large calendar on the wall ticking off the days of Advent. Some of the children had drawn Christmas pictures, but these had been abandoned halfway through so that they could make get-well cards for Stella, which Miss Kemp had collected up to give to Felix next time she saw him. All the children had been distressed to learn of the accident and she had been besieged each morning for news.

'It will be good to have someone new to distract them,' she said to Grace and Mrs Warren. 'I don't want them harping on the accident. And they still need to have their Christmas – neither Felix nor Stella would want that spoiled.'

'I'll be here tomorrow, promptly at two,' Joyce said briskly. 'I'll bring my script and some ideas for costumes, and the words of some nice easy carols. You need have no fear, Miss Kemp – the Nativity Play is safe hands.'

Russell Tozer arrived at six o'clock as promised, to take Maddy back to the hospital. They set off in the car he and his father had hired and drove across the moor to Plymouth. People were already putting lighted Christmas trees in their front windows, and there was even one at the entrance to the hospital. A little group of people were singing carols around it as Russ and Maddy went in, and Russ dropped a few coins in their tin. They were collecting for presents for the local Children's Home.

'Stella and I were taken to two different Children's Homes after our father died,' Maddy said listlessly as they trudged through the corridors towards Stella's ward. 'She stayed at hers until she was eighteen and went to college, but I was adopted by Fenella and lived with Dottie. We never knew why they separated us and wouldn't even let us know each other's addresses. They thought it was better for us, but how could it be? It was cruel.' Her voice shook. 'I thought I'd lost her for ever. And now...'

'But you hadn't lost her – and you're not going to lose her now,' Russ said quietly, gripping her arm. 'She's regained consciousness, and that's a wonderful sign. She'll get over this, Maddy – it might not be quick, nobody can promise that – but I'm sure as I'm standing here with you now

49

that she'll get over it.'

Maddy stopped and turned to face him. They looked into each other's eyes for a moment and then she drew in a deep, shaky breath and nodded.

'I'm praying all the time, inside, that she will. But – oh, Russ, I'm so *frightened...*'

Her voice broke and he caught her in his arms and held her close, one hand stroking her back gently as she sobbed against his coat. He laid his cheek against her hair and closed his eyes for a moment; then, when he felt her take in another long, shuddering breath and draw away, he loosened his hold so that she could step back. He looked down into her tear-stained face and said, 'Come on, sweetheart. Let's go and see her now. You can sit with her while I take Felix home and bring Dottie back for the night. Between us, we'll get your sister through this – you'll see.'

She nodded and tried a wavering smile, and they walked on together along the corridor, with Russell still holding her hand firmly in his.

Felix was sitting outside the ward door when they arrived. He looked up and gave them a wan smile, moving up along the wooden bench so that they could sit down. Maddy took her seat beside him and clasped his hands in hers.

'Felix, you look so tired. How is she?'

'I don't know. They're all round her now – doctors, nurses, specialists...' He leaned his head back and closed his eyes. 'She's woken up again a couple of times... She knew me, Maddy... She tried to smile. The doctor said it was an excellent sign, but ... she looks so white and so *tiny* in that bed... I can't leave her...'

'Felix, you have to. You can't stay here all the time. You must go home and get some rest and some proper food.' She was repeating all the things that Dottie had said to her. 'It's no good making yourself ill as well.' She gazed anxiously at his pale face and glanced round at Russell. 'Look, Russ is here, he'll take you home and I'll wait till he comes back with Dottie. She's going to stay the night. Stella will still have one of us nearby. We won't leave her alone. And you can come back tomorrow.'

'Tomorrow?' he said listlessly. 'I can't look as far ahead as tomorrow.'

Maddy and Russ exchanged glances.

'He needs to get out of here for a while,' Russ muttered. 'He'll crack up if he stays here, thinking of nothing but what's going on behind that door.'

'I know.' Maddy turned back to Felix. 'Felix, you have to go back to Burracombe. There are people who want to help you there. You have to be strong, for Stella. Please.'

There was a long silence. Then Felix nodded, slowly, and began to rise to his feet. At the same moment, the door opened and they all turned to face the doctor who was coming out.

He looked almost as tired as Felix, Maddy thought. She rose and took a quick step forward and he answered the question in her eyes.

'She's sleeping now. I hope she'll sleep for a good many hours. Mr Copley, I really think you should go home and get some rest yourself.'

'That's just what we've been telling him,' Maddy said. 'But we don't want to leave her without anyone at hand, just in case she wakes up. I'm staying for an hour or so while my friend takes Felix home, and then he's going to bring Miss Friend – our landlady – back to stay the night. Stella's very fond of her.'

'She won't be very comfortable,' the doctor warned dubiously. 'There's nowhere but this bench here to sit. And the staff don't really like–'

'Dottie knows that. She's going to bring some blankets and cushions,' Maddy said firmly. 'We want Stella to know there's always someone here for her.'

'Can I go and say good night?' Felix asked. 'I won't wake her. I just want... I just want one more minute with her.'

The doctor nodded, and Felix went quietly through the door. In a moment, he came out, with tears on his cheeks but otherwise calm. He nodded to Russell, and the two men turned away, while Maddy settled herself on the bench.

'I'll be back in an hour or so,' Russell said quietly, and touched her shoulder.

'Take as long as you like,' Maddy answered, and covered his hand with her own. 'I don't mind how long I stay here, to be near Stella.'

Their eyes met in a long look, and then he took his hand away and walked down the corridor after Felix.

Maddy watched him go, and then put her hand on her shoulder again, as if to retain the warmth he had left there; just as she felt she could retain the warmth that had stolen into her heart.

Chapter Four

Bernie and Rose had finished decorating inside the pub and were turning their attention to the tree outside. Tom Tozer had brought them a good tall one and helped Bernie fix it into a half-barrel, and it stood to one side of the door. Bob Pettifer, who had just finished his electrician's apprenticeship in Tavistock, was unravelling several coils of large coloured bulbs on a cable.

'You sure that'll be safe, out of doors?' Bernie asked, eyeing it doubtfully. 'I don't want nobody electrified on my account.'

'It'll be as safe as houses,' Bob assured him. He was a tall, spindly young man, just turned twenty-one, with curly ginger hair and a long, rather lugubrious face covered with a mass of freckles. 'I reckon it'll look proper handsome when 'tis lit.'

'Well, that's what my missus and Dottie Friend wants. Cheer up the village, that's what they say, and we're hoping young Miss Simmons'll be home from the hospital in time to see it. Course, you won't know her all that well, being as how you left school years ago now.'

'I was in that pantomime we did – *Robin Hood*. I was a Merry Man.'

Bernie looked at his long face and grinned. 'And a merrier-looking man I never saw in all my born days. All right, Bob, you get on with what you'm doing, and if you make a good job of it there'll be a pint on the house for you after you've done.'

Bob continued to unravel his cables and then climbed the tall stepladder to wind them around the branches of the tree. Half the village seemed to come by as he was working, and everyone had something to say about it.

'You going to be the fairy, then, Bob?' one wit enquired, seeing him perched at the very top.

'More like a hobgoblin,' someone else suggested, and there was a general laugh. Bob was not the best-looking boy in the village, and nobody ever thought it necessary to hide the fact. He was used to such taunts, however, and twisted his rubbery features into a ferocious grimace.

'You wait until the next time your electrics go wrong. Be laughing on the other side of your faces then, you'll be.'

'Looks like you are already,' one of his old schoolmates called out. 'I dunno what you were doing when the wind changed, Bob, but whatever it was, you shouldn't have been!'

'Very funny, I don't think.' Bob climbed carefully down a rung or two. 'Here, you might as well make yourself useful instead of just standing around – hold this and walk round the tree with it.'

'Wouldn't it have been a better idea to start at the bottom?' his tormentor asked, doing as he was told and getting tangled with several spiky branches.

'I had to make sure the lights would reach the top, didn't I? No good running out halfway up.'

'So how d'you know they'll reach the bottom, then? You going to stand there all over Christmas, holding two bits of wire together to keep 'em going?'

Bob gave him a look and came down two more rungs, arranging the bulbs more artistically as he did so. His helper handed him the cable and together they wove it in and out of the branches until they ran out of bulbs close to the lowest branches. Bob fastened the cable to the trunk and stood back to appraise his work.

'I reckon that'll look a treat when 'tis all lit up. Just got to run the wire indoors and make sure 'tis all waterproof and we can switch it on. Thanks, Reg. Bernie says he'll let me have a pint on the house tonight – you can share it if you like.'

'You mean you'll give me half?' Reg asked, following him through the door.

'No – you can watch while I drink it.'

Rose came to the door to view their work and nodded with satisfaction. 'Just what we wanted. Dottie'll be pleased, too. We'll have the switch-on when her comes in. Might ginger up a few of the folk that lives round the green to put their lights up as well.'

'My mum says it's a bit early for Christmas,' Bob remarked, kneeling to work on the socket. 'She never puts our decorations up till the week before. Says they gets all dusty if you puts 'em up too soon.'

'Wouldn't hardly be worth doing it just for the last few days,' Rose said. 'Not in a pub. Anyway, it gets customers into the Christmas spirit.'

'Talking of Christmas spirit...' Reg said encouragingly, and she shook her head at him.

'You can forget that, Reggie Dodd. I promised Bob a pint for his work, but it don't seem to me you done much. Just walked round the tree a time or two, holding a bit of wire, that's all you done.'

'There's no gratitude in this world,' the young man said mournfully. 'Well, I'll hang on for a bit anyway, just in case you has second thoughts. Anyway, does anyone know how the schoolteacher is? Last I heard, her was in a coma and not likely to ever come round.'

'You'm behind the times, then,' Rose said. 'Latest news is she opened her eyes and spoke to young Mr Copley. There's a long way to go before her's up on her feet, but we all got to send her our hopes and prayers. Mr Harvey's saying some for her in church on Sunday, special.'

'Reckon that do any good, then?' Reg asked sceptically.

'Of course it do! It's been proved time and time again. Look at the time my old Auntie Maisie had that stroke. Doctor'd just about given her up, he had, but we all said prayers for her in church and three months later her was up on her feet as good as new. And what about when old Miss Bellamy fell out of her apple tree backalong and hurt her ankle? Could have been crippled for life, but us all said our prayers and her's as spry as ever now. It just goes to show.'

She went back to the bar and the two boys winked at each other.

'So what do you reckon it goes to show, then, Bob? Shall us go to church on Sunday and say prayers for Miss Simmons?'

56

Bob finished what he was doing and got to his feet, almost bumping his head on a low beam. He stood for a minute or so gazing reflectively down at the socket he had just attached, and then said in his slow, thoughtful way, 'Reckon us might as well, Reg. It won't do no harm and it might do a bit of good. Miss Simmons is a real nice young lady, and I don't like to think of her laying there in that old hospital bed, not able to move or speak, and maybe stopping like it for the rest of her life. Reckon whatever us can do, us should, even if it do give Mr Harvey a bit of a fright to see us walking into his church.'

'It'll give him a fright to see *you* walking in, that's for sure,' Reg said with a grin. 'He'll think one of they old gargoyles has fallen off the roof and come to get him!'

Dottie arrived at the inn just after twelve and paused to admire the tree. Bob and Reg were inside by then, enjoying the pints that Rose had pulled for them, and the three of them looked round as the little woman bustled in.

'What do you think of our handiwork, then?' Bob enquired. 'Pass muster, do it?'

'It's proper handsome, and it'll look lovely when 'tis all lit up.' Dottie went behind the bar, took off her coat and tied a white apron around her plump body. 'You done a good job there, boys.'

'See?' Reg said to the landlady. 'I told you I deserved a pint as well.'

'And you got one,' Rose said smartly. 'Much against my better judgement, I may say.' She turned to Dottie. 'I didn't expect you in here now, after you've been all night at the hospital. You ought to be at home getting a bit of rest.'

'I couldn't settle down, somehow. I dropped off in the chair for an hour or two but I reckon I'm better up and about, doing something.' She rubbed her face wearily. Her normally rosy cheeks were pale and her eyes heavy. 'Maybe I'll get a bit of a nap this afternoon.'

'How is the poor maid, anyway?' Rose asked. 'We keep hearing rumours but I reckon you'll know better than anybody.'

'Well, much the same, as far as I can tell. She opened her eyes once or twice and said a few words to Felix, but then the doctors said she was better off asleep and I think they give her something. Not that she needed it, to my mind, but apparently it's a different sort of sleep to just being unconscious. They told me there wasn't no need for me to stop there all night, but I'd said I would and it didn't seem right for nobody to be there. I managed a bit of sleep and then I come back to Burracombe when young Russell Tozer brought Maddy in this morning. He's been a tower of strength, that boy,' she added. 'And so's Joe. I don't rightly know how us would have managed without those two.'

'Reckon he've got an eye for that maid,' Bob observed, wiping froth from his lips. 'Mind you, I don't blame him – turned out a real stunner, her has. Funny to think us used to play conkers with her down the lane, when us was all tackers together, innit, Reg?'

'Right sparky little thing she was,' his friend

agreed, draining his glass. 'Remember when her got stuck up that old oak tree, going after some kitten? Old Mr Prout had to get his longest ladder out to bring her down. Always in some scrape or other in those days, she were.'

Bob nodded. 'And since then her's had no end of trouble. First losing her chap and now her sister's laying at death's door. It don't hardly seem fair, do it?'

They put their glasses on the bar, thanked Rose again and departed. The two women looked at each other.

'What do you reckon really?' Rose asked quietly. 'Is she going to get over it? It'll be a tragedy if she don't, and just before Christmas as well.'

'I don't think anyone knows yet,' Dottie replied. 'It's a good sign that she's come round, and Felix is sure as sure that she knew him, but they don't want her stopping awake too long just yet. Proper sleep's healing. I feel so sorry for that poor young man,' she added fervently. 'He'm at his wits' end, and got so much to do in the parish as well. But for all his daft ways, he've got a lot of strength, and a lot of good friends to rally round him. Us'll all do our best for them both, that's for sure.'

The door opened and a crowd of farm labourers entered, stamping the mud off their boots as they came in. Rose and Dottie moved to their positions behind the bar and stood waiting for a flurry of orders.

Russell made yet another journey to the hospital in Plymouth that afternoon, to take Felix in and bring Maddy home. As he settled her in the front seat and tucked a rug around her, she gave him a wavering smile and said, 'You've been so good to us, Russ, both you and your father. It's not been much of a holiday for you, has it – all this running backwards and forwards to the hospital.'

'We had a pretty good time before the accident happened,' he said, getting into his own seat. 'And we're not here just for a holiday – Dad wanted to be part of his old home again, and he wanted me to be part of it too. I reckon that includes helping out wherever we can.'

'Well, you've certainly been a help to us these past few days,' she said, leaning back and closing her eyes. 'Oh, I feel so *tired,* and yet I've hardly done a thing.'

'I guess you do,' he said, steering the car through the traffic. 'Just worrying about someone you love can be pretty exhausting, and I bet you didn't get much sleep last night. You need to take care of yourself, Maddy.'

'Dottie says that too, but I don't notice her doing the same thing. I think we all feel that we've just got to be strong enough to manage, while Stella's so ill.'

'You still need to take care,' he repeated. 'And you know, if she really is improving, the doctors won't want you waiting there so much. It's their job to look after her and yours to look after yourselves. Life has to go on, Maddy.'

Maddy didn't reply, and he glanced at her and saw that her eyes were still closed. He wasn't sure if she'd heard his last words or not and wondered if she had been annoyed by them. Perhaps it was a little too soon for such a reminder.

He thought of the night when he had fetched her from Exeter – it seemed as if a lifetime had passed. He had been by her side when she had first arrived at the hospital, as they sat waiting through that long night, as he took her home afterwards and brought her back. Even in the midst of such dread, he had been aware of her reaching out for reassurance and consolation, and had been ready to give it. He believed he had managed, somehow, to give her what small comfort she could accept, and he wanted with all his heart to give her more. All that she wanted and needed. Always.

This is my woman, he realised suddenly. My girl. This is the one I want to spend my life with. And I believe she'll feel the same, when all this is over. One of these days, she'll look at me, and she'll know – we'll both know.

But when would it be over, enough for Maddy to look outside of herself and recognise him for her man? How much time would it take?

In less than a month, he and his father would be setting sail to go back to America. A lot could happen in that time – Christmas, the New Year and, it had been planned, the wedding of Stella and Felix. In normal circumstances, that would be more than enough to set the wheels of romance turning. But now?

He shook his head slightly, and sighed as he concentrated on his driving.

Chapter Five

In the village school, now their cards for Stella were complete, the children were working on Christmas cards to give to their families. Their desks were strewn with sheets of thin coloured card, paintboxes and scissors, and the atmosphere was one of dedicated industry.

'What are you getting for Christmas, Shirley?' Jenny Coker enquired that morning as she was drawing a church, which she intended to paint before cutting it out and sticking it on a red card. She contemplated it proudly. 'I'm getting a new scooter, and my brother Micky's having a bike.'

'I don't know. We never knows until it's Christmas Day.' It wouldn't be a bike or a scooter, Shirley knew that. Her father's intermittent earnings never ran to such luxuries, especially with six children in the family. 'Our Joe wants toy soldiers and a Rupert book.'

'Do he still believe in Father Christmas?' Jenny asked. At nine, she and Shirley had reluctantly given up their belief a year or two earlier, but Joe Culliford was only six.

'Yes. We'm not telling him yet. It's better he should think of it for himself,' Shirley replied, sounding like a wise old woman. 'We're all going to hang up our stockings, same as usual. You're never going to get that weathercock to cut out proper, Jenny. The pole's too thin.'

Jenny had suspected the same but was stung by the criticism. 'Bet I can, then. Anyway, what's yours meant to be? Looks like a weathercock that's fell off the church.'

'It's a robin,' Shirley said indignantly. 'Anyone can see that. Look at its red breast.'

'My mum says it's rude to say "breast".'

'Not when it's a robin. It just means "front" then. Anyway, it's not as rude as "tit", and you said that this morning when we were doing the bird table.' Shirley dipped her brush into the fish-paste pot of water they were sharing and rubbed it fiercely on the square of red paint in the box. The square was almost completely worn away, leaving only two corners of colour left. 'You've used up nearly all the red on your old weather-cock. And nobody's going to see it, anyway, on that red card.'

'I never! It was half gone when us started. And you've got to have red on a weathercock.' Jenny wiped her brush and began to cut round the church with a pair of scissors. She cut out tiny windows, which would look lit with red when placed against the card, and then came to the tower. Shirley watched critically.

'There!' Jenny said triumphantly as her scissors followed the narrow line and came to the weathercock. 'See, I said it would be all right – *ow!*'

She turned indignantly as Billy Lillicrap, sitting just behind her, gave a sudden lurch and jogged her elbow. The scissors sliced across the church, taking half the tower and the weathercock with them, and the jar of water was knocked over,

63

sending a stream of murky water across the desk the two girls were sharing and flooding all their cards beyond repair. They stared at the wreckage in dismay and then turned as one girl and fell upon the clumsy boy.

'You done that on purpose! You've spoiled all our cards! We won't have nothing to give our mums now, and I was doing that church special. You're a horrible, horrible little toad and I'm going to tell Miss of you straight away!'

'Miss', who could not have failed to notice the sudden uproar, was already on her way with a cloth, which she handed to Jenny. 'Here you are – wipe it up and I'll give you some more card. Yes, you as well, Shirley. Billy, whatever were you doing? Well, you shouldn't have been standing up, then you wouldn't have slipped over. You'd better take all your things over to the table in the corner. Yes, I do mean now.' She glanced round as the door opened and Joyce Warren peered in. 'Yes, Mrs Warren?'

'I just wondered if this might be a good time for a little rehearsal,' Joyce said, quite diffidently for her. 'We could all run through one or two of the carols together before the children go home.'

Miss Kemp gazed at her. 'I thought you were coming in this afternoon.'

'Yes, I am, but I popped in to see if you needed a hand. You've got all the babies in here, as well as your own class. We could practise "Silent Night".'

'Well, we could, but the children are making cards just now.' Miss Kemp looked around the room, at the heads bent industriously over their desks. A moment or two ago they had all been transfixed by the accident to Jenny's water pot, but now it was as if their concentration were absolute.

'I don't think there'll be time,' she said, and heard a soft sigh of relief sweep the room. 'We'll have to clear everything up first, you see. But thank you for offering. We'll rehearse this afternoon, as planned.' She turned back to her class and said brightly, 'Did you hear that, children? Mrs Warren is coming back straight after dinner, and we'll all rehearse together for our carol service and Nativity Play. So you must hurry up and finish your cards now, because we won't get another chance.'

They looked back with wooden expressions and bent again to their labours. Only Jenny and Shirley continued to gaze at her, their faces filled with woe.

'I'll never get another church card done by dinnertime,' Jenny said in despair, and Shirley echoed her dismay.

'There's not enough red left in our paintbox for me to do another robin. He'll look like a blooming sparrow with no red breast.' She remembered Jenny's admonition and hesitated. 'I mean ... *front.*'

Robin Tozer told his mother all about the rehearsal when she came to meet him at the gate to the school playground that afternoon.

'...and we're going to sing "Silent Night" as Joseph and Mary lead the donkey into Bethlehem to find the No-room-at-the-Inn. It's going to be at the Bell, where Daddy and Grandad go after bellringing.'

Joanna looked down at him, somewhat bemused.

'What is, Robin?'

'The No-room-at-the-Inn, of course,' he said patiently. 'Haven't you been listening, Mummy?'

'Yes, of course I have – but you won't really be going to the Bell. You'll be doing the Nativity Play at the school, like they did last year. Remember we went to see it?'

Robin shook his head. 'No, we're going round the village doing it. We're having a proper donkey, not just Micky Coker with big ears fixed to his head, and we're going to knock at all the doors and they'll tell us to go away–'

'I wouldn't be a bit surprised,' Joanna said. 'But–'

'And then we'll go to the Bell, and Mr Nethercott will come to the door and say there's no-room-at-the-inn, and Mary will cry, and then Mrs Nethercott will say, yes there is, they can go in the stable, and we'll all go round the back and the Virgin Mary will have the baby Jesus and lay him in a manger – I said we could use Grandad's, out of our stable – and then the shepherd and the wise men will come and everyone will bow down and worship him.' He paused for breath and then added, 'What *is* a Virgin Mary, Mum? Is it like Mr Warren, who gives out hymn books in the church?'

'No, Mr Warren is a *verger*, Robin.' Joanna looked at him again in some perplexity. 'Are you sure about this? I haven't heard anything about going round the village.'

'Mrs Warren only decided this afternoon. Even Miss Kemp doesn't know. She was doing something else while we were practising.'

Joanna's lips twitched. Joyce Warren had been either very clever or rather silly, she thought. Miss Kemp might have thought it a good idea, or she might not, but by the time all the children had gone home with the tale, it would be hard to retract it.

'Suppose it's snowing? Or raining.'

'We won't care about snow,' Robin said confidently. 'It was snowing then, it says so in that carol about shepherds washing their socks. And Mrs Warren says I've got to wear a tea towel. One of those with little squares all over it.'

'Yes, we can find you one of those.' Checked tea towels were an inevitable part of the Nativity Play costumes. 'But I wouldn't be too sure about going round the village, Robin. If Mrs Warren's only just thought of it, it might not happen that way. She'll need to ask Miss Kemp first – and Mr and Mrs Nethercott, and all the people whose doors you're going to knock. They might not all want to do it.'

'But it's the *Nativity* Play,' he exclaimed in outrage. 'And Mrs Warren *said*.'

Joanna smiled again. He was probably right. Joyce Warren, with her forthright and rather domineering manner, usually did get her own way. If nothing else, the Nativity Play would be interesting, and it would certainly help to take the children's minds off their other teacher, Stella Simmons.

'I think it will be lovely,' she said, and found, rather to her surprise, that she did.

After some initial surprise and a little consideration, Miss Kemp too thought it was quite a good idea. She talked it over with Grace Harvey, who had another suggestion to make.

'Why not combine it with the village carol-singing? The children's families would be coming anyway, and we could sing carols at the various houses to bring people out, and then the children can perform the appropriate parts of their play. We may even find the rest of the villagers joining us as we go round, and the final scene in the stable would be really touching.'

'That does sound a good idea,' Miss Kemp agreed. 'It will involve everyone, not just those with children at the school. I have to admit that I was slightly concerned about Mrs Warren's ideas, but this really is a rather good one.'

'She does tend to be a little enthusiastic at times,' Grace smiled, 'but she means well, and she's certainly prepared to put in a lot of effort. I think you'll find that this is going to be a Nativity Play to remember.'

The fact that the play was to be combined with the carol-singing meant that some of the older children, who had left the village school to go to either the grammar or the secondary modern school in Tavistock, would be able to join in. Micky and Henry Bennetts, who were still singing in the church choir as their voices hadn't yet broken, agreed that they would go, along with Micky's father Alf, the village blacksmith, who had a deep bass voice that he could switch easily to a falsetto when playing the dame in the pantomimes.

'It'll be good fun,' Micky said. 'Mrs Nethercott says she'll bring mince pies and hot cider punch out to the stable when the play's finished. There might be sausage rolls, too.'

'OK,' Henry said. 'Here, what about asking Mr Tozer if us could ring the bells too? I mean, it's really Christmas Day, when you come to think of it, isn't it – the day Jesus was born. It'd sort of finish things off proper.'

It was practice night on Friday and they asked then. Ted Tozer and Travis Kellaway, who had been teaching the boys to ring for the past few months and were pleased with their progress, looked at each other and nodded.

'That's not a bad idea,' Ted said thoughtfully. ''Tis only a few yards from the pub stable to the church. Us could nip up as soon as the play finishes and have a short peal, and then go back for the punch and mince pies, and maybe a bit more of a sing-song inside. The kiddies will all be going home to bed by then, of course.' He looked meaningfully at Micky and Henry, who scowled. 'And you needn't look so grumpy. You'll get your fill, no need to worry about that.'

'It'll make a real celebration of it all,' Travis said. 'The village needs a bit of cheering up, and Stella will be pleased to know that her children are doing such a good job. When is this play going to be, Micky?'

'Next Thursday, Mr Kellaway. School breaks up on Friday and they has their party then.'

'When's Fur and Feather?' Norman Tozer asked. 'Us can't clash with that.'

'That's not till Wednesday week.' Ted looked at Travis. 'You'll be providing a few birds for that, I take it.'

'I certainly will. Hope for a brace or two of hare as well.' Fur and Feather was the annual Christmas whist drive, with prizes of various game which would come in handy for celebrations. The whist club met each Wednesday in the village hall, playing ferociously, but never was competition more savage than at the Fur and Feather.

'And it's the Women's Institute Christmas do on the Tuesday before Christmas, and the Mothers' Union on Monday. I reckon us can fit in a bit of ringing to go with that old play and carol-singing on Thursday.' Ted nodded at the boys. 'I'll see it's right with the vicar and you can mention it to your dad, Micky, seeing as he couldn't be here tonight. I hope his thumb'll be better by then.'

'It will,' Micky assured him. ''Twere only a bit of a tap with a hammer, and it weren't even the big one. He reckons the swelling'll have all gone down by Sunday.'

'Right, then.' Ted turned back to the ringing circle and took the tenor rope in his hands. 'Better stop all this chitter-chatter and stand to again, or our ringing won't be fit to be heard come Christmas. I want to practise that new peal again, that Travis has made up. You two boys had better ring too, since I dare say you'll want to do a bit of showing off in front of your mates next week. And watch your back strokes, Henry –

you'm still coming in too quick and clipping the bell in front. Let her rise up a bit before you pulls.'

Henry nodded, and the boys took their places at their accustomed bells. During normal practices, when they rang the traditional Devon call changes, every ringer stayed on the same bell each time, but during the more complicated 'method' ringing that Travis had introduced, and for which they had a separate practice, they were allowed to swap around. Ted Tozer, like most tower captains, had strict ideas about the striking and still didn't really approve of the new-fangled 'scientific' method of ringing, which was so much more difficult to strike well, but he could see that it kept the boys interested and he valued Travis's presence in the team too much to forbid it. As yet, they still tied the clappers to the bells for their method practices, so that no sound could be heard outside, but he knew that they would soon want to leave them free, so that they could hear the music they were making.

It would be a while before that day, however, and although he kept a stern eye on the progress the two boys were making, he was secretly pleased with them. They learned quickly and didn't fool about – at least, while he was there. He had a suspicion that Travis had caught them up to larks a time or two, but nothing had been said and no harm done. They needed to understand that bells could not be trifled with. Someone who didn't know what they were doing could cause a lot of damage and even kill themselves. Ted was satisfied that Travis had made the boys realise

71

this, and they were shaping up to become good members of the band.

'Look to,' Travis said, taking the rope's end and the sally in his hands and glancing round to see that everyone was ready. 'Treble's going... She's gone.'

The ropes began to move and the notes of the bells sounded high in the church tower to send their call across the village and out into the darkness of the fields and moors beyond. They sounded across the Burra Brook and all the way to Little Burracombe, where Felix had come back from the hospital and was standing at the vicarage door, breathing in fresh cold air to try to clear the smell of the hospital from his lungs, and thinking and praying, as he always was now, for his dear Stella's recovery. The chimes sounded faint and silvery in the air, almost as if the stars above his head were singing to him. And it seemed to him that they were sending him a message; a message of hope that all would yet be well, and that the bitter darkness of winter would not last for ever.

Chapter Six

On Saturday morning, Russell came to take Maddy for a drive. She needed some fresh air and a change of scene, he said, and the hospital had begun to take a firm line over Stella's visitors. Her doctors had decided that she needed an operation, possibly more than one, on her legs and spine and wanted her to have as much rest as possible before they began. They did not want more than one visitor at a time, and then for only short periods during the normal visiting hours. It had been agreed that Maddy and Felix should be the only ones to visit for the next few days, and as Felix had his church duties to perform on Sunday, he was going in later today. He was also going to hire a car to replace Mirabelle until it was decided whether she could be repaired.

Dottie watched them go and then turned back into the cottage. She had decided to give the place a thorough cleaning, after the neglect of the past few days. She had just tipped the tea leaves out of the pot, squeezed them dry and sprinkled them on the carpet when she was startled by a knock on the back door. She opened it to find Joe Tozer standing there.

'Joe! Whatever be you doing here? You've missed that boy of yours, if that's who you're looking for – just gone off together for the day, they have, in the car.'

'I know.' He glanced past her into the kitchen. 'It was you I wanted to see. Can I come in for a bit, Dottie?'

She looked down at her apron and the dustpan and brush she held in her hands. 'Well, of course you can, but you'll have to mind where you put your feet. I'm in the middle of brushing the living-room carpet. I'll have to carry on, now I've started.'

'That's all right.' He followed her into the room and watched as she got down on her knees to brush up the damp tea leaves. 'I remember my mother used to swear by tea leaves to bring up the dust, and Alice still does it too. You wouldn't have to do it if you lived in America, though. You'd have a vacuum cleaner.'

'They've got vacuum cleaners up at the Barton,' Dottie said, brushing vigorously, 'but it's not worth it for a little place like this. Anyway, it don't do me no harm to do a bit of housework – keeps me healthy.'

'There's other ways of keeping healthy. Dottie, can't you stop that now and sit down? I want to have a talk.'

'I can't leave wet tea leaves all over the carpet,' she objected, but she finished sweeping the last of them into her dustpan and got up stiffly, her knees creaking. 'I suppose you wants a cup of tea as well. Or coffee, being as you're an American now.'

'Tea'll do fine,' he said with a grin. 'It's one of the great things about coming home, that I can get a proper cup of tea again. It don't matter how you try to teach 'em in the States, they never really get the idea of using boiling water. They make good coffee, mind.'

Dottie took the dustpan outside and emptied it on to the compost heap. She came back in and filled the kettle, and started to take cups and saucers down from the dresser. She took the biscuit tin from the alcove cupboard and set it on the table, then turned back to the range to make the tea. She left it to brew for a few minutes while she opened the larder door and took out a jug of milk.

'So what d'you want to talk about?' she asked at last, when they each had a cup of tea in front of them. 'And have one of these biscuits. They're flapjacks, made with peanut butter.'

'Sounds good.' He took one and bit into it. 'Mm. You know, Dottie, there's no one to touch you for baking. You could have made a career out of it.'

'I pretty nearly have,' she said drily. 'Always baking for someone, I am – if it's not cakes and biscuits for George Sweet's shop, it's jam tarts and sponges for the WI tea or the Mothers' Union – not that I'm a mother – or for Stella to take over to young Felix. Hollow legs, that young man's got. Although I don't reckon he'll be needing my bits and pieces for much longer, with all they Little Burracombe women mooning over him.'

Joe said nothing, and after a moment Dottie sighed and asked, 'All right, Joe, out with it – what is it you want to talk about?'

'The same thing I've been wanting ever since I came back to Burracombe and saw you coming down the village street, looking as pretty as ever,' he responded. 'I want you to come back to the States with me – as my wife.' He leaned across the space between them and took her hands in his. 'We missed our chance all those years ago, when we were young. Don't let's miss it again.'

Dottie stared down at his hands. She said, 'You've had a happy life, though, Joe. You married a good woman and you've had a family. I don't reckon you missed all that much.'

'I know. I've been lucky. I'm not saying there's only one woman for each man, or one man for

75

each woman – we've both seen enough to know that's not true. You can find happiness twice. But we'd have been happy together, Dottie, you know we would. And we still could. You told me the other day you'd think about it. So now I'm asking you again. Please, Dottie, won't you say yes?'

'Oh, Joe,' she said, feeling her throat swell with tears, 'I *have* thought about it. But it's the same as I told you then – it's too late. My life is here in Burracombe. I know everyone here. The village is my family. I can't leave it all and go to a strange place where I won't know anyone else, and where life is so different. I'd be out of place there. I'm too old to make a big change like that.' She withdrew her hands and picked up her knitting.

'You'd have family. You'd have me and Russ and the girls. And we're not so very different, you know, in America – we do speak English!'

'You may think so,' she said wryly. 'But your whole life is different, Joe. You live in a town, for a start.'

'Corning? Why, it's just a small place, not much bigger than Tavistock. Everyone knows each other there. There's the glassworks and a nice hotel and two railways, but it's still a small town, with lots going on. They're doing summer theatre performances now in the big auditorium at the Glass Center, as well as concerts, banquets, square dances, boat shows – you name it, it happens there. Everyone gets together all the time. And the shops are nice, too. There's a real good store, three storeys high, where you can get everything you want.'

'That don't sound much like Tavistock! Don't

you see, Joe, you'm talking about a city life. Corning may be a small city, and I'm sure 'tis very nice, as cities go, but I'm a village person. Village life is what I understand.'

'You lived in London, when you were working for that actress.'

'Yes, I did, and glad enough I was to come back to Burracombe where I belong.' She paused, concentrating on starting a new row, then said gently, 'I know what I'm like, Joe, and what I need to make me feel comfortable and happy. And I've got it here. If I moved away, I'd just be miserable. I know I would.'

'Even if you were with me?' he asked quietly.

'I'm afraid so, Joe. I just couldn't make the change. Not at my age.'

There was a short silence. Then he said, 'And suppose I were to stay here?'

Dottie looked up at him in surprise. 'Why, Joe, you'd never want to do that. You've been away over thirty years. Corning's your home now, same as Burracombe's mine. How could you settle back here, where nothing ever happens?'

'Well, I'm not so sure about that,' he said. 'Seems to me plenty happens. I know what you mean, though, Dottie. It's pretty quiet on the whole. But maybe I'm ready for that now.'

She shook her head. 'You're not, and you never will be. And what about *your* family? No, Joe, we made our choices back then and I don't see as we can change them now. I won't say I didn't regret it,' she added honestly. 'Many's the time I wished I hadn't sent you off the way I did. But us can't go back and alter things now.' She put down her

77

knitting and squeezed his hands gently. 'You're right to say we've got a second chance, but it's not a second chance of marrying. It's a second chance to be friends again. Real, special friends.'

'We'll always be that,' he said, a little sadly. 'And I reckon I'll always wish we were something more. Maybe you're right, and it'd be a shame to uproot you and then find you were unhappy. But I don't reckon it'd be that way at all...' He paused, as if thinking, then said slowly, 'How about this, then? Suppose you come over for a holiday? No strings attached. Just to stay for a while and meet the girls and see where I live. We might even take a trip somewhere together. How about that?'

Dottie had picked up her knitting again. She lowered the needles and stared at him. 'A holiday to *America?* It'd have to be longer than a week.'

He laughed. 'It would take you a week to get there! No, I reckon you'd need two or three months to really get to know the place.' His grip tightened. 'Why not think about it, Dottie? Later on in the year, perhaps – in the fall, when the trees are all in colour. New York State's a picture then, and we might go down to Vermont or New England. They're real pretty at that time of year.' He watched her face for a moment. 'All this worry over Stella will be behind you then, and I reckon young Maddy will be making her own life too. You might even find you've got a good reason for coming.'

'Maddy and Russ, you mean? Well, I won't say I haven't noticed the way the wind's blowing there. But it's early days, Joe. It's not quite a year since she lost her young man, and there's Stephen Napier too, always been sweet on her he has, and ready to step forward the minute she gives him the signal. I don't reckon your Russ should put too much store on anything happening there, not yet awhile anyhow.'

'Maybe, and maybe not. But she's not the only one coming to Corning. There's young Jackie, too. Now Ted and Alice have agreed to her coming over, she's full of plans. But I reckon she'll be a bit homesick now and then, and glad to see a familiar face.'

'She'd have to be pretty homesick to want to see mine,' Dottie observed, frowning over a dropped stitch. 'I've always been fond enough of Jackie Tozer, but I've never had much to do with her since she's growed up, and hardly ever seen her since she went to work in that hotel in Plymouth. Anyway, she surely won't still be there when I come over in the autumn – that's if I come at all,' she added hastily. 'I haven't said I will yet, so there's no need for you to look so pleased, Joe. Jackie's only going for a month or two, isn't she? That's what Alice told me t'other day, anyway.'

'That's what the plan is,' he agreed. 'But I reckon once she's in America she'll want to make the most of it – stay a bit longer, travel about a bit. She's a bright young woman, Jackie is, and she's not going to want to come tamely home and go back to being a hotel receptionist in Plymouth once she's got a taste of the big wide world.'

Dottie gazed at him in consternation. 'But that's just what Ted and Alice were afeared of! If they knew she was planning to stay away, they'd not let her go for a minute.'

'Oh, I don't think they're in much doubt about it,' he said, a little ruefully. 'But Jackie pretty well held them over a barrel – pointed out that once she's twenty-one she won't need their permission anyway, and if they wouldn't agree to her going before that she'd just stop coming home. It was a bit strong, if you ask me, but the girl feels it's her life and she's got a right to it. And there wasn't much they could do but agree.'

'That's blackmail,' Dottie said, horrified. 'The naughty girl! But there, her's always been headstrong. They never wanted her to go to Plymouth in the first place, you know.'

'It's one of the things I've noticed, coming back to England after all these years,' Joe said thoughtfully. 'Young women are much more independent these days – more like American girls. They don't want to do ordinary jobs in shops or offices while they wait to find a husband. They want to do a bit more with their lives. They want careers.'

'There's always been careers for young women,' Dottie objected. 'Even when I was young, you could go to be a teacher if you had the brains. Or a nurse, like young Val Tozer as was. Why, there's even been women doctors. And I went to a woman dentist once, in London, though why anyone should want to spend their lives peering into people's mouths and seeing all them bad teeth is something I've never understood.' She paused, then added: 'It's the war that's done it, you know.'

'Done what? Made people's teeth bad?'

'No!' She punched him on the arm. 'Made

80

women more independent. We had to do so much more when the men all went off to fight. Women did all sorts of jobs they'd never done before – worked in factories, drove buses and lorries, worked on the land like Joanna Tozer, took over responsibilities they'd never have been allowed before. It started during the First World War – they more or less had to give us the vote after that, and that gave us a bit more say in things. But then the Second War started and we really showed them what we could do. We wouldn't have won the war if it hadn't been for women, you know. The country couldn't have carried on without us.'

'Women always have been important,' he said. 'Just in different ways... Dottie, it's so good to be able to talk like this. It's something I've missed a lot – just sitting by the fire, talking quietly and sensibly with someone around my own age. You with your knitting – the cat purring in front of the fire. It's home to me.'

'It was once, Joe,' she said quietly. 'But you left it behind, and America's your home now. And your house is a fine, big place, not a little cottage like this.'

Joe sighed and looked at the fire. 'It's isn't just the house. It's the people in it. One person in particular.'

Dottie laid her knitting down on her lap and looked at him. 'You still miss your wife.'

'Well, sure I do. We were together a long time and she was a good wife. I loved her, Dottie, it would be wrong of me to say anything different. But I loved you too, all those years ago, and that

81

never really went away. And since I came back to Burracombe–'

'No,' she said, and laid her hand on his arm. 'Don't say it, Joe, please. You've said enough – I don't need no more.'

'I don't want you to think you're just a substitute,' he said in a low voice. 'You were my first love, Dottie. Nobody ever forgets their first love.'

'But times have changed,' she said gently.

There was a long pause. At last he gave her a quick look and asked, 'Why did you never marry, Dottie? You must have been asked.'

'Now and then, maybe.' Her eyes were on her knitting again. 'But oh, I dunno, Joe. Nobody ever really took my fancy, I suppose. And then I met Fenella Forsyth, the actress, and went to London as her dresser, and I spent most of my time in her dressing room, sewing and mending and all that sort of thing. I never seemed to meet anyone else.'

'You must have done. There must have been people in and out all the time.'

'Not people who'd take a second look at a maid up from Devon,' she said wryly. 'Anyway, it never happened... And then the war started and I came back to Burracombe and the Barton filled up with evacuee kiddies – that's how Maddy first came here, and Miss Forsyth being a friend of old Mrs Napier, she used to come here to visit and took a fancy to Maddy and adopted her, and asked me to look after her while she was away entertaining the troops. And ... well, I suppose time went by and I just settled down and never thought about marriage. Not that I felt upset about it, mind!' she

82

added fiercely. 'I've had a good, contented life, and nobody can ask more than that.'

'As long as it wasn't me that put you off,' he remarked, and she tilted her head to give him a sideways look.

'And it's no use you fishing for compliments, Joe Tozer! I know what you wants me to say – that I never met any man to match up to you. Well, I'm not going to say it. You'm quite proud enough of yourself already.'

Joe laughed, but there was a trace of guilt in his voice as he said, 'Well, maybe I was, and maybe I would have been pretty flattered to think that was true. But I wouldn't really have wanted you to be lonely on my account, Dottie. I wanted you to be happy. And it came as a pretty big surprise to meet you here that first day we arrived, and find you were still Dottie Friend. I was certain you'd have been married with a flock of young 'uns.' His voice dropped a little. 'I'm sorry you weren't. You'd have made a lovely mother.'

'Well, that's as maybe,' she said a little gruffly, concentrating on her knitting again. 'But I had Maddy, don't forget. She was like a daughter to me. And so's her sister Stella.' She laid the knitting down again and looked at him, not ashamed to let him see the tears in her eyes. 'Oh, Joe, talking with you like this, I'd let that poor maid go right out of my head.' She drew in a shaky breath. 'Is she *ever* going to get over this, d'you think?'

Chapter Seven

The same thought was running incessantly through Felix's head. Pray as he might, and strong though his faith remained, he knew that people did die, and they didn't always wait to grow old to do it. Stella's own parents had died in their thirties, her baby brother had died at only a few months old, and Maddy's sweetheart Sammy had been killed less than a year ago. Whatever your faith in God, you knew you were not immune, and nobody was immortal.

Yesterday, the doctor had advised him to go home and not come in again until the next official visiting hour, which was on Saturday afternoon.

'Now that Miss Simmons has woken, we'll be able to proceed to the next stage of her treatment,' he had said, standing by Stella's bed. Her eyes were closed but she'd opened them again for a few seconds, and, once more, Felix had been sure that she knew him and was glad he was there. Now, he was holding her hand and could feel her fingers tremble very slightly in his. 'X-rays, tests, operations – these must be done at the right time, and without visitors to greet the doctors with anxious faces every time they step out of the ward. I know it seems hard, Mr Copley, but the medical teams need to be able to get on with their work.'

Felix had nodded. He understood this, but it was cruelly difficult to stay away when all he wanted was to be at Stella's side, to be with her through whatever ordeals she faced. She looked so alone, so small and white in that high hospital bed, and it tore at his heart each time he was forced to leave her.

He looked down at her pale face now and saw her eyelids flicker again. With a leap of excitement, he bent towards her and said, 'Stella. Stella, darling, it's me, Felix. Tell me you know I'm here. Please, sweetheart, say something to me so that the doctor knows you're getting better.'

Her colourless lips moved and a faint whisper breathed through them. Felix glanced swiftly up at the doctor, who also leaned down and spoke, more firmly than Felix, as though his words were important.

'Miss Simmons, I'm Dr Jenkins. I want you to listen carefully and answer a few simple questions.' He paused, watching Stella's eyes, and Felix saw her gaze transfer slowly from his own face to the doctor's. 'Do you know your name?'

'Stella,' she breathed after an agonising pause. 'I'm Stella. Stella ... Simmons.'

'Good. Very good. And do you know who the Queen is?'

'The Queen,' she whispered. 'Queen Elizabeth ... she was crowned...'

'Good. And what is the name of the Prime Minister?'

'What–' Felix began, but without taking his eyes from Stella's face the doctor lifted a hand to silence him.

'The Prime Minister?' he repeated encouragingly. 'What is his name?'

'Win ... Winston ... Winston Churchill...'

The doctor looked pleased. Then he said, 'And do you know where you are?'

'I think ... I think I'm in hospital.'

'Yes, you are, and we're going to make you better. Now, do you know *why* you are in hospital?'

Stella's face twisted as if she were in sudden pain, and she closed her eyes and turned her head away. Felix, seeing the effort that even so small a movement cost her, burst out in an angry whisper, 'Why are you doing this? Why are you asking her all these questions? Can't you see–'

'Please,' Dr Jenkins said, lifting his hand again. He looked down at Stella and touched her shoulder lightly. 'Well done, Miss Simmons. Just one more question and then you can go back to sleep. Do you remember anything that happened before you woke up in hospital? Do you remember the accident?'

'Accident?' she whispered. 'I don't know... What accident...? I don't remember an accident... I don't know why...' Her voice, faint as it sounded, was becoming agitated, and she opened her eyes again, casting them about as if searching for something, or someone. Felix, still gripping her hand in his, began to protest again, but the doctor shook his head and drew him away.

'Let her sleep now,' he said and, reluctantly, Felix bent to lay his lips on the ashen cheek and followed him from the room.

Once the door had closed, he opened his mouth to burst out again, but the doctor stopped him. 'I know what you want to say, but believe me, we have to ask such questions to find out if she has amnesia. I would have preferred to do it at some other time, but she was conscious and I couldn't miss the opportunity. I'm sorry it was upsetting.'

'But the Queen?' Felix asked in bewilderment. 'The Prime Minister? Why ask *those* questions?'

'Questions to which everyone knows the answers. Once we've established that the brain is functioning on that level, we can pass on to others. She knows who she is, and she seems to know who you are – all good signs. But she has no memory of the accident.'

'She had a knock on the head,' Felix said, but a small worm of fear was beginning to uncurl deep inside him. 'Surely that's normal.'

'It certainly can be,' the doctor agreed, 'but we have to be sure, and we have to ask the questions. There'll be more, I'm afraid, when she wakes again. It's part of the process we need to go through while determining her treatment.'

Felix stared at him, trying to take in his words. 'You said – *amnesia?* Do you really think she's lost her memory?'

'It's a possibility we have to consider. We can't know for certain until she's properly conscious.'

'But – do you mean she might not be able to remember her own life? She might not be able to remember *me?*'

'It's rare for that to happen,' Dr Jenkins replied, 'but – yes, until we can know for sure, it has to be considered.'

'And she may never remember?'

'The memory does usually return, over time, but–'

'But not always!' Felix cried. 'Sometimes it never comes back – and Stella may never know any more about me than my name! She may never remember that we loved each other, that we were going to get married!'

He turned away, thrusting both hands over his forehead and into his hair. The doctor watched him for a moment, then came closer and laid his hand on the back of Felix's shoulder.

'Go home,' he said quietly. 'You're exhausted. Go home and rest, have a good meal, and then come back tomorrow. It almost certainly won't be that bad, but in any case, you need your strength. Go home.'

Felix nodded dully. He did as he was told, making his way to the bus stop, since there were no more trains for an hour, and trudging the last mile from the main road into the village. He had reached the vicarage in darkness, made himself some toast and fallen into bed in a stupor of exhaustion, only to lie half waking, half in nightmare all night, and sleeping too heavily at last as the late December dawn sent cold grey fingers of light between his bedroom curtains.

Basil Harvey came to see him later in the morning and insisted that he return to the Burracombe vicarage for lunch.

'Grace is expecting you. She's made shepherd's pie especially.'

Felix smiled faintly. Shepherd's pie was one of his favourite meals. He said, 'I'll have to let the hospital know where I am. I'll ring and give them your phone number. Just in case ... in case they need to get in touch with me.'

'Of course.' Basil waited while Felix made the call, asking at the same time if there had been any change. He thanked the person at the other end and put the phone down. 'Anything new?'

'No, she's still asleep, but the doctors are going to be seeing her soon.' Felix ran his fingers through his fair hair. 'I don't know if I ought to come, all the same. There's so much to do here. Parish things...' He glanced distractedly around his cluttered study. Post lay unopened on his desk, and there was a pile of notes from the parish helpers who had been in and out, trying to keep his work from amassing too much. 'And I've got to make some decision about the wedding. I just don't know...'

'You can talk it over with Grace and me if you like,' Basil said firmly, taking him by the arm. 'You have to eat, Felix, and it won't take any time to walk over the Clam to Burracombe and have lunch with us. The fresh air and exercise will do you good, too.'

Felix nodded, more as if he were too weary to argue than because he agreed, and the two walked down the vicarage drive and along the little lane that led to the old footbridge across the Burra Brook that separated the two villages. The bridge, which had once been no more than a large tree trunk and was still called by its old name of 'Clam', was about twelve feet above the swiftly running river, which was capable of rising several feet when in flood from the rains that descended from higher up on Dartmoor. Today, it was reasonably shallow, flowing as brown and sinuous as an otter between its banks, with the sunlight shimmering through to create a shifting pattern of greenish-white over smooth, flat slabs of granite. The banks were hung with winter-dead grass, trailing wisps of fern and torn brambles, which were caught and tugged by the current yet clung obstinately to their roots. A flicker of brown and white caught Felix's eye, and he saw a dipper flash upstream and stop to flirt its tail on a rock before diving into the water.

At certain times of the year, you could see salmon making their way upstream to spawn and die. There were water voles too, and if you were very lucky, you could catch a glimpse of electric blue as a kingfisher flashed past. In February, snowdrops carpeted the Devon banks with bells of pearly white, and later in the spring the banks were thick with primroses and violets. But today, it all looked lifeless, and although he knew that it was no more than an illusion, that plants lay dormant beneath the brown soil and would soon come bursting into life, he felt a great despondency settle over his spirits. It was as if his whole world were failing and moving beyond his reach.

'Come along, Felix,' Basil said quietly, taking his arm. 'It's too cold to stand here for long.'

As they walked through the village, they encountered a number of people who wanted to know how Stella was, but Basil waved them gently aside, murmuring that there was no more news yet but she was sleeping, and they understood that Felix didn't want to stop and talk. All the same, Felix was glad to reach the haven of the vicarage and take off his coat in the warmth of the hallway.

Grace came out of the kitchen to meet him.

She put her hands on his arms and kissed his cheek.

'Felix, I'm so glad you came. We're eating in the kitchen – it's warmer there. Now, how are you?' She stood back and regarded him. 'You're looking very tired.'

He rubbed his face. 'I don't think I've slept much, these past few days.'

'Have you actually been to bed? Or have you just been dozing in a chair? You need to look after yourself, you know. It won't help Stella if you wear yourself out.'

'I know. People keep on telling me that.'

Grace smiled. 'I'm sorry. You must be tired of hearing it. Now, come along and have a sherry before we eat. It'll warm you up.'

They went into the big kitchen, where Grace had laid the table with a red checked cloth and put a decoration of scarlet-berried holly and tiny glittering Christmas baubles in the centre. The range cooker was giving out a welcoming warmth and the savoury smell of cheese-topped shepherd's pie filled the air.

'Oh, this is nice,' Felix said, sitting down at the table. He looked around at the big dresser with its rows of colourful plates and dishes, at the cupboards and shelves with their displays of bottled fruit and preserves, and thought of his own vicarage in Little Burracombe, where he had hoped that Stella would reign as Grace did here. The kitchen there was just as big, but seemed bleak without a woman to bring it to life, just as the entire house seemed bleak without the love and laughter he had looked forward to so much.

Grace saw his face change and glanced at her husband. Basil moved quickly to the dresser and lifted a bottle of sherry.

'You will have one, won't you? And then we'll have a talk about what you're going to do next.'

'Thank you.' Felix accepted the glass and looked at the golden liquid. There was a moment of hesitation as they all wondered what toast to make, and then Basil said quietly, 'To Stella, and a full recovery', and they touched glasses and murmured together.

Basil sat down at the table while Grace turned back to the range to finish cooking the vegetables. He gazed thoughtfully at Felix and said, 'Have the doctors given you any real idea what progress Stella is making?'

'Not really. Obviously it's a good sign that she's woken up and that she knew me. The doctor asked her a few questions, like who the Prime Minister is and that sort of thing, and she managed to answer. But she's very tired and weak, and she's in pain from the broken bones, and she doesn't remember anything about the accident.'

'That's probably just as well,' Grace said, straining a pan of carrots at the sink and tipping them into a dish. 'It must have been a nightmare.'

'It was. And she was barely conscious when the doctor was asking her. But suppose she loses more of her memory?' He looked at them with fear in his eyes. 'Suppose she forgets about her life before the accident? Suppose she forgets Maddy and Burracombe ... and me?'

'Now, that isn't very likely,' Basil said, leaning over to touch his arm. 'People don't often forget everything that's ever happened to them. She may not remember the accident, and as Grace says, it may be for the best if she doesn't. Such memories can only be upsetting. But she'll remember you and all the people she loves, I'm sure. You just have to give her time.'

'I suppose so,' Felix said, sounding unconvinced. 'And there are other people to think about as well. It wasn't just us – there was that poor boy Rob, too. I must go and see him. Perhaps I could go after lunch, while I'm in the village. Is he still at the Barton, do you know?'

'I believe so,' Basil said. 'I ran into Hilary earlier, and she told me he was staying for Christmas and then going back to France with his family. I don't think they're sending him back to Kelly College now, since it's so near Christmas anyway.'

'Christmas!' Felix said in a horrified voice. 'How on earth am I going to manage? All those services – and the teas, and everything?' He buried his face in his hands. 'It all just seems to be so much – I don't know where to start...'

Again, Basil and Grace glanced at each other. Then Basil laid his hand on the younger man's shoulder and said, 'Felix, you don't have to manage. Not all by yourself. We're all here to help. What about your family? There are plenty of clerics amongst your relatives. Can't they send someone to take some of the services?'

'They've already offered. One of my cousins says he'll come. But it's my first Christmas in Little Burracombe and I really wanted to do it all myself. With Stella there as well, it was going to be so *joyful*. But now...' He shook his head, unable to go on, and Basil's hand tightened.

'It can still be joyful, if Stella continues to improve. But you must be ready to hand over some of your tasks. You need your energy for Stella as well as for the parish – you're her best medicine, you know, as long as you can remain strong.'

Felix lifted his head and looked at him.

'Do you really believe that?'

'Yes, I do,' Basil said firmly. 'You can give her strength just by being there and holding her hand. Your own faith will strengthen you both.'

His simple words, spoken with quiet certainty, found their way into the coldness of Felix's heart and warmed it as the sherry warmed his blood. He felt the tears hot in his eyes and pressed the heels of his hands against them, but they seeped through and left a salty trail down his cheeks. Basil said nothing, but kept his hand steady on his shoulder, and Grace came to his other side and put her own hand on his other shoulder. He sighed and rested his cheek against her side and she held him there for a few moments.

'I'm all right now,' he said at last, leaning away from her and taking his hands from his face. 'Thank you – both of you.'

Grace moved back to the sink and drained the cabbage. She put the vegetable bowls on the table and took the shepherd's pie from the oven. The plates were warming on the top of the range, and she brought them to the table and began to serve the food.

'This is so good,' Felix said, tackling his plateful. 'I didn't realise how hungry I was.'

'I don't suppose you've been eating properly,' Grace told him. 'But I'm sure there are plenty of your own parishioners ready to help you.'

'I know. It's just that I don't really know them very well yet. Here, I feel as if I'm at home.'

'And so you are,' Basil said. 'At home with friends. You must always feel able to come to us, Felix, whenever you want to. And now let's eat before this delicious food gets cold.'

They didn't talk about the wedding after all. To Felix, it seemed wrong to discuss it with anyone before he could talk to Stella again, and as Basil said to his wife after the young vicar had gone, everyone who knew about the accident must be aware that it was likely to be postponed. There was really nothing that could be done at this stage.

Felix had decided to use the train to go into Plymouth. The branch line ran only a mile or so away and was often more convenient than the bus, and he needed to find a car hire firm before going to the hospital. He had decided that if Mirabelle could not be repaired, he would manage without a car – a bicycle was good enough to get around the parish, or, if getting to more remote places proved difficult, he could buy a small motorcycle. For a young vicar like himself, a car was a luxury, and Mirabelle had been a present from one of his uncles. But while Stella was in hospital, a car was a necessity, or he would spend a lot of time waiting for buses and trains.

Before catching the train, he had time to go to see young Robert Aucoin at the Barton. He walked up the drive and pulled the bell at the front door, and after a few moments Hilary opened it.

'Felix! How are you?' A look of concern crossed her face. 'It's not bad news, is it?'

'No – no, she's still the same. As far as I know, anyway.' A shadow touched his heart as he thought of Stella's possible loss of memory. 'I'm going in to visit her in an hour or so and I wanted to see young Rob. How is he?'

'He seems to be all right, thank goodness. Do come in, Felix. I'll call him – we've just had lunch. I think he's going over to Wood Cottage to see Jennifer and Travis soon.'

She closed the front door behind him and went to the stairs. 'Rob! Felix – Mr Copley – is here to see you.'

There was silence for a moment, and then a door opened and closed and the French boy appeared at the top of the stairs, looking uncertain. He came slowly down towards them.

'It's all right, Rob,' Felix said, going to meet him at the foot of the stairs. 'Nobody's blaming you for what happened.'

'If I hadn't run away from school...' he said in a small voice, looking at Felix with large, frightened eyes. 'You wouldn't have had to go to Exeter to fetch me.'

'No, and if the ponies hadn't run across the road, we wouldn't have hit them,' Felix said. 'They weren't your fault, were they?'

The boy smiled faintly. 'No, but–'

'There are all sorts of things that could have happened differently,' Felix said. 'If we hadn't stopped for lunch at that farmhouse – if I hadn't had a second helping of pudding. Once you start that kind of thinking, there's no end to it, Rob, so it's best not to start. What's happened has happened, and the main thing is that nobody is blaming you. So you must stop blaming yourself – all right?'

'Yes,' he said, still in an uncertain voice. 'But that isn't the main thing really, is it, Mr Copley? The main thing is that Miss Simmonds was hurt. She *will* get better, won't she?'

The appeal in his voice chimed in with Felix's own desperate need for reassurance. For a moment, he could not speak, then he pulled himself together and said quietly, 'I hope so, Rob. I believe she will. For the time being, that's all any of us can do – hope and believe. And pray. Can you do that – for Stella, and for me?'

Their eyes met in a long look, and then, slowly, the boy nodded his head. Felix reached out and laid his hand on the dark hair and they stood very still for a moment, united by their fear as well as by their hopes and prayers, and then Felix withdrew his hand. He turned to Hilary.

'I have to go now. I want to organise a hire car before I go to the hospital. But I'll telephone you the minute I get any news. How's your father?'

'He's pretty well,' Hilary replied. 'The attack wasn't a bad one, and as long as he takes it easy, he'll be back to normal in a few days. The problem is *getting* him to take it easy, of course,' she added wryly. 'He ought to have learned by now, but you know what he's like.'

Felix nodded. 'He's never been used to being

inactive. Nor to not being in control. Well, I'm sure you know how to cope with him. And I'm sure he's pleased to have this young man around again.' He turned his attention back to Robert. 'When is your mother arriving?'

'Just before Christmas. I don't know which day.'

'She hasn't let us know exactly yet,' Hilary said. 'There must be a lot to arrange, with the children coming as well, and so much baking to do for the patisserie. Felix, don't let us keep you any longer. You must be anxious to get to Plymouth.'

'Yes, I want to catch the train.' He looked at his watch, then touched Rob's head once more. 'Now, you're to stop worrying, d'you understand? Go and have a happy afternoon with Mr and Mrs Kellaway.'

'And Tavy,' Rob said, a smile breaking out on his face at last.

'Tavy?' Felix repeated, at a loss. 'You're going to the river?'

'No, not the *River* Tavy,' Hilary said, laughing. 'Tavy's Jennifer's dog – the Jack Russell Travis gave her to keep her company when he's out. She's just a puppy at the moment and Rob's helping to train her.'

Felix smiled and turned to go. He left the Barton feeling better; relieved that he had eased the boy's mind and comforted again by the warmth of good friends. His time as curate in Burracombe had been well spent, he thought; he hoped that he had brought as much to the people who lived there as they had given to him.

The branch line ran from Launceston to

Plymouth. Felix was on the platform at the halt with time to spare, and watched the little engine come puffing along the single track. He climbed aboard one of the two carriages and settled down in a corner, with several people who were evidently going to do their Christmas shopping. He smiled briefly at them, then gazed out of the window, hearing their cheerful chatter but unable to join in.

The line ran through beautiful countryside. Before reaching Tavistock, it passed the dramatic chasm and waterfalls of Lydford Gorge, and then ran along the edge of the moor before arriving in fields and woods. Near Shaugh Prior there was a siding which allowed two trains to pass each other; the engine driver would be handed an iron loop at the station, which entitled him to use the line, and then hand it back as he went by, leaving the line free for the train coming the other way. Shortly after that, the train passed the tumbling waters of two rivers, the Plym and the Meavy, as they poured like molten brown glass to collide and merge in a foam of broken water over a clutter of rocks. A little further down, as the water settled into a smooth flow, a heron stood on the bank like an old man, clad in a tattered grey coat and hunched against the raw cold of the December afternoon.

When they arrived in Plymouth, Felix left his fellow-travellers to walk to the car hire office. Half an hour later, he drove out in a Baby Austin, which felt very sedate after Mirabelle, and made at last for the hospital.

His heart was beating fast as he parked and

walked through the doors. He had had no news of Stella since telephoning from the vicarage that morning. Had she woken again and found him not there? Was she still making slow, but hopeful, progress? Or would the news send him once more plunging to the depths of despair?

Chapter Eight

Hilary saw Rob off on his walk to Wood Cottage and was about to turn to go back indoors when the sound of a motor engine turning into the end of the drive caught her attention. She waited and, to her surprise, saw her brother Stephen's sports car approaching. He swept to a halt in front of the steps and jumped out. 'Steve! I didn't expect you today.'

'I felt a bit guilty after we talked the other day. I can't stay long – have to go back tonight. But I thought I ought to see Dad again, and we need to talk things over – about Christmas, and Rob. Where is he?'

'You've just missed him. He's gone over to the Kellaways. He gets on well with them. Anyway, come in – have you had lunch?'

'I had a sandwich on the way.' He followed her into the house. 'I'll see him before I go, I expect.'

'I don't know. He usually stays to tea with them. D'you want to see if you can catch him up? He went across the field.'

'No, I won't do that. I just wanted to make sure

he was OK, and I'm sure he will be if he's with the Kellaways. I wouldn't say no to a coffee.'

They went to the kitchen and he sat down at the table while Hilary put the kettle on. She glanced at him as she did so, and saw that he had rested his hands on the table and was staring at them pensively. She made the coffee and poured out two cups, bringing them to the table and sitting down opposite him.

'Are you worried about Christmas, Steve?' she asked.

'A bit. I know there'll be quite a houseful, with the other two kids as well, but ... well, it's a queer situation. You have to admit that. Baden's son, half French even though he's been brought up entirely in France, his half-brother and sister wholly French ... and his mother. Marianne. We're going to be a bit outnumbered, Hil.'

She gave him a wry smile. 'It's not the children you're worried about, is it?'

'No, of course it's not. If they're anything like Rob, we'll get along fine. He's a nice enough kid, though a bit hard to read at times. I sometimes think there's more going on in that head than he lets on. But Marianne ... well, you know how difficult that's going to be, Hil.'

'I do. But nobody else does. And if she's got any sense, she won't refer to it at all.' Hilary thought of the early morning when she had caught Marianne leaving Stephen's bedroom, and the subsequent anxiety until they knew that there were to be no consequences of their brief affair. 'It's over, Stephen. We know what she intended, but it didn't work, and she won't get a second chance.'

She gave her brother a sharp look. 'She won't, will she?'

'No, she won't. You can be sure of that. I've never been more ashamed in my whole life. She was after feathering her own nest – if Dad didn't leave the estate to Rob, and she had a child by me, I'd have had to marry her and she'd have been sure of a place here.' He shuddered. 'To think I nearly got caught in her nasty little trap! No, nothing like that will happen again, but it's not going to make for an easy atmosphere at Christmas.'

Hilary sighed. 'Well, we'll get through it as best we can, and after that they'll all be going back to France and we'll only see Rob during the holidays. And maybe after a while Dad will think again about leaving him the whole estate. He'll never leave him out, of course, but he might decide that a decent bequest would be enough.'

'Only if he gets another grandson,' Stephen said moodily. 'And that doesn't seem very likely, the way things are going for you and me.'

'Oh, come on, Steve. You're only twenty-four. There's plenty of time for you to find a wife, even if it's not...' She hesitated.

'Not Maddy,' he finished for her. 'But that's just the trouble, isn't it? It's Maddy I want, and somehow she seems to be going further and further away from me.' He sighed deeply and added, 'I called at Dottie's on the way here, hoping to see her, and you know what Dottie told me? She's gone out with that American – Ted Tozer's nephew.'

'I believe he's been taking her to the hospital,'

Hilary said carefully. 'He and his father have been real rocks, using their car to run people backwards and forwards. I don't think it means anything.'

'I'm not so sure,' he said. 'Dottie looked pretty embarrassed when she told me. And the father was there too – Joe, isn't it? They both seem to be getting their feet under Dottie's table.'

'Joe and Dottie knew each other years ago. They were children together. It's natural that they should want to talk over old times.'

'It looked a bit more than that to me,' Stephen observed. 'Not that there'd be anything going on there – they're both in their sixties.'

Hilary smiled. 'It has been known. But I can't see Dottie leaving Burracombe. Steve, I think you ought to make an effort to see Maddy properly. She needs her friends at a time like this, and you've known her since she was a child – much longer than Russ Tozer has.'

'I don't know if she wants to see me.'

'Of course she wants to see you! Look, she won't be staying out all day – they'll be back by dark, I'm sure. Go down to Dottie's again later on. Let Maddy know you really care. She's not going to know that if you stay away from her.'

'I suppose I could,' he said, without much enthusiasm.

'Oh, for goodness' sake, Stephen!' Hilary exclaimed in exasperation. 'Whatever's the matter with you? Show a bit of gumption. You'll lose her if you don't.'

'I think I've lost her anyway,' he said in a depressed tone. 'Honestly, I do.'

'Then you've nothing else to lose by making a bit of effort now, have you?' she said firmly. 'Now look, you'd better go and have a word with Dad. And stop worrying about Christmas. There'll be too much going on for Marianne to get her claws into you again, and nobody else will notice if you steer clear of her as much as possible. We'll fill the time up with stockings and church and Christmas dinner and games – it'll go in a flash. And you can always say you've only got two or three days' leave.'

'It'll be true, too.' He finished his coffee and stood up. 'Oh lord, Hilary, I haven't even asked about you. You're coping all right, are you?'

'Oh yes,' she said. 'I'm coping all right. But then I usually do, don't I?'

'Yes,' he said, looking at her a little doubtfully. 'You usually do. I don't know what we'd do if you weren't here. It's lucky you're not thinking of running off and leaving us.' He narrowed his eyes a little. 'You're not, are you?'

'What on earth makes you say that?' she exclaimed, taken aback and wondering suddenly if her guilt showed in her face. Stephen knew her pretty well, but surely even he could not have divined her secret just from looking at her.

'Oh, nothing. There's no need to look so alarmed. I'm only joking. Only there seems to be something different about you, somehow.'

He grinned, but as Hilary returned his look, she felt a surge of irritation. She controlled it until he left the kitchen, but then went to the sink and banged the milk pan down hard on the wooden draining board.

Good old Hilary, she thought bitterly. The main-stay of the family. The anchor that holds everyone in place. But just suppose she did think of running off – how would they manage then? What would any of them think if they knew about David?

Was she never going to be able to live her own life?

Stephen had intended to spend most of the after-noon with his father. Gilbert had been almost pathetically pleased to see him, and he felt a twinge of guilt at his recent neglect. True, he had come hotfoot as soon as he'd heard about the heart attack, but he'd stayed only a few hours and then gone back to the RAF station with a sense of relief. Gilbert had been more concerned then with Rob's absence, and once again Stephen had felt no more than an also-ran in his father's affections. First Baden, now Rob ... Not that he'd ever matched up to the expectations Gilbert had made it so obvious he held for him.

But today, the air seemed a little clearer at the Barton. Decisions had been made, and although they hadn't been the decisions Gilbert had wanted, even he seemed to feel a little easier for them. Perhaps he'd already been regretting his earlier actions.

'I gather Rob's none the worse for his experi-ence,' Stephen said, sitting down in the armchair opposite his father. 'Hilary says you're not sending him back to Kelly.'

'Didn't work out,' Gilbert said fretfully. 'Maybe it was my fault, expecting him to settle down like an English boy would, but I thought it was for the best. He needs a decent education.'

'I think he'll get a reasonable one in France,' Stephen said mildly. 'He's a bright boy – never struck me as being badly taught.'

'No, I suppose not. I was being too hasty, I know. Hilary never stops telling me... But it was like a miracle, having Baden's son turn up out of the blue like that. A gift from God.'

'Yes, it must have been,' Stephen said quietly, and his father shot him a sharp look from under bushy grey eyebrows.

'Not casting any aspersions on you, Stephen. But you made it very clear you weren't interested in the estate. What was I to do – hmm?'

'Well, let Hilary take it over, as she wanted to do. She's been making a good job of running it, hasn't she?'

'With Kellaway's help.'

'Even *before* Travis came,' Stephen said steadily. 'She was making a darned good fist of it, Dad, and you ought to admit it. You could have done a lot worse than leave it to her.'

'Maybe so, maybe so. But Baden's son–'

'Would be the legitimate heir, I know. But Dad, suppose he doesn't want it? It might not be just the school he was trying to run away from.'

Gilbert stared at his son. His brows came down low as he barked: 'You're not implying he was running away from *me*, I hope!'

'No, not from you,' Stephen said, although he wasn't at all sure. 'But possibly from the whole situation. You were putting a lot of pressure on him, you know. Telling him he was going to have to learn to manage a big estate in a country he'd never visited before. Arranging his life for him before he'd had a chance to think for himself. He's only twelve, after all. It must have come as a tremendous shock.'

'His mother knew the situation.'

'I don't think she fully realised it. She thought Baden's home was a farmhouse. She probably thought we were more like Ted Tozer. Worth coming to see, but not likely to have much to give away. But once she saw the house...'

'You talk as if Marianne is nothing more than a gold-digger!' Gilbert exclaimed indignantly.

Stephen said nothing for a moment. Then he said, 'Well, I don't think Rob is, anyway.'

'What *do* you think, then?'

'I think he's a confused young boy who's been thrown into a world he doesn't understand and who just wants to go home to his own family and finish growing up. And I think he's still missing his father,' he added carefully.

'But he never *knew* his father!'

'He knew Jacques Aucoin. Jacques brought him up as his own son, from birth. He knew the truth, but he treated Rob exactly as he treated Philippe and Ginette. Of *course* Rob thought of him as his father, and of *course* he misses him. He didn't just spring up out of the earth aged twelve.'

Gilbert scowled at the fire and leaned forward to throw on another log. After a few moments, he looked up at Stephen again and said, 'So you think I'm right to let him go back to France?'

'Yes, I do,' Stephen said, thankful to have something to agree with at last. 'He can come back in the holidays, after all – they have long ones in the summer there. He can still learn about the estate. But if you really want my opinion...' He hesitated. His father had never shown much interest in his opinions before.

'Well? And what *is* your opinion?' Gilbert demanded, in a tone that implied he wouldn't put much credence to it now either. 'Out with it.'

'Well, I think you should just let him come back and enjoy himself here. Make friends...'

'That's what he was supposed to do at Kelly!'

'Yes, but how many of those boys live locally? He seemed to make friends readily enough in the village.'

'And look what happened then! They took him down a disused mine and nearly killed him. I wanted him to mix with something better than the village boys.'

Stephen looked at him thoughtfully. Then he said, 'Boys like Micky Coker and Henry Bennetts are good value. They get up to mischief, but what boy worth his salt doesn't? At least they didn't bully and torment Rob. He could do a lot worse than make more friends like them.' He pushed the log a little further into the fire, and it crackled and sent a shower of sparks up the chimney. 'I think you forget that they're probably the sort of boy he mixes with at home.'

'Village boys, you mean. Farm labourers and such.'

'Alf Coker isn't a farm labourer – he's a blacksmith. A skilled man, working for himself. And Henry Bennetts' father is a forester. But even if they were farm labourers, would that be so bad? Working-class children have more opportunities now – they can go to grammar schools, take the School Certificate, stay at school until they're eighteen and even go to university if they're bright enough. You know, if you'd sent Rob to Tavistock Grammar, things might have been very different.'

'*Tavistock Grammar!*' Gilbert expostulated. 'But he's a *Napier!*'

Stephen saw that he would get no further with this argument. Instead, he said mildly, 'Well, it doesn't matter now. I think you're doing the right thing to let him go back to France anyway. And he seems to get on with the Kellaways, so he'll have plenty of opportunities to learn about the estate.' He paused, then added rather diffidently, 'Actually, Father, there was something else I wanted to talk to you about.'

'Oh? What's that, then?'

Already he was sounding less interested. Stephen sighed, but now he'd started, he would have to continue. He ploughed ahead.

'You know I'll be leaving the RAF next year.'

'Good lord, already?'

'I've been in two years. You know that.'

'Humph. Suppose so. Lot's happened in those two years.'

'A lot happens in any two years,' Stephen observed. 'Anyway, sometime in the next few months, I'm going to have think seriously about my plans when I come out.'

'Thought you'd decided all that. Canada or America, isn't it? Didn't you have some idea of setting up some kind of air freight business? Don't know where you got that from, mind.'

'Yes, I did and it's still what I'd like to do. But

109

I've been thinking of putting it off for a while.' He stopped, his heart suddenly beginning to pound. Once he had said this, there was no going back. He would be committed. 'I've been thinking of doing what you've always wanted me to do – come back here and help run the estate.'

There was a long silence. Stephen drew in a shaky breath. Now you've done it, he said to himself. There'll be no way out now. The old man will get his claws into you and you'll be hooked for life, like poor old Hilary. He closed his eyes, already regretting his words, and offered up a silent prayer that he would not be trapped as his sister was.

Gilbert looked up at last and met his eyes in a hard stare. His brows came down and he lifted his head slightly, as if to see past the bushy grey hairs. He said, 'And what's brought this on? Seeing young Rob about to snatch it all from under your nose?'

'That's a pretty unpleasant thing to say,' Stephen said after a moment. He was trembling inside, and his jaw tightened, but he kept his voice quiet. He's been ill, he thought, looking at the formidable figure in the armchair, the thick, lowering eyebrows, the mane of silver hair. He may look like a lion, but he's not strong enough for an argument. I shouldn't have said anything.

Yet he'd only said it because he'd thought it might please his father, might give him a way out of the dilemma he had found himself in, with a French grandson he believed to be his legitimate heir but could not be sure of. Rob's defection from Kelly College had upset him badly, and with the boy now returning to France, Gilbert must be feeling his grasp slipping. A few weeks in the summer holidays would not be enough to instil in Rob the deep and passionate feeling for Burracombe that landowners such as the Napiers must have in order to keep their estates running and in good heart.

'Unpleasant?' His father snorted. 'And hasn't it been unpleasant for me, all these years, losing my eldest son and having to watch my younger one fritter his life away? Oh, you worked hard at Cambridge, I suppose – you must have done, to get a degree in mathematics. And you're doing well enough in the RAF, I'll give you that, but once you're back in civvy street, what are you planning to do? Go off to Canada and run some tinpot little air freight service that'll bankrupt you in no time.'

'You don't know that. There's a need for such things, and I've got the flying know-how to run it. In any case, haven't you been listening to a word I've said? I'm prepared to give all that up and do what you say you've always wanted me to do – work here, on the estate. Take over, if you and Hilary want me to.'

'And why decide that now? Seems an odd time to choose, after all. You refused point-blank all the time you thought the estate was safely tied up for you and your sister to inherit. She'd have gone on running it, and you'd have sat back and collected your share of the money. But now Rob's on the scene, everything's different, isn't it?'

Stephen stood up. He found that his body was cold, as if ice had entered his blood, and he was shaking. He stared down at his father.

'I've always known you didn't think much of me,' he said in a tight, hard voice, 'but you've never said anything quite so hurtful as that. As a matter of fact, Rob hardly comes into it at all, except that I feel damned sorry for the poor little blighter. The main reason I decided it might be a good idea to come back was Hilary.'

'*Hilary?*'

'Yes.' A voice somewhere inside was telling him to stop now, not to say things that could never be taken back, but a stronger urge had taken over and was driving him on. He spoke quickly, bitingly. 'You've battened on to her long enough. She came back from the war to look after Mother and she's never been able to get away since. You've never given a thought to her and whether she might want to live her own life.'

'Utter nonsense! I've told her time and time again to get out and find herself a husband.'

'As if they grew on trees! Father, times have changed. Women can have careers now – they proved what they could do during the war, and they're just not prepared to sit at home and be an obedient wife to some arrogant fool who thinks he's God's gift. Hilary wanted to *do* something with her life. You took that chance away, but she's not too old to do it now. And if I came back–'

'What you don't seem to understand,' Gilbert said, and although his voice was controlled, it was a cold, frightening control, 'is that your sister *enjoys* running the estate. She's made that very clear. And what *I* don't understand is why you've suddenly begun to worry about her now – just at the time when Rob's turned up with a better claim than either of you.'

'A *better* claim?' Stephen drew in a deep breath, then reminded himself that there was no point in pursuing this argument. They would just go round in circles. 'Yes, Hilary enjoys running the estate, but you don't let her. You brought in Travis Kellaway. She's had to fight every inch of the way to keep her place here. And now you're proposing to leave it to a boy none of us knew even existed, and who might decide to do almost anything with it. Break it up, sell it off – who's to stop him? And even if he keeps it on and does run it himself, where does that leave Hilary?' Stephen stopped for breath. 'That's why I am thinking of coming back. So that she can take her chance now. You ought to look at her sometime, Father. She's run ragged. And there's something different about her – something restless, unhappy. As if she's almost at the end of her tether. I tell you, if nothing is done soon to help her see her way ahead, she may do something desperate.'

Gilbert flung him a look of angry scorn. 'Don't be so ridiculous!'

'I'm *not* being ridiculous.' He heard his voice rising and made an effort to bring it down to a normal level. 'But it's obvious you'll take no notice of me, and I shouldn't have said anything, not when you've just been ill again. I wouldn't have, if I'd thought it was going to turn into an argument.' He couldn't help the bitterness creeping into his voice as he added, 'Should have known better.' He turned and walked to the door, still trembling.

113

Gilbert grunted. He did not look at his son again, but as Stephen reached the door, he said, 'You'll be here for dinner tonight, I take it?'

Stephen laid his hand on the doorknob. 'No, I won't. I've got to go back – only got a few hours. I'll see you at Christmas.' He looked back, remembering his good intentions when he had first come into the room, and added, 'I really didn't mean it to turn into a row, Dad.'

There was no reply. Gilbert Napier was staring into the fire and gave no sign that he had even heard, let alone had any answer to give. Stephen sighed, opened the door and went out into the hall.

Outside the door, he hesitated. He was half inclined to leave immediately and return to the RAF station, without even seeing Hilary again. She was nowhere in sight and he assumed she had either gone out or was in the office, or maybe the kitchen. In any event, she obviously hadn't hung about to see him again and he felt irritated, neglected and generally out of sorts, as if nothing he could do would be right. I'll go back, he thought. I know where I am at the air station; there's always someone to talk to or have a drink with, and there's usually a bit of rough-housing on a Saturday night. I can't do any good here. I'm more at home there.

He walked towards the front door, but hesitated again as Hilary's words about Maddy came into his mind. He ought really to go and see her, if only for friendship's sake. What sort of a friend would he be, to avoid her when she was in such

114

distress? It would be common politeness to go down to Dottie's and ask after Stella, see for himself how Maddy was bearing up and offer any help he could give. It would be downright unkind not to go.

Hilary had said they would be sure to be back by dark. It was nearly four o'clock now, with the early December night already throwing its shadow over the countryside. He made up his mind, opened the door and strode out, past his waiting sports car and down the drive to the village road.

There were no lights in the village save those that beamed out from cottage windows, and they were few since most people lived in the back rooms of their homes, keeping the front parlours for 'best'. But Christmas lights shone in a colourful pattern outside the Bell Inn and its doors were flung wide, throwing a warm yellow glow on to the village green and creating twisting shadows from the gnarled limbs of the great oak tree. As he drew nearer to Dottie's cottage, a little further on, he saw that there was a lamp in the front window, as if to guide weary travellers home, and he guessed that Maddy had not yet come back. Presumably she had been at the hospital during the afternoon and would be tired and probably rather upset when she did return. Once again he hesitated, a few yards from the cottage, wondering whether to wait here, to knock at the door and ask Dottie if he could wait inside, or simply to give up and go away.

As he paused there, he heard a motor approaching along the village street and drew back hastily into the shadow of an overhanging tree. A car appeared round the bend and he realised that it was coming to a halt here, outside Dottie's cottage. He drew back a little further, and watched as the engine stopped and the driver's door opened.

A tall figure got out and went round to the passenger's door. For a moment, Stephen was uncertain as to who it was, and then he realised.

It was the American – Ted Tozer's nephew. And the passenger he was helping out so solicitously was Maddy.

Stephen made half a movement forward and then checked himself. He saw Russ Tozer put his hand under Maddy's elbow to help her out of the car. He saw Maddy stand there, quite close to the other man, looking up at him; and although he could not see the expression on her face, he knew what it must be simply from the stance of her body and the tilt of her head.

He felt a sinking in his breast. She doesn't need me, he thought. Not my comfort nor my love. She doesn't need anything at all from me.

He watched the two go up the short garden path and round to the back door of Dottie's cottage, and then he turned away and walked back the way he had come, back to the Barton to collect his own car and return to the RAF station, which it seemed to him now was the only real home he had.

Chapter Nine

'I'm happy to say that she seems quite a lot better,' the doctor told Felix. He had appeared beside him as Felix approached Stella's room, and touched his arm, asking him to step into the office for a moment. Felix had followed him, his heart thudding with anxiety, and the doctor's first words had sent a huge wave of relief washing through him. But before he could express his thankfulness, the other man had held up a warning hand.

'It's still early days, mind, and the brain is an unpredictable thing. We must take things very carefully. But she woke again this morning and was able to talk a little.' He smiled. 'She asked for you.'

Felix was half on his feet. 'I must go to her at once.'

'No, not just for a moment. I mentioned the brain – now, we don't know if Stella's brain is actually damaged. Obviously, with such deep unconsciousness for so long, there must be a degree of concussion, but it may be no more than that.'

'But her memory? You said she asked for me.'

'She whispered your name, and she knows she has a sister called Maddy. But she still has no memory of the accident, and we don't yet know how far back the loss goes. She may never remember that.'

'So she could have forgotten our engagement –
and that we're getting married in January.'

There was a slight pause, as if the doctor were
debating Felix's last words. Then he went on,
'There's no fracture of the skull, which is a good
thing. But we know she has other injuries – two
broken ribs, a fractured collarbone and a broken
tibia – that's the lower part of the leg.' Felix
nodded impatiently. 'She'll suffer quite a lot of
pain from those, but they will heal. Indeed, the
healing process has already begun. Our main
problem is her spine. We still don't know the
extent of the damage there.'

'Is she paralysed? Do you know that yet?'

'We think it's possible there could be some
paralysis. With the other fractures as well, it's
difficult to tell, since we can't move her too much.
But her leg is in plaster, and her ribs are strapped
up now, so she should be more comfortable.'

'Yes, thank God,' Felix said in heartfelt tones. He
felt as if a huge burden had rolled away from his
shoulders. At least Stella was going to get better,
and he could only pray that she would regain her
memory – although he knew that it would be
better if the accident itself always remained a
blank in her mind. He looked at the doctor and
said, 'Do you have any idea how much paralysis
there might be? Will it get better?'

'That we just can't say at present. My opinion
at the moment, and you must realise that I could
be wrong, is that it will be confined to her legs.
There was some crush damage there and it's
difficult to know what condition the nerves are
in. As for whether she will regain movement, or

118

how much she will regain, that's something we shall have to wait and see. A lot depends on Stella herself.'

'In what way?'

'Well, on how much she wants to get better and how much she's prepared to work towards it. She's going to be in quite a lot of pain, and we'll do what we can about that, of course, but she'll still need to do a lot of hard work, and it won't be easy. Some people just can't face the demands of working on their own body – the exercises, the pain, the sheer level of determination that's necessary. Others refuse to be beaten. Sometimes it seems that motivation is the key – what regaining movement will mean to the person. Some, quite unconsciously, I'm sure, seem to take the decision that they're happier as they are.'

'Happier as they are?' Felix echoed. 'Bedridden? In a wheelchair for the rest of their lives? Surely nobody would want that.'

'Not knowingly, I'm sure, but if life has been difficult for them, if the challenges of being in full health seem too much, it's as if their brain decides, at some deep level, that being helpless is a better option. No more decisions to be made – no more worry about working, earning a living, looking after a family. Being looked after instead. There have been some cases in my own experience where that has appeared to be the only answer – where the patient seems to have decided there's not all that much to live for if they do get better.'

Felix stared at him, then shook his head. 'Stella won't do that. She has everything to live for. We were getting married after Christmas.' He correc-

119

ted himself. 'We *are* getting married.'

'Yes, so I understand, and I'm sure you're right. Stella does have everything to live for. But ... not too soon after Christmas, I think. You should consider postponing the wedding. I'm sorry.'

'Postpone?' Felix said, his heart sinking. He had known that it would come to this, he had thought the doctor was about to say so earlier, yet he still felt himself rejecting it. 'But the arrangements are all made. The invitations have been sent out, the reception's organised. We can't postpone it.'

'I'm afraid you must. I don't think Stella will be fit enough to leave hospital that soon. You should think about another two or three months, at least, and there's no guarantee that she'll be walking even then. If ever,' he added quietly.

'Another two or three months! But ... can't we get married in hospital?'

The doctor shook his head. 'You know as well as I do that a patient has to be terminally ill and unable to go to a church or register office for permission to be given for a hospital wedding. Stella is not, in my opinion, in danger of her life now. I'm afraid there is nothing for it.' He rose from his chair. 'I'm sorry to be giving you bad news as well as good. But I think you will agree that the good far outweighs the bad. Your fiancée is alive and seems to be in full possession of her senses. Once we know what the extent of the damage is to her spine, we can begin a proper course of treatment. And you *will* be able to get married – I'm sure of that. You'll just have to wait a little while longer.'

Felix nodded reluctantly. 'Yes. I see that. Thank

you, Doctor. It's good of you to take the trouble to explain it all to me. Of course I'll wait, for as long as I have to. And now I'd like to go and see Stella, if I may.'

'Of course.' The doctor went to the door and opened it, ushering Felix through. Outside, they both paused for a moment, and then he laid his hand on Felix's shoulder and said quietly, 'I think you're right about your fiancée, Mr Copley. She's a very brave and courageous young woman and she knows just what she has to live for. Off the record, I'm sure she will overcome this and you'll be getting married just as you wanted. We'll certainly play our part, and I believe you and Stella will both play yours.'

'We will,' Felix said with conviction, and shook the doctor's hand. 'With God's help, we certainly will.'

He turned towards the door of the ward. Most of the visitors had gone in now and were sitting by the beds as he walked towards the small room where Stella had been put. She was lying flat, the bedclothes heaped over her legs, and his heart twisted with pity as he saw the bandages and plasters that swathed her slender body. Her eyes were closed as he approached, but when he stopped by the bed she opened them. They looked like enormous hollows in the paper-white of her face.

'Stella,' he whispered, drawing the hard little chair nearer to her bed and sitting down so that his face was close to hers. His heart thudded as he wondered how much she would remember about him and the love they shared, and he wondered how he would bear the pain if she knew him only

121

as a friend, even a stranger. 'Stella, my darling...'

'Felix,' she murmured. 'Oh, Felix, why am I here? What happened to me?' Her eyes searched his face, and she added in a tone that went straight to his heart, 'Have we had our wedding yet?'

The question, uttered with such poignant fear that she might have forgotten one of the most important days of her life, filled Felix with both pity and elation. Paramount was his relief that she knew him and knew that they had been planning their wedding; but alongside it was an overwhelming sorrow that she was suffering such distress. For she obviously knew that she had lost the memory of some part of her life, yet neither she nor anyone else yet knew how much of it had disappeared. How frightened she must be, he thought, and how alone she must feel.

He held her hand warmly in both of his and said softly, 'No, darling, we haven't had our wedding yet. We were still planning it when we had the accident.'

'The doctor said there'd been an accident,' she said in the faint, weak voice that was all she could manage. 'Was it in the car? Mirabelle?'

'Yes. We'd gone to fetch Rob from Exeter and we were coming back across the moor. It was dark and icy and we ran into some ponies.' He hoped he was not bringing the nightmare back to her mind. Grace was right, it was better that she should not remember that terrible crash, the ponies' screams, the head smashing through the windscreen in to Stella's lap... 'But before that, everything was all right,' he went on quickly. 'Do you remember going to Exeter, darling? Do you

122

remember meeting Rob at the railway station?'

A tiny frown gathered between her brows and he knew that she did not. 'Do you remember Rob? The French boy living with the Napiers – Hilary's nephew?'

'Rob,' she whispered. 'Rob ... stuck down the mine with Micky Coker...'

Felix smiled, thankfulness washing over him. 'That's right. You do remember him. And you remember me, and Maddy, and our wedding, so that's all right. You needn't worry about it any more.' And nor do I, he thought, almost weak with relief. 'It will all come back, as you get better. And you *are* going to get better. We will have our wedding – but perhaps not as soon as we planned.'

'I'm going to be here for months,' she murmured. 'My leg's broken – it'll be weeks before that's healed. And there are other things, too... Felix, I don't think I'm ever going to be able to walk again.'

'Of course you are! You mustn't even think that.' He clasped her hand, leaning closer. 'You're going to get completely better, as if the accident had never happened, and we're going to be married just as we planned, with a rainbow of bridesmaids to show all our friends that the storm has passed. Even if we have to put it off for a little while, it's still going to be a marvellous, happy day. And we'll have our honeymoon and then go back to the vicarage and live happily ever after. I promise you, Stella.'

She smiled a little, but shook her head very slightly. 'Nobody ever lives happily ever after, Felix.'

'Some people do,' he said stoutly. 'And anyway, we'll be together. That's all I want really, darling – for us to be together, facing whatever comes to us. Happiness isn't something you can arrange, it just comes along by itself while you're living your life, but it only comes if you live the best way you can. And that's what we shall do.'

'You're a dear,' she said softly, and squeezed his hand. Then her eyes closed again and she whispered, 'I'm awfully tired. Do you mind if I go to sleep now?'

'Of course I don't. I'll just sit quietly, and be here when you wake up again.'

He kept her hand in his, letting his grasp slacken as he felt her hold grow loose, and watched her face as she slept. Despite the blow on her head, there was no sign of bruising on her face, and she looked as peaceful and serene as if she were naturally asleep and uninjured. It came to him that he had never actually seen Stella asleep before, never been able to let his gaze linger on her pale complexion, her soft mouth, the faint tinge of blue beneath her eyelids. He wanted to stroke the alabaster skin, bring some roses back into that ivory pallor, smooth away the tendril of soft brown hair that had escaped from the bandages that swathed her head. But he was afraid that even the lightest touch of his fingertips might wake her, and he knew that she needed to sleep, if only to escape from the pain that must constantly be with her.

'The doctor says we'll have to postpone the wedding,' he told Dottie and Maddy later. 'He says she won't even be out of hospital in time.'

'Oh, my dear,' Dottie said sorrowfully. 'Mind you, I'm not surprised. 'Tis less than a month off, after all.'

'A *month!*' he said. 'She's going to be in hospital for a whole month! Maybe even longer. She's got to have operations and heaven knows what, and even after that they don't know if she'll be able to walk again. My Stella, in a wheelchair for the rest of her life. How will she bear it?'

'She'll bear it, because she's the sort that will bear anything,' Dottie said sturdily. 'But you'm just looking on the black side, Felix. You don't know that it'll come to that. I dare say her'll be out by Easter and you can have your wedding then.'

'She wanted an Easter wedding,' he said miserably. 'It was me who wanted to rush things through now.'

'And that had nothing to do with the accident, so you needn't start blaming yourself for that,' she said firmly. 'But you did ought to start thinking about letting people know. There's all those invitations you've sent out, for a start, and the booking at the Bedford Hotel.'

'I don't know how I'm ever going to get it all done!' Felix exclaimed, running his fingers through his hair. 'There's so much to do – Christmas services to prepare, and it's Sunday tomorrow. I can't expect Basil to take my services for me, he's got his own church to look after... I won't even be able to go in and see her... But you're right, everyone will have to know. If only I could give them another date... I hardly know where to start.'

'I'll help you,' Maddy said. She had been sitting quietly until now, dismayed by Felix's words but aware that Dottie was a better comforter than she could ever be to the distressed young man. 'If you give me the list of invitations, I'll write to them all and tell them what's happened. And I'll go and see Stella tomorrow, before I go back to West Lyme.' She turned to Dottie. 'I must go back. The Archdeacon's been very kind, but he has a lot to do as well and I oughtn't to desert him like this – he must wonder sometimes if I'm really working for him at all! I'll come again next week. Unless – unless...' Her voice quivered, and Dottie swiftly laid a hand on her arm. 'You will let me know if I need to come back, won't you?' she finished shakily.

'Of course I will, my bird. But it seems as if her's turned the corner. There might be a long road to travel yet, poor maid, but her'll get there, you see if her don't. Now then,' she added, turning back to Felix, who was standing by the fireplace, his arm resting on the mantelpiece as he gazed broodingly into the flames, 'you're to come and sit down this minute, if you please. I don't remember giving you permission to leave the table.' She was using the voice she often used to Felix, as though he were a small boy and she his nanny, and he smiled faintly and did as he was told. She took away his plate, tipped the crumbs on to an old enamel plate to put out for the birds, and gave it back to him with two slices of bread and butter on it. 'Now, you put something on that – there's Marmite here, or a pot of fish paste, sardine and tomato it is, your favourite – and get some food inside you. There's some more rock cakes and some of my scones, and my own strawberry jam. You can take a few back with you. And what are you doing for your dinner tomorrow?'

'Oh, I expect I'll be asked back somewhere. I usually am. I must give my own parishioners some attention too,' he said, spreading Marmite on his bread. 'Sometimes I forget I don't really belong to Burracombe now.'

'Not belong to Burracombe!' Dottie exclaimed, outraged. 'Why, of course you belong to Burracombe, Felix, and so you always will. Well, if nobody asks you to dinner tomorrow after church, you come right over here, d'you hear me? There'll be enough to go round, and Maddy'll be here too, won't you, maid?'

'No, I'll go in early to see Stella and then go straight back on the train from Plymouth. Visiting hours are from two till four tomorrow, so if I leave here at one I'll be in plenty of time. I'll take a sandwich with me. And then Felix can have his Sunday dinner and come in a bit later. Bring that list of invitations with you, Felix.'

'I'll be there by three,' he said. 'Thank you, Maddy. I didn't want her to feel I'd abandoned her for that first hour. She might think I don't want ... that I've changed my mind...' His voice shook and he laid down his piece of bread and rested his forehead on one hand.

'Of course she won't think that,' Dottie said forcefully. 'Now, you eat your tea and stop fretting.'

Obediently, Felix ate his bread and Marmite

127

and then, to please Dottie, another rock cake. But the food, usually so delicious, tasted like ashes in his mouth and he swallowed the last few crumbs with difficulty. Then he stood up.

'I'll go back now. There must be any amount of things wanting my attention. I'll see you at the hospital, Maddy. And don't worry about my dinner, Dottie – I'm sure someone will want to look after me.'

Maddy went to bed early, worn out by the emotion of the past few days. The moon was full, and she opened her curtains and lay gazing at it, awed by the huge pale globe. It looked almost near enough to touch, as if she had only to reach her hand through the window to stroke its lustrous face. Stella's face had looked like that, as pale as a pearl, as still and as cold; and as remote. Maddy's fingertips could touch her skin, but she could not reach through to the mind and the personality of her sister. She had seemed as distant as the moon.

Poor Stella, and poor Felix. They had been so close to happiness, and now it seemed to have been snatched away from them. It was a feeling that Maddy knew all too well; she too had been close to happiness, had felt it brush her with its glimmering wings, and then lost it in the flutter of an eyelid. Lost it in such a similar way, too – an accident on the road. Sammy had been knocked down and killed by a lorry that had no chance to stop as he rushed blindly across the road to save a man's life, while Stella had been hurt in a car that had no chance to avoid the ponies that had loomed up out of the foggy darkness of a December night.

But Stella would get better. Already she had opened her eyes, had known Felix was there, had smiled the faintest touch of a smile. Her injuries were terrible, but she would get better. She must...

Maddy turned over restlessly, away from the moon with its cold, pale stare. She needed time to think over the events of the past few days, time to get her thoughts into order, to come to terms with it all. The dreadful moment when she had first heard about the accident, the scramble to leave the Archdeacon's house in West Lyme and come to Burracombe, that first visit to the hospital, not knowing what awaited her there, afraid of what she would see. She had imagined her sister's face swollen and bruised, perhaps disfigured for life. She had imagined being too late, finding her already gone.

It was odd that it should be a stranger who could give her most comfort. Felix had tried, of course, but he was too wrapped up in his own distress. Dottie had taken her to her bosom at once, but she had been as anxious as Felix about the injured girl. The only person who was able to give her his full attention was the American, Russ Tozer.

Maddy had tried not to think too much about Russ, after that first meeting soon after he and his father had arrived in Burracombe. They'd been invited to Dottie's cottage to tea, Joe Tozer having apparently known Dottie years ago, when they were both young and before he'd emigrated to America. Maddy wasn't much interested then, for she was still grieving over Sammy, but even in the midst of her grief she had been unable to ignore Russ's good looks and the warmth of his smile – a warmth that had spread to his eyes as he looked into hers.

Maddy had looked away hastily. She'd seen that kind of interest in a man's eyes before, more than once, and before Sammy she might have responded. But there was no heart in her now for flirtation, and she'd made sure that their eyes didn't meet again that evening.

And then he had met her train and brought her to Burracombe, and during that journey she'd become aware that his warmth went deeper than a look, and during the next few days, as he made it his business to transport her to the hospital in Plymouth whenever she needed it, she had found herself resting more and more in his strength, and her heart, frozen in its sadness, had begun to thaw.

By now, there was almost an understanding between them. Soon he would be returning to America. He had hinted that she might go too, to visit him and his family, and she knew that the hint was for more than a simple, friendly visit. There could be a life for her there, if she wanted it – a life far away from all she had known, from the cruelty of a war which had robbed her of her parents and brother; from the loss, perhaps, of her one remaining relative, her sister. For if Stella did not survive, Maddy would feel very alone.

She wouldn't be truly alone, of course she wouldn't. There was Dottie, who had been like a mother to her when she was a small, frightened

130

evacuee, and Fenella Forsyth, the actress who had adopted her. But Dottie's cottage could no longer be a home for Maddy, who had travelled the Continent with Fenella, and Fenella herself was now married and living in France. Maddy needed more than either of those. She needed what she should have had with Sammy – love, a home of her own, a family to gather around her.

Perhaps, she had begun to think lately, she might have that after all.

As Russ had driven her through the cold, bleak countryside that day, taking her for lunch in a warm, elegant hotel already decorated for Christmas, treating her with tenderness, she had felt a sense of homecoming, and knew that if he chose this moment to propose to her, she would very likely accept him. She almost hoped he wouldn't, for it was too soon and she was afraid she might regret it, yet she was disappointed when he said nothing. Probably he too knew that it was too soon, that she was still too anxious about Stella. She'd caught his look once or twice, as if he were on the verge of speaking, and had looked away quickly, afraid to give him any encouragement. Yet when they arrived at Dottie's door as the early December darkness fell, she felt a wistful longing. Say it now, she'd begged him silently, say it now before things change again and we lose our chance...

He helped her out of the car and they'd stood together at the gate, very close, his hands resting on her shoulders and hers on his forearms. She looked up at him, her lips slightly parted, and she'd caught a gleam of light in his eyes. He was

131

about to speak, she knew it, and her heart kicked.

And then she'd heard a sound, so faint that she wondered if it was her imagination. She turned her head, thinking it was Dottie's cat come to greet them, and saw in the shadows of the trees a darker shape, very still. For a brief moment there was stillness, and then the shape moved and she knew who it was. How she knew, she could never again remember – a flash of the wings on his tunic, perhaps, or the general overlaying of a deeper shadow on other shadows, a shape that she knew well, that had been important to her once, almost as important as Sammy. Or maybe nothing tangible at all.

Stephen.

He was there, waiting for her. She made a swift, small movement towards him, and then checked herself and turned away. She looked up again at Russ, but the moment was gone. With one hand he opened Dottie's gate and with the other he guided her through. When she looked back, the shadow beneath the trees had vanished, and there was a coldness around her heart.

Maddy turned over in bed and looked again at the moon. It had moved in its passage across the sky and looked smaller and further away, but it was still as cold, still as remote, still as inaccessible, and she no longer felt she could reach out and touch it.

Chapter Ten

Sunday dinner was a kind of celebration, Alice Tozer thought as she handed the dish of roast potatoes to her brother-in-law. Almost like a tiny Christmas, starting every new week off on a good note. Most people had meat of some sort, although during the war it had been a very small portion indeed. And it was still on ration, even though the war had been over for eight years now. Who could possibly have thought it would go on so long!

But there had always been vegetables available in the country, and in town too if you could grow your own in your back garden or on an allotment. 'Dig for Victory', that's what they'd said, and there'd been that advertisement with a picture of a man's boot thrusting a spade into rich soil. As long as you had fresh vegetables, grown with plenty of manure, you'd be all right.

That was what Alice thought, anyway, and as she watched her family tuck into the mounds of golden potatoes, green cabbage and bright orange carrots, it seemed to her that the Tozer family was doing quite well for itself. It was true that Jackie wasn't here – she seemed to work longer hours than ever at that hotel, especially with Christmas so near – and poor Joanna and Tom were still grieving over the loss of their baby, Susannah. But there it was – these things happened. Alice's own mother had lost three babies, two of them still-born and one a miscarriage, and Ted himself should have had a twin. You just had to take it on the chin, as Tom would say, and get on with your life. And to do her credit, Joanna did seem to be doing that now. The surviving twin, Heather, helped a lot. At eight months old, she was a joy to behold, with her round face that seemed always to be smiling, and her deep, infectious chuckle that made you laugh just because it seemed so in-congruous coming from a little baby. She was chuckling now, as she sat in her little high chair at Joanna's elbow, chewing on a strip of crackling from the roast pork.

There was Val's baby too – young Christopher, three months old, murmuring to himself in his pram by the staircase – and Robin, who had grown up alarmingly since he'd started school. All of them to keep the family on its toes, and herself and Ted green.

Without Jackie, there were twelve of them – herself, Ted and Minnie; Tom and Joanna and their two; Val and Luke with Christopher; and Joe and Russ. Eleven around the table and baby Christopher nearby. That was what Alice liked – a big family sitting round the kitchen table enjoy-ing a good home-cooked meal together. The best thing in life, she thought, feeling a deep content-ment warm her heart. And she wondered yet again why her daughter Jackie didn't seem to feel the same. Why couldn't she see that a family life, with a good husband and a quiverful of children, was the best, most satisfying way for a woman to live? Why did she want to go off and work in a hotel in Plymouth, away from her family? And why, for heaven's sake, did she want to go to America and travel the world – and maybe never come back to Burracombe at all?

Alice sighed. It was beyond her understanding, but there it was. Jackie had always been the restless one, and she wasn't going to change now. And at least she was alive and healthy, and seemed happy. Maybe, like Joanna, Alice had to take it on the chin and get on with her own life.

'It'll seem strange without you and Russ here after Christmas,' she said to Joe. 'You've fitted in just as if you'd never left the place.'

'Don't know about that, Alice,' he said, pouring gravy over his meat and potatoes. 'There's been a lot of changes, both in me and in Burracombe. And yet, in some ways, the place hasn't altered a bit. Even some of the youngsters look like the ones me and Ted used to know. It's a funny thing about family resemblances – I reckon if you went back a hundred years, maybe even two or three hundred, you could walk down the street and see Cokers and Bennettses and Friends, just like today.'

'Maybe you could,' she said thoughtfully. 'But then there's incomers to take account of – like Joanna, and Luke. Robin's a Tozer through and through, but Heather's a bit of a mixture, and Christopher looks more like his father.'

'Yes, but back in history there weren't so many incomers. People stopped where they were born, and grew old and died there.'

'Most people do now,' Alice observed. 'Two world wars have made a difference, though. Folk like you, emigrating because there was nothing here for you after you'd done your bit, and people like Joanna, who came here as a Land Girl and never went away again. Which we're proper thankful for,' she added, smiling at her daughter-in-law, who was trying to persuade Robin to eat his cabbage. 'Tell us about the Nativity Play, Robin.'

'Yes, how's it coming along?' Tom enquired from the other side of the little boy. 'I bet the Baby Jesus ate his cabbage, don't you?'

Robin gave his father a withering glance. 'He couldn't – he was only born that night. Anyway, they didn't have cabbage in Bethlehem.'

'Well, tell us anyway,' Russ encouraged him. He had taken a great liking to his young cousin. 'You're a shepherd, aren't you?'

'Yes. I wanted to take a lamb, but there won't be any new ones yet. I'm going to borrow the one from Mr Foster's shop.'

'What lamb's that?' Joe asked. He knew that Bert Foster ran the village butcher's shop, but he hadn't been inside it since he was a boy, when Bert's father ran it. 'They don't keep sheep, do they?'

'It's a papier mâché one that he stands on his counter,' Joanna explained. She turned back to her son. 'Has Mr Foster said you can borrow it?'

'Yes, I asked him when I went in with Granny to get the pork. He says I can have it but nobody else is to carry it. He doesn't want it broken.'

'I don't suppose he does. You'll have to take great care of it. They're going all round the village,' Joanna explained, just in case there was anyone in the family who hadn't heard all about this from

Robin. 'Calling at different houses, singing carols and asking for lodgings – for Mary and Joseph, of course, not for themselves – until they get to the Bell Inn, and then they're going round the back to the old stable. I thought at first it was a strange idea, but now I think it will be rather nice.'

'I think it sounds proper handsome,' Minnie said. 'I'm going to go and watch.'

'I don't know about that, Mother,' Alice said doubtfully. 'Do you think that's wise? It'll be cold and dark.'

'I can wrap meself up, can't I? And I'm not frightened of a bit of dark. It's not going to be in the middle of the night, is it, not with all they little tackers from the babies' class going. Anyway, I want to see our Robin being a shepherd.'

'I want Great-Granny to come,' Robin said, and they smiled at each other across the table.

'Well, all right,' Alice said resignedly. She had never beaten her mother-in-law in a battle of wills yet, and Minnie wasn't likely to give in now, for all she was almost ninety years old. It was as much as they could do to persuade her to have a lie-down in the afternoons. 'We'll all go.'

'Sure we will,' Joe said. 'Wouldn't miss it for the world. What are the rest of the plans for Christmas, Alice? We seem to have got a bit out of step, with all this travelling down to the hospital in Plymouth and back.'

'And a real help you've been too,' Alice said, with a glance at Russ. 'I know poor young Maddy must have been glad of a shoulder to cry on. Anyway, about Christmas – there's plenty happening in the village in the next fortnight, what with all the goings-on in the village hall, and the carol services and such. There'll be one at the Chapel as well, and that's usually a rousing sort of do. And the handbell ringers'll be going round the night before Christmas Eve, as well as the carol-singers and the school play. Folk will have been saving their pennies for weeks to keep in a pot by the door, to share out. And then there's Christmas Day itself...'

'Which is what he was asking about,' Tom said with a grin.

'...and I always like to go to early service, at seven o'clock. It gives me a little bit of peace and quiet before all the rumpus starts. Ted and Tom ring for that.'

'Only Dad this year,' Tom said. 'I want to be here for Robin to open his stocking. And Heather – she's old enough to enjoy it too.'

He slipped his arm behind Robin's chair to lay his hand on Joanna's shoulder, and she smiled at him a little mistily and looked down at her plate. Alice noticed the look and felt a pang of pity for her. There should have been two babies to enjoy their first Christmas, not one, and although she knew Tom and Joanna would always be grateful for Heather, they would never stop grieving over her twin, who had died suddenly in her pram last Easter Day.

'I'm going to hang up one of Granny's stockings,' Robin said, now eating cabbage without really noticing it. 'It's her lucky stocking, isn't it, Granny? And a pillowcase, in case Father Christmas brings me too many presents to go in a stocking.'

'That's right, Robin,' Alice said. 'And then

there'll be the dinner to get ready while you men get the outside work and milking done, and bring in plenty of logs for the fire later on. I've already picked out which geese look the fattest.' Alice reared several geese every year, choosing the finest for the Squire's table and the second for their own.

'Will Jackie be home for Christmas?' Russ asked, helping himself to another potato.

'Not Christmas Day, I'm sorry to say. They're busy then, she says. Why folk should want to eat their Christmas dinner in a hotel is a mystery to me, but apparently some of them do. Posh people with luxury kitchens, who don't even know how to turn the oven on, I dare say.' Alice's voice was tight with disapproval. 'But she'll be home for Boxing Day, so we'll have to be grateful for that. And then it won't be long before she's off back to America with you.'

'Only a couple of weeks now,' Joe agreed. 'But you mustn't worry, Alice. You know we'll take care of her.'

'Oh, I know that – while she's with you. But what happens if she decides to up and go off on her own? I don't like to think of her roaming round a huge country like America all by herself. It's not right, at her age.'

'We'll just have to try to make sure she doesn't,' Joe said reassuringly. 'Corning's a nice place to live. She'll find plenty to do there. We could probably find her a job to keep her occupied, and she'll soon make friends. I don't reckon she'll want to go off anywhere else.'

'You don't know our Jackie like we do,' Alice told him. 'Restless as a cricket, always has been.

Wants her own way, and won't let go until she's got it – like a terrier, she is.'

'She's a great kid,' Russ told her. 'Honestly, Auntie Alice, you don't need to worry about Jackie. She won't get into any trouble. She'll always land on her feet.'

Val, who was the only one there who knew about a time when it looked as though Jackie *was* in trouble, yet had landed on her feet, pursed her lips. Her sister was only nineteen and had no experience of life other than in Burracombe and, for the past year or so, Plymouth. Val could understand her mother's anxiety, but she also knew there was nothing to be done about it. As Alice had said, Jackie always did manage to get her own way, in the end.

'So what else happens at Christmas?' Joe asked, diplomatically changing the subject. 'D'you still play games like we used to when we were boys, Ted?'

'Oh yes. Us likes the old traditions. Charades and all those sorts of things. And us has a sing-song round the organ. Alice can play a treat, and our Val's not bad.'

'The organ?' Russ asked, mystified. 'You mean the church organ?'

They all laughed, and Joe shook his head.

'You've seen it, surely. It's in the front parlour. Just a small one, nothing like the church organ, but it's got a good tone. A lot of Devon homes have got an organ in them.'

'That?' Russ said, surprised. 'I thought it was a big old desk!'

'You used to be able to get a good tune out of

140

it yourself, if I remember rightly,' Ted said to his brother.

'Oh, I'm years out of practice. To tell the truth, I'm surprised we've never heard anyone play it while we've been back. Don't you ever slip in there and practise a few tunes, Alice?'

'Only when everyone's out of the way,' she said firmly. 'But I'll play at Christmas, of course. Now, does anyone want any more vegetables? And there's a slice or two of meat left if you're really hungry, only remember to leave enough for us all to have cold tomorrow, with a jacket potato and some bubble and squeak. Pass your plates over then, if you've all had enough.'

She took the plates to the deep sink by the window and brought a large pie out of the larder. It was still warm and smelled of plums.

'These are the ones Robin and me picked in the summer,' she said. 'There was a good crop this year. Who wants a piece?'

Everyone did, and by the time dinner was finished, they were all full. Tom declared that he didn't think he'd need another meal before Christmas, and Joanna raised her eyebrows and told him he'd be hungry again by teatime. Ted took his *Sunday Express* and went to sit by the fire, where he fell asleep within ten minutes, Minnie went upstairs for her own rest, Joanna and Val went to Val's room to feed their babies, and Alice started to pump water into the sink for the washing-up. Joe pushed her firmly aside.

'Russ and me'll do that. You sit down and have a rest. You've been slaving away all morning over this great meal.'

'I'll help,' Luke offered, but Joe shook his head.

'You and Tom take young Robin out. I know you like to have a walk round the fields on a Sunday afternoon. We'll come and find you when we've done this.'

He poured hot water from the kettle into the cold water already in the sink and rolled up his sleeves. Alice sat a little uncomfortably in her chair, watching as he began to wash the dishes. 'It seems funny to me to see a man doing that sort of work, Joe,' she said. 'Do all Americans help their wives like that?'

'Not all,' he said with a grin, 'but I always used to give Eleanor a hand, especially towards the end, when it was all she could do to cook the dinner. And you got to remember I don't have a wife now, so I have to shift for myself. Dab hand at the domestic skills now, ain't I, Russ?'

'He sure is,' Russell told his aunt. 'Puts on a good dinner when he sets his mind to it. And he's making sure I go the same way, too. I'll make some lucky girl a good wife one of these days!'

Alice laughed, thinking that she knew who the lucky girl was likely to be too, although a lot of water would have to flow under the bridge before Maddy Forsyth agreed to leave her sister and go to America to live. Then she thought of Jackie, and her smile faded. Joe, glancing round to smile at her, caught her expression and understood it.

'You really don't need to worry about young Jackie,' he said quietly. 'We'll take care of her. But she's an independent young woman and she'll go her own way whether she stays in England or travels to some other country. And America ain't the only place youngsters can go to seek their fortune these days. Australia's looking for more people too, and that's even further away.'

'I know,' Alice said, and sighed a little. 'I've had the feeling for some time now that our Jackie's like a caged animal. She's always been a bit different from the rest of us Tozers. More like you, I suppose, Joe. I hoped she'd find some nice boy nearby and settle down, but it don't look like that's going to happen, and the next best thing is that she should be with family, even if that does mean she goes away.' She watched the two men working at the sink for a moment longer and then added, 'I trust you, Joe, but I'm not going to ask you to do the impossible. If her own family can't hold the maid, 'tis unfair to expect you to do it. She'll go, with our blessing, and it's her own self we got to trust after that. But Ted and me, we both know she couldn't do better than go with you, and we're grateful that you'm willing to take her on.'

Joe left his task and came over to her, wiping his hands on the checked tea cloth that Robin had requested for his headdress in the Nativity Play. He laid his damp hand on her shoulder.

'More than willing, Alice. She's a lovely girl, and wherever she goes and whatever she does, she'll do well. One of these days, mark my words, we're all going to be proud of your Jackie.'

143

Chapter Eleven

Felix had, as expected, been invited to Sunday lunch by one of his parishioners. It wasn't, unfortunately, one of those he would have liked to be invited by, but the tall, elegant woman was first in line as he stood at the church door and he couldn't refuse. He could see from the expressions on the faces of those behind her that there would have been other, more appealing, invitations extended, and he could only hope that these would be more successful another time. Then, picturing an unseemly rush to be at the front of the queue at the church door, he felt his lips twitch and thought of Stella's reaction to such vanity. *As if half the congregation were competing to ask you to lunch!* he could hear her saying, and the brief flash of humour vanished in a pang of grief.

'Thank you, Mrs Lydiard, I'd like that very much. I'm afraid I'll have to leave soon after two, though – I want to be at the hospital by three.'

'Of course. Poor little Miss Simmons. You must be so anxious.' She pressed his hand with her long, slim fingers. 'I'll hurry on, then, and have everything ready for you when you arrive.' She flashed a smile at the rest of the congregation, lining up behind her with varying degrees of impatience, and Felix marvelled at the discreet triumph in her face. Surely I'm not such a catch as all that, he thought, and reminded himself that

144

it wasn't him, personally, that she was setting out to ensnare. It was his position as vicar.

Felix had not been long in Little Burracombe, but he was beginning to identify the different types amongst his congregation. Everyone had their own personality, of course they did, but all the same there were amongst any group of people certain types. And in any church, there were inevitably a few who seemed to consider it their right to be in the inner circle around the vicar. It seemed to give them an added sense of importance.

Olivia Lydiard was one of these. She reminded him a little of Joyce Warren, in Burracombe; both liked to have their fingers in as many village pies as possible, sat on several committees and chaired more than one. But where Joyce Warren was big, bustling and bossy, Olivia Lydiard was more subtle. Tall, slender and elegant with her blonde hair, china-blue eyes and sweet smile, she was the wife of a retired naval captain, and had spent many years attending and effortlessly organising events on a social scale far beyond those of the solicitor's wife. What Joyce aspired to, Olivia had left behind, and Felix was well aware that she could be dangerous. But he did not come from a long line of clergymen and bishops for nothing; he had met both types before and didn't intend to be manipulated.

He shook hands with the rest of his congregation, accepting their compliments on his sermon and answering their enquiries about Stella. They were all sympathetic and he knew that they must be wondering about the wedding, but there was nothing he could tell them about that yet. He knew it would have to be postponed, but the knowledge was too fresh and painful to discuss with people who were still, after all, strangers.

Olivia Lydiard, however, did not consider herself a stranger. On his arrival at the large detached house which stood on the edge of the village, she pressed a glass of sherry into his hand and urged him to sit in the corner of a comfortable sofa by a wide curved bay window looking out into the garden. She sat opposite him and asked immediately after Stella.

'Poor little soul. She's so young, isn't she? It seems so cruel, to be robbed of so much, just when you were about to begin your life together.'

'We're still going to begin our life together,' Felix answered. 'The accident hasn't changed that. It may delay things a little, of course, but that's all.'

'Oh, that *is* good news. I heard – well, never mind what I heard.' She brushed a slim hand down her silk skirt, and he thought that only a woman like Olivia Lydiard would be wearing silk at a time of year when most women were in tweeds and twinsets. But Olivia did not have to worry about being cold. Her large, solid house was warmly heated, and when she set foot outside, she was swathed in furs.

'What have you heard?' he asked, feeling a prickle of annoyance. It could only be gossip, for nobody who knew the facts about Stella's condition would have discussed it at large.

'Why, nothing definite,' she said, confirming his thoughts. 'Just what people are saying. But you know what *people* are like.'

'Yes, I do, and usually I find it best not to listen if they've "nothing definite" to say.' He was uncomfortably aware that his voice might be betraying his irritation and that he was in danger of being rude to his hostess. 'It's good of them to take an interest,' he added, and realised that he was now probably sounding sarcastic. I shouldn't have come, he thought miserably, staring at his sherry. I should have stayed at home and eaten that shepherd's pie that Grace Harvey gave me yesterday to heat up.

'But of course we take an interest,' Olivia exclaimed. 'You're our vicar and we were looking forward so much to welcoming Miss Simmons as your wife. Such a dear girl... So she is going to make a complete recovery, then?'

Felix was caught. He could only answer this direct question honestly, and he said, 'Nobody knows yet, Mrs Lydiard. There's some damage to her spine. I believe they're planning to operate in the next few days and then I hope we'll know more. But whatever happens, you may rest assured that you'll be able to welcome Stella here as my wife. Nothing is going to stand in the way of that.'

Olivia Lydiard gazed at him. 'I see... But if she's bedridden...'

'A word I particularly dislike,' he answered strongly. 'It smacks of someone who has abandoned and been abandoned by normal life, and it's one which I am sure will never be applied to Stella.'

'Oh, of course, of course,' she said hastily. 'And,

147

as you say, until they know for certain... Would you like a little more sherry, Vicar? Or may I call you Felix? I feel we are going to be such friends.'

'Of course you may,' he said, feeling quite the opposite but recognising that she was trying to recoup the situation. 'And I won't have any more sherry, thank you. I have to drive to the hospital in an hour or so, and wine makes me sleepy in the afternoons.'

The door had opened while he was speaking and they both turned in some relief to see Captain Lydiard entering. He was tall, with silver hair and bright blue eyes – just what you'd expect of a seafaring man, Felix thought, amused as always when people slotted almost too easily into their stereotypes.

'A stiff pink gin, that's what you need,' the Captain said, bearing out this first impression. 'Sherry's no drink for a man.'

'I'm afraid that would send me to sleep even more quickly,' Felix replied, standing up to shake his hand. He had met the Captain before, in church, and at the reception that had been organised to welcome him to the village after his induction service, but they had not had much conversation before. He met the direct blue gaze and felt a liking that surprised him. The Captain was a different kettle of fish from his wife, but not, Felix thought, one to trifle with.

'Well, I'll have one, if you've no objection.' The Captain went to the sideboard and poured himself a drink, then came over to the big window, where he stood swirling his glass in his hand and looking out at the garden. There was a wide lawn, bordered by shrubs and trees; the flower beds were empty at this time of year, but Felix guessed that in the summer they would contain strictly laid-out formal beds of herbaceous plants (probably red, white and blue) and that there would be beds of stiff standard roses all lined up and looking ready to set off at a quick march.

'Have you lived long in Little Burracombe?' he asked, to steer the conversation into safer waters. My goodness, he thought, I'm beginning to think like a sailor myself.

'Came here when I retired in forty-seven. Knew the area, of course, from my time in the Service. Looked for a place in Crapstone – know it? Nice little spot near Yelverton, not too far from Plymouth. Lot of naval officers' quarters there, good neighbourhood – our sort of people, you know – and quite a few decent properties to buy, but nothing available when we were looking, so we settled on this house. It suits us well enough – easy to get into Plymouth, and Tavistock's a nice little town with one or two good shops. We can see plenty of our friends.'

'A car is essential, of course,' Olivia said, smiling. 'I don't know how we'd manage without the Bentley.'

'I suppose you'd have to use the bus,' Felix suggested, and saw her shoulders move in a very delicate shudder.

'Well, in an *emergency*... Luckily, we haven't had to resort to that so far. And we'd have to go over to Burracombe for the train, so that isn't a lot of use. And public transport is really very limited when you want to visit friends in the country.'

A gong sounded from the hall, and Olivia rose to her feet. 'That will be lunch. Do come this way, Felix.'

Lunch was served in the elegant dining room that Felix expected – a warm room with tall windows looking out on to another part of the garden, and a long, highly polished table set with gleaming Wedgwood china, silver cutlery and crystal glasses. There was a joint of beef in front of the Captain's place, and Olivia and Felix sat on either side while he carved. Roast potatoes, carrots and cauliflower steamed in bowls which they handed to each other as the Captain served the meat, and a jug filled with rich gravy to pour over.

Felix, who had been dreading not being able to eat the meal, found that he was hungry after all. At least Dottie will be pleased, he thought, as he ate, and it's certainly very good. Not that it's any better than one of Dottie's Sunday dinners, but the Lydiards' cook is well up to her standard. I wonder what her name is.

'It's Mrs Sweet,' Olivia told him in answer to his question. 'She's a cousin of the baker in Burracombe – cooking seems to run in the family.' She wagged a playful finger at him. 'You're not to poach her, mind!'

'Oh, I don't think I shall be looking for a cook,' Felix said, accepting a second helping of roast potatoes. 'Dottie Friend's been teaching Stella...' His voice faded as he wondered when, or even if, Stella would be able to put her lessons into practice; then he said, 'I'd like some more horseradish sauce, if I may, please.'

The meal progressed to gooseberry crumble and custard and finished with coffee. By now, Felix was growing anxious about the time and would have cheerfully forgone the coffee, but Olivia Lydiard seemed to have forgotten his hurry. She apologised that the garden wasn't worth looking at in the middle of December and suggested a tour of the house instead. At this, Felix cast a glance of entreaty towards the Captain, who immediately got up from the table, saying, 'We ought to let Copley go now, dear. He has to visit his fiancée in the hospital, don't forget.'

'Of course!' Mrs Lydiard was on her feet at once. 'Felix, my dear, do forgive me. I was so much enjoying your company, I quite forgot the time. Now, are you sure you want to drive that little hire car all the way to Plymouth? You wouldn't like James to take you in the Bentley?'

'No, indeed – I'm quite happy to drive. That's what the hire car's for.' He shrugged into his coat and shook hands with them both. 'Thank you so much for the meal, and please give my compliments to Mrs Sweet. It was very kind of you to ask me for lunch.'

'We're happy to have you, at any time. Come again next Sunday,' Mrs Lydiard said as she showed him to the front door. But Felix smiled and shook his head.

'That would be delightful, but I must be fair to my other parishioners. I know several of them want to invite me as well.' He laughed a little. 'That's until you tell them how much I eat!'

Olivia Lydiard echoed his laugher with a pretty trill that he was sure she must have practised long and hard until it came naturally to her lips. 'I shan't breathe a word. Now, be sure and give my best regards to your dear little fiancée and tell her she must get better soon. We're all longing to have her in the village. James, why don't you walk back to the vicarage with Felix? Unless you're quite sure about the Bentley?'

'Quite sure, thank you,' Felix said, and the two men set off together along the drive. It was only a short walk to the vicarage, and for a moment or two neither of them spoke. Then the Captain cleared his throat.

'Don't mind Olivia,' he said gruffly. 'She misses the company of the other wives. Officers' wives, I mean. She was always rather looked up to when I was in the Service, and she enjoyed organising them all. Sometimes forgets we're in civvy street now.'

'That's quite all right,' Felix said, rather surprised. 'There are always a few ladies in any parish who like to take the vicar under their wing and get him organised. They're very useful.'

'Well, that's all she wants, really,' James Lydiard said. 'To be useful, I mean. Running a house and chairing one or two village committees isn't always enough for a woman like Olivia. If she'd been born a man, she'd have risen to the top of the tree. Difficult for a woman like that.'

'Yes, I suppose it is,' Felix said, and bade the Captain goodbye at his gate. He went into the house and changed into a sports jacket and grey flannels, then made straight to the little car he had hired, anxious to get on the road to Plymouth and wondering how Stella had been since he saw her

152

yesterday. But although his thoughts were mainly of her as he drove across the moor and through the quiet Sunday streets of the city, he was also thinking of Olivia Lydiard.

The Captain was right, he thought. Olivia Lydiard was intelligent as well as elegantly beautiful, and was probably at her best organising and running things. Making friends with the vicar and running a small Women's Institute, estimable though that organisation was, probably left her feeling frustrated and useless when she knew she was capable of so much more. He wondered what she had done during the war. As a naval captain's wife, she had probably held quite a responsible position and even after the war would have had numerous tasks to do in organising social events. Yet would that have been enough? Once a party was over, it was more or less forgotten. He had got the impression that Olivia Lydiard could, if given the opportunity, have achieved so much more.

In a sense, he thought, she was caught in the same kind of trap as Hilary Napier – a woman who had had a taste of the wider world and then found herself confined. And then he realised he was approaching the hospital. His thoughts turned entirely to Stella, and he forgot the tall blonde woman who had commandeered him for Sunday lunch.

'I hope you know what you're doing, taking our Jackie on,' Tom observed to his uncle as they walked up to the Standing Stones. Joe and Russ had caught up with them just as he and Luke, with Robin trotting beside them, crossed the lane, and they walked in single file up the narrow, twisting path through the wood. 'She's a wilful little baggage when she's a mind for it.'

Joe grinned. 'I can see that. But I've got two daughters of my own, remember. I know what young women can be like when they want their own way.'

'And brother, do they want their own way!' Russ said feelingly. 'I tell you this, Tom, the house has been a darn sight quieter since those two got married and moved out.'

Luke laughed. 'You make me glad Val and I have got a son. Not that we wouldn't like a daughter as well, mind. After a couple of years, anyway.'

A faint shadow crossed his face as he spoke, and Tom noticed it and said, 'Val wouldn't necessarily have the same problems another time, Luke.'

'I know. You can't help worrying about it, though. Same as you worry about your little Heather.'

Tom nodded. Then he said, 'Well, I reckon it's different worries our Jackie'll be giving Uncle Joe. From what you say, Corning's too much like Tavistock to hold her. She'll be wanting to head off to New York itself.'

'We won't let that happen,' Joe said. 'Not straight away, anyway. Maybe we'll take her for a visit sometime.'

'Corning's a bit bigger than Tavistock anyway,' Russ added. 'She'll find plenty there to occupy her.'

'I wouldn't mind being a fly on the wall in your

house, with Jackie and Dottie Friend both staying there!' Tom said with a grin. 'Bit like chalk and cheese, I reckon. Jackie won't want Dottie breathing down her neck.'

'No, I've been wondering about that too,' Joe admitted. 'Might be better if Jackie went to stay with one of the girls after the first week or two. They've both got plenty of room, and they're nearer her age. She'll have fun with them. Anyway, Dottie's not said she'll come yet.'

'But won't Jackie have someone nearer her age at your house too, Joe?' Luke enquired. 'Someone told me Maddy Forsyth might be going as well.'

'Now where did you hear that?' Russ exclaimed, and they all laughed.

'You're in Burracombe, remember? All you have to do is think about something and it's all round the village. Anyway, not much gets past my mother and Gran – and you and Maddy have been getting pretty thick just lately.'

'I just wanted to help her,' Russ protested. 'She needed to get to the hospital to see her sister.' He looked at their faces and grinned. 'Well, all right, I have asked her to come over for a visit. But I'm not at all sure she's going to come. Not while her sister's still in hospital, anyway.'

'You'd like it to be more than just a visit, wouldn't you, though?' Tom challenged him. 'Come on, admit it! You're pretty sweet on her.'

'Maddy's a special sort of a girl,' Russ said. 'She's had a rough time this past year, but I reckon she's nearly ready to come out of that now and look ahead, and I don't mind admitting

I'd like to be around when she does.'

'You've got some competition,' Luke observed. 'Stephen Napier's always had a soft spot for Maddy, and he seems to have been coming home quite a bit just lately.'

'That's because of his father,' Tom said. 'I reckon he's missed his chance with Maddy. All the same, I don't know as I approve of you Yanks coming over here and taking all our best girls. What did they say during the war – "overpaid, over-sexed and over here"? Seems to me history's repeating itself.'

Russ aimed a punch at his head and he ducked away, laughing. The two young men began a chase along the path, and Robin joined in, shouting with glee. They joined forces to capture the small boy and threw him to each other like a ball while Joe chuckled and Luke began a running commentary, like a radio sports reporter.

'And the English team wins by a head!' he shouted as Tom caught his son and held him aloft like a giggling, squirming trophy. 'Well done, England.'

'And that's the game over for today,' Tom said, lowering Robin to the ground. 'We'd better turn back for home now. It'll be dark soon and your granny'll be getting tea ready. I saw Mummy making a chocolate cake earlier, and we don't want to miss that, do we?'

'Chocolate cake!' Robin yelled, and set off at a run. The men followed, strolling along and sniffing the cold December air. The temperature was falling fast now, as darkness crept over the landscape, and the clouds were massing in the south-west like charred edges on the burning orange of the sunset.

'Reckon there's snow on the way,' Tom observed. 'Better have a word with Dad about getting some of the stock down off the moor. You can help with that, Russ – if you're not too busy being a taxi service to Maddy Forsyth.'

'She'll be back at West Lyme by now,' Russ said, but his tone was thoughtful. He'd hoped that Maddy was coming round to the idea of going to America, but Luke's words had disturbed him. Was Stephen Napier really such a threat? You could never, he thought, take anything for granted where women were concerned.

'... and so I thought I'd come over and see you for myself,' Tessa Latimer said, standing on the church path after evensong and smiling up at Felix. 'It's ages since I've been home and Burracombe just doesn't seem the same without you. And Stella, of course,' she added. 'I was so sorry to hear about the accident. How is she?'

Felix looked at the young woman in some bemusement. Although he'd met her plenty of times before, of course – as the village doctor's daughter she was well known in the village, and had been at a number of social occasions held either in the Latimers' home, at the Barton or in the vicarage – he'd never thought of her as more than an acquaintance. Now she was gazing at him as if they were old friends, and obviously intended to walk back to the vicarage with him, which meant that he would be obliged to invite her in.

Felix sighed. This was one of the disadvantages

of being a vicar, he thought. You were completely at the mercy of other people, especially after a service. First Olivia Lydiard and now Tessa Latimer, who had come all the way over from Burracombe especially to see him and must therefore be given special attention. She had waited while he greeted his parishioners and, with as much regret as he could summon up, refused yet more invitations to supper, and now fell into step beside him as he went back into the church to change out of his cassock. She was clearly not going to let him escape.

He went into the vestry and leaned his forehead against the cool stone wall for a moment. The day seemed to have gone on for ever, with the early Holy Communion service, matins, lunch at the Lydiards' and then his visit to Stella, and all through the service he had been looking forward to a quiet evening alone, reading or just listening to the radio. The Light Programme on Sunday evenings always gave him a sense of peace – first, *Grand Hotel* with Tom Jenkins and the Palm Court Orchestra, with singers like Olive Groves and Owen Brannigan, and then *Sunday Half-Hour*, with hymns, a few prayers and a short address. There was usually a music programme following these too, and he almost always went to bed feeling refreshed and ready to start a new week next morning.

Of all the companions he might have chosen for this evening – given that he couldn't have Stella – Tessa Latimer would have come very late to his mind.

Still, here she was, and it was a kind thought that

had brought her here, and perhaps she had changed while she'd been away. In any case, she knew that he was engaged to Stella, and although that wouldn't have stopped the Tessa he'd known from embarking on a flirtation, surely in the circumstances even she wouldn't try to take advantage...

Felix shook himself and began to take off his robes. It wasn't the first time a young woman had set her sights on a vicar, especially a young vicar, and it wouldn't be the last. Surely he had learned by now to deal with it. Anyway, he was probably doing Tessa an injustice. She had returned from her finishing school in Switzerland, heard about the accident and come over purely in a spirit of friendship, to see how he was. He scolded himself for being uncharitable and even unchristian, and determined to take her friendship for what it was.

Tessa was wandering around the church when he emerged, looking up at the big east window, the only stained glass in the church, depicting the Virgin Mary to whom the church was dedicated. The rest of the windows were plain, slightly opaque so that the congregation would not be distracted by outside views, just for letting in light. She turned towards him as he came out, smiling. She was small, with blue eyes that looked grey or even green in certain lights, and a cloud of dark hair framing her face. Her smile had an impish quality that Felix realised was both provocative and attractive, and he forgot his resolve and wished again that she hadn't come.

As they walked down the church path, she tucked her arm into his. 'I was really upset to hear

159

what had happened. It must have been dreadful.'

'Yes, it was.' He was thankful for the little gate leading from the churchyard into the vicarage garden. At least none of his parishioners would see him walking arm in arm with Tessa Latimer – none, that is, except for old Ivy Ellacombe, whose cottage looked straight out into the churchyard. But her curtains were drawn against the December darkness and she was probably sitting by her fire, tucked under a crocheted rug in her sagging armchair and listening to the programmes on the wireless that he had planned to listen to himself.

He disengaged his arm from Tessa's and opened the vicarage door. 'Will you come in for a cup of tea?'

'I'd love to. But surely you'll be having some supper, won't you? I don't want to keep you from your meal.'

He hesitated. 'I've got some shepherd's pie to heat up. Mrs Harvey gave it to me yesterday. I'd be happy to share it with you.' There wasn't really enough for two, but he could make it up with some cheese and biscuits. But Tessa shook her head.

'We had high tea at home before I came over. Mummy and Daddy always do that so that they don't have to eat when they come home from church. Why don't we have some tea while you're waiting for it to heat up?'

And then perhaps she'll go, Felix thought with relief. He hung both their coats up in the hallway, then led her through to the kitchen and filled the kettle before taking the shepherd's pie out of the larder and putting it into the oven. The range was already hot, of course – it was the main source of heating for the big, draughty vicarage – and the pie wouldn't take more than twenty minutes.

'You don't mind staying out here, do you?' he enquired. 'It's the warmest room in the house – I spend a lot of time here.'

'So I see,' Tessa said, smiling and looking at the papers piled untidily at one end of the kitchen table. 'I should imagine you practically live in the kitchen, don't you!'

'I do, rather,' he confessed. 'Of course, it'll be different when Stella's here.' He stopped abruptly and turned to make the tea.

There was a short silence; then Tessa said quietly, 'How is she really, Felix? Have you been to see her today?'

'I was there for much of the afternoon. She was asleep most of the time. She woke up once or twice.' His voice shook a little, remembering the white face, the bewildered eyes. 'I think she knew I was there, but...'

'Oh, *Felix*.' Tessa came to his side, laying her hand on his arm. He looked down at her and saw that her face was soft with compassion. 'But I thought – Dad told us that she'd woken up a day or two ago, and knew you.'

'She did. I thought she did, anyway. But today ... she hardly seemed to understand anything at all. It's as if she'd slipped right back – slipped almost out of reach...' His voice shook again and he turned instinctively towards the comfort of the arms she held out for him. 'And I had to leave her there. I had to *leave* her there.'

'Oh, Felix,' she said again, softly, and held him

close for a moment. Then she stepped away and asked, 'What did the doctors say?'

'I didn't see a doctor. The nurse said she was just sleeping and it was nothing to worry about. She said Stella would probably be like that for a day or two and then start to recover again. Delayed shock ... I don't know. But I'd felt so hopeful. I thought she was going to be all right.'

'And so she is,' Tessa said firmly. 'Now, you come and sit down.' She pushed him into the old rocking chair that had been left by the previous vicar's wife, with most of the rest of the vicarage furniture, and stood close to the range. 'I'll make the tea. You need someone to look after you.'

'Oh, there are plenty of people willing to do that,' he said wearily. 'Almost too many, in fact.'

Tessa poured boiling water into the teapot. 'Is that a hint for me to go?'

'No,' he said quickly, 'no, of course not. It's good to see you, Tessa.'

She went to the kitchen dresser and took two cups from the hooks under one of the shelves. 'I shan't stay long, all the same. I'll sit here with you and drink my tea and make sure you eat your supper, and then I'll go. You need an early night – you look exhausted.'

'I'm all right.' He took the cup she handed him and sipped the hot, sweet liquid. 'Stella's trying to make me give up sugar.'

'Time for that when she's better,' Tessa said briskly. 'You need all your strength now.' She turned one of the chairs away from the table and sat down, surveying him thoughtfully. 'She is going to be all right, isn't she?' she asked after a

162

moment. 'I mean, there's all kinds of rumours flying around.'

'What sort of rumours?'

'Well – that she had a bang on the head and that's why she's been unconscious for so long. And some people are saying that she might not walk again. I didn't know whether to tell you or not,' she added quickly, seeing the flush rise in his face. 'But I think you ought to know what people are saying.'

'Well, you can just tell them to stop saying it,' he said angrily. 'They've no right to go talking about Stella like that. It's gossip, and I bet I know who's doing most of the gossiping.'

'They don't mean any harm,' she said. 'Everyone likes Stella, and you too. They're just concerned, and you know how stories get about.'

'I do, but all the same... I don't like the thought of it, Tessa. What does your father say?'

'He says we just have to wait and see. He says nobody can tell what the damage is until she wakes up properly.'

'That's what the hospital doctors say too, so if you hear any more gossip, I hope you'll tell them that from me.' He was still angry, and he gulped down some tea that was still too hot and spluttered a little. 'Oh, blast.'

'She does have some broken bones, though, doesn't she?'

'Yes, her leg's broken and they're going to operate on that tomorrow.' He sighed. 'So she'll be unconscious again tomorrow evening, I suppose. But it's my day off, so I'm going in while they do the operation and I hope she'll wake up while I'm there.' He paused and took a more careful sip of tea. 'In fact, I shan't come home until she does wake up. I want to make sure she knows me again.'

'Would you like me to come with you?' Tessa asked, and he glanced up at her in surprise.

'You don't want to do that.'

'I will, if it's any help.'

Felix paused. It was a kind offer, and Tessa was being surprisingly comforting, but he reminded himself that she had never been more than an acquaintance. 'It's all right, thank you, Tessa. I'll be quite OK on my own. Besides, I don't know how long I'll be there.'

'Well, if you change your mind,' she said. 'I'm home now until after Christmas, so I've plenty of time. Consider me at your disposal.' And she gave her that impish smile. 'Now, what about that shepherd's pie?'

Felix made up his mind. 'I'll have it later,' he said, taking the hot dish from her and putting it back into the warming oven. 'I'll see you home first.'

'Oh, there's no need for that. I can walk back by myself. I thought I'd stay for the evening – you must be so lonely here by yourself.'

'I've got some work to do,' he said, looking at the pile of papers on the end of the table. 'I've been neglecting it these past few days. Really, Tessa, I can't let you walk home by yourself, all across the Clam and up through the fields. I'll come with you and have my supper when I get back.'

He went out to collect their coats and helped Tessa into hers. She was looking faintly mutinous, but as she slipped her arms into the sleeves she turned and smiled up at him.

'You won't mind if I come again, will you, Felix? We've always been such good friends, and I really do want to help you if I can. Daddy says you mustn't be allowed to worry too much, so if there's anything I can do to cheer you up...'

He looked down at her gravely, wondering if she really knew how provocative her manner was, how flirtatious her glance. It wasn't that she attracted him at all – he was too much in love with Stella, too desperately anxious about her – but he could not but be aware of her attraction, and he knew that other people would see it too. To allow her to visit him here was to court danger from the village gossips, a danger he could well do without.

'I'm sure we'll run into each other over the Christmas period,' he said at last. 'But you know how busy it is for a vicar. I've any amount of things to attend, as well as special services, and I must get in to see Stella as often as I can... But I won't forget, Tessa. I'll let you know at once if there's anything you can do.'

He stepped away, leaving her to shrug into her coat, and pulled on his own thick jacket. Then he took his torch from the dresser and led the way to the front door.

A walk across the Clam to Burracombe in the company of Tessa Latimer and then home again wasn't the way he had planned to spend his evening, but at least there was the shepherd's pie to look forward to when he finally returned. He might even be in time to hear the last part of *Sunday Half-Hour.*

Chapter Twelve

As Stella was wheeled into the operating theatre next day and Felix sat tensely in the hospital corridor, the children of Burracombe school were busy rehearsing their Nativity Play.

Joyce Warren had swept everyone else along with her enthusiasm, and Miss Kemp had found herself agreeing to rehearsals taking place every afternoon that week. With the play due to be performed on Thursday evening, time was getting short and everyone was anxious that it should go well. Robin Tozer, who had a rhyming couplet to say, plagued the family to listen to him and could be heard chanting his lines all over the farmhouse.

We've come to see the newborn child,
The Baby Jesus, meek and mild.

'It ain't exactly Shakespeare, is it?' Tom remarked when he heard this gem of poetry. 'Still, I suppose it's all right for little ones to say. Does everyone in the play have some words, Robbie?'

'Yes. Joseph's got the best part, though,' he said rather grudgingly, and everyone laughed.

'I expect he's being played by an older boy,' Joanna told him. 'Maybe it will be your turn when you get into the top class.'

Robin obviously didn't think much of this

166

suggestion, but went off cheerfully enough with his tea towel and dressing gown to play the part of a shepherd. Tom had made him a miniature crook, and he would have Bert Foster's papier mâché lamb on the night. For the time being, he had to make do with his old teddy bear.

'That looks a bit daft,' Billy Madge said when he saw this. 'A shepherd coming to see the Baby Jesus with a teddy bear! Folk'll think you'm proper mazed.'

'I shan't have it when we're going round the village,' Robin retorted. 'It'll be a proper lamb then. This is just for rehearsal.'

'And quite right too,' Joyce Warren said, overhearing. 'As long as you've got something to carry, so that you know how it will feel, it doesn't matter what it is. Now, what about the donkey? Is that all arranged, Wendy?'

Wendy Cole nodded importantly. Her aunt owned a donkey called Jack, which she had agreed to lend for the occasion. It was apparently a docile creature, and Wendy had told Miss Kemp that she knew it well and was accustomed to handling it. Since it lived a little way out of the village and wasn't familiar with any of the other children, Wendy had therefore been given the part of Mary, and Billy Madge was to play Joseph.

'I hope you'll be able to manage him,' Joyce said to Billy. 'You and Wendy will have to lead him all the time. I don't think we can risk Wendy riding him.'

'I could,' Wendy said. 'I've ridden him before.'

'But only in his field,' Joyce pointed out. 'Not round the village in the dark.' She glanced a little anxiously at the sky. 'I do hope we're not going to get bad weather. It's turned very cold. Now, you will all come well wrapped up, won't you? Dressing gowns aren't as warm as overcoats, so you'll want plenty on underneath. Nobody wants to catch cold and not be able to come to the school party the next day, do they?'

The children agreed that they didn't, and the rehearsal went ahead. Joyce and Miss Kemp had decided that it would be sensible to practise actually going round the village, so after dinner they all put on coats, scarves and gloves and set off, with Robin rather self-consciously carrying his teddy bear and Billy Madge's father's sheep-dog Fly taking the part of the donkey.

'Miss Kemp and I have arranged which doors you will knock on,' Joyce Warren explained. 'Not everyone will be in this afternoon, but they've all promised to be there on Thursday evening. For this afternoon, I'll say their words.'

They finished at the Bell Inn, where Rose was sweeping up in the bar after the lunchtime opening and Bernie was down in the cellar working on the beer barrels. They both came out as the children approached, and Bernie took them into the old stable.

'Not used much now,' he said. 'There were a time when farmers from way off would come in on their horses of an evening or a dinnertime and put 'em in here while they had a drink, but not many do that now. It'll be clear for your bit of a play.' He turned to Mrs Warren. 'I done what you asked and got Ted Tozer to bring down some straw bales for folk to sit on if they wants. We'll put 'em over there. And he's bringing his old manger down too. I suppose you got a Baby Jesus?'

'Betty Culliford's bringing her doll,' Miss Kemp said. She'd had some doubts about this, as the Cullifords weren't known for giving their children quality presents – they did most of the shopping at jumble sales – but Betty had pleaded so eloquently that she'd given in. After all, she thought, Joseph and Mary must have looked quite weary and travel-stained by the time they reached Bethlehem, and wouldn't have had grand raiment to dress their baby in. One set of swaddling clothes looked much like another, and only the doll's face would be seen. She just hoped it wasn't too battered.

The actors straggled their way back to the school, where they sang their going-home hymn still wrapped in their coats, since there wasn't much point in taking them off for just a few minutes, then Miss Kemp rang the bell and they all streamed out into the playground. Joyce Warren, who had played the piano for the hymn, put on her own coat and Miss Kemp locked her desk and smiled at her.

'It seems to be going very well, Mrs Warren. You've worked very hard with the children.'

'They're dears.' She paused, then added, 'Most of them, anyway. The Crocker twins...'

'Yes,' Miss Kemp said ruefully. 'The Crocker twins... I hope we've done the right thing in allowing them to be two of the Wise Men. It's not exactly type-casting! But it's often better to give such children something to do, rather than try to keep them in the background and hope they behave. At least we shall be able to *see* them – and see which is which, what's more, with Edward playing Melchior.'

'Unless George does it!' Joyce said. 'Not that it really matters, as long as they behave themselves. You do feel happy about the idea of the play going on all through the village, I hope?'

'I do now. I must admit I wasn't sure to begin with, but now I think it will be a great success.' The teacher hesitated. She didn't want the solicitor's wife to know what she had really thought about having to accept her help in the school, but honesty compelled her to go on. 'I really am grateful to you for all you've done to help us. I had no idea you had teacher training, and I confess I had some doubts – but you've more than proved yourself. Did you ever take it up after leaving college?'

Joyce shook her head. 'I never went to college. I stayed on at my boarding school as a trainee teacher with the younger ones when I was eighteen. Then the First World War broke out, and I volunteered as a nurse, and then I met Henry and married him when the war ended. I was twenty-two then, and of course there was no question of me working after that. I was sorry, because I enjoyed working with the children, but I always hoped we'd have our own family and that would more than make up for it. Unfortunately, it wasn't to be...' Her voice trailed away and Miss Kemp glanced at her, hearing the wistfulness in her voice. For a moment, she wondered whether to ask more, but before she had made up her mind, Joyce said briskly, 'It's been a great pleasure to help you here, but you'll be getting a new teacher after Christmas, won't you? Stella would have been leaving this term even if the accident hadn't happened.'

'Well, in a way we shall,' Miss Kemp said with a worried little frown. 'The governors appointed her a few weeks ago. Quite an experienced young woman, a few years older than Stella. I was hoping she would have been able to come and meet the children before term finishes, but she still has her present job to go to. She'll be here a day or two before the new term begins. Unfortunately, we're not sure that she'll be permanent. She couldn't say how long she would stay in the area – until Easter, certainly, but after that she might have to leave us again. Family problems, I understand.' She shook her head anxiously. 'It's not at all ideal, but there were just no other suitable applicants.'

'Oh dear. That doesn't sound very satisfactory. And does she have any lodgings? I suppose Dottie Friend...'

Miss Kemp shook her head. 'No, Dottie had already decided to keep her spare room free for a while, in case either Stella or Maddy need it. I believe she's found a room in Tavistock, although I have to say, I'd feel happier if she were here in the village.'

'I see,' Joyce said thoughtfully. 'Well, I mustn't keep you here chattering – you must be wanting to get home to your tea, and I have Henry's dinner to cook. I'll look in tomorrow, in case there's anything you want me to do, and we'll have a final dress rehearsal on Wednesday, in the school. And

171

then it will be the Big Day!'

Joyce made her way home, thinking about the conversation. Until now, she'd never really known how much she had missed taking up the teaching career she'd set her heart on at school. The smallest children, the infants, were the ones she liked best and wanted to teach. Little children of five, hardly more than babies, coming to school wide-eyed and looking ridiculously tiny in their new school clothes. The boys almost swamped by their school caps, the girls with frocks made too long, for them to grow into. The children at Burracombe didn't wear a school uniform, in fact since the war not many primary schools did, they just wore their ordinary clothes, but the little ones usually had new home-made jumpers and skirts or grey flannel shorts and pullovers to start them off. And the babies' class still looked almost too young to be away from their mothers.

Joyce Peters, as she had been then, was an only child and had always longed for a brother or sister. She'd spent her time arranging her collection of dolls and toy animals in rows facing her, and had taught them to read and write using a blackboard she'd been given one Christmas and forcing pencils into their stiff fingers or soft, floppy paws. Her parents had viewed these activities with amusement, evolving into tolerance when her school reports talked about their daughter's ability to stand in front of a class of younger children and give lessons almost as good as the teacher's, and finally anxiety and downright anger when she told them she wanted to become a teacher herself.

'Nonsense!' her father had said roundly. 'What

172

do you want with a job? Your mother needs you at home with her.'

'I don't want a job,' Joyce had said. 'I want a career, as a teacher. I've talked to the head-mistress, and she says I can go back to school as an assistant teacher, with the prep classes. I won't be paid much, but I'll have my keep and—'

'Stop!' her father roared. 'What on earth do you think you're talking about? Pay? Keep? What do you want with pay and keep? I'll make you a decent allowance and you can stay at home with your mother and do what girls of your class have always done.'

'And what's that?' Joyce asked. 'Learn to arrange flowers and order meals and tell the housemaids what to do? I don't *want* that sort of life, Father.'

'Well, what *do* you want, then?'

'I've told you. I want to be a teacher.'

Her parents looked at each other in bemuse-ment and her father turned away. He picked up the silver cigarette case that stood on the sideboard, took out a cigarette and lit it. Then he turned back to his wife, who was sitting on the sofa, her face threatening to crumple into tears.

'I'll tell you what's brought all this on,' he said, jabbing a finger at her. 'It's all this damned suff-ragette nonsense. They're feeding the girls with it at that school. Votes for women, and all that twaddle. It's turning their brains.' He wheeled back to his daughter, who stood defiantly in the middle of the carpet. 'Don't tell me they never mention those Pankhurst sisters and their dis-graceful acts. And that idiotic woman Emily Davison, throwing herself in front of the King's

173

horse and getting herself killed.'

'Of course they tell us about them. They're teaching us. Father, what's the point of sending me to school if you don't want me to learn about the world? What's my education *for?*'

'What's it for? I'll tell you what it's for, and it seems to me it's time your teachers understood that too. I pay them to teach you the kind of accomplishments a well-brought-up young lady needs – a little French, a smattering of mathematics to help her understand her own household accounts, an appreciation of music and art and enough English literature to enable her to make intelligent small talk, and the skills she'll need to run a home and be a good wife. I don't pay them to fill your head with politics and rubbish about votes for women.' He glared down at his wife. 'I think I'd better have a word with Miss Jones.'

He walked out of the room, leaving Joyce and her mother alone, and Joyce knew that there would be no use in further argument. But as she too left the room and went out to walk her fury off in the garden, she knew also that she wasn't ready to give in yet. Something would happen to change things, she was sure, and she would achieve her ambition to be a teacher.

The thing that happened was the outbreak of war, just a few months later. With growing disbelief, Joyce's parents read in the newspapers about young women nursing, working as bus conductors, entering factories and even enrolling in something called the Women's Defence Relief Corps – backed by Lord Kitchener, of all people! – which had two sections: a civil section, which sent women to do jobs that had until now been done by men, and a military section, which trained them in marching, signalling and even the use of arms.

Nothing more nor less than common soldiers, George Peters said disgustedly, and decided at once that his daughter would be better off in a good school, teaching reading and writing to small girls. Joyce had got her way.

By now, though, she wasn't so sure she wanted it. The WDRC sounded so much more exciting, and even if she didn't go into the military section, she could drive an ambulance or a motorcycle, carrying important papers, maybe even be sent to France like other women she'd heard about. It was becoming obvious that the war wasn't going to be over by Christmas – perhaps not even by the following Christmas – and as more and more men were recruited, so many of them never to return, more and more jobs became open to women. More and more opportunities.

She was young and strong; her conscience and her driving energy forced her to leave her safe, comfortable shell and look for something else to do. She volunteered as a nurse in the Voluntary Aid Detachment and found herself in one of the big London hospitals, tending soldiers who had been sent home from the front line; soldiers with terrible wounds, soldiers who had lost limbs or eyes, soldiers whose mutilations would leave them without any means of earning a living and would (although Joyce didn't know that then) send them to stand blind or crouch legless on heaps of dirty blankets on street corners, selling matches or begging for pennies to buy their food. She ministered to them while they were in hospital, feeding them if they couldn't hold their own forks or spoons, cleaning up after them and changing their soiled beds.

She never told her parents what she saw in that hospital. They were appalled that she had volunteered for such work and didn't want to hear about it. Their only gratitude was that she was too young to be sent to France, as some of the older VADs were, and they looked forward to the day when the madness would cease and Joyce would return to be their biddable daughter, staying at home and looking for a husband, even if it was too late for her to be presented at Court or do the Season.

None of that happened, of course, because by the time the war ended, she had met Henry Warren.

Henry had been in the Army. He had been wounded at the Somme and then a month later, more seriously, at Passchendaele. After that, he was deemed unfit for further action and sent to the hospital where Joyce worked. They were not supposed to fraternise, but there were ways and means, and when Henry was drafted into a desk job in London, they kept in touch. They married as soon as he was demobbed and back in his father's solicitor's office in Tavistock.

That was the end of Joyce's teaching career. Married women were not welcomed in that, or any other sphere of work. The war had left too many single women – girls who had not had the chance to marry, and older women who had been widowed. Those jobs not taken back by the returning men were kept for these women. Besides, Henry took the common view that no decent man would allow his wife to work, and Joyce bowed to the inevitable and looked forward to the day when she would have her own children to look after and teach.

The children had never come along, though. Nobody knew why; perhaps it was due to Henry's war wounds. In the end, it was just one of those childless marriages, and Joyce had to direct her energies in other ways – sitting on committees, running women's organisations. Gradually, the bright, determined girl who had longed for nothing more than seeing a row of small faces before her, eager to learn, turned into a domineering and bossy woman who could be relied on to get things done but never quite understood why people didn't like her as much as she wanted.

During the past week or two, however, she had begun to find that girl again. Helping at Burracombe school, working with the children, enthusing them with her ideas, had reminded her of her early ambitions, and she felt a sudden sadness at their loss. I ought to have been a teacher, she thought. I could have been like Miss Kemp, running my own school – a big boarding school or a little village school like this one, I wouldn't have minded, so long as it was my school. I would have done a good job, I know I would.

The only thing that had stopped her was that small difference in title – the fact that she was Mrs, and not Miss. And that hadn't changed even now – look at Stella Simmons. Even if she'd wanted to, even if she recovered from this dreadful accident, she couldn't go on teaching after she married Felix. Women still weren't really expected to do such a thing. Most husbands still didn't want them to.

We have such potential, she thought, turning into her own gateway. It's so wrong that we should be pushed to the background, when so many of us could do as good, or better, a job as men.

Meanwhile, she had her own small triumph – the Nativity Play – to come. And then, on Friday, the school would break up for the Christmas holidays. After that, she would have to hand over the reins to the new teacher and revert to being Joyce Warren, the bossy woman with a finger in every pie in the village, who had more brains and energy than anyone had ever realised, and never enough to do with them.

Chapter Thirteen

As Joyce Warren was walking home from the school, Stella was waking up in her hospital bed after her operation. Felix was beside her, his hand gently clasping hers and his anxious gaze fixed upon her face. She turned her head, muttered something and suddenly her eyes were open and she was staring at him in bewilderment.

'Felix?'

'Darling!' he said. 'Oh Stella, my darling – you

know me!'

'Of course I know you. But...' Her head moved again and she winced. 'I don't know ... what's happened...? Why does my head hurt...?' She flinched again. 'My back ... my leg...'

'You can feel your legs?' He tried to keep the eagerness out of his voice. If she could feel her legs, even if they hurt, it would mean there would be no paralysis. 'Darling, can you feel your legs?'

She stared at him again, but the brief light faded from her face and she seemed bewildered once more. Her voice was feeble. 'I don't know ... I don't know what's the matter with me ... why...?' And then she turned her head away from his and said peevishly, 'Go away. Go away... Leave me alone...'

Felix drew in his breath, but the nurse was beside him, gently moving him aside. He looked at her in distress but she shook her head and murmured, 'She isn't properly conscious yet, Mr Copley. Don't take any notice.'

'But she knew me. She knew I was here.' He felt the tears come hot to his eyes. 'Why did she tell me to go away?'

'She's confused. It doesn't mean anything.'

'And her legs. If she can feel them...'

'We shan't know that until she wakes properly. It could be quite a while, Mr Copley. Now, I must fetch the doctor...' She gave him the look that he knew meant he should go outside now, while she and the doctor attended to their patient. He sighed and got up stiffly, only now realising how long he had been sitting there, holding Stella's hand. He looked down at her, thinking how long it seemed since he had seen her on her feet, walking beside him, laughing up into his face, treating young Rob with tenderness and understanding in his distress.

'It could still go either way, couldn't it? he said quietly to the nurse. 'She isn't out of the wood yet.'

The nurse gave him a quick glance, then looked away. She made no reply; she didn't have to. He nodded slightly and went out, his heart still heavy, standing aside for the doctor, who was making his way in.

'I'll be just outside,' he said, and the man paused and looked into his face.

'I think you should go home. Try to get some rest. She's unlikely to wake again before the morning.'

'I'll wait until you've seen her,' Felix said. He felt almost too tired to stand, let along drive himself home in the hire car, but he knew the doctor was right. 'I just want to be sure. Then I'll go home.'

He sat on the hard wooden bench outside the room, leaned his elbows on his knees and rested his face in his hands. He wanted to pray, but the words wouldn't come. He could only offer up the weariness of his body and the anguish of his heart, and hope that it would suffice.

'I think she's turned the corner,' Hilary said to David later that evening. She was in her father's study again, speaking to David in his surgery in Derbyshire. 'Felix telephoned about an hour ago. He stayed with her until they made him come home, but he says she woke up and knew him, and the operation on her leg was a success.'

'And what about her spine?'

'I don't know. He thinks she could feel her legs, though – that's a good sign, isn't it?'

'It could be. And how's Felix?'

'Difficult to tell, over the phone. He sounded terribly tired.' It was strange to think that David had never met these people who meant so much to her, had never even known they existed until a few days ago. 'He said one of the parishioners had been to the vicarage and left him a casserole in the oven. He was going to eat some of that and then go to bed.'

'That's the best thing.' David paused, then said, 'And how are you, my darling?'

Hilary felt tears prick her eyes. She had become so accustomed to being the strong person, the one everyone turned to, that to hear concern for her in a voice was strange. And this was more than concern – it was love. Love such as she had not known for many years, thought never to know again. Two of the tears rolled down her cheeks and she brushed them away with her free hand, but they had opened a pathway for more to follow and she drew in a shaky breath, not wanting David to know she was crying.

'I'm fine,' she said, trying to keep her voice light. 'Busy, of course. Getting ready for Christmas, you know.'

'You're crying,' he said abruptly. 'Hilary...'

'I'm all right. Really. Just tired and worried about Stella. And Rob. He's so quiet. Well, he's always quiet, but – I don't know. He seems different. And it's difficult to know what to do with him – he's at home with nothing much to do, and all his friends here are still at school. Travis is being very helpful, taking him about the estate, and of course that's good for him, to see how it works and so on, but... I just wish I could do more to help him.'

'Perhaps he'll be better when his mother's there,' David said. 'When does she arrive?'

'Next Tuesday – the twenty-second. And he'll have his brother and sister as well. That should do him good. He must have missed them, all these months. We really didn't consider him at all, with all these plans we made for him.'

'You mean your father didn't,' David said, and she sighed.

'I suppose that's true. But then he never does take much notice of other people. And he's another problem. It's only a few days since his attack. He still needs to be careful. But with Christmas coming, and Rob's mother and her other children on their way...' She rubbed her palm against her forehead. 'I'm sorry, David. You don't want to hear all my problems.'

'I do,' he said. 'I want to hear everything. I just wish I could be there with you, to help. I wish I could be with you all the time.'

'David, please don't.'

'I can't help it. And you feel the same. Don't you.' It was not a question.

'Yes,' she whispered. 'I feel just the same. Oh, David. *David...*'

'We've got to meet again. I can't go much longer without seeing you.'

'After Christmas. Maybe when Marianne and the children go home. I could go as far as Dover with them and then stay a day or two in London on the way back.'

'A night or two,' he said, and she felt the hot colour rise up her neck and into her cheeks.

'A night or two... It sounds like heaven. But what about Sybil?'

'I'm sure Sybil will have other fish to fry,' he said bitterly. 'She won't even notice I'm not here. Darling, you do realise we have to talk seriously, don't you? Very soon.'

'There's nothing to talk about. There's nothing we can do.' The brief flash of ecstasy evaporated into dull despair. 'We can't even do what we're doing now – not for ever.'

There was a long silence, and then he said quietly, 'We have to talk, Hilary. We have to.' He waited, but she could not answer, and then he said, 'I'll see you after Christmas. Let me know when you'll be in London. I'll see you then – and we'll talk. Whatever happens, we must talk.'

'Yes,' she said at last. Her voice was very low. 'Yes. After Christmas. Goodbye, David.' And then, in a whisper as thin as spider's silk, 'I love you.'

She put down the phone and leaned her forehead on her hand. The tears dripped on to her wrist and soaked into the sleeve of her jumper. Her throat ached with them and her chest felt tight and full.

I wish this had never happened, she thought. I wish I had never gone to that reunion and met David again. I should have stayed at home and never known he was there, never known we could still feel like this about each other.

It was like a fire that had been thought to be out for years but had been gently smouldering. It had only needed one tiny breath of wind to set it aflame again, and now the blaze was too fierce to control.

It could burn us both up, she thought. It could destroy everything. And there's nothing I can do to stop it.

Tessa Latimer was waiting at the vicarage door when Felix arrived.

'I know you didn't ask me to come again,' she said as he clambered out of the hire car and stared at her. 'But you were just being polite, weren't you? And when Daddy told me you'd telephoned to tell him how Stella was and were on your way home, I felt I had to come.'

Felix sighed and fitted his key into the lock. 'You didn't have to, Tessa. It's kind of you, but–'

'You need someone to look after you,' she said firmly. 'Someone to make you a cup of tea and give you something hot to eat without you having to do it yourself.'

'I don't have to do it myself.' He led the way into the front hall, with its black and white Victorian tiled floor and the row of coathooks on the wall. He shrugged out of his overcoat and hung it up, then took the one that Tessa was holding out to him. Clearly she meant to stay, and he was too tired to argue. 'One of the ladies has left a beef casserole in the oven for me. Vicars are usually pretty well looked after. Too well, sometimes.'

'You still have to do it yourself.' She followed him into the big kitchen. 'Sit down, Felix, and I'll make you some tea, and then I'll put your casserole on a warm plate and I'll wash up afterwards. Would you like me to light the fire in one of the other rooms? This house is freezing.'

'I know. The kitchen's the only warm room in the place. I need to do something about it before ... before Stella...' He swayed slightly, and Tessa caught his arm and pushed him gently into a chair at the table.

'Sit there.' She moved quickly about the kitchen, filling the kettle with fresh water and setting it on the hot plate. The big range kept the kitchen warm, and when the door was left open, the heat seeped slowly through the rest of the house, but it wasn't enough to warm the passages, the downstairs rooms, the bedrooms. The previous vicar, Mr Berry, and his wife had heated the other rooms by lighting fires or plugging in electric fires, but the cost of electricity must be enormous and to keep fires burning took a lot of work. 'You need central heating,' she observed.

'It's supposed to be put in sometime this year. But I don't know – there'll be so much upheaval, installing all the pipes and those big, heavy radiators. Stella's going to need peace and quiet.'

'She's also going to need a warm house,' Tessa said severely. She placed a large cup of steaming tea in front of him. 'There. Drink that while I see to the casserole.'

Felix sipped his tea and watched her moving about the kitchen. She was a pleasant sight – slim and pretty, with a rich fall of dark hair waving gently on her shoulders. She had deep blue eyes which warmed into a smile when she turned and met his gaze. He glanced away quickly, then chided himself and looked back to return her smile. It was, after all, very agreeable to have a friendly young woman here, ministering to his needs.

'It's good of you to take this trouble,' he said. 'I hadn't realised how tired I was.'

'You look exhausted.' She was putting a plate into the warm oven, where the casserole was bubbling gently. 'Have you got any wine?'

'I don't know. Probably not. I don't keep much in the house – there might be a bottle in the dining room, I suppose.'

She left the kitchen and he sat slowly drinking the tea, thinking over the events of the day. After the doctor had attended to Stella, he had been allowed back into the room to sit with her, holding her pale, limp hand and watching her face. She had been given a sedative and wasn't likely to wake for some hours, the doctor had said. They wanted her to rest, to remain immobile for as long as possible. He might as well go home.

Felix had stayed stubbornly where he was. He wanted to be there if she woke again, even if she were sedated immediately. After today, he would only be able to come in during normal visiting hours, afternoon or evening, and then for no more than an hour. Unless her condition deteriorated...

'That's not likely now,' the doctor said. 'She's stable, she came through the operation well, she's not critical any more. Not in that sense, anyway.'

'In what sense, then?' Felix asked quickly, and

the doctor screwed his mouth to one side.

'In the same sense as we've always been concerned for her. The damage to her spinal cord is still not completely clear. That's another reason why we want to keep her as still as possible.' He paused. 'We may decide to put her into a full body cast.'

Felix stared at him. 'You mean a plaster cast? Her whole body?'

'That's right. It may well be the best option.'

'But ... how long would that have to be for?'

'For as long as proves necessary,' the doctor said. 'Now, if you'll excuse me...'

Felix nodded dumbly and the doctor walked swiftly away, his white coat flapping. Felix went back into the room and sat down again by Stella's bed. He tried to imagine her encased in plaster of Paris from neck to thigh, and the tears came to his eyes. His Stella, trapped in a rigid cage for weeks, maybe months. How could she bear it?

There was no doubt in his mind now that the wedding must be postponed. And when Stella was fully conscious again, when she was able to understand what had happened to her, she would have to be told. He would have to tell her.

Tessa came back into the kitchen, brandishing a bottle of sherry. 'This was all I could find. You can have a glass with your meal. Have you finished your tea?'

'Yes,' Felix said, looking at his cup with some surprise. 'Thanks, Tessa.'

She filled the wine glass she had brought with her and placed it in front of him. 'There.'

'That's an awful lot of sherry,' he said.

'It'll do you good.' She took the warm plate and casserole from the oven and ladled out a rich beef stew, filled with chunks of meat, bright orange carrots, golden swede and white, peppery turnip. There was a jacket potato too; she split it, spread it with butter and laid the whole dish in front of him. 'Now, I want to see that plate cleared.'

'Or I won't get any jelly,' he said with an attempt at humour.

'Or you won't get any jelly *or* custard,' she replied, smiling. 'Do you mind if I have a sherry too?'

He shook his head and then turned as they heard a sound from the hallway. The front door clicked shut and footsteps sounded across the Victorian tiles. The kitchen door opened and a tall, slender woman wrapped in a fur coat came in. She stopped on seeing the pair sitting at the table, and her eyebrows rose.

'Mrs Lydiard...' Felix said.

'Good evening, Felix,' she said, drawing off her gloves. 'Good evening, Miss Latimer. I saw the light on so just called in to see that you were all right. I see you've found the casserole I left in the oven.'

'Yes. It's very good.' He had barely taken one mouthful. 'And it was very good of you to bring it over for me.'

'Oh, I didn't bring it myself,' she said. 'I sent Mrs Sweet over earlier this afternoon. She understands these old ranges better than I do.' She glanced around the kitchen. 'It's warm enough in here, but this is such a cold house, Felix. You'll have to have something done about it if Miss

Simmons comes here.'

'It's not *if*,' Felix said. 'It's *when*. And I'm hoping to have some proper heating put in.'

'Don't stop eating, Felix,' Tessa broke in. 'Mrs Lydiard won't mind, will you, Mrs Lydiard? After all, she sent the casserole over for you.'

'Of course I don't mind.' The light-blue eyes took in the bottle of sherry and the two glasses on the table. 'I should have thought to send some wine as well.'

'I don't drink very much wine,' Felix said, beginning to eat, although he felt uncomfortable at being the only one. 'Not on a vicar's stipend. But perhaps you'll have a sherry, Mrs Lydiard.'

'I told you yesterday,' the blonde woman said, watching as Tessa went out of the kitchen and returned a moment later with a small sherry glass. 'It's Olivia. I thought we were friends now.' She smiled as Tessa grudgingly poured sherry and handed her the glass. 'Thank you, my dear. I suppose you came over to give dear Felix what help you could.'

'That's right,' Tessa said. 'I've known him ever since he first came to Burracombe, of course. We're *old* friends.'

Olivia Lydiard smiled again, very slightly. 'It's very kind of you, but Felix does have his own parishioners now, all very eager to give him whatever help we can.'

'I'm sure you are,' Tessa returned, 'but there's nothing like real friends at times like this.'

There was a small pause. Felix wished he could be alone to battle with the meal that had been put in front of him. It was tasty and hot, and he knew

189

he must be hungry, but every mouthful was an effort to chew and swallow. He listened to the barbed exchange between the two women, perfectly well aware of the undercurrents, and wished they would go and leave him alone. He wished he could be forthright to the point of rudeness, like his uncle the Dean, who would have made no secret of his feelings.

'Still,' Olivia said smoothly, 'you may as well go home now that I'm here. You've got quite a long walk by the road.'

'It's all right,' Tessa said. 'I'm not going to go that way.'

'You're surely not going to walk through the woods and over the Clam all by yourself? In the dark? It's very icy out there.'

Felix stirred himself and said reluctantly, 'I can see Tessa home.'

'Oh, but *surely*–' Olivia said, turning swiftly and putting her hand on his shoulder, but Tessa broke in as quickly.

'There's no need, Felix. Daddy's coming to collect me.'

'Your father?'

'Yes. You didn't think I'd ask you to drag yourself out again, did you? I told him I'd like to come over when we knew you were on your way home, and he said he had to visit a patient in Little Burracombe and he'd pick me up on his way back. He'll probably be here any minute.' She glanced at Olivia and added, 'He said you ought to be left in peace for a while, to rest.'

'Yes,' Felix said, seizing his opportunity just as the front doorbell sounded. 'I think that's just what I need. Let your father in, would you, Tessa, and then I'll ask you both to excuse me. All I want to do is finish this delicious meal and go to bed.' He looked at Olivia, who seemed about to offer to stay until he had finished. 'I'll have the dish washed and ready for you tomorrow. There's another meal in it anyway.'

Charles Latimer came in then, looking slightly surprised to find Olivia Lydiard there. He went to Felix, gestured to him to stay in his seat, and put one hand on his shoulder.

'How are you, my boy?'

'I'm all right. A bit tired. Thanks for bringing Tessa here and taking her home again.'

'More thanks for taking her home than for bringing her, I imagine!' the doctor said with a grin. 'And you're looking more than "a bit tired". You're looking all in. Time you finished your meal in peace and got some sleep.' He nodded at his daughter, who began to put on her coat. 'May I give you a lift home, Mrs Lydiard?'

'It's only a few steps,' she began, but Charles Latimer smiled and put his hand under her elbow.

'I think it's best if we leave Felix now. I'm sure he's very grateful for your help, but as you can see, he's worn out.'

'Very well,' she said, turning away reluctantly. She looked at Felix again. 'I'll call in tomorrow morning.'

'Thanks, but there's really no need. The verger's coming at nine and I've got a heap of correspondence to deal with, and there are bound to be other parish matters. And of course I'll be going to see Stella in the evening – in the afternoon too, if I can manage it.'

Charles ushered the two women out of the kitchen and then returned. He looked at Felix gravely.

'You'll let me know as soon as there's any more news, won't you? I'll try to get down to see Stella myself in a day or two. And be sure to look after yourself too, my boy. You've got to keep up your own strength.'

Felix nodded and made an attempt at another smile. The doctor patted his shoulder once more and left. Felix heard the front door open and close, the voices fade, the doctor's car start up and drive away. He pushed away his half-eaten meal, leaned both elbows on the table, and rested his face in his hands.

He wanted nothing more than to go upstairs and fall into his bed, but he felt almost too weary to move from where he sat. He knew he could eat no more tonight. At last he lifted his head and saw the half-full glass of sherry standing before him.

He picked it up and drained it. Then he refilled it, stood up as stiffly as an old man, and carried it out of the room and up the stairs to his bedroom.

Chapter Fourteen

By Thursday afternoon the excitement in the school had not only reached fever pitch, it had passed it and left it behind.

'I shall be thankful when it's all over,' Miss Kemp confessed as she and Grace Harvey took a few minutes' break with a cup of tea in the main classroom after lunch. 'I have never known the children so excited about their Nativity Play before. They always enjoy it, of course, but this year you'd think they were going on the London stage. It's completely taken over their minds.'

'Joyce has done a very good job with them,' Grace said. 'I would never have thought she had it in her. Look at her now, surrounded by them out in the playground.'

Joyce Warren had offered to do playground duty and was standing outside the door with a crowd of small children around her, clamouring for her attention. Her face was flushed and smiling, and she looked a different person to the woman Miss Kemp and Grace Harvey had known for so long.

'She's come into her own,' Miss Kemp said slowly. 'She's told me a little about herself during these past few days, and I have to say it's taught me a lesson. We shouldn't judge people from what we see, Grace – especially those who have been through both world wars. If they're old enough to have experienced those, they can't help but have

193

an interesting, sometimes tragic and often admirable history.'

'I've often thought that.' Grace nodded. 'And Joyce always wanted to be a teacher, didn't she?'

'She would have made a very fine one,' Miss Kemp said. 'You have only to look at her now... Oh, *what* are those naughty Crocker twins doing now? After all the trouble the babies took to build their snowman...'

The village had woken on Wednesday morning to find themselves covered by a blanket of white. Nobody was particularly surprised, for it had been threatening for days, and they had turned philosophically with spades and shovels to clear it from their front paths and from the village street. The children had greeted it with whoops of joy and been out of bed and dressed and throwing snowballs at each other almost before it was light, while some of the bigger boys had already started to make ice slides which threatened the life and limbs of older villagers. In the school playground, Miss Kemp had allowed the children to make a row of snowmen, one for each year, which were lined up along the wall to watch the goings-on with round faces, eyes made of bits of coke from the pile used to keep the stoves going, and noses of carrots filched from kitchen vegetable baskets.

There had been a few hours of tension while Miss Kemp deliberated as to whether the Nativity Play could go ahead – if it snowed again, it could be too deep for the procession through the village, and the donkey had to be considered too – but the desperate pleas of the children and the efforts of a few volunteers led by Jacob Prout to make sure the way was clear had finally persuaded her. 'As long as it's not actually snowing at the time,' she cautioned. 'If it is, we'll have it in the school-room as usual.'

'Us could still have it up at the pub,' Billy Madge urged. 'It'd be a crying shame if Mr Nethercott went to all that trouble to get the stable ready and us never used it.'

'That's true,' said Joyce Warren, who had been as anxious as the children that nothing should disrupt their plans. 'So many village people are willing to be involved and it really is very special to have the snow. It makes it all the more real.'

'As long as it's not snowing heavily,' Miss Kemp repeated firmly, and then added, 'If it is, we'll have it at the stable. And since we've all got to get to the stable first, we may as well knock on a few doors along the way. But I can't promise anything about the donkey.'

'We could just postpone it if the weather's really bad,' Grace suggested. 'Have it one day next week instead. It won't matter that school's broken up – the children will all still be in the village.'

Fortunately, apart from a few light showers which covered the road nicely with a fresh dusting of white, there was no more snow, and by the end of afternoon school the sky had even begun to clear. The children were set free to race home and have their tea before returning with their various costumes and props, and as they gathered in the playground, hopping with excitement, the first few stars began to appear.

The donkey was due to be brought to the play-ground just before the procession began, and soon a crowd of children, dressed in various garbs as shepherds, angels, Wise Men and assorted villagers of Bethlehem, was milling about at the gate watching anxiously along the village street. Most people had risen to the occasion and set lanterns on their garden walls or at their gates, and the flickering yellow light streamed out across the rumpled snow. Cottage windows were lit as well, and as the carol singers appeared round the corner, wrapped in thick coats and carrying their own lanterns, the entire scene looked like a Victorian Christmas card.

'And here comes the donkey,' Joyce cried, as the children sent up a huge cheer. 'Oh, isn't he *sweet!*'

The donkey came plodding steadily along the street, led by Wendy Cole's uncle. Its back was covered by a colourful blanket, with two or three cushions, and its bridle had been woven with bright strips of crochet made by Wendy's aunt.

The children surged forward and Miss Kemp rang the bell which she had thought wise to bring with her.

'Stand still, please,' she commanded. 'You'll frighten the poor creature to death. Really, anyone would think you'd never seen a donkey in your lives.' She ushered them back to the gate and went forward to thank Mr Cole, who handed the bridle over to her.

'You're quite sure it will be safe for the children to be in charge?' she asked. 'Wendy assures me she knows the donkey well, but you know what children are.'

'None better,' he said with a grin. 'Had seven of

me own. But Jack here ought to be all right, he'm a quiet enough beast. The only trouble you're likely to have is getting un to move in the first place.'

'He seems to be walking very nicely now,' Miss Kemp observed. 'And he's beautifully dressed. Thank you so much, Mr Cole. It's very kind of you to lend him to us.'

'That's no trouble, Miss,' the farmer said with a grin. 'And you'll be finishing up at the pub, is that right? I'll be waiting for you there.'

Miss Kemp watched him walk away, thinking that 'finishing up at the pub' wasn't quite the way she would have liked to describe the school Nativity Play, and turned to lead Jack towards the throng waiting at the gate. Again they surged towards her, and she held up her hand.

'Please, children! You can all come in twos – *twos*, I said – and say hello to Jack, and then we'll get into our proper order and start the procession. Mrs Warren, you're in charge now. If you'll lead the way, Mrs Harvey and I will come along with the children. I think I'd better follow behind, to make sure there are no stragglers.'

The convoy was now ready to set off, with the donkey in the lead. Wendy had insisted that she could ride him, and after some consultation and a careful examination of the colourful blanket and the cushions, Joyce and Grace deemed it safe and lifted the little girl on to the donkey's back. She sat there proudly in her blue gown and her baby sister's white christening shawl as a head-dress, holding the crocheted reins, and beamed down at Joseph in the person of Billy Madge wearing his father's striped dressing gown and baggy blue pyjama trousers. In fact, almost all the children seemed to be dressed in nightwear of some sort, with plenty of warm clothes underneath.

Their excitement kept them warm too, Joyce reflected, as she gave the signal to move off. As she gazed around at the ring of faces with their flushed, rosy cheeks and bright eyes, she felt a rush of warmth of her own, an affection for these village children whom she had grown to know so well in the past week or so, and a gratitude for the opportunity that had been given her. I'd rather it had come any other way than by that dreadful accident, she thought, but I can't deny I'm happy to have had it.

'Come along then, children,' she cried, waving them into action. 'Let's start! And remember, you're not in Burracombe now – you're in Bethlehem. You've walked miles from your own villages to get here, and now you've arrived, hungry, thirsty and tired, in the bitter cold, you've got to find somewhere to stay. But other people have got here first and nearly every bed in the village has been taken. And Mary – poor Mary – is about to have a baby.'

There was a short pause while they all digested this and imagined themselves in their roles. Then Robin Tozer, dressed as a shepherd with a brand-new tea towel wrapped around his head and clutching his papier mâché lamb under his arm, spoke up.

'Her ought to have a cushion stuffed up her frock then. Her don't look a bit like her's going to have a babby. Her's much too skinny!'

As the cavalcade moved through the village, the carol singers formed themselves up in front of the children and sang as they went. Their voices floated through the cold, crisp air, reaching in through every cottage window, and doors began to open all along the narrow street, with people standing at them waving and smiling. Micky Coker and Henry Bennetts darted up the short garden paths, holding out their collection buckets, and the cheerful clink of coins upon metal could be heard on every side. Only a few doors remained closed, and at each of these houses Billy Madge marched up the path and knocked firmly on the door.

The first house was Constance Bellamy's, which stood almost opposite the school. The players and singers crowded into her garden and stood round the door, with Wendy clinging rather precariously to the donkey and Joyce Warren standing near, in case she fell off.

The door opened and Miss Bellamy's brown, wrinkled face peered out. 'Who are you? What do you want?'

She sounded so fierce that Billy quailed for a moment. Then he remembered that she was supposed to be acting too, and he said loudly, 'My name's Joseph and I be a carpenter from Bethle'em.' (No amount of coaching by Joyce had persuaded him that 'I am' would be better than 'I be'.) 'This is my wife Mary an' she'm havin' a babby, can we come in?'

'Certainly not!' Miss Bellamy exclaimed in horror. 'The very idea!' And she slammed the door.

It was so effective that even Joyce stood non-plussed for a moment or two. Some of the children giggled nervously, one or two of the younger ones began to cry, and it was not until Joseph recovered himself and said philosophically, 'She always were a mardy old bat' that the company pulled itself together and turned to trail back down the short drive.

'*It came upon the midnight clear, That glorious song of old,*' the singers crooned as they made their way to the next closed house. This was the black-smith's forge, where Micky lived, and Alf Coker himself came to the door, his sleeves rolled up to display brawny arms and a heavy scowl darkening his face. One of the smallest infants squeaked and moved behind Grace Harvey to cling to her skirt, and Grace wondered briefly if this really had been such a good idea after all.

Joseph repeated his words, getting only a few of them wrong, and indicated his wife, still seated rather crookedly on the donkey. 'Us can't find a room anywhere,' he said pitifully, 'and the babby's due any minute.'

'Well you can't stop here,' Alf said brusquely. 'A blacksmith's forge ain't no place to have a babby.'

'It do look nice and warm,' Joseph improvised, peering past the smith at the fire still burning inside. 'And 'tis freezing brass monkeys out here.'

Most of the children, who had never heard this phrase before, looked baffled at the reference to monkeys, but Joyce, who had learned a good deal of naval and military slang during her time in the hospital, groaned faintly and covered her face with her hand. Alf Coker's lips twitched but he kept the scowl on his face and said, 'Aye, and it's too cold to stand out here argufying. You'd better try somewhere else.' And he too closed his door.

The trek continued. The carol singers were doing well with their collection, for everyone was ready with a few pennies to throw into their buckets, and only those whose doors remained closed by prior arrangement made no contribution, having done so already when Joyce Warren and Grace Harvey went round to enlist their help earlier. At each house, Billy Madge became bolder, diverging more and more wildly from his script, and forcing the unlucky householders to think quickly to outwit his pleas for accommodation. At the last house, which happened to be the vicarage, Basil Harvey came to the door, his pink face beaming under his fuzz of white hair, to be confronted by a Joseph who was now so firmly entrenched in his part that real desperation sounded in his voice as he stepped forward and demanded to be let in.

'You can't leave us out here in the snow! My Mary's just about all in – look at the state of her. If she has her babby out here it'll die, and whose fault will that be? Yours – and you'm a *vicar!*'

Basil stared at him, completely taken aback by the indignation in the young voice. Floundering feebly for a moment or two, he almost stepped back and let them in; then he caught Joyce's stern eye and recollected himself.

'I haven't got any room,' he said firmly, thinking guiltily of the comfortable rooms behind him and the warmth of his fire. 'You'd better try the pub.'

'The pub?' Joseph echoed unbelievingly. 'You want the babby Jesus to be born in a *pub?*'

There was a moment of silence. Basil tried frantically to remember his lines. Hadn't Joseph been meant to turn meekly away at this point, leaving Basil to close the door and then, after a few minutes, open it again to join the increasing crowd following the procession through the village? What else was he supposed to say?

'Yes!' he said at last, panic taking over completely. 'The pub! And take that donkey with you! Look what he's doing on my path!'

He shut the door, hearing the outbreak of giggles from outside, and wondered just why the exchange had had so much effect on him. It had seemed so real – the children arrayed in their tea towels and dressing gowns, the carol singers ranged behind them with their faces lit by the lanterns they carried. Little Robin Tozer with his papier mâché lamb. And Joseph and Mary – he could not think of them as Billy Madge and Wendy Cole – Joseph and Mary with their donkey, tired and desperate, and Mary so close to giving birth...

They're just children, he reminded himself. You see them every week, almost every day. They're just playing the parts. And yet...

And yet, for a moment as he'd gazed at them standing in the snow, lit by lanterns and starlight, they'd seemed transformed; and he had felt himself wafted back in time to that night nineteen hundred and fifty-four years ago, when the original scene had taken place, when it had indeed been real. There had been a brief touch of magic –

almost, he thought, of holiness – touching the little group, and he had known then just how it must have been for the young couple, so desperate, yet so close to the greatest miracle the world had ever known.

The sound of singing faded and he pulled himself together, tore his coat from the hallstand and opened the door to follow the singers along the last part of their journey. They had been all through the village now and the younger ones were tiring, yet the most important, the most exciting part was yet to come. And it was to come in the pub.

The children went into the stable first. Joseph had knocked on the door of the Bell Inn and Bernie Nethercott had come out, to listen rather more sympathetically. 'I'm sorry,' he'd said when Joseph finally ran out of arguments, 'every bed's been took. But you could go in the stable, if that'd do.'

'The stable?' Joseph said sceptically. 'Well, I dunno...'

Wendy, who was getting more and more uncomfortable on the bony back of the donkey, decided that it was time to intervene. 'We don't have time to argue, Joe,' she said. 'I'm going to have this babby any minute now, so us'd better get into the stable if that's all there is and get on to the next bit.'

Joyce thanked her silently, and even Miss Kemp, with whom Wendy had never been a favourite, decided that there must be some good in the child after all. They filed in and Bernie showed them the manger and filled it with clean hay. He'd already arranged bales behind it, and the rank and file settled themselves there while the shepherds, angels and Wise Men stood to one side and waited.

There was a slight hiatus.

'Well, come along,' said Joyce. 'Angels first, then the shepherds.'

'But her ain't had the babby yet, Miss,' Joseph said. 'Us can't do nothing more until her's had the babby.'

This really is very hard work, Miss Kemp thought. Next year, we're having it in the school as usual, no matter what anyone else says. She looked around.

'Where's Betty? She was supposed to be bringing the baby, wasn't she?'

'Please, Miss,' one of the smaller Cullifords said, 'our Freddy dropped it in the pig bucket this morning and our mum had to give it a bath. It weren't dry when us come out, so she said she'd bring it up here.'

'For heaven's sake!' Miss Kemp said. 'Why did no one tell me? And where is she now? And where's Betty?'

'Her wouldn't come out without it. I don't reckon it were dry,' her informant said. 'Anyway, it had a big smear of summat over its face from the pig bucket and our mum said she didn't think she'd be able to get it off.'

Miss Kemp groaned. 'So now what are we going to do? Joseph – I mean, Billy – is quite right. We can't do the rest of the play without a baby.'

'Please, Miss,' said a small voice somewhere

close to her knees. She looked down and saw Janice Ruddicombe, the little girl who had suffered from polio and wore a built-up boot, standing next to her holding out a small bundle. 'Please, Miss, you could have my dolly.'

Miss Kemp took the bundle. It was a baby doll, wrapped in a fragment of blue blanket and wearing a green knitted bonnet. It was obviously much cherished, for its button nose and pouting red lips were almost rubbed away, and its yellow hair was rather grubby, but it was a doll, and a baby doll at that, and beggars, she reminded herself, could not be choosers.

'Thank you, Janice,' she said, remembering that this was the child who had been chosen to be one of Stella's bridesmaids. 'Thank you very much.' She passed it along the line to Joyce. 'They aren't exactly swaddling clothes, but...'

'It's wonderful,' Joyce said thankfully. 'And look, the blue is just the same blue as Mary's cloak. It'll do beautifully. Thank you, Janice, very much.'

The play was now in its final stage. The actors were all in position, quiet now, aware of the importance of these concluding moments. Joyce handed the baby doll to Mary, who laid it reverently in the manger, and then sat down on a bale of hay and leaned over it, one hand on the baby's face, her hair slipping out from beneath her headdress to fall half across her cheek. Joseph moved to her side and stood with a hand laid protectively, even proudly, on her shoulder, and one by one the shepherds and the Wise Men came forward to kneel and present their gifts.

Robin came last, standing his papier mâché lamb beside the manger, and then the angels began to sing in soft, high, childish voices, the only carol that was possible at just this moment.

'Away in a manger...'

The carol singers joined in at the third verse, and then Edward Crocker, who had surprised them all during rehearsals with his voice, began the first notes of 'Once in Royal David's City'. Again, the carol singers waited until the second verse, and as they finished the hymn, the bells began to ring, their chimes clear and pure in the cold, still air. There was silence in the stable as they rang, and more than one person, gazing at the shining faces of the children in the mellow light of the lamps, found their eyes damp with tears.

The bells stopped and there was a stir of movement. Miss Kemp moved forwards and, before anyone could speak, held up her hand. 'Children, that was lovely. You've all done very well indeed. It was the most beautiful Nativity Play we've ever done in Burracombe and we all know who we must thank.' She turned and held out her hand to Joyce Warren, who stood with unaccustomed diffidence to one side. 'Mrs Warren, who came to help us at the last moment, and whose idea all this was. And Mrs Harvey, who has been a tower of strength in these past two weeks. I don't know what I would have done without you both.' There was a burst of applause, and she waited until it died down, then continued. 'And there is one person we must remember specially tonight. We must remember our dear teacher Miss Simmons, who would be so proud of you. I know you've all been very upset by what happened to her, but the good news is that she's getting better.' There was another outburst of cheers. 'It will be a while before she can come home, but she's had an operation on her broken leg and the doctors are very pleased with her. I'm sure that's one of the best Christmas presents any of us could wish for, and I wish you all a very happy Christmas, and thank you for coming to see and help with our play.'

A third roar of applause greeted these last words, and then Bernie Nethercott stepped into the lamplight and held up his hands.

'I'd just like to add my good wishes to those what Miss Kemp's just given you,' he said. 'And I'd like to ask you all not to rush off home just yet awhile. Rose is coming in with a few mince pies and sausage rolls and Dottie Friend's right behind her with a jug or two of mulled ale and cider, and some cocoa for the kiddies. So stop here for a bit – 'tis nice and warm, and if 'twas like this in that stable in Bethlehem, I don't reckon 'twere too bad for Joseph and Mary. And I don't reckon they'd have been human if they hadn't had a bit of a party that night, what with all them angels and whatnot bringing them presents – so 'tis only right we should have a shindig and all. And you'm all very welcome. Happy Christmas!'

'Happy Christmas!' they all shouted, and then in came Rose and Dottie with the food and drink.

'It's been a wonderful evening,' Grace said to Joyce as they stood together eating mince pies and drinking hot cider. 'You really have done a marvellous job.'

'I don't think I've ever enjoyed myself so much in my life,' Joyce said, looking round at the eagerly chattering children. 'I only wish I could have been doing it for years.' She sighed. 'But once Christmas is over, there'll be the new teacher coming to take over. I shan't be needed any more.'

'Don't you be too sure,' Grace said. 'Miss Kemp has got her eye on you now. I think you'll be needed quite a lot more.'

Chapter Fifteen

The school party the next day could have been an anticlimax after the excitement of the Nativity Play, but the children were still too thrilled with their success to feel let down, and chattered about it incessantly as they wolfed down sausage rolls, sandwiches and fruit jelly in the classroom. The partition between the two rooms had been pulled back and the desks and tables ranged around the walls and laid with sheets as tablecloths for the feast, leaving a large space for games. The best moment came when Jacob Prout, dressed as Father Christmas, suddenly entered with a huge sack and proceeded to hand out presents.

'They aren't very much,' Miss Kemp said to Joyce Warren, who was organising some of the babies to act as elves and take the gifts to their appointed recipients. 'Just little things, so that they've got something from Santa.'

'That's the important thing,' Joyce said, watching as the children tore off the wrappings and aware that Miss Kemp paid for these gifts from her own pocket. 'It's so sad that Stella can't be here, though.'

'I know. But Hilary Napier called in this morning and told me the latest news – she came through the operation well, apparently, and the doctors are very pleased with her. There's a long way to go yet, but it does look more hopeful.'

'Oh, that *is* good.' Joyce hesitated, then said, 'I did hear there might be some paralysis...'

'I don't think they know that for sure yet. Hilary didn't mention it.' Miss Kemp's attention was distracted by a sudden dispute in the far corner of the room. 'I might have known it – the Crocker twins again!' She set off through the throng, clapping her hands loudly. 'Edward! George! Whatever you're doing, *stop it at once!*'

Joyce smiled. The play and the party had both been very successful, but there was no denying that she, Miss Kemp and Grace Harvey were all exhausted now and glad that the term was over. From today, the school would be closed, and the children the responsibility of their own parents for nearly three weeks.

And after that? Miss Kemp would be back here, with the new teacher, but she and Grace would have returned to their own daily lives and have little more contact with the school and its children. She sighed, and then turned to attend to a small child who was holding out a Mars bar.

'Please, Miss,' Janice Ruddicombe said, 'this is

for you. For Christmas. Because you helped us with our play.'

Joyce gazed down and felt the tears come into her eyes. She reached out and took the chocolate and then bent to kiss the little girl.

'Thank you, Janice,' she said. 'Thank you very much. It's one of the nicest Christmas presents I've ever had.'

With only a few days to go before Christmas, the village was now in a frenzy of preparation. Puddings, cakes and mincemeat had been made weeks ago, but there were plenty of things that couldn't – or shouldn't – be done until the last moment, and little enough time now to do them in.

At the Tozers' farm, Alice Tozer's geese, fattened all through the summer and autumn and already on order for various villagers, were killed and ready to be plucked. The family sat together in the outside kitchen, as it was called, to do the task together, Joe and Russ sitting on a hard wooden bench with the others, each with a heavy bird across his lap and pulling out soft feathers until they filled the air like a snowstorm of drifting white. Joanna had stayed indoors to be near the children, but Minnie was plucking too, despite Alice's protests.

'I've never missed doing the birds yet and I don't reckon to miss it now,' she said firmly, allowing Ted to carry out her own kitchen chair, with the flat wooden arms and several cushions. 'Specially not with my Joe and his boy here. 'Tis a once-in-a-lifetime party with they two.'

'Once in my lifetime, that's for sure,' Russ said with a grin.

'Don't say that,' Alice reproached him. 'Now you know where we are, you'll be coming over all the time. This won't be your last Christmas in Burracombe.'

'Probably not. And I hope the next one will be happier. Not that it isn't great to be here with you all – that couldn't be better. I was thinking about that poor schoolteacher and her sister.'

Mostly about her sister, Alice thought, glancing at him. 'We'll give you a proper Devonshire Christmas,' she said, finishing the goose she was plucking and setting the naked body aside. 'One that'll make you want to come back as soon as you can.'

The door opened and they all looked up, surprised to see Jackie standing in a flurry of snowflakes. She came in quickly, shutting out the cold draught, and unwound the long scarf Minnie had knitted for her last year. Her face was pink with cold and she took off her thick gloves and rubbed her hands together.

'It's freezing out there! Joanna told me where you all were, so I came straight in.'

'Well, this is a nice surprise,' Alice said, beaming. 'Didn't expect to see you here this side of Christmas – I thought they'd be keeping you run off your feet in that hotel.'

'We had a change of shifts, so I thought I'd come back and help with the plucking. It doesn't seem like Christmas without pulling out a few feathers. Shift up, Tom.' She settled herself on the bench beside her brother and helped herself to a bird. 'Looks like I was just in time.'

'We've broken the back of it,' Alice nodded. 'Only a few to go now. And how be you, Jackie? You're still all right for getting home after Christmas, I hope?'

'I'm all right, Mum, and Miss Millington says I can come home after my afternoon shift on Boxing Day.' Jackie made a face. 'Don't know how I'll get here, with hardly any trains or buses running, but I suppose someone will fetch me over, will they?'

'Be glad to,' Russ said. 'And then it won't be long before you'll be leaving for good and coming with us on the *Queen Elizabeth,* back to the States.'

Ted grunted. He still wasn't entirely happy about Jackie's jaunt to America, but he had been forced to accept it with good grace. He'd had a talk with Joe and they'd agreed to go halves on the fare, which was still a lot of money for Ted to pay out, but he'd been determined not to be beholden to his brother. 'She'll have to be satisfied with a bit less for her wedding, whenever that happens,' he'd said grumpily to Alice. 'Not that it would surprise me if the maid up and got wed over there without even telling us. That's just the sort of thing her'd do.'

'Ted, you don't mean that!' Alice had exclaimed in horror. 'For one thing, it's eighteen months before our Jackie turns twenty-one, and she's said she'll only be gone a few months. You don't really think she'll stop longer, do you?'

'I don't know what to think about what's in our Jackie's head any more,' he'd said heavily. 'All I do know is that nothing will surprise me. You'd better make up your mind to it, Alice m'dear, once her gets on that ship and sails away, her'll be out of our reach and out of our control, and us'll just have to rely on her own good sense, if she's got any, and the way us brought her up. We done our best and nobody can do more.'

Alice thought of this conversation now, as the family sat plucking Christmas geese as they had done for as long as she could remember, and for generations before that. The outside kitchen was really more of a small barn, and not heated at all except by the small paraffin burner Ted had put near his mother's chair, but the warmth of their bodies and the feathers of the geese created their own warmth, and the little stone building seemed snug and cosy. It wasn't just that sort of warmth, though, she thought, looking around at the ring of faces lit by the glow of the old hurricane lamp, it was the warmth of a family together, doing something useful towards the best family occasion of the year. It was always good, but this year it was even better, with Joe and Russ sitting alongside them for all the world as if they'd done it every year. But what would it be like next year, without them? And what if Ted's fears were right and Jackie wasn't there then either?

She decided it was best not to look ahead. You never knew what was round the corner anyway, and there was no sense in spoiling this year by worrying about the next. She heaved the last goose on to her lap and began to pluck the fine down from its breast.

Hilary Napier was preparing for the busiest

Christmas that the Barton had seen for years. Not since before the war, when her mother had been alive, had it been filled with visitors at Christmas, and never with such visitors as these. She was looking forward to it with trepidation, but at least Rob could be involved in the preparations and distracted from his recent troubles at school.

'You'll have to tell me how you celebrate Christmas in France,' she said cheerfully as they brought the decorations down from the attic. 'We want to make it as nice as possible for you all.'

He looked at her blankly. 'Isn't it the same everywhere?'

Hilary stared him over the armful of tangled paper chains she was carrying. 'Well, no. I don't think it is. Different countries have different customs. Look, I'll tell you what we do here and you can tell me what's different.' She passed him the paper chains and delved in a pile of boxes for the Christmas lights that had been used and carefully put away again every year since she was a small child. There were some glass baubles somewhere too – purple and gold and red and silver, shaped like perfect spheres which glittered in the light, or like balls with segments cut out to reveal a fluted curve of colour. There were even two or three angels or cherubs to be hung from the branches of the tree where they would float, blowing eternally silent trumpets of shimmering glass so fine and delicate it was a miracle they had survived for so long.

'On Christmas Eve,' she said as they trooped down the stairs to the drawing room where the tree was to be erected, 'children hang their stockings up by the fire, or at the ends of their beds, for Santa Claus to put their presents in. They usually write to him a week or so earlier, saying what they would like, and put their letters into the fire to go up the chimney. Oh, and they often put a glass of sherry and a mince pie out for him too, because he has such a long journey all in one night.' She paused, recollecting that Robert was twelve years old and had probably stopped believing in Santa Claus several years ago. 'It's all just tradition, of course,' she added. 'Anyway, they wake up very early on Christmas morning to see if he's come, and if he has they open all their presents and wake the whole household with the sound of toy trumpets and drums or anything else noisy they've received – there's nearly always something noisy – and Christmas begins. Later on the grown-ups have their presents, and sometimes the children have their bigger presents then – the stockings just have small gifts – and then there's Christmas dinner, with a turkey or a goose and a Christmas pudding. And then we play games and sing carols and other songs.' She stopped and looked at him. 'Is that how you celebrate Christmas?'

'Something like,' he said, dumping his pile of paper chains on the small sofa. 'But we put out shoes, not stockings, and we go to Midnight Mass and have a feast afterwards. Don't you go to church at all?'

'Yes, of course. I just forgot to mention it. We do have a midnight service in the village church, and then there's a Communion at eight o'clock and matins at eleven.' A thought occurred to her. 'Will you be wanting to go to Midnight Mass in

215

Tavistock, at the Roman Catholic church?'

'Yes, I expect Maman will want to do that,' he said. 'But how will we get there? You won't want to wait for us for over an hour. And what about the feast?'

'I suppose I could go to the midnight service at St Eustachius'. I've always rather wanted to. But there won't be a feast, I'm afraid,' she added firmly. 'Your grandfather will never be able to eat a big meal at such a late hour, and I'm not at all sure I'd want to, either. I'll make some sandwiches to come back to, and that will be all.' She busied herself untangling the Christmas lights, which seemed to have spent the past year winding themselves into knots. 'You know, it might be better if we don't try to mix up our two sorts of Christmas but just show you what an English Christmas is like. I think that's what your grandfather wants to do, anyway. You wouldn't be too disappointed if we do that, would you?'

'No, not at all,' he said tranquilly, and removed the tangle from her hands. 'I think we would like that. And I shall be going home with Maman and Philippe and Ginette afterwards, anyway.' With deft fingers, he untangled the knots and stretched the wire out so that the lights lay in a line. They were quite plain lights, simply small coloured bulbs of red and blue, but they had been strung on the Napier Christmas tree every year for almost as long as Hilary could remember, and she was fond of them and wouldn't have dreamed of replacing them with the more fancy sets that were slowly becoming available in some of the larger shops.

'I wonder if they all work,' Rob said. 'Shall we plug them in to see?'

'Yes, let's. There's a two-pin socket in that corner – that's where we usually have the tree.' She watched as he carried the lights to the corner she had indicated and pushed the small plug into the socket. The lights glowed with colour and she exclaimed with delight. 'Oh, that's lovely. It's really beginning to feel like Christmas now.'

Rob unplugged the lights and smiled at her. 'When shall we fetch the tree?'

'Travis said he'd take you to get it tomorrow morning. You have to go over to Hanger Woods, where we always grow a few conifers. It'll need to be set up and then we can decorate it the day after.'

'And Maman and the others come the day after that,' he said. 'Can we put up all the decorations too, before they come?'

'Of course. And we should think about their presents, Rob. We ought to go shopping one day.'

He stared at her in dismay. 'Oh, Tante Hilary! I have no money.'

'Don't you?' she asked, surprised. 'But what about your pocket money while you were at school?'

He hung his head and whispered, 'I spent it on the train fare to London. I am sorry...'

Hilary looked at him and felt a prickle of compassion. 'Oh, Rob. Of course you must have done. I'm sorry – it never occurred to me.' In all the drama of the discovery that he had run away from school and gone to London in a bid to return to France, her subsequent recovery of him

217

via David, and then the horror of the accident, she had completely overlooked the fact that he must have used almost every penny he had to pay his fare. How had he expected to pay his way to France from there? She shook away the thoughts of Rob, alone and penniless in London, and thanked heaven that David had been there to come to the rescue.

'I'll give you some more money,' she said. 'You should have some for the holidays anyway, and Father always gave your father and Stephen and me extra for Christmas presents. You'll have enough to buy everyone something.'

He frowned. 'I should have earned it. At home, Maman makes us earn our pocket money.'

Hilary felt a grudging respect for Marianne. Not that she had anything against her as a mother, she acknowledged. Rob was a nice, well-mannered boy, even if it was hard to tell what he was thinking sometimes.

'Well, you can earn yours,' she said cheerfully. 'You can go with Mr Kellaway this afternoon and tomorrow, and help him on the estate, and when you've brought the tree back you can help me set it up and put up all the decorations. Then you can help me get the bedrooms ready for your mother and sister and brother, and by the time we've done all that, you'll have earned your money and we can go shopping.'

And that will have kept you nicely occupied for the next three days, she thought, by which time Marianne and the other two children will be here and you can spend your time with them while I get on with all the other things I have to do.

It seemed an eternity since she had last spoken with David. He was as caught up in pre-Christmas festivities as she was, although his were of a rather different nature – a round of cocktail parties, dinners and formal dances run by organisations such as the local Rotary Club or Sybil's cronies, as far as she could gather. Apart from one or two parties being held by local landowners and friends of her father, which she had declined on account of his health, hers were of a much simpler nature. And that's how I like it, she thought. Almost without noticing it, I've slipped out of that world and don't have any desire to slip back in. Times are changing, and I'm changing with them.

In fact, she thought, she had changed more than she'd realised. From a properly brought-up young woman, with moral values instilled in her by parents who had been born during Queen Victoria's reign, to someone secretive, deceitful and prepared to commit adultery. To have an affair. To be a *mistress*.

She tried to feel ashamed. Well, she *was* ashamed, she insisted to herself. Deeply ashamed. And yet ... lurking beneath the shame, the anxiety, the knowledge that it could destroy both her and David's reputations, if not their lives, was a thrill of excitement, of delight in the new experiences, the new knowledge of herself that came with every morning as she woke and thought of him. A different Hilary had been born, or maybe had been there all the time, desperate to break out. The Hilary who had left home and the life her parents had planned for her and gone to war, finding independence, finding herself. That Hilary had

219

almost been lost when she came back again after the war and had felt compelled to stay, to look after first her mother and then her father, to run the estate, to take second place to a manager...

It's as if I've been born again, she thought, wondering if she dared ring David that night, if he would still be in his surgery. David has brought me back to life. David has rescued me, and whatever happens to us after this, I will always love him for that.

There was no time to telephone him, however. Her father stayed up later that evening, playing chess with Rob, who was, Gilbert said, not half a bad player. After that, Rob went to bed and Hilary tried to persuade her father to do likewise, but he refused.

'I don't need to be packed off early like a two-year-old. Nothing wrong with me now. I've done precious little all day, don't begrudge me an evening of peace and quiet by my own fire. There won't be much peace and quiet once Marianne and her other two arrive.'

'I don't suppose there will, which is why I think you should rest as much as possible now.'

'I *am* resting. I'm sitting in a comfortable armchair with my feet up in front of a roaring fire. I tell you, Hilary, there's only so much time a man can spend in bed without going insane. See what's on the wireless, there's a good girl.'

Hilary found the *Radio Times* in its leather cover. 'There's *Ray's a Laugh* at half past eight on the Home Service, or *Ignorance is Bliss* on the Light Programme, and *A Midsummer Night's Dream* on the Third Programme. Or we could watch television – there's a play and a quiz programme.'

'Too irritating,' he grunted. 'I always want to throw something at the set. Don't know why we bought the damned thing.'

'We got it to see the Coronation. And there have been some quite interesting things on since then. Well, which would you like?'

'None of them.' He seemed in a cantankerous mood tonight, Hilary thought, and hoped it didn't mean he was going to have another attack. 'Get out the cribbage board and we'll have a couple of rounds before we go to bed. You've got a lot of work on, with all these visitors coming – you need your sleep as much as I do.'

He was right, Hilary thought, as she got out the cards and the board with its coloured pegs, but she wasn't likely to get it. Alone in bed at night gave her the only chance she had to think about David, to picture his face, hear his voice and remember the hours they had spent together, walking in Hyde Park, and making love in the hotel room. She lay awake quite deliberately, re-living each moment in her mind until at last she could stay awake no longer. And since it was obvious that she was not going to have a chance to telephone him, that was all that was left to her.

Chapter Sixteen

Felix hadn't the heart to put up Christmas decorations. He felt as though he should, but the
thought of actually doing it was enough to exhaust
him. Besides, he didn't have any. He had never
had his own home before, and had always spent
Christmas either with his own family or with
someone in the parish he was working in at the
time. Since he had come to Burracombe, Basil
Harvey had made him welcome, and last year
Stella had been with him too. That was probably
what they'd have done this year, if it hadn't been
for the accident. And next year, he thought, they'd
have been buying or making new decorations
together for the Little Burracombe vicarage.

Next year, that's what we *will* be doing, he told
himself firmly. Stella will have recovered by then
and we'll be married, and all this will be behind
us.

'You know you're welcome to come to us on
Christmas Day,' Grace Harvey had told him.

'Thank you. But I'll be going into the hospital
straight after matins. I don't know how long
they'll let me stay, but I want to be with Stella as
much as possible.'

'Well, we won't be having dinner until after the
Queen's Christmas broadcast – Basil thinks it's
disrespectful to listen with dirty plates on the
table. So we'll eat at four, and if you're not there

we'll keep a plate hot for you. Do say yes, Felix. You know perfectly well that if you don't, you'll just go home and eat baked beans on toast, and you can't do that, not on Christmas Day.'

Felix smiled. 'I don't think I'll be given the chance. Dottie's invited me and so have the Napiers – you know young Rob's family will be there, don't you? – and Joyce Warren has almost twisted my arm off, and that's before we even begin to think about all the parishioners in Little Burracombe. People really are so kind.'

'Well, you must go wherever you feel most at home,' Grace said. 'What about Maddy? I assume she's coming to the village for Christmas. Will she be going to the hospital too?'

'Yes, and she's staying with the Napiers. I was rather surprised that they invited her, since they've got the French family staying too, but I think Hilary feels a little overwhelmed by it. And of course, Maddy used to stay there a lot as a child, when Hilary's mother was alive – Mrs Napier and Fenella Forsyth were great friends, so I'm told.'

'I wonder she isn't staying with Dottie. She usually does, doesn't she?'

'Yes, but Dottie's going to be so busy at the Bell – they're having a party there in the afternoon, after closing, for anyone who hasn't got family to go to. She did tell Maddy she'd be welcome, but Maddy decided to go to the Napiers. So I think, on balance, I ought to accept Hilary's invitation. Maddy's been such a tremendous help to me over the wedding. She's sent a letter out to everyone who was coming, to tell them it's been postponed. It's a pity we couldn't give them a new date, but that will have to wait for Stella to decide.'

'So long as you're going somewhere,' Grace said. 'I really don't want to think of you alone in that great vicarage over Christmas. What are you doing on Boxing Day? Apart from going to the hospital, that is.'

'Oh, I've got company then,' he said, his face brightening. 'My parents are coming down to stay for a few days. They haven't been able to come sooner because of Father's services and so on, but he's got plenty of cover for the Sunday after Christmas and he'll help me with mine. And Mother will make sure I have a good breakfast and eat my greens!'

'That's very good news. They must have been so worried about you and Stella. They'll be glad to be able to see you both for themselves.'

As well as the preparations going on in every home, there was a succession of parties in the village hall, from the Fur and Feather whist drive to the Women's Institute Christmas party. Each member was allowed to bring one guest to this, and thus the entire village was represented, from the Cullifords to the Squire. Hilary had been doubtful as to whether her father was up to it, but Gilbert had insisted she took him as her guest.

'Just don't play any rough games,' she cautioned him. 'You know what these WI parties are like.'

'Rough games at a WI party?' he said in astonishment. 'They're not likely to be playing British Bulldog, are they?'

'No, just things like Musical Chairs, but even

that can get quite rough when there's only one chair left. I've seen some nasty pushes happening, and you know what Ivy Sweet's like when there's a prize at the end of it.'

He chuckled. 'Oh, I know what Ivy Sweet's like, all right. I've known her since she was in ankle socks and a pinafore. She didn't have red hair then, mind.'

She didn't have a red-haired little boy, either, Hilary thought, but she didn't say so out loud. That would have been repeating gossip – of which there'd been plenty when a few people had seen Ivy Sweet in the Horrabridge pub where she worked, flirting with the pilots from Harrowbeer airfield. One of them had had red hair, so it was said, and he and Ivy had been especially friendly...

Hilary shook herself. Even thinking it was bad enough, and she was uncomfortably aware that such gossip could quite easily be applied to herself and David. You had to be seen for gossip to start, of course, but she often thought of the November day when Joe and Russ Tozer had come upon herself and David sitting together in that café in Hyde Park. Nothing had ever been said, and there was no reason for them to suspect anything untoward, but it only took one word, spoken in the wrong place and with the wrong ears listening...

Joe and Russ were at the WI party too, invited by Alice and Minnie. Luke had offered to look after the children, so Val invited her father as her guest and Joanna brought Tom. The village hall was full and there was a festive tea laid out on the long trestle tables, with plates of ham and salad and bowls of trifle as well as mince pies, sausage rolls, Swiss roll, butterfly cakes, chocolate sponges and a large Christmas cake for which everyone in the WI had contributed some dried fruit.

'I don't know how they do it!' Hilary said in amazement. 'Rationing's hardly over and yet they produce a feast like this. I hope nobody's stinted their own Christmas for it.'

'It's surprising what you can do if everyone gives what they can afford,' Joyce Warren smiled. 'And George Sweet is always very good to us. And we've had some wonderful things from the Tozers this year.'

'That's our Joe,' Alice said, overhearing her name. 'Wrote to his girls to send over some parcels, he did. You wouldn't believe what they put in the post.'

Chairs were drawn up to the tables and everyone tucked in. Hilary kept a watchful eye on her father, at the other end of the table, but he seemed to be enjoying himself hugely, laughing uproariously at something Alf Coker was telling him. If only he could be like this all the time, she thought, watching as he crossed his arms to pull crackers with Alf and Jessie Friend, on his other side. I'm sure he'd get much more pleasure from life. But no – once Christmas was over, he would revert to being the Squire again, expecting fine men like Alf and Jacob Prout to touch their caps to him, forgetting that he had sat at the same table with them, wearing an orange paper crown and laughing at their jokes.

The meal over at last, the tables were cleared

and folded up and the chairs pushed into a circle for the games to start. Pass the Parcel was always a good ice-breaker – if there was any ice to break after the meal – and Grace Harvey played popular song tunes on the tinkling old piano in the corner, sitting with her back to them so that she couldn't see who had the parcel when she stopped. It was Russ Tozer who tore off the last wrapping and, amidst cheers and laughter, held up a wooden spoon. 'I'll be able to bake as good as any of you now!' he declared.

Next, they played Finish the Sentence, in which the aim was actually not to finish the sentence spoken one word at a time round the circle by the players. The story grew wilder and wilder, with plenty of 'ands' and 'buts' until at last Dottie Friend could bear it no longer and brought the sentence to a triumphant end, having to stand on one foot for a full minute as a forfeit and managing only forty-five seconds before she almost fell over.

'We're now going to play One Minute, Please,' announced Joyce Warren, who was WI president that year. 'I'm sending round a hat with slips of paper in it, and I want you all to take one. If there's anything written on it, you have to speak on the subject for a full minute or pay a forfeit. If the paper's blank, you've had a lucky escape!'

The hat was passed round and people fumbled inside, picking out slips of paper which they opened with trepidation and gazed at with expressions either of relief or of varying degrees of dismay. Basil Harvey was first to go.

'It's hardly fair,' he protested, getting up, with

his white hair sticking out from under the green paper hat he'd got out of his cracker. 'I'm used to talking to you all.'

'You'm not used to keeping it down to a minute, though, Vicar,' Jacob Prout called out. 'Usually you got us trapped for a good half-hour!'

'I don't think I can even talk for a minute on this subject,' Basil said plaintively. 'It's "Teaching Your Kitten to Fly"!'

There was a roar of laughter and he proved quite right, floundering to a stop after only three sentences and being made to perform a waltz with Ivy Sweet, who had drawn a slip of paper bearing only a red cross and now found out what it meant. She was a good, rather showy dancer though, and the vicar was led back to his seat slightly pink in the face and breathless.

'Well done, Vicar!' Joyce cried. 'Now, who's next? Oh, it's the Squire – and what's your subject, Colonel Napier?'

'I'm not sure...' Hilary began, but her father waved her into silence. He rose from his seat, holding his piece of paper and looking slyly smug.

'My subject,' he declaimed in his usual strong voice, 'is the Battle of Waterloo!'

There was a burst of laughter at this, and Joyce looked both nonplussed and amazed. Before she could speak, however, he had begun; and it was clearly a subject he knew a good deal about. His audience had learned more about the Duke of Wellington than they'd ever thought they wanted to know before Joyce found her own voice and intervened.

'That was excellent, Colonel,' she said, holding

up one hand. 'Unfortunately, you seem to have got hold of the wrong piece of paper. "Waterloo" was meant to be a word in our next game, Charades. It seems as though they've got rather mixed up.'

There was a roar of laughter and Gilbert Napier sat down, still holding his piece of paper. Jacob Prout, hardly able to contain his mirth, called out, 'Do that mean he've got to pay a forfeit, Mrs Warren? After all, he did talk on the wrong subject, didn't un?'

'Well, I was going to ask him to kiss the prettiest girl in the room,' Joyce admitted, 'but since he did after all manage to talk for more than a minute...'

'Seemed more like quarter of an hour to me,' someone muttered.

'...I think he should be excused.'

Gilbert stood up again. 'And what if I don't want to be excused?' And to everyone's delight, he marched across the circle and gave Minnie Tozer a smacking kiss on the cheek.

The party wound on to its usual close, with everyone singing first a few carols and then some of the old songs they all knew so well. 'Tavern in the Town', 'Clementine', 'The Ash Grove', 'Widecombe Fair' and at last the song that Alf Coker always sang, in his deep baritone voice, – the bellringers' song, telling the story of a competition held many years ago in the Devon village of Ashwater.

''Twas in Ashwater town, The bells they did sound, They rang for a belt and a hat laced with gold, But the men of North Lew ring so steady and true, There never was better in Devon, I hold...'

'Except in Burracombe,' Ted Tozer added at the end, as he always did. 'But then, us couldn't get a team along that day – too busy milking.'

'It was a lovely evening,' Val said as she and Luke walked home from the farm. Christopher was in his pram, well wrapped up in his shawl and blanket, and hadn't stirred all evening, his father said. He would just need a feed when they got indoors and then he'd sleep through the night. 'You should have seen Colonel Napier! He was really enjoying himself. I sometimes think Hilary coddles him a bit too much.'

'Well, he has had two heart attacks, and Dr Latimer told him to take it easy. You can't blame her for wanting him to be careful.'

'I don't, but he needs to get out of the house and see people. It would take his mind off himself and what's going to happen to the estate. It's just about all he thinks of, Hilary says. It's not good for him.'

'It's a pity the weather's so cold,' Luke observed. It hadn't snowed again, but it was still below freezing, and the track, although now well trodden, was icy in places. 'He can hardly go out for a walk, and there's not much else he could do outside. Doesn't Dr Latimer go and play chess with him sometimes?'

'Yes, but the doctor's very busy at the moment. Everyone is, with Christmas so near. Still, the relatives from France are arriving tomorrow, apparently, so that should give him something different to occupy his mind.'

'If it doesn't kill him off altogether!' Luke said with a grin. 'I'm not sure I'd fancy a house full of visitors with two children I'd never met before, and French at that. He'll be praying for peace and quiet and a dull life by Boxing Day.'

Val laughed. 'Perhaps. I'm not at all sure Hilary's looking forward to it, anyway. She doesn't like Marianne very much as it is. And when I remarked that it was a good thing Stephen was coming, as he could help entertain them, she gave me the funniest look. But she wouldn't say anything – just made a face and left it at that. I think she'll be glad when Christmas is over.'

'Mm.' They walked in silence for a moment or two, enjoying the crunch of frozen snow beneath their feet and the sparkle of the stars above their heads. 'Is Hilary all right, Val? I thought she looked rather strained. More than I'd have expected from just having visitors at Christmas, I mean. She can usually cope with anything like that with one hand tied behind her back.'

'I know what you mean. I've thought it once or twice myself lately. For a few weeks, in fact. But she's had all those problems with Rob, and then her father's heart attack – I don't suppose it's any more than that. She just needs a bit of time to herself, that's all.'

'Well, none of us will get much of that this side of Christmas,' he said cheerfully. They came to their cottage and he opened the gate and pushed the pram up the narrow path. 'There's far too much to do.'

'Tomorrow we'll be putting up our own decorations,' Val said. 'I can't wait to see Christopher's face when he sees them. He's just old enough now to enjoy coloured lights and sparkly baubles.'

'And next year he'll be fifteen months old and running about, and will enjoy it even more,' said Luke, but Val shivered suddenly.

'Don't let's wish his babyhood away too quickly, Luke. It'll go all too soon as it is. Let's just make the most of every minute we have now.'

He looked at her in surprise. 'What's the matter?'

'Oh, nothing really,' she said, but her voice trembled a little. 'I just thought then of poor Joanna. She should have two babies seeing the decorations and enjoying their first Christmas, but she's only got one. It's bound to be upsetting for her.'

'Yes,' Luke said soberly. 'You're right. It's all too easy to forget that, when we're so happy ourselves. Even though Jo has two lovely children, there'll always be a gap where Susannah should have been. We must never forget it, Val, because Tom and Joanna never will.'

Chapter Seventeen

The French visitors arrived the next day, late in the afternoon, just as dusk was closing in. They had travelled by ferry to Dover and come the rest of the way by train, and Hilary and Rob drove to Tavistock to meet them.

'It is a very long journey,' Marianne said when they had greeted each other with kisses and Hilary had been introduced to Rob's half-brother and sister. 'The children have enjoyed it, but they're tired now.'

'Well, we'll soon be home.' They loaded the suitcases into the back of the Land Rover and set off. 'I hope your mother and sister are well,' Hilary asked politely as they drove out of the station and down the hill into the middle of the town. 'Christmas will be very quiet for them without you.'

'They will be busy enough. We did much baking before I came away, for the patisserie, but there will be plenty more for them to do. We must go back a day early, so that I can help them prepare for New Year and Epiphany.'

Hilary wondered if Marianne's terse note was due entirely to weariness. They had not parted on good terms after her previous visit, and Hilary had no reason to be pleased to see her, but she was Rob's mother and must be made welcome. She sighed and let in the clutch. It was not going to be an easy Christmas.

'*C'est* Tavistock,' Rob was telling his brother and sister. '*Elle est notre ville. Quand je–*'

'Robert!' Marianne said sharply. 'Speak English, please. It is impolite to your aunt to speak in French.'

He looked at her, startled, and whispered, '*Pardonne-moi, Maman.* I am sorry – I am just excited to see Philippe and Ginette again.'

'Perhaps so, but we have agreed to speak English all the time we are here. It will be good for the younger ones, too. They need to practise.'

There was a short silence. Hilary broke it by saying, 'I'll bring you all into town tomorrow if you like, to have a look round. I need to do some

233

more shopping.'

'I will not come,' Marianne said. 'I wish to speak with your father. It will be a good opportunity.'

Hilary glanced sideways at her. Clearly, whatever Marianne wanted to say to Gilbert was to be said to him in private, with Hilary safely out of the way. She wondered what it could be. There had been too little time since the accident to do more than let Marianne know that Rob had come home early from school, and she had been told none of the details. She was clearly displeased, however; her lips were folded tightly together and her dark eyes stared straight ahead. She was wearing what looked like a new costume, Hilary noticed; when she had first brought Rob to see them, in June, her clothes had been carefully looked after but old. She remembered that her father had given Marianne a handsome present when she had gone back to France, leaving Rob with them, and it was easy to see where some of it had been spent. And why not? Hilary knew that Gilbert would expect his daughter-in-law to be well turned out. That was what the money had been for.

'We're just coming on to Dartmoor now,' she told the children as the Land Rover rattled over a cattle grid. 'That grid is to stop ponies and sheep from coming off the moor. I expect Rob's told you in his letters about the wild ponies, hasn't he?' Too late, she thought of the ponies that had been involved in the accident and wished she hadn't spoken. But they could hardly pretend the animals weren't there.

'He says they are free to go wherever they like,' Philippe said. He was small and dark, like his

234

mother, with her large eyes and soft, curling hair. 'But that's just a story, *non?*'

'No, it's quite true. They do all belong to someone, and they tend to stay in their own part of the moor, but apart from that they're quite free to wander.'

'I would like a pony,' Ginette said. She had a rather high voice and was a smaller copy of her brother. She would look exactly like Marianne when she was older, Hilary thought, and wondered if she had inherited her nature too. 'Robert says you have horses. Will you let me ride one?'

They really did speak astonishingly good English. Marianne had explained on her first visit that her father had been a teacher of English and had brought the family to England many times before the war. She had maintained the language in the knowledge that one day Rob would come to England to meet his father's family, and she had certainly done a good job.

'I think we can find a pony for you. Rob's learning to ride too. But the weather isn't really right for it now – the ground's too hard and icy. Perhaps if you come later in the year...'

And now I've invited them back, she thought with an inward groan, before they've even reached the house! Well, we would have had to do it anyway. They're part of our lives now.

But what of her own life? The life she so desperately wanted to lead with David – away from Burracombe and all the responsibilities that had been heaped upon her head?

'Who else will be here for Christmas?' Marianne enquired. 'Will Stephen be at home?'

'Yes, he will,' Hilary answered shortly, hoping that Marianne had no ideas about renewing her attempted seduction. 'And Maddy Forsyth. I'm not sure if you met her in the summer. She used to stay with us a lot – her adopted mother and my mother were friends.'

'Her adopted mother?'

'Fenella Forsyth, the actress. She lives mostly in France now – Maddy's spent quite a lot of time there, in the Loire valley.'

'Oh, yes. I do not know that part,' Marianne said dismissively. 'But why then does this ... Maddy? ... not go to France to be with her adopted mother?'

'Mainly because her sister's in hospital, very ill.' Hilary remembered why Stella was in hospital and glanced quickly in the mirror, biting her lip, but Rob was deep in conversation with his brother. 'I'll tell you more about it when we're at home and you're settled,' she added. 'Look, Ginette, there are some ponies!'

'Ponies!' The French girl craned her neck. *'Mais ils sont ravissants.'*

'English, please,' Marianne said sharply.

'Oh, let them talk French if they want to,' Hilary said. 'It's natural to them. Their English is so good, I'm sure they'll use it when they're with the family. And we do know a little French ourselves anyway.' In fact, Gilbert spoke it fluently and Hilary and Stephen had both done well in the language at school and spent holidays in France with their mother before the war.

They were almost in Burracombe now. The narrow road that led from the main road had been cleared of most of the snow by Jacob Prout,

236

assisted by some of the farm workers, but it was still icy and Hilary drove carefully. It would not do to have another road accident, and she still had to explain to Marianne what had happened to cause the first, and how Rob had been involved. She turned along the drive at last and drew up in front of the house, relieved to be safely back and hoping that her father was feeling fit to receive visitors after his high jinks at the WI party the evening before.

The door at the top of the steps opened and light flooded out from the hallway. Marianne, who had her hand on the handle of the car door, ready to open it, looked up and her eyes widened.

'Stephen!' she exclaimed, and at the tone in her voice Hilary's heart sank. 'Hilary did not tell me you were already home. What a pleasant surprise.'

She jumped down, lithe as a cat, and ran up the steps towards him. Stephen cast Hilary an agonised glance and stepped back, but Marianne threw her arms around his neck and kissed him.

Hilary, staring up at them, saw that there was someone else silhouetted behind Stephen in the hallway. As he disentangled himself from the Frenchwoman's arms, the figure came forward and looked down. Her dark blue eyes were huge in her white face.

'I hope you don't mind,' Maddy Forsyth said in a quivering voice, 'but I came a day early. I hope I won't be in the way...'

Chapter Eighteen

'The Archdeacon and his wife wanted to come
and see Felix,' Maddy explained as Stephen went
out to bring in the luggage, helped by the children. 'They were so anxious about him and Stella.
So they said I might as well come too. I telephoned, but you'd already gone out, so I spoke to
Mrs Ellis. She said she was sure it would be all
right. But I can go away again if it's not. I mean,
you've got your family here, you don't really want
me hanging around as well.'

'Of course we want you!' Hilary exclaimed, as
her brother dumped a large, battered suitcase on
the hall floor. 'Don't we, Stephen? And where
would you go, anyway?'

'I'm sure Dottie–'

'There's no need,' Hilary said firmly. 'You'll
stay here, as arranged. I know Dottie will want to
see you but she's going to be terribly busy over
the next few days, and it's years since you stayed
with us. We *want* you here. Now, you met Marianne during the summer, didn't you?'

'Yes, just briefly.' The two women shook hands,
Marianne's gaze travelling over Maddy's dress. 'I
hope you had a good journey.'

'It was no worse than one can expect,' Marianne said with a shrug. She turned to Stephen,
who had brought in all the luggage and was closing the front door. 'Am I in the same room as

before?' She slanted a glance up at him and he turned away, colouring.

'Yes,' Hilary said quickly. 'We'd better get your things upstairs and then you can settle in. I hope you won't mind sharing with Ginette. Philippe is in with Rob.'

Marianne looked displeased. 'I thought I would have the room to myself.'

'You know we only have six bedrooms now. We had extra bathrooms put in after the war, and the other two have been used as box rooms for years. I didn't think you would mind sharing with your daughter.'

The Frenchwoman flicked her eyes at Maddy, clearly thinking that if she had not been staying, there would have been room for herself and Ginette to be separate, but she said no more. Maddy, who had caught the look, blushed and glanced at Hilary, who frowned and said rather curtly, 'Get these cases upstairs, will you please, Steve? I'll bring this holdall and show the children their rooms and the bathrooms. Maddy, would you mind letting Mrs Ellis know we're here and ask her to take some tea into the drawing room?'

Maddy did as she had been asked and stayed in the kitchen to help the housekeeper. The teacups were already set out on a large tray, and Mrs Ellis had made some sandwiches, scones and cake, which were on the big wooden table, with clean tea cloths laid over them. Together they buttered the scones and loaded the trolley.

'I'll take it in if you like,' Maddy offered. 'You've got so much to do.'

'Oh, I don't mind that. 'Tis what I'm paid for,

after all. But 'tis a long time since the Barton saw a busy Christmas like this, what with visitors from abroad and the party tomorrow night. And children in the house, too! That's what Christmas ought to be.'

'I know. I hope it won't be too much for the Colonel, having all these people around.'

'Miss Hilary won't let that happen. She's told me she means to make him rest every afternoon and not stay up late at night. Now, I think that's everything. A pot of strong breakfast and a pot of Earl Grey, and plenty of hot water. I wonder if they'm ready yet.'

Maddy opened the kitchen door to listen. 'I can hear people coming down the stairs. Shall I do the trolley?'

'No, but you can go ahead and open the doors for me if you don't mind. I'd like to say hello to Mrs Aucoin, anyway. She did some baking with me back in the summer, you know.'

'Of course.' Maddy had forgotten that Marianne ran a patisserie in the little French town where she lived. 'Perhaps she won't mind helping over Christmas too, then. You'll be at home with your own family, won't you?'

'I will. I did offer to come in on Christmas Eve and Boxing Day, but Miss Hilary would have none of it. Said there were enough able-bodied folk in the house to lend a hand, and I deserved to be at home for a change. So it looks as though you'll be peeling Brussels sprouts and potatoes, Maddy!'

Maddy laughed. 'I shan't mind. Dottie brought me up well.' She held the door open while the housekeeper bustled through with the trolley. 'You have a good time with your family, Mrs Ellis, and forget about us. Your daughter's baby's just the right age to enjoy Christmas, isn't she?'

'Little Meggie? Yes, she's just coming up to her first birthday. Loves all the decorations, and what her little face is going to be like when she sees her presents ...' Mrs Ellis paused at the foot of the stairs, beaming upwards. 'Why, Mrs Aucoin, 'tis a real pleasure to see you again. And these are your other two, then – what a fine-looking pair, but nothing like their brother, are they?'

'They're hardly likely to be, since Robert resembles his own father.' Marianne softened the terseness of her reply by coming down the stairs, her hand held out and a smile curving her red lips. 'It's good to see you again too, Mrs Ellis. And you have made cakes for us, too – see, children? I am going to offer Mrs Ellis a job in our patisserie, if she will come to France!'

The housekeeper laughed. 'I'm afraid I'm too settled here. And I'd never leave my little Meggie – that's my baby granddaughter,' she added to the children. 'Rob met her once in the kitchen when my daughter brought her over to see me. She's grown a lot since then, mind.'

The drawing-room door opened and Colonel Napier looked out. 'So there you are. I wondered what all the chattering was about. Glad to see you, Marianne, my dear. Come inside and let's have a look at you. And the youngsters, too. Hilary, I don't know what you're thinking of, keeping them out in this draughty hallway.'

'We're just coming, Father.' Hilary smiled at the

241

housekeeper. 'Thank you very much, Mrs Ellis. I'll send the children to see you in the kitchen later, if you're not too busy. And Marianne will want to have a good talk with you too, I'm sure.'

It was clear that the Frenchwoman had made a good impression on the housekeeper, and Hilary was relieved that it should be so. Without at least some harmony in the house, this would be a very difficult Christmas indeed.

The Napiers' Christmas began officially with a drinks party the day before Christmas Eve. The three children were given high tea at five and sent off to bath and change into their best clothes. Colonel Napier took the view that children should be seen and not heard, and better still not seen at adult parties, but Hilary had overruled him.

'They're our family and our guests. We can't pack them off to the nursery at the top of the house – those days are past. Anyway, if Philippe and Ginette are as well-mannered as Rob, and they certainly seem to be, they'll behave perfectly. French children are quite accustomed to being with adults.'

'I've no objection to Rob being present,' Gilbert said. 'He's my grandson and has his own position in the family. It's the younger two...'

'Well we certainly can't pack *them* off by themselves,' Hilary said firmly. 'It would be most unkind. I'm sorry, Father, but if you want to have this party – it was your wish, remember – you'll have to have the children present. That's all there is to it.'

Gilbert scowled but didn't argue any further,

242

and when Hilary saw the three children, their faces scrubbed, their hair freshly washed and looking thick and soft, their clothes neat – although she did rather wish French boys wore their short trousers a little longer – she felt happy that they would be a credit to both their English and their French families.

The guests began to arrive soon after six. Most of them already knew Rob, who dutifully introduced his brother and sister and offered bowls of crisps or nuts. Hilary was pouring sherry and Stephen shaking cocktails with wildly fantastic names – 'they're all the rage in the mess' – while Gilbert stood near the fireplace, receiving his friends and neighbours, and then settled on the big leather sofa, where a few cronies could join him. Maddy, looking rather pale, sipped a dry sherry and explained to Charles Latimer that Felix was coming to collect her soon to go and visit Stella.

'That's why I'm not really dressed for a party,' she said, indicating her blue jumper and skirt. 'I didn't really think I should come, but as I'm staying in the house, it seemed silly to sit in another room just for the sake of a frock! And it's nice to see everyone.'

'And how is Stella?' Mary Latimer enquired, coming to stand beside her husband. 'Charles tells me she came through the operation very well.'

'Yes, so Felix says. I wished I didn't have to go back to West Lyme last weekend, but there were things I had to do for the Archdeacon before Christmas. He's been so good, letting me have so much time off. I don't feel I've given him value for money at all.'

'I'm sure you have,' Dr Latimer said. 'And we're all doing whatever we can for Felix. Our youngest daughter's been over to see him once or twice, you know.'

'Has she?' Maddy said in surprise, glancing across the room to where Tessa, dressed in a sheath of black that showed her smooth white shoulders and long legs to their best advantage, was talking animatedly to Travis Kellaway. Her two older sisters, Erica and Felicity, were sitting on the sofa, one either side of the Colonel. 'He didn't mention it.'

'I expect he has more important things to talk about,' Mary said, smiling. 'From what I hear from friends in Little Burracombe, there's a steady stream of parishioners beating a path to his door. He probably has as much as he can do to snatch a few minutes to himself.'

'And how are you, Maddy?' Charles asked. 'You're looking a little pale, you know. You have to take care of yourself as well.'

'Oh, I'm all right,' Maddy said, but her tone was listless and he looked at her more closely. He was aware that Maddy had lost her fiancé Sammy Hodges less than a year ago, had suffered a broken arm in the same accident and had been very upset not long afterwards by learning that Sammy's father and stepmother were expecting a baby. And now Stella's accident... It was too much for a young woman to bear alone.

'I mean it,' he said seriously. 'It's a good thing you're staying here over Christmas – Hilary and

244

Stephen will look after you. And there's Madame Aucoin, too, and her children. You should have a good time together.'

'Yes, I suppose we should,' Maddy said, and then seemed to shake herself a little. 'I mean, of course we will. We've already had fun decorating the tree together – Rob went out with Travis and brought it in from the woods. It looks very pretty, doesn't it?'

They turned to admire the tree standing in the corner of the room. It was over eight feet tall and reached almost to the ceiling, with just room on top for the big golden star that had graced Napier Christmas trees ever since anyone could remember. The coloured bulbs trailed down the sides, lighting up the sparkling baubles, and Ginette had tied countless ribbons in tiny bows to the tips of the branches. A pile of gaily wrapped parcels was heaped around the scarlet tub it was standing in.

'The children are having shoes as well as stockings,' Maddy went on. 'Rob wanted a proper English Christmas, but the other two want their own traditions too, so we're doing both. Hilary and I had to dash into Tavistock yesterday to find more little presents to put in them!'

'And are they settling in well? Do they speak as good English as Rob does?'

'Very nearly. His has improved through living here, of course, but they've all been well taught. They seem very nice children. Their mother's brought them up well.'

'I dare say Madame Aucoin is pleased to have you to talk to, as well,' Mary Latimer observed. 'You've spent a good deal of time in France, haven't you?'

'Yes, although not in her part.' Maddy glanced at her watch. 'Felix should be here at any minute. Will you excuse me, please? I don't want to keep him waiting.' She smiled at them and slipped away, going over to Hilary first to let her know she was leaving. Hilary, who was talking to an old army friend of her father's who lived in Tavistock, nodded and laid her hand on the younger girl's shoulder for a moment.

'Give Stella my love, won't you? Tell her I'll come and see her as soon as I can after Christmas. And bring Felix back for some dinner – we'll keep it hot for both of you. We'll be eating late anyway.'

Maddy nodded and slipped out. Hilary found Marianne at her elbow.

'She has gone to visit her sister? The little Maddy?'

'Yes, that's right. Felix must have arrived. Have you met Brigadier Stanhope? Brigadier, this is Madame Aucoin, Baden's wife – widow.'

The Brigadier, a robust man in his late seventies with a large white moustache and steel-grey eyes beneath bushy white brows, looked down at Marianne and held out a strong hand for her to shake. She tilted her head to one side and smiled up at him.

'It is a pleasure to meet you, Brigadier. That is an Army rank, *non?*'

He blew into his moustache. 'It is indeed. And one I'm sure your husband would have reached, had he lived. Tragic loss to us all. Tragic. But I'm sure Gilbert must be very pleased you've brought young Robert into the family, where he belongs.'

'I think so. But Robert is French as well as English, you know. He has two families. He's a very lucky boy.'

'Of course, of course. But he'll be staying in Burracombe now, won't he? Learn our ways, learn about the estate, get a decent education?'

'He had a very good education in France,' Marianne replied, with a distinct edge to her voice. 'I think our system suits French boys very well. Perhaps better than yours.'

Hilary glanced at her uneasily. Marianne had carried out her promise to have a private discussion with Gilbert while Hilary took the children to Tavistock, but there had been no time for Hilary to ask her father what they had talked about. She could only deduce from his grim face at lunch that it had not been pleasant. She wondered what Rob had told his mother – had there been time for him to recount the stories of the bullying he had endured? Well, it was all over now, and her father had already decided that Rob should go home and complete his education in France.

'There's a lot to talk about still,' she said to the Brigadier. 'Meanwhile, we want to give our visitors a real taste of an English country Christmas. We've even got snow – although it's getting a bit dirty now. We need another fall to freshen it up.'

'God forbid,' the Brigadier snorted. 'Had enough snow to last me a lifetime. Thinking of spending the winter abroad next year – Spain, maybe, or Malta. Got quite a few friends in Malta.'

'That sounds a good idea,' Hilary said. 'Some winter sunshine would do my father good too, but I know he'd never agree to go. Perhaps you could persuade him, Brigadier.'

'Not a bad notion, at that. I'll have a chat with him now.' The old army man stumped across to the sofa where Gilbert was sitting with Grace Harvey. Hilary turned to Marianne.

'I hope you're enjoying yourself. The children are behaving very well.'

'Of course.'

'Did your talk with my father go well?'

Marianne turned her dark gaze on Hilary. 'As well as I expected it to go. He is a difficult man, your father.'

He was, but Hilary didn't feel inclined to agree with the Frenchwoman's assessment. 'He has a right to his opinions.'

'And so do I.' Marianne's tone was composed and her eyes met Hilary's steadily. 'And Robert is my son.'

Hilary felt nonplussed. She had no idea now what Marianne wanted from them. To begin with, it had seemed clear enough – a place in the family for Rob, which had been granted all too readily when Gilbert had declared him to be the rightful heir to the estate – and an allowance such as would have been due to Baden's widow, even though she had married again before Rob was born. She had left at the end of the summer, apparently content to leave her son behind to start his education in the unfamiliar setting of an English public school, and this visit was intended as a purely social one, to show Rob the English way of celebrating Christmas and to include the most important members of his French family. Yet from the moment she had arrived, it seemed that Marianne had a hidden purpose, that she was angry and determined to make changes. Hilary was baffled.

'Perhaps you and I should have a talk too,' she suggested. 'You know we only want to do what is best for Rob, but if there's anything you're not happy about...'

'We will talk,' Marianne stated. 'Tomorrow.' Her eyes roamed around the room and she added casually, 'Stephen is looking well, I think.'

'Yes – yes, I suppose he is.' Hilary followed her gaze. Tessa Latimer was standing with him now, one of his infamous cocktails in her hand, laughing up at him. He was looking down at her rather gravely, but as Hilary and Marianne watched, his face broke into a smile and seemed to come to life. Tessa laid her hand on his arm and rested her face against his shoulder for a moment, as if her laughter were too much for her.

'A flirt, that one,' Marianne said dismissively. 'He will not be taken in by her, I think.'

Hilary felt a surge of anger. Talk about pots calling kettles black, she thought furiously. Her voice was cold as she said, 'I don't think Stephen is likely to be taken in by any woman now. He's learned his lesson.'

At that moment, Stephen glanced across the room towards them. His gaze sharpened as his eyes met Marianne's and then his eyelids came down, concealing his expression. Marianne smiled a little and turned her limpid glaze back to Hilary.

She seemed about to speak, then to change her mind. At last, still with that tiny smile, she said, 'We shall see,' and moved away. Over her shoulder, she remarked, 'I must go and talk to someone else. It is bad form for the family only to talk to each other, *n 'est-ce pas?*'

Hilary stifled a sigh and found Rob beside her, the other two children trailing behind him. They're bored, she thought, and no wonder. After the first few minutes of a grown-up party, with the guests doing nothing but stand about with drinks in their hands, talking a language which is not your own, the enjoyment begins to pall. She smiled at them, wondering what to suggest, but Rob spoke first.

'Tante Hilary, may I take Philippe and Ginette to the Long Gallery?'

'Yes, of course,' she said, relieved. 'Take a plate of snacks and some more drinks, and you can have a picnic up there.'

They grinned at her and scuttled away, weaving through the other guests like puppies let off the leash. Really, they were no trouble at all, she thought. As long as they had something to do, they were almost invisible. She must find ways to keep them occupied tomorrow, and then it would be Christmas and the day would look after itself.

'Your glass is empty,' a voice said in her ear, and she turned to find her brother at her side, his cocktail shaker in his hand. 'Want a top-up?'

'No thanks! Goodness knows what lethal concoction you've got in there. I'll stick to sherry, though I think I've probably had enough of that too.' She glanced around at the throng. 'People should be starting to leave soon, anyway. Better not ply them with any more drink or they'll be here for ever.'

'A fine example of hospitable Christmas spirit, I must say,' he said with a grin. 'What's the matter, Hil? Are you tired of this sort of thing?'

'I think I am, rather,' she said slowly. 'It all seems so meaningless. People standing about shouting remarks at each other, and nobody actually listening to a word. Most of them don't meet from one year's end to another, except for at parties like this – what's the point of it? If they were really friends, they'd see each other at other times and do proper things together. It's just a charade.'

He stared at her. 'You really are in the dumps, aren't you! Don't you think it helps people to get together and get to know each other? If they didn't, we'd all be living in our own separate compartments, never making friends at all. The world can't work like that.'

'I suppose not. But there are other ways of getting to know each other. Clubs and societies, where people are all interested in *doing* something. The Garden Club that they've got going in Little Burracombe. The Bridge Club. The whist drives – the pantomime. The bellringers' practices. Those are places where you really make friends, Steve. Not at smart parties, where people just come to see and be seen, and to show off.'

'You sound a bit disillusioned,' he said. 'Are you all right, Hil? I've thought once or twice lately that you seem a bit off colour. Is it getting too much for you, having Rob here?'

'Oh, Rob's no problem. Well, he has been, I suppose, but it's not really been his fault. We haven't

251

been fair to him, Steve, but I hope things will be better now that Father's seen the sense of letting him go home again. No, it's not that. It's–' She stopped, knowing what the real problem was but unable to share it, especially here and now. 'It's nothing – just the accident, you know, and worrying about poor Stella. But I must admit I'll be glad when Christmas is over.'

'It's not easy having Marianne here again, is it?' he said quietly.

'No, it's not, but it must be harder for you.' She met his eyes. 'You're not going to let it happen again, are you? I can see she's a very attractive woman.'

He gave a short laugh. 'Not to me! Not any more. I had a real fright back in the summer – thinking I might have to marry her. I'm not likely to let that happen again.'

'It was what she intended.'

'I know it was. But I don't think she's in any doubt now. Not that she's pleased about it – you know what they say about a woman scorned.'

'Hell hath no fury,' Hilary agreed. 'But you don't think she'd actually *do* anything, do you? I mean, what *could* she do? Apart from...' Her voice faded and she stared at him, suddenly thinking of that mysterious talk Marianne had been having with their father. 'Steve, you don't think...'

Stephen nodded grimly. 'That she might tell Father about it? Yes – it had occurred to me. And even if she hasn't, there's always the possibility, isn't there? She'll always have that to hold over me.' He moved restlessly. 'I don't know how I could have been such a stupid idiot.'

Hilary sighed. 'Well, it's done now and there's no point in worrying about it. I don't think she's told him yet, anyway, or he'd have been in a foul mood and probably cancelled the party. And I don't really think she will. He's not a fool, Steve – he knows what women like Marianne are like. He'd be as likely to blame her as you, and then she'd have thrown away all she came for.'

They were silent for a moment, then she said quietly, 'It's not just having Marianne here that's making it a difficult Christmas for you, is it? It's Maddy as well. You're still fond of her, aren't you?'

He gave her a wry look. 'A bit more than fond. But what's the point? Even if she is getting over Sammy, there's that American chap on the scene now. What chance do I have against someone like that?'

'Every chance in the world,' Hilary said steadily. 'Don't give up, Stephen. I've seen her looking at you a few times since she arrived here, and I'm not sure that Russ Tozer has made quite as much headway as it seemed at first. They've been thrown together over the accident, when he was able to take her to the hospital and be with her, but you're here now. Try having a talk with her – you may be given another chance.'

Chapter Nineteen

In the Tozers' farmhouse, Robin was awake before anyone else. He lay for a moment in the darkness, wondering why his tummy felt as if it were full of butterflies, and then remembered that it was Christmas Day. His heart beat fast as he wondered if Santa had been yet, and as he moved his feet experimentally and felt a lumpy weight at the foot of his bed, he gave a squeak of delight and scrambled out from under his eiderdown. He crawled down the bed and felt for the stocking that had hung there, so limp and empty, when he went to sleep, and his groping fingers encountered a variety of shapes – knobbles, smooth round curves, straight edges and long, thin tubes.

Grabbing the end of the stocking, he slid from his bed and pattered over to the door of his room. His parents slept next door and he pulled down the handle and burst in.

'He's been! He's been! Can I open my stocking now? Can I look?' Urgently, he took hold of his mother's shoulder and shook it. 'Mummy! *Mum!* Wake up – he's *been!*'

Joanna stirred and reached out for the table lamp that stood beside her. Tom grunted, muttered and turned over and Robin, dancing with impatience, shouted again.

'Mum! Dad! He's *been!* Can I get into your bed? I want to see my presents!'

'For goodness' sake,' Joanna mumbled. 'It's only a quarter to five.' She struggled to sit up, brushing hair from her eyes. 'I *told* Daddy not to–' She stopped abruptly.

'Told him not to what?' Robin asked; then, without waiting for an answer, 'Can I come in, Mummy, can I?'

'Yes, of course you can.' She pulled him on to the bed and he snuggled in between her and Tom. 'Happy Christmas, sweetheart.'

'Happy Christmas, Mummy.' He poked Tom on the arm. 'Happy Christmas, Daddy!'

'Ssh, not too loud,' Joanna cautioned. 'You'll wake Heather. I'm surprised you haven't already.'

As if on cue, the baby, sleeping in her cot at the foot of the bed, moved and whimpered a little. Joanna reached down to her, murmuring softly, and she settled again.

'Mummy,' Robin implored, and she laughed, shook Tom's shoulder and pulled her pillow up behind her.

'Come on, Tom. Robin wants to open his stocking. Happy Christmas, love,' she added, giving her husband a kiss, and as Tom opened his eyes at last, they looked at each other for a moment, sharing a thought for the child who was not there and would never open a Christmas stocking. Then she turned back to Robin and put her arm around him. 'Come on, then, let's see what Father Christmas has brought you.'

Robin gave a little sigh of ecstasy. This was his favourite moment of all, warm and snug in bed with his mother and father, with all of Christmas stretching before him like a series of bright

255

parcels to be opened throughout the day – the stocking itself, breakfast with the family, church with carols and everyone smiling and wishing each other a happy Christmas; playing with his new toys in front of the fire before the big Christmas dinner with the huge goose; a walk in the afternoon with Daddy and Uncle Luke and anyone else who wanted to come, muffled up against the cold and throwing snowballs at each other; tea with jelly and Christmas cake round the big table; and then games in the evening with the whole family joining in. He gave a little wriggle of pleasure at the thought of it all, and then, letting the moment go like a bright, glittering bubble, reached into his stocking, pulled out the first little parcel, and thus declared Christmas open.

Jacob Prout had been invited to spend the day with Jennifer and Travis in Wood Cottage. He joined Travis and the other bellringers to ring for the morning service, then went back with them in the Land Rover. Jennifer went straight to the kitchen to see that the joint of beef, which Travis and Jacob both preferred to poultry, was roasting. Tavy, the little Jack Russell, was lying close to the Rayburn, a look of dreamy bliss on her face as she drank in the rich smell, and Jennifer moved her back to her basket in the corner of the kitchen.

'You're in the way and you might get hot fat dropped on you. I'll make sure you get some meat, don't worry.'

She had laid the table in the dining room before going to church, but she went back to have another look, delighting in the rich red colour of the new tablecloth, the glint of the cutlery that had been a wedding present from the Napiers, and the place mats with the hunting scenes on that Val and Luke had given them. Travis had bought a bottle of red wine, which stood glowing like a ruby in the centre of the table, flanked by two small holly wreaths that Jennifer had made herself, each with a candle in the middle. The facets of the lead-crystal wine glasses that Jennifer had inherited from her grandmother would sparkle like diamonds when the candles were lit, and the deep burgundy colour of the wine would be like fire inside them.

It was their first Christmas in their own home, their first Christmas together, and Jennifer went back to the kitchen determined to make it one to remember. It had begun well some hours earlier, with Travis waking her with a cup of tea and a rectangular parcel about six inches long, wrapped in gold foil.

'Happy Christmas, sweetheart. And many more of them.'

'Oh, Travis,' she said, offering her lips for a kiss. 'Happy Christmas to you too. But you didn't need to give me a present. You've already given me two rings and a necklace!'

'Those were for getting engaged and then married,' he said. 'This is for Christmas. And I think you'd have felt rather hurt if I hadn't given you anything! Open it, love.'

She unwrapped it carefully, not wanting to tear the shimmering paper, and found a box inside. Slowly, she lifted the lid.

'A watch! A gold watch! Oh Travis, you

shouldn't have! It must have been terribly expensive.'

'It was,' he agreed. 'There won't be any house-keeping money until Easter at the earliest... Do you like it?'

'I love it.' She held it up, admiring the thin gold bracelet. 'It's beautiful. But I shall be afraid to wear it.'

'You're to wear it as often as possible. That's the thing to do with expensive things – then they get cheaper every time you put them on. By the time you're eighty, this watch will have cost nothing at all.'

Jennifer laughed. 'Oh, Travis, you are a fool! Now I suppose I'd better give you your present, or *you'll* be hurt.'

'Well, you can drink your tea first,' he said, but she shook her head at him and reached down the side of the bed, bringing out a larger parcel, wrapped in red. 'That looks remarkably like a book.'

'I hope you like it,' she said anxiously. 'You mentioned it one day. It is the right one, isn't it?'

Travis tore off the paper and stared at it in delight. 'It's exactly right! I've been wanting this for years. However did you find it?'

'I asked the second-hand bookshop man in Tavistock, and he found it for me.' She leaned on his shoulder as he reverently turned the pages. 'The pictures are beautiful. They're woodcuts, aren't they?'

'Yes.' Each plate, illustrating a different game bird or countryside scene, was protected by a film of tissue. 'You know, this book is really rare.

I'm amazed you could get it. And it must have cost at least as much as a gold watch.'

'If it did, we're equal.' She drew him to her for another kiss. 'Come back to bed for a while, Travis. There's no hurry to get up, is there?'

'None at all,' he said, doing as she suggested. 'As long as we're in time for ringing. And we mustn't forget that Jacob is coming to dinner.' He kissed her again. 'Happy Christmas, darling.'

'The happiest Christmas ever,' she had replied.

Travis and Jacob were now poring over the book in the living room, and the watch was back in its box. I'll wear it this afternoon, Jennifer thought, when we've had a walk and I get changed. I can't wear it while I'm cooking! She drained the parboiled potatoes, tossed them in the saucepan to roughen their edges, and then tipped them carefully around the joint in its big roasting pan. The other vegetables were ready for cooking when the meat came out of the oven to rest, the pudding was steaming, and all that was needed was for the Yorkshire pudding batter to be made. As she looked round the kitchen, checking that all was in order, Travis put his head round the door.

'Can you come in for a few minutes? I want to give Jacob his present, and he says he's got something for us.'

'Yes, I'll come now.' She untied her apron and followed him into the living room, with Tavy at her heels. A bright fire burned in the grate and Jacob was in one of the armchairs beside it. He started to get up when Jennifer came in, but she waved at him to stay where he was.

'Here you are, Jacob,' Travis said, producing a

259

long, thin parcel from behind the sofa. 'A happy Christmas to you!'

Jacob took the object and looked at it thoughtfully. 'Now, whatever can this be? 'Tisn't a football, that's certain, nor yet a picture. I dunno what it can be.'

'Well, open it and see!' Jennifer said, laughing, and he unwrapped it and revealed a walking stick with a sheep's-horn handle. 'Honestly, I don't know what else you thought it could have been.'

'Now that be what I call a good stick,' he said, turning it this way and that. 'And that's some handsome carving on the handle. Proper handsome, that be. Thank you both very much.' He handed Jennifer a large box. ''Tis nothing much, mind, but hopefully 'twill keep you warm through the winter.'

Together, Jennifer and Travis opened the box and lifted out half a dozen dark green bottles. 'Home-made wine!' Jennifer said. 'Well, it certainly will. Thank you very much, Jacob.' She leaned over to kiss his wrinkled cheek. 'And you know what I think we should do now, don't you?'

'I hope you do,' Travis said, holding one of the bottles to the light and reading the handwritten label Jacob had stuck to it. 'I was going to suggest a sherry, but I think we should broach this instead. A glass of parsnip wine each – does that sound a good idea?'

'It sounds a very good idea,' Jennifer said, and a few minutes later, when Travis had filled a small glass each, she raised hers and gave them a toast. 'To the two most important men in my life. Happy Christmas!'

Stephen had not forgotten Hilary's advice to let Maddy know that he really cared about her. 'Show a bit of gumption!' she'd told him in exasperation. 'You'll lose her if you don't.' And when he'd replied gloomily that he'd lost her all ready, she'd told him crisply that in that case he had nothing to lose by making an effort. But now, even though she was staying in the same house over Christmas, it didn't seem likely that he was ever going to get a chance to talk to her alone until at breakfast on Christmas Day, after the children had had their presents, she said that she wanted to go to the hospital with Felix, to see Stella.

'I must see her on Christmas Day,' she said. 'They'll be doing all sorts of things there – the doctors dress up and go round the wards, and the nurses sing carols – but she needs to see her family as well.'

'Is Felix taking you?' Hilary asked. 'He told me he'd be going straight after Matins. But I think he's intending to stay as long as possible – he said we must have dinner without him if he's not back.'

'I'd like to stay too, but I'm not sure if we'd both be allowed. They're going to be very busy. I suppose if I can't stay in the ward, I can wait outside until he has to leave.'

'You don't need to do that,' Hilary said quickly. 'Stephen will fetch you – won't you, Steve?'

Stephen looked up from his bacon and eggs, startled. He cast a swift glance at Maddy, and saw her colour. She doesn't want me, he thought, and looked down at his plate again.

'Oh, would you, Stephen?' Maddy asked. 'I really just want to see her, to say hello and wish her – well, it seems odd to wish her a happy Christmas, but it doesn't seem right not to! But I needn't stay more than half an hour. She gets tired very quickly – and you don't want to be away from the family for too long.'

'Of course I'll fetch you,' he said, his heart leaping. 'I'll take you as well. We'll telephone Felix and let him know he needn't come over. He can go straight there himself then.'

'There,' Hilary said in a satisfied tone. 'That's all arranged. It fits in very well.'

Marianne spoke. 'Oh – but I had hoped that Stephen would take us to church in Tavistock. How will we get there now?'

'I'll take you myself,' Hilary said. 'I've been to Holy Communion in the village church, so I needn't be there for matins. And I'll come to collect you straight afterwards.' She sighed a little. She was already feeling tired after their late night, when she had taken the French family to their Midnight Mass in Tavistock and then attended the service at St Eustachius' before bringing them home again. It had been after one o'clock before they had got to bed and she had been up soon after seven to set the breakfast table and go to the early service, feeling guilty at having abandoned Basil for the larger church in town at midnight.

Still, dinner wasn't planned until six – earlier than usual because of the children – so there would be plenty of time for preparation, and plenty of helping hands, and she was determined that everyone should have the Christmas they wanted. More than that, she was determined that Stephen should have some time alone with Maddy, and what better opportunity than a drive to Plymouth and back in his sports car, where they could not be interrupted by the predatory Marianne.

I just wish I could talk to David today, she thought, feeling the now familiar longing sweep over her. But there was no chance of that. She did not know when she would hear his voice again.

Stephen and Maddy went to church that morning and sat in the Napier pew with Gilbert. The argument between Stephen and his father had been set aside for the time being, and Gilbert had given his son an old hunter watch owned by his own father as a Christmas present. Stephen had gazed at it in surprise, wondering if it was a peace offering. His own gift of an antique chess set he'd come upon in a dusty old shop in Salisbury had certainly been intended as such, and he was thankful to see that his father obviously liked it. He had been setting out the pieces on their board when Stephen had gone into his study to say it was time for church.

'Nice pieces,' he'd remarked, letting his fingers rest on the queen's crowned head. 'Very nice pieces.'

'I'm glad you like it, Dad.' They'd walked out into the hall to find Maddy coming down the stairs towards them, wrapped in a dark blue winter coat with a fur collar. 'Happy Christmas.'

Gilbert nodded. 'And to you, my boy. And little Madelaine here.' He'd always refused to shorten

Maddy's adopted name. 'Let's hope we all have a happy Christmas. And a new start for the new year. Nineteen fifty-three's not been the easiest one we've had, any of us.'

'No,' Stephen said quietly, taking Maddy's hand and tucking it into his arm as he remembered what a very hard year it had been for her in particular. 'No, it hasn't. And I'll second that. A new year and a new start, for us all.'

Maddy remembered his words as she knelt between the two men for silent prayer. The church was filled with old friends, people she had known since her childhood, and their warmth seemed to wrap itself about her like a soft fur cloak. The tranquillity of the moment, after the clamour of the bells and the resonant notes of the organ, seemed to settle upon her like downy white feathers, and she felt a cool peace stealing into her heart – a peace she had not known since that terrible moment when Sammy had fallen into the path of the lorry. Perhaps I *can* make a new start, she thought. Perhaps there is happiness for me, after all. She felt Stephen's arm touch hers as they knelt, and peeped sideways at his face, unaccustomedly grave. She thought of the years they had known each other, of the steadfastness of the love he bore her, and her heart warmed towards him.

Perhaps ... perhaps... Perhaps, after all...

Chapter Twenty

Felix was already by Stella's bedside, her hand cradled in his, when Stephen and Maddy arrived. He glanced round and smiled at them, and Maddy saw that Stella was awake, propped up on a stack of pillows, and that she even had a little colour in her cheeks.

'Stella! Happy Christmas, darling. You're looking so much better.' She kissed her sister's cheek gently and Stella laughed. It was a rather frail, wobbly laugh, but a laugh just the same.

'You only saw me yesterday. I can't be looking that much better.'

'You are. Isn't she, Felix?' Maddy sat down on the chair at the other side of the bed. 'And look who else has come to see you.'

Stella smiled and held out her free hand. 'Hallo, Stephen. It's good to see you. And good of you to bring Maddy.'

'It's a pleasure,' he said, and meant it. They hadn't spoken much on the drive in, but their silence had been companionable and he'd slowly relaxed. 'I'm just surprised to find myself at the head of the queue.'

'What queue?' Maddy demanded. 'I didn't see a queue forming.'

'Well, Felix would have brought you, and I'm sure that young Tozer would have jumped at the chance.'

'He couldn't. He had to stay with the family.' She spoke carelessly, but Stephen's heart sank a little. It sounded as if she'd asked him and he'd regretfully declined. So he'd been ahead of Stephen after all.

'Anyway, that doesn't matter,' Maddy went on, taking Stella's hand in hers. 'What matters is that we're here and you're looking tons better, and it's Christmas. Everybody sends you their love and I've got a whole bagful of presents for you. Mostly chocolates, I think.'

'I hope not. I'll get terribly fat lying here doing nothing.' Stella looked at the pile of colourful parcels that Maddy was distributing on her bed. 'Mind my plaster. Unwrap them for me, would you?'

'All right.' Maddy began to tear off the paper. Some of the parcels were indeed chocolates, but there were other presents too – two or three books, a little dressing case for toiletries and a pretty nightdress sewn and embroidered by Dottie. Hilary had sent a wrap of cobweb-fine cashmere and Val and Luke one of Luke's paintings of Burracombe which could be propped on her bedside table. Jacob Prout had sent a bottle of parsnip wine, which Stella said she thought had better go home again, as she didn't think they would let her have it in hospital.

'All things I can use in here,' she said, tears in her eyes as she surveyed her prizes. 'People are so thoughtful.'

'They all love you, that's why,' Maddy said, leaning over to give her another kiss. 'And we all want you home again as soon as possible. Then we'll have another Christmas, specially for you!'

The door opened and the small room was suddenly crowded with nurses, all singing carols. One of the doctors pushed through them, dressed as Father Christmas, and handed Stella a present out of his sack. She unwrapped it to find a small teddy bear with one leg heavily bandaged.

'We couldn't get plaster to stick,' the doctor told her solemnly. 'But you can take off the bandages when we take off your plaster, and he'll be as good as new.'

'Just like you!' Stephen said, and she smiled at him. But there was doubt in her smile, and he looked quickly at Maddy and Felix, wondering if they had seen it too.

'Yes,' Maddy said, and squeezed her hand tightly. 'Just like you...'

On the way home, Stephen said, 'She *is* going to get better, isn't she? Completely, I mean?'

Maddy was silent for a few minutes; then she said, 'To be honest, Stephen, I don't think anyone knows. Not even the doctors. Her spine was damaged, you see. It wasn't broken – they've found that out now – but there's a lot of bruising, and they don't know just how badly the spinal cord may have been affected. They're still afraid of paralysis.'

'But surely they'd know by now! She's conscious – she can tell them if she can't feel her legs.'

'That's just it,' Maddy said. 'She can't.' Her voice trembled. 'She can't feel anything below her waist. And she may never be able to feel anything again.'

Stephen cast a glance at her and saw the tears pouring down her cheeks. He pulled over quickly on to the moor's edge, and drew her into his arms.

'Maddy, Maddy. Oh, my darling. I'm so sorry.' As he held her, he marvelled at the feel of her small body so close to him, closer than he had ever believed it could be again. But this was no time to give way to his own feelings. Maddy was in need of comfort, desperate need, and it was his job to give it to her. He would like it to be his job for the rest of their lives, but that was for another day.

'I just hate seeing her like this,' Maddy sobbed against his chest. 'She's always been my big sister, always looked after me when we were little, and even though we lost each other for all those years, it was just the same when we found each other again. She's looked after me all this past year, when I've been so miserable and selfish, and now she's the one who needs looking after and there's nothing I can do.' Her voice rose in a wail. 'I can't do anything to help her.'

'I know, darling, I know. But you do help, you know, just by being there, by going to see her and being you. You made her feel better this morning, with your smile and your jokes about the presents. You make everyone feel better.'

'I don't. I make people miserable. I do, Stephen. You don't know – about Ruth and Dan and how horrible I was about their baby. And all the other things I've done – the people I've hurt – when I was wallowing in my own misery. I was even horrible to Stella and Felix. And Dottie. How could anyone be horrible to Dottie? And now Stella's the one who's suffering and – and I can't do anything about it.'

'I've already told you, you can and you do.' He produced a large white handkerchief. 'Dry yourself up a bit, sweetheart, and let's just sit here quietly. There's no hurry to go back.'

'I promised to help Hilary with the dinner.'

'Hilary's got plenty of help. Marianne's a cook, remember? And most of the vegetables were done yesterday. Darling, you're in no fit state to go back there just yet. Tell you what, let's go for a walk.'

'A walk?' Maddy looked startled, then she glanced through the car window at the moorland that surrounded them. There had been no more snow, but the frost had turned the surface to glittering spicules of crystalline ice, like shards of glass sprinkled across the soft contours of the valley slopes. The sky was a pale cerulean blue as delicate as the wing of a blue tit, and the air was sharp and cold, like wine taken straight from the fridge.

'A walk...' she repeated. 'Oh, Stephen, that would be so lovely.'

'You've got your sheepskin boots on, haven't you?' He grinned at her. 'Then let's go.'

They scrambled out of the car. Most of the snow had sublimated off in the dry weather, leaving a thin crust that crunched beneath their feet. Stephen took Maddy's hand and they walked away from the car, following a pony track between gorse bushes whose prickly branches seemed encased in ice, like shimmering filigree. A small

269

flock of finches scattered into the air before them as they walked, and a group of ponies, pawing the ground with their hooves to reach the grass beneath, lifted their heads and watched in the hope that they might be bringing food.

'Poor things,' Maddy said. 'It must be terribly hard for them in this weather.'

'I think they've been fed,' Stephen said, indicating a few wisps of hay still lying on the snow. 'And I expect the sheep have been taken lower down to the fields.'

They strolled quietly along. Stephen, feeling her small hand resting in his for the first time for over a year, felt as if they were walking a bubble, surrounded by a fragile shell of rainbow colours that could be shattered by a touch. He wanted to keep her in that bubble, close beside him, safe from all the grief and sadness that had beset her, safe from the anxiety over her sister. He glanced sideways at her and saw her lift her face to the weak warmth of the sun and breathe in deeply, her eyes half closed. Her face, which had been so pale, was touched with faint rosy colour, and as he watched, Stephen was shaken by a sudden wave of love and longing so powerful that he trembled and almost stumbled in the snow.

'Maddy...' he said, but she had begun to speak at the same moment and he stopped, aware that he could all too easily break the spell.

'This is so lovely,' she said quietly. 'I didn't realise how much I missed the moor, and just walking. Not going anywhere – just walking, with someone you...' She stopped.

Stephen waited a moment, then prompted

gently, 'Someone you...?'

Maddy didn't answer at first. Then she turned her head and looked at him with clear eyes. 'Someone you feel happy and comfortable with,' she said. 'I'm sorry, Stephen. I know what you'd like me to say, but I can't go any further than that. Not just now.'

'I know you can't,' he said. He was still holding her hand and he lifted it, caressing the fingers with his other hand. 'Happy and comfortable will do very well.' For the time being, he added silently. 'You ought to be wearing gloves,' he added, but she shook her head.

'You're keeping my fingers warm. Oh, Stephen...' She stopped and leaned her head against his shoulder. 'What's it all about? Why do these terrible things keep happening? It seems to have been going on all my life – the war, Mummy and Daddy, baby Thomas... He was born in an air-raid shelter, you know, during a raid. A man along the street helped... And then he died in another raid. Poor little baby, he hardly knew what it was to be alive.' Her voice broke. 'And my mother died with him. Stella and I had to go to Bridge End and live with an old vicar.'

'That can't have been much fun,' Stephen said. He had heard some of this before, but he wanted Maddy to go on talking. He began to walk again, leading her along the narrow pony track.

She smiled. 'It was, actually. The Budd boys lived there too – Tim and Keith – and the vicar was like an overgrown schoolboy himself. He used to go across to the church to take early service with his pyjamas still on. You could see the bottoms peeping out under his cassock. And we used to sell him our sugar at a farthing a teaspoonful. Or maybe it was a ha'penny. I think that time at Bridge End was the happiest of my childhood.'

'And it was there you met Sammy.'

'Yes, it was. He was such a funny little scrap then. He lived in April Grove too, at the other end from the Budds, but his mother was terribly ill and died and his father – Dan – couldn't look after him properly. He used to go to sea on the minesweepers and leave Sammy on his own for days at a time. In the end, he had to be evacuated and he went to live with Ruth Hodges. I used to play with him there.' She smiled again. 'Ruth had an African grey parrot called Silver – she's still got him – and I made Sammy bring him out for a picnic one day. We nearly lost him and Ruth was terribly upset. I think it was the only time she was really cross with Sammy, and it was that day that Dan came out to visit him for the first time and found him crying into a bowl of bread and milk. He nearly took Sammy back with him there and then.'

'But he didn't.'

'No. He realised that Sammy was really happy with Ruth and came out again, lots of times, and eventually he and Ruth got married and Dan works at the blacksmith's forge in the village now.' She stopped. 'You know all this already, Stephen.'

'Not all of it. I never wanted you to talk about Sammy before.' He hesitated. 'I was jealous, I suppose.'

'But you don't mind now? You're not jealous any more?'

Stephen thought for a moment. He had told Hilary that before he could go any further with Maddy, there must be complete honesty between them. He said, 'I'm still a bit jealous, yes, because you loved him and it was him you were going to marry. But I don't mind you talking about him. I want you to. I think it will be good for you, and – and I think it will be good for us, too.'

'Us?' she said in a small voice.

Stephen stopped again. He looked down at her gravely. 'Yes, us. If there is an us. I'm still not sure, you see. Because now there's someone else, isn't there?'

Maddy was silent. She turned a little away from him and gazed out across the sparkling white moors towards the glitter of the sea in Plymouth Sound. A small, sudden breeze caught her hair and whipped a few tendrils across her face. He could see only a part of her profile and her expression was hidden.

At last she turned back. Her eyes were very serious as she said, 'I don't know, Stephen. I honestly don't know. Russ has been very good to me and I know he'd like there to be an us with him and me. But we've only known each other a matter of weeks, and not at all really until the accident. And I – I've been in such a muddle. First over Sammy, and then over Ruth and Dan's baby – I don't suppose you knew they were having a baby, did you? I behaved so badly over that. And then the accident, and Russ... I felt there was something between us, you see. And he's new and different and rather exciting...'

'American,' Stephen supplied drily.

273

'Yes, I suppose that makes him exciting,' she admitted. 'But now – being with you again... I just don't know, Stephen. I need more time, I'm afraid.' She looked at him again with that clear gaze. 'I seem to be always asking for more time.'

'You have all the time you need,' he told her, and then he added, 'But if you do think there could be an us for me and you ... well, there are things you need to know about me. And maybe it would be fairer to tell you them before we go any further, so that you can be sure you want to.'

'Things I need to know?' she asked. 'What things?'

He shook his head. 'Not the time or the place now. It's Christmas Day, remember? And Stella was looking so much better. Maddy, we've been serious long enough. Let's forget all those past sorrows now and enjoy ourselves. And when we're ready – when *you're* ready – we'll talk again. And we *will* talk. There's got to be complete honesty between us before we can move any further forward.' He touched her cold cheek with one fingertip, then bent to kiss her lips, as lightly as a butterfly. 'Darling, you're frozen. Come on – I'll race you back to the car. It's time we went home and helped Hilary with the Christmas dinner.'

He set off, with Maddy in pursuit, laughing and calling to him to wait. When they arrived at the car, she was pink-cheeked and laughing. He leaned against the bonnet and waited for her, and as she reached him she slapped him on the arm.

'That wasn't fair! You had a start.'

'I know. I'm sorry.' He caught her in his arms and held her against him, feeling the slenderness of her body even through their thick coats. 'Oh, Maddy,' he exclaimed before he could stop himself, 'I do love you so much! You know that, don't you?'

She tilted her head and looked up at him, the laughter fading from her eyes. They stared at each other for a long moment, and then she said softly, 'Yes, I do. And I promise you that I'll let you know the minute I feel ready to talk.'

She reached up both hands and put them on either side of his head, then drew him down to her. The kiss this time was no butterfly kiss, yet neither was it passionate. It was warm, tender and – yes, and loving. After a moment, she pulled gently away.

'Let's go home, Stephen. I want to call into the Bell and let Dottie know how Stella is today. Take me home.'

'Yes,' he said, feeling that there was more to her words than she had allowed herself to say. 'Let's go home.'

Chapter Twenty-One

The rest of Christmas Day passed in traditional fashion for the inhabitants of Burracombe. The Tozers had their dinner and listened to the Queen's Christmas broadcast together, sitting round the big extending table in the parlour, which was used only on special occasions. Basil and Grace Harvey, who didn't like to listen to their monarch with used plates on the table, heard it while their turkey 'rested' and the vegetables simmered on the stove. Dottie Friend, who was spending the day at the Bell with Bernie and Rose, listened in their kitchen, after the pub had closed, and the Napiers and their guests sat in the drawing room at the Barton, paying respectful attention to the young Queen who had come so suddenly to the throne nearly two years earlier and received her crown only six months ago.

'All the way from New Zealand,' Dottie marvelled as they heard the words recorded from Government House in Auckland. ''Tis wonderful when you think of it. And they'll be away on their tour for six months – just imagine all the things they'll see.'

The Queen herself seemed equally awed, yet completely composed as she spoke, her voice as clear as if she were in the next room. And all over Burracombe, all over Britain and all over the world, her people listened.

Last Christmas I spoke to you from England; this year I am doing so from New Zealand. Auckland, which I reached only two days ago, is, I suppose, as far as any city in the world from London, and I have travelled some thousands of miles through many changing scenes and climates on my voyage here.

Despite all that, however, I find myself today completely and most happily at home. My husband and I left London a month ago, but we have already paid short visits to Bermuda, Jamaica, Fiji and Tonga, and have passed through Panama. I should like to thank all our hosts very warmly for the kindness of their welcome and the great pleasure of our stay.

In a short time we shall be visiting Australia and later Ceylon and before we end this great journey we shall catch a glimpse of other places in Asia, Africa and in the Mediterranean.

So this will be a voyage right round the world – the first that a Queen of England has been privileged to make as Queen. But what is really important to me is that I set out on this journey in order to see as much as possible of the people and countries of the Commonwealth and Empire, to learn at first hand something of their triumphs and difficulties and something of their hopes and fears.

As I travel across the world today, I am ever more deeply impressed with the achievement and the opportunity which the modern Commonwealth presents.

Like New Zealand, from whose North Island I am speaking, every one of its nations can be justly proud of what it has built for itself on its own soil. But their greatest achievement, I suggest, is the Commonwealth itself, and that owes much to all of them. Thus formed, the Commonwealth bears no resemblance to the Empires of the past. It is an entirely new conception, built on the highest qualities of the spirit of man: friendship, loyalty and the desire for freedom and peace.

To that new conception of an equal partnership of nations and races I shall give myself heart and soul every day of my life.

I wished to speak of it from New Zealand this Christmas Day because we are celebrating the birth of the Prince of Peace, who preached the brotherhood of man.

May that brotherhood be furthered by all our

thoughts and deeds from year to year. In pursuit of that supreme ideal, the Commonwealth is moving steadily towards greater harmony between its many creeds, colours and races despite the imperfections by which, like every human institution, it is beset.

And now I want to say something to my people in New Zealand. Last night a most grievous railway accident took place at Tangiwai which will have brought tragedy into many homes and sorrow into all upon this Christmas Day.

I know there is no one in New Zealand, and indeed throughout the Commonwealth, who will not join with my husband and me in sending to those who mourn a message of sympathy in their loss. I pray that they and all who have been injured may be comforted and strengthened.

'Oh, how sad,' Dottie said, tears in her eyes as the Queen came to the end of her speech and the National Anthem began to play. 'Those poor souls. But what a lovely speech it was, and the poor young woman must be so tired too, with all that travelling she've done. Imagine seeing all those places! Well, I hope everyone who heard it will take notice, that's all. Us don't want no more wars and fighting. Us just wants a bit of peace and quiet to live our own lives and look after each other.'

Her sentiments were echoed in all the other homes where the wireless had brought the Queen's words to her subjects. At Wood Cottage, Jacob Prout cleared his throat and Jennifer wiped her eyes; in the vicarage, Basil and Grace folded their hands and bowed their heads in prayer; in the Napiers' drawing room, Gilbert harrumphed and the others looked sober. Maddy took out a handkerchief and blew her nose, and Hilary brushed her hand across her eyes.

'But how strange,' Marianne said after the strains of the National Anthem had died away, 'that she should leave her young children and go so far away, for so many months. I do not think I could do that.'

'I don't think she has much choice,' Hilary said. 'She has to do these things.'

'But could she not take them with her? She is a mother, as well as a queen, is she not?'

'It's not the same for them,' Stephen said. 'Prince Charles and Princess Anne must be looked after by nannies most of the time. I don't suppose they see much of her even when she's at home.'

Marianne sniffed. 'I do not call that being a good mother. I would not want to leave my children for so many months, when they are so young. I am glad to be taking my son back to France with me after Christmas, and he's glad to be coming, *n 'est-ce pas*, Robert?'

Rob, who had sat dutifully still with his brother and sister to listen to the broadcast, was now stretched out on the floor playing Ludo. He looked up, startled.

'I am sorry, Maman. I wasn't listening.'

'It is of no matter.' She flipped her fingers and he went back to the game. But there was a challenge in her eyes as she looked around at the adults. 'This is what I wanted to say to you all. I have not been happy about leaving my son here, and I know he has not been happy either. He has been miserable.'

There was an uncomfortable silence. Hilary glanced at her father, who was scowling.

'I don't think this is the time–' she began, but Gilbert interrupted.

'We've already had this out, Marianne. I did what I believed to be best for the boy and I still believe it would have been best, if he'd been willing to persevere at the school. However, he doesn't wish to do that and you want to take him back to France, and that of course is your privilege. As far as I can see, there's no need for any further discussion, and certainly no need to bring it up on Christmas Day.'

'It is not important enough, is that it?' Marianne demanded. 'My son has been bullied and made miserable, but it must not be discussed. Tsk!'

'Please,' Hilary said, putting out a hand. 'Marianne, we're all sorry that Rob was unhappy at the school, but Father's right – this is Christmas Day, a day for peace as the Queen's just said, and we want it to be a happy one for you all. If you do still want to talk about it, we will, but please let's leave it until after Christmas. For the children's sake, if nothing else.'

By now, the atmosphere in the room had tensed and the children had stopped their game and were staring, wide-eyed. Hilary looked exasperated, Marianne sullen and Stephen at a loss. Then Maddy dropped to her knees beside Ginette and said, 'You need four for a really good game of Ludo. Let's start again, shall we?'

The children looked at her a little uncertainly,

then Philippe, who had taken a fancy to Maddy since the first moment he had arrived, said, 'Yes! Let's do that. Maddy, would you like to have the blue? It is the colour you like best, *je pense.*'

'You're right,' she said, surprised. 'However did you know that?'

'Because you look prettiest in it,' he said shyly, yet with a wicked twinkle in his eyes, and she laughed.

'Philippe, you'll break all the girls' hearts when you're a little older. Tell you what, let's take the board over there, where there's more room and we shan't be interrupted by grown-up talk.'

'Grown-up talk?' Ginette echoed. 'But you are a grown-up, *n'est-ce pas?*'

'I sometimes wonder about that,' Maddy said gravely. 'But even if I am, today is Christmas and nobody should be a grown-up at Christmas. *N'est-ce pas?*'

The two younger children picked up the board and pieces and carried it to the other side of the room. Maddy rose to her feet and found Rob looking at her gravely.

'What is it, Rob?' she asked quietly. 'You're not upset about what we were saying, are you?'

He shook his head, but it was an unconvincing shake. 'I was just thinking ... it's so strange. I have two families, but Philippe and Ginette have only one. I was thinking that perhaps they are the lucky ones.'

Maddy gazed down at him and felt the tears come to her eyes. She brushed them away swiftly and then put her hand on his shoulder.

'It's not easy, Rob. I know that. Everything that

changes takes a while to get used to.' Briefly, she thought of herself and Sammy, and then of Russ Tozer and of Stephen, who was watching her now, a sober look on his face. 'But time does help. You will get used to it and I hope that after a little while, when everything's settled down, you'll come to believe that you are the lucky one. We can never have too much family to love us, Rob. Remember that. And I know that all your family, *both* your families, do love you. You must never doubt that.'

They looked into each other's eyes for a moment, and then she smiled and gave him a little push.

'Come on,' she cried gaily, 'the others are waiting to play Ludo, and I'm going to beat you all!'

When Ted Tozer came in from milking later that afternoon, the family were in the long living room, with a fire blazing at one end, playing Monopoly. Russ, who had been helping him so that Tom could have the afternoon off, went on upstairs to wash and change, and Ted looked around the room. It was decorated with home-made coloured paper chains, with holly over the mantelpiece and coloured lights twinkling on the Christmas tree in the corner. The presents that had been given and received earlier were in neat piles on a shelf, and the Christmas cake, which had been iced the week before, stood resplendent on the sideboard. Joanna had done it this year, intending to make a smooth white topping, but as usual had ended up roughing the surface with a fork to look like snow, which everyone said they liked better anyway. It went better with the tiny red cottage with a snow-covered roof, which was dwarfed by the giant robin that towered over its chimney.

'Well, you do look cosy in here,' Ted said, surveying the room. 'Where's your mother, Tom?'

Tom shook the dice, moved the miniature pig that had been borrowed from Robin's farm set, and landed on Mayfair. 'She went out to make some tea. Tell her to come back, it's her turn now.'

'Don't tell her too quick, though,' Joanna said. 'He's hoping I won't notice he's landed on my property. *And* I've got a hotel and five houses on it, too. That's – how much rent is that he owes me, Luke?'

'More than I can afford,' Tom said gloomily. 'One more like this and I'll be bankrupt. How is it I always end up with the cheap places, and nobody ever lands on them anyway?'

Ted went out to the kitchen and found Alice standing by the range, waiting for the kettle to boil. She glanced round as he came in and brushed her hand across her eyes.

'Here, what's this?' he asked, coming over to her. 'Not having a cry, are you? Whatever for, on Christmas Day? I thought everyone was having a good time.'

'They are,' she said, sniffing a little. 'That's just it.' She turned to look at him. 'We're having such a lovely Christmas, Ted, but I keep thinking what next year's going to be like. It's going to be so different.'

He stared at her. 'Well, Joe and Russ won't be

here, I know, but they've never been before and us managed to enjoy ourselves.'

'It's not just them,' she said, dabbing her eyes with a hanky. 'It's our Jackie. Where will *she* be, come next Christmas?'

'She'll be home here with the rest of us,' he stated. 'Where else d'you think her'll be, for goodness' sake?'

'I don't know. I just got a feeling... She might be still in America. Or she might be somewhere else. *Anywhere* else. I just think that once she leaves us, she isn't never going to come back. Not to live with us.'

'Well, her don't actually live with us now,' he pointed out. 'Her's at that blessed hotel all the time. Her's not even here today.'

'That's just it, isn't it? Not with her family on Christmas Day because of that job of hers. And in a fortnight she'll be off to America with Joe and Russ and out of our control. I just don't know what she'll get into her head to do after that.'

'None of us do,' Ted said. Privately, he understood very well what Alice meant, for he felt just the same himself, but it wouldn't do to let this fear of what might happen in the future interfere with the pleasures of today. 'And that's why 'tisn't no good worrying about it. Us got to live in the present, not a future what none of us can see anyway. All sorts of things might have happened by then. You knows as well as I do that none of us knows what's waiting round the corner, good or bad.' He put his arm round her shoulders and gave her a hug. 'Now come on and make the tea, or that kettle will have boiled dry. Our Tom's losing all his money hand over fist and you'm missing your turns.'

Alice nodded and wiped her eyes dry. 'I know I'm being foolish, Ted, but looking at them all round the big table, laughing and enjoying theirselves so much – well, it just sort of came over me. It was as if I *could* look ahead for a minute and see that next year there'd be some of them missing. Joe and Russ, I know, but someone else too – and I thought it must surely be our Jackie.' She leaned against him for a moment. 'It's not been an easy year, this one. Losing that poor little babby, and Joanna and Tom being so upset. None of us have properly got over that yet, and to have Jackie going so far away...'

'I know, my bird. But it's all been talked through and decided, and we've got to put a brave face on it. And she'll come back. She won't stop away for ever.' He hoped he was speaking the truth. 'Our Jackie's a home bird at heart, even if she do want to fly a bit now. Mark my words, her'll be here next Christmas and there'll be nobody missing from the table. Nobody at all.'

Chapter Twenty-Two

With Christmas over at last, Marianne began to make preparations for returning to France, taking Rob with her. Maddy, passing his room, saw him through the open door, staring at a pile of possessions on his bed. She hesitated for a moment, then knocked softly and said, 'Can I come in? You look as though you need some help.'

He turned and gave her a half-smile. 'I seem to have so many things to take home. I don't know where they all came from.'

Maddy laughed and came to stand beside him. 'It's always the same. I'd only been at West Lyme a month when I found I had twice as much stuff as when I first went there. Do you have to take them all back, though? I mean, you'll be coming to Burracombe again, won't you?'

'Yes, for part of the holidays. But I can't decide which things I shall want when I'm at home. There are my books ... and my father's Meccano ... and the model railway Uncle Stephen gave me for Christmas... How can I pack all of those?'

Maddy glanced at his rather battered pre-war suitcase. 'I'd say you can't. You'll just have to leave some behind and look forward to using them when you are here. Look, why don't you start by collecting the things you brought with you when you first came, and decide which of those you want to take back, and then think about the things you like best. Perhaps not the model railway,' she added. 'There is rather a lot of it – you'd need a whole suitcase just for that.'

'Yes, and there isn't really room for it at home. We have only a small house, and so many of us to live there.' Regretfully, he set the boxes containing the railway to one side. 'But I could take my Meccano. It will help me with my engineering studies.'

Maddy looked at him. 'You want to be an engineer?'

'It is what I wanted to be,' he said, and paused before adding, 'before I came to Burracombe.'

'And now?'

'I don't know,' he said a little helplessly, but his eyes went to the box containing the Meccano set.

'Did you say that was your father's?'

'Yes. So I think perhaps it means he wanted to be an engineer too.'

'I don't know,' Maddy said. 'I don't think it means anything, really. Most little boys had Meccano sets. I think Baden just wanted to run the estate.'

Rob turned to her. 'Did you know my father?'

'No, he was k– He died before I came to Burracombe. But I heard about him, of course. Your grandmother used to talk about him a lot, and Stephen's told me quite a bit.' Mostly about how Gilbert had tried to mould Stephen into a second Baden, and the disappointment Stephen believed he had been to his father when he couldn't do so. But she couldn't say that to Baden's son. 'I think he was a very fine man,' she said after a moment.

'I know. But nobody seems to know what he *really* wanted to do, when the war was over.'

Maddy felt helpless. 'Why – stay here and learn to manage the estate, I suppose. That's what the Colonel wanted him to do. He would probably have stayed in the army for quite a while first. It seems to be what the Napier men did.'

The boy stirred. 'But did they *want* to do that?'

Maddy gazed at him. 'Well – I suppose so. Your grandfather did, didn't he?'

'Perhaps,' Rob said. 'Or perhaps he has forgotten.' He stared pensively at the Meccano box

287

for a minute or two. 'I think perhaps none of them really thought about it. They grew up here, they went to school' – his expression twisted a little – 'and they went into the army. And then they came home to Burracombe. They did not think that they could do anything different.'

'No, I suppose they didn't,' Maddy said doubtfully. 'But then, they didn't have to, did they? Their future was arranged for them. They didn't have to wonder what to do or try to get jobs, or pass exams or anything like that. They were really very lucky.' Or maybe very unlucky, she thought suddenly, to have their lives so arranged for them.

'Unless they hated being in the army, and then running the estate,' he said. 'Perhaps some of them did. Perhaps my father did.' He gave her a challenging look. 'Uncle Stephen would.'

'Well – yes. But he didn't ever think he would have to, so it was different for him.' She remembered something Stephen had let drop during Christmas dinner. 'I think he'd be ready to do it now, if he had to.'

Rob shook his head. 'No. He has said he would do it, perhaps, because he knows his father wants it, but he would hate it. I think I would hate it too.'

Maddy stared at him in dismay. 'But *Rob*...'

'I know. My grandfather wants to leave the estate to me, because my father would have inherited it and therefore so must I. But I haven't *lived* here, Madelaine. I haven't grown up here. And I am not English – I am French. I don't know English ways – not well enough for this.' He waved a hand at the pile of possessions, at the family photographs on the walls, at the picture of Baden that Gilbert had given him in a silver frame. 'I can't be like the boys I met at school. I'm different.'

'But after a while...' she said helplessly. 'You'd *learn* to be the same as them.'

'I do not *want* to learn to be the same as them!' he cried with a sudden flash of temper. 'Why should I? I saw those boys at school and I would *never* want to be as they are, never. I am *proud* to be different. I'm proud to be *French*. I'm proud to be *myself*. And I shall be proud to become an engineer.'

He fell silent, and they looked at each other. Then Maddy said awkwardly, 'So what will you do, Rob?'

He shrugged. 'I will go home to France, back to my own studies. I'll come back here for holidays and because I have family here. I know that part of me is English and I want to feel comfortable in England, for my father's sake. But I shall always be French really, and I shall make my own life, in the way that I want to make it. And if I want to be an engineer when I am older, then that is what I shall be.'

His voice was quieter now, and firm, and as Maddy gazed at him, she believed it. She thought of what Stephen had told her, about the discussion he had had with his father which had turned into an argument, and wondered what he would do if he heard Rob talk like this. Would he really throw away his own plans and settle down on the estate? And what of Hilary? Maddy too had noticed that she was different these days, as if she had something other than Burracombe on her mind. She had always seemed content to manage the place, either alone or with Travis, but now she seemed slightly out of touch with estate matters. Was she losing interest? Was she, too, thinking of leading her own life at last?

'Let's have another look at these things and decide what you want to take back with you,' she said, turning back to the bed. 'We'll make a pile here of things that have got to go. And this, I think should be first.' She picked up the Meccano.

'Yes,' Rob said. 'I am certainly taking the Meccano.'

'Did you know,' Maddy asked Stephen later that afternoon, 'that Rob wants to be an engineer?'

Stephen looked uncomfortable. 'Well, yes. I mean, he's talked to me about it, a bit. But that was some time ago – I thought he might have changed his mind by now.'

They were walking the two old dogs in the grounds. Marianne and the other two children were still packing and Rob had gone to say goodbye to Travis and Jennifer. It was that lull between Christmas and the New Year when the tumult and hard work of preparation was over and nobody wanted to do anything but relax and gather strength for whatever life had in store for them next. Maddy had been to the hospital to see Stella that morning, and was thinking of going to have tea with Dottie when Stephen caught her at the door and asked her to go for a walk with him.

'You can go to Dottie's after that. In fact, I'll come with you, but these two old fellows need a bit of exercise first. They're both getting fat and lazy.'

'Well, they're Labradors, aren't they?' Maddy said, rubbing Barley's ears. 'And they don't go shooting any more. Travis takes his own dogs.'

The wide, sweeping lawn in front of the house was almost entirely green now, with just a few shreds and patches of white left to remind them of the snowfall before Christmas. Around its edges, the branches of the deciduous trees were starkly bare against a sombre grey sky, while the evergreens brooded like ancient monks withdrawing into hooded cloaks.

Maddy was wearing a deep blue mohair coat with a big shawl collar which she could draw up round her ears. It was nipped in close to her small waist and swirled around her legs as she walked. She wore fur boots and gloves with a scarlet beret that matched, and her glossy fair hair streamed down over the wide collar like golden silk. The cold air had brought rosy colour to her cheeks and her eyes were as blue as her coat.

Stephen took her gloved hand and tucked it into the crook of his arm. The two dogs ran lumberingly ahead a little way, then slowed to a plodding walk. They went along a narrow path into the trees and Stephen and Maddy followed them.

They had walked for about five minutes in silence before Maddy brought up the subject of Rob's ambition. She said, 'Why did you think he'd change his mind?'

'Well – having Burracombe handed to him on a plate. It's a lot to give up, especially when you've been fairly hard up all your life. Marianne and her sister work hard in that patisserie.'

'I wonder what Marianne thinks of it,' Maddy said thoughtfully. 'I got the impression that she'd be happy for Rob to inherit.'

'Oh, I'm sure she would,' Stephen said a little bitterly. 'Very happy indeed. And I don't imagine that she even knows what he's thinking now. I don't suppose he's told her.'

'She knows he hasn't been happy here.'

'That was at school. He's happy enough at Burracombe.' He glanced at her. 'When did he tell you he wanted to be an engineer?'

'This morning. He was trying to decide what to take back to France with him. I think he really means it, you know. He says he wants to be himself. It's as if he feels like a puppet, with your father pulling his strings.'

'Well, isn't that just what my father does to everyone? It's why I wanted to get away.'

'And do you still want to? You told me on the way back from the hospital that you'd offered to come back when you finish your National Service, if he wanted you.'

'I know, and look where that led,' Stephen said gloomily. 'No, it would never work. We both know that. I broke away when I went to Cambridge and again when I joined the RAF, and he's never forgiven me for either. We'd never be able to work together. But I felt sorry for Hilary. I felt I had to offer, at least.'

A red squirrel ran up a tree in front of them, and they stopped to watch as it turned on a branch and chattered crossly at the dogs. Overhead, two pigeons took off from the tree, clapping their wings as if applauding the brave animal, and the squirrel gave up his scolding before running effortlessly up the tree trunk and taking a flying leap into space. The dogs, who had chased many a squirrel in their time and even caught a few, looked at each other and seemed to shrug their burly shoulders, as if to agree that it wasn't worth the bother.

Maddy said, 'So you won't come back. And Rob doesn't seem to want to. So where does that leave Burracombe – and Hilary?'

Stephen sighed. 'It leaves Burracombe in much the same position. It could be run just with a manager, you know, provided he was a decent, honest sort of chap, which Travis is. But as for Hilary... I just don't know. She seems different lately, as if she's trying to make up her own mind about something. Maybe she's thinking of leaving too...' He turned to her. 'What *I* want to know is where it leaves us.'

'Us?' Maddy said uncertainly.

'Yes,' he said. 'Look, Maddy, I didn't mean to say anything so soon, and I know you said on Christmas Day that you'd let me know when you felt ready to talk – but I'm away so much, I hardly ever see you and I'm so scared of losing you again. Please, even if you don't want to say anything to me, please listen to what I want to say to you.'

She looked up at him. His eyes were serious and she thought suddenly that he had changed in the last few months. The laughing, flippant Stephen she had known was still there, but the

293

lightness was overlaid with a new maturity. She wondered what had happened to cause this. I wouldn't have known, she thought. I've been so wrapped up in myself all this past year, I hardly know what's happened to anyone else at all.

'Go on,' she said quietly.

'You know how I feel about you,' he said. 'That's not changed and it's never going to. I know I didn't go about things the right way – trying to lure you away from Sam Hodges by taking you to smart restaurants in my smart car and all that. It didn't mean a thing to you, did it? None of that was what you wanted.'

'No, it wasn't,' Maddy said. 'It was fun and I enjoyed it, but those things weren't real to me, and you weren't real either – not in the way that Sammy was. He'd never had any of that, you see – he'd had a poor childhood in Portsmouth, and even when he went to Bridge End to live with Ruth, they lived very simply. But he learned *values* with Ruth, the sort of values my family had too, and the Budds, and lots of the other people we knew back in April Grove. And Dottie too, and all my friends here in Burracombe. Money and smart possessions didn't mean much to any of us because we didn't have them and didn't think we ever would. What mattered to us was being honest and decent and – well, *true.*'

'I know. And that's why you preferred him to me. And you were right.' He paused. 'But I think I've learned a lot in the past few months. About myself and about how things are and how they could be. I've learned that there's got to be complete honesty between us if there's going to be anything at all.' He stopped again. 'I've been a bit of a fool too, and I've learned from that as well.'

'A fool?' she said, but he shook his head.

'That's something I'll have to tell you about one day. But not now. All I want to know today is – well, if there's any chance at all for me. Or if you're going to go off to America.'

'America?' she echoed, startled, and a deep flush ran up her neck.

'Yes,' he said, watching her. 'With Russ Tozer. Don't tell me it isn't on the cards.'

'I – I don't know. I mean – we haven't talked – we hardly know each other...'

'That's not the impression I got seeing you together at the hospital,' Stephen said a little grimly.

Maddy was silent for a moment, then she said, 'You're right, Stephen. We owe each other honesty, so I'll be as honest as I can. And the truth is, I don't really know. I did think, when he first took me to see Stella and I was so upset – well, he was very kind to me then. And I thought – yes, I did think there might be something for us. And he's talked a little about me going to America – just on a visit, that's all. Jackie's going, and he even thinks Dottie might.'

'*Dottie?*'

'Yes. Apparently she and Joe Tozer were good friends before Joe went away originally – more than friends, Russ thinks. Joe wants her to go, anyway. So I wouldn't be on my own if I went and it could be just a visit. A holiday. And it does sound lovely.' She stopped.

'I can see that,' Stephen said, looking at her wistful face. 'If anyone needs a holiday now, it's you, Maddy. So ... will you be going?'

'I don't know,' she said, looking up at him. 'I truly don't know.'

There was another pause. Then Stephen said, 'Let me put my cards on the table, Maddy. I love you and I want to marry you. I think I could make you happy and I know you'd make me happy. I shan't keep asking you because I think once should be enough, but I'll wait for as long as you want, so long as you promise to give me an answer one way or the other as soon as you do know.' He stopped and took a breath, his eyes searching hers.

'Oh, Stephen,' Maddy said a little faintly. 'I – I don't know what to say.'

'Just don't say no,' he replied with a twisted grin. 'Not straight away, anyway.'

'What – what would you be doing?' she asked. 'I mean, when you come out of the RAF? Will you come back to Burracombe?'

He shook his head. 'I don't think so. Dad knows I'm not cut out for it, and so do I. But I'd stay if you wanted me to,' he added quickly. 'With you beside me, I could do it – I could do anything.'

'And if not?'

'Well, you know I've been planning to go to Canada and set up an air freight business. We could do that together. Start a whole new life in a new country. Or if you don't like that idea, we could stay around here – they'll be developing the airport at Plymouth in the next few years. I could go into commercial piloting there, or I could join one of the big airlines. There'll be plenty of opportunities for a chap like me.'

'It sounds exciting,' Maddy said wistfully.

'It's going to be. I've had a good training in the RAF, Maddy. It's changed my thinking. I did well in maths at Cambridge, but I don't want to sit in an office doing accounts or anything like that. And maths is essential for flyers. But the important thing is, I'm a *good* flyer.'

Maddy shivered suddenly, and they began to walk on. After a moment or two, she said, 'What did you mean about being a fool?'

'It's not something I want to talk about much,' he said reluctantly. 'I will tell you, if you think we could get serious, but if not...'

'No,' she said. 'I think you must tell me anyway. You can't let me start to feel serious about you – if I'm going to – without knowing the things you have to tell me.' She looked up at him and said, 'I've been a fool too, you know. Ruth Hodges – Sammy's stepmother – is expecting a baby, and when she and Dan told me, I flew into a terrible temper and walked out of the house and wouldn't speak to them for months. I thought they were doing it to replace Sammy, you see. But I was just being very silly and horribly selfish.'

'Were you? I don't think so. I think it was quite natural to feel that way, when you were still so upset.'

'Perhaps, but I think I was being selfish and spoilt. Anyway, it's all right now – I've made it up with them. I went to see them and apologised and they forgave me.' She looked at him. 'I expect whatever you did can be forgiven too.'

Stephen looked rueful. 'I'm not so sure. It was a lot worse than that.'

'Did you hurt anyone?' she asked, and he thought for a moment and then shook his head.

'No, I don't think I did – not really.'

'Then it wasn't worse, because I did hurt someone. I hurt two people who had been very kind to me. So ... what was it?'

Stephen heaved a sigh. He held her hand more closely within his arm and said, 'It was Marianne.'

'Marianne?'

'Yes. Back in the summer. She – she wasn't altogether certain of what Dad was going to do about Rob, you see, and she wanted to make sure of her position in the family. So she decided to take matters into her own hands and – well, make sure, I suppose.' He stopped, staring down at the path, his face dark. 'She came into my room one night,' he said at last. 'She'd been making a play for me all along and – well, I wasn't man enough to resist, I'm afraid.'

Maddy caught her breath. After a minute or two, she said, 'She stayed all night?'

'Yes,' he said miserably. 'All night.'

The little wood had fallen very quiet, and darkness was seeping in between the trees. They turned and began to walk back along the narrow path. The dogs had already started back, and were waiting at the edge of the lawn. Maddy stopped just inside the wood, and Stephen stopped with her.

'Why? Why did she do that?'

'I think,' he said heavily, 'that she wanted me to

make her pregnant.'

'Stephen!'

'I know. It never occurred to me then – I was too bemused. I'd never met anyone like her before, you see. She wasn't ... she's not like you, Maddy, all open and honest and above board. Anyway, it didn't work, thank goodness, because a day or two later she found she wasn't pregnant, and Hilary found out about it and she went back to France. And I've taken very good care not to let myself get into such a position again.'

'I'd noticed you didn't seem to like her much,' Maddy said thoughtfully.

He looked down at her. 'I don't. I never did, really. But she knew just how to get at me.' He paused. 'So ... does it make any difference? I told you I'd been a fool.'

'I know. I wasn't really expecting anything quite like that, though.' Maddy gazed across the lawn to the house. Lights were beginning to come on in the windows and it looked welcoming, tranquil, as if nothing ever happened within its walls. 'I don't know, Stephen. I just don't know. I'll have to think about it.'

He stared at her. 'I've spoiled it, haven't I? Ruined it – just when I thought... Oh, *hell!*' He let go of her hand and turned away, running his fingers through his hair. 'I shouldn't have told you. I should have kept it to myself. I'm nothing but an *idiot!*'

'No!' She caught at his arm. 'No, don't think that. You said there had to be honesty between us and you were right. And it might easily have come out – Marianne herself might have told me, just out of spite – and it was better that I heard it from you.' She drew him back towards her. 'I just need time, that's all. Time to get it settled in my mind, and time to think about all the rest, too. And it's not so easy just now – not with Stella still in hospital.'

'Oh my God,' he groaned. 'I'd even managed to forget Stella. What on earth must you think of me?'

'I'm not thinking any more about it now,' she said steadily. 'Not unless there's something else you ought to tell me.'

He shook his head.

'Nothing.'

'Then let's take these two poor old dogs back to their fire,' she said, slipping her hand through his arm again. 'And have a pleasant last evening together. Tomorrow you're taking me back to West Lyme, and after that I'll have time to think. I promise I *will* think,' she added seriously. 'I won't play with you any more, Stephen. I'll think very, very hard about all you've told me. About Russ, too. And I won't keep you waiting any longer than I have to for an answer.'

Chapter Twenty-Three

The next morning was one of departures for the Barton. Maddy and Stephen left first, in Stephen's sports car, for West Lyme. Stephen would have lunch there with the Archdeacon and his wife, before going on to the RAF station at White Cheriton, and Maddy would settle back into her duties. She had promised Stella, however, that she would be back after the New Year to see her sister and spend the first weekend of January with Dottie.

Hilary, Marianne and the children were the next to leave. Travis came round with the Land Rover and packed them all in, with their luggage, to take them to the railway station in Tavistock. Hilary was to see them as far as the Dover train and spend the night in London before returning home.

Her heart was beating fast as she helped load the suitcases into the Land Rover. She had managed at last to speak to David the night before, and he was coming to London to meet her after she had said goodbye to the French family. He couldn't stay overnight, but they would have a few hours together before he returned to Derby. The thought of seeing him again, of being able to look into his eyes and touch his hand, feel his kiss on her lips, was like fire in her blood, and she was sure that everyone must see the difference in her.

Her father, of course, noticed nothing. He had come to breakfast looking grim, and requested that Rob sit at his right hand at table. He was clearly upset that the boy was leaving, and Hilary felt sorry for him. His hopes and dreams for a second Baden to take over the running of the Burracombe estate seemed to lie in ruins around him, and once again he appeared to feel that the inheritance faced an uncertain future.

'It's too early to give up hope,' she'd told him

the previous evening when she'd gone to his room to say good night. 'Rob's still a child. And all this has come so suddenly to him – it's no wonder he's confused.'

'If he'd only stayed at Kelly,' Gilbert had mourned, referring to the school where Rob had spent less than one term. 'He'd have been all right then. All those things the other boys did to him – they weren't real bullying. It was just a ritual they all go through at first. By the time he'd gone back after Christmas he'd have found real friends, friends that would last all his life.'

Hilary didn't answer that. She'd been genuinely shocked at the 'rituals' boys seemed to think it necessary to inflict upon their fellows, and sympathised with Rob over his reaction. She said, 'He's been brought up differently, and such a lot of changes were too much for him. He'll be better off in France. And he'll be here during the holidays. He can learn as much about the estate then as he would if he were away at school in England and only home during the holidays.'

Gilbert shifted restlessly on his pillows. 'That's if he wants to. I'm not at all sure he does. He likes it here, I'll grant you that, and he enjoys going about with Travis – did well on the Boxing Day shoot too, apparently – but I don't think his heart's in it. Not as his father's was.'

'And you can't expect it to be,' she stated. 'Baden grew up here, and he had a special position in the family. He was your eldest son and it was always assumed that he would take over. Rob grew up in France, in an occupied country for the first five years of his life, with German soldiers in the house and in the streets. His life was different from anything we can imagine and he didn't know what the future would bring. He didn't even know Burracombe existed. Even when he was told, and when Marianne brought him over in June, they had no idea about the extent of the estate. She thought it was just a farm.' She paused, but her father didn't speak, and she looked at his face and thought how tired he looked. 'Father, you're still not over your attack. You shouldn't be worrying like this. Go to sleep now, and let what will be, be. There's really no more we can do about Rob now.'

He heaved a deep sigh and then nodded. 'I know.' Then he reached out his hand and laid it on hers. 'You're a good girl, Hilary. Think perhaps I haven't always been fair to you.'

Hilary felt tears sting her eyes. 'You don't have to say that, Dad.'

'Think perhaps I do,' he said. 'Taken you for granted.' The medication he was still on, to help him rest, was taking effect and his eyelids began to droop. 'Leave me alone now. I'll probably go to sleep.'

'Yes,' she said, getting up from her chair and bending over to give him a kiss. 'You go to sleep, and sleep well. I'll see you in the morning.'

She turned at the door and looked back. His eyes were already closed and he was breathing quietly. Hilary went out into the passage and closed the door behind her.

This morning he looked rested, but she could see that he was still despondent over Rob's imminent departure. Rob seemed to feel it too as he sat by his grandfather, helping him to bacon and eggs. They had always got on well together, partly because Gilbert had taken the boy to his heart from the first moment he had seen him. It was as if he had been given his eldest son back again, and he'd refused to see any difference between the two.

It had been bound to end in tears, Hilary thought. Right from the start, her father had been doomed to disappointment. Even if Rob had been – still might be – interested in taking over the estate, he was not Baden and never could be. Their backgrounds were too different.

The reality had been brought home to them all now, by Rob's despair at the school his grandfather had insisted on sending him to, and by his attempt to escape, with all its consequences. He still felt guilty over the accident and Stella's injuries. Felix himself had come to see him last night on his way back from the hospital, to assure him again that nobody blamed him, but Hilary thought he had been only half convinced. It would be good for him to be back in France, she thought, where all these events would be far away and his other life would become real to him again.

Marianne, too, was looking dour. Whatever hopes she had entertained were also dashed this morning, and the glances she kept giving Stephen were bitter, almost vindictive. He had taken care never to be alone with her, but had failed the evening before, when Hilary had gone to say good night to her father. He had made to follow her, but Maddy had spoken to him then and the opportunity had passed.

'I'm going to bed too,' she said. 'I'll see you in the morning, Stephen. I'll be ready to go straight after breakfast.' She had turned to Marianne, holding out her hand. 'Goodbye, Marianne. I hope you have a good journey home.'

Marianne took her hand and smiled. 'I'm sure we shall, thank you, Madelaine. May I say what a pleasure it has been to spend Christmas with you?'

Maddy hesitated, confused by the barbed tone. She smiled uncertainly, muttered something and escaped from the room. Marianne watched her go and then turned back to Stephen.

'So at last we are alone. I thought we would never have the opportunity.'

He made to pass her, but she moved gracefully to stand in front of the door. She tilted her head and challenged him with her eyes.

'Does she know about us, the pretty little Madelaine?'

'Why do you ask that?' He stepped away from her.

'Because it is apparent that you have an interest in her. And she in you, perhaps?'

'I don't think,' Stephen said, walking away to stand by a side table and fiddling with a pen that lay there, 'that that's any of your business.'

Marianne opened her eyes at him. 'Oh my! So sensitive! Perhaps I have touched a nerve, *n'est-ce pas?*'

Stephen turned to face her. 'Marianne, I don't want to discuss Maddy with you. In fact, I don't want to discuss anything with you. We've both got a long day tomorrow, so why don't we go to bed?'

He realised what he had said the moment the words left his mouth, and bit his lip, flushing painfully. Marianne burst out laughing.

'What a very good idea, *mon ami!* I thought you would never suggest it!'

'I'm not suggesting it now,' he said savagely, 'as you very well know.'

'You did not *suggest* it in the summer,' she said, 'but you did not turn me away when I came to your room.'

'That's in the past. Over.'

'Perhaps it is,' she said, crossing the room to stand close to him. 'And perhaps it is not.'

Stephen turned swiftly away. He heard her soft laugh and cursed himself. Even now, angry as he was, he could not help his male response to her closeness, her dark beauty, her provocative stance. He could smell the deep musky perfume she wore, so different from Maddy's light floral scent, the aroma of a female animal making ready to receive her mate. He could feel the warmth of her body and see the invitation in her eyes.

'Go away, Marianne,' he said, despising the hoarseness of his voice. 'There's nothing here for you. Not as far as I'm concerned, anyway.'

Her dark eyes narrowed. 'Are you quite sure of that, my Stephen?'

The words, which she had spoken so seductively when she had come to his bed in the summer, were like a fan to the smouldering self-disgust he had been feeling all over Christmas. He felt his body tremble and stepped away quickly, afraid that he would strike her. Enraged, he faced her and his voice was like the lash of a whip.

'Am I sure?' he demanded. 'Yes, I *am* sure – more sure than I've ever been of anything. You trapped me once, or tried to. You won't do it again. I'm surprised that you even try.'

Marianne laughed again. 'Oh, I don't wish to trap you, *mon ami*. It was a mere whim anyway, nothing more than that. A marriage between us two would have been a disaster, *non?* No, I simply amuse myself – it makes me laugh to see how I can still set you on fire, even when you try so hard to resist me.' Her eyes moved slowly down his body and Stephen felt himself flush again. 'And it makes me laugh to think that you will never be really free of me. Robert will always be a part of Burracombe now, and so shall I.'

Stephen took a deep breath. When he was sure his voice was under control, he said in a low, bitter tone, 'You were my brother's wife, Marianne. You bore his child. And yet still you find it amusing to play with me – his brother.' He paused, knowing that all the scorn and contempt he felt for her was showing in his face and in his eyes; yet he kept his voice quiet as he said, 'You are quite despicable.'

He turned and walked towards the door. He opened it and went out of the room, closing it behind him. He did not look back, so he did not see the stricken anger in her face; nor would he have cared if he had.

This morning, he did not even glance at her, so he did not see in her eyes the spite that Hilary saw. Maddy saw it too and wondered what had happened between them last night. It had been a risk, leaving them alone together, but she had felt it essential for Stephen to be able to prove to himself that he could resist the Frenchwoman before their own relationship could progress. From the dark glances Marianne was giving him now, it seemed that he had, and Maddy felt a glow of warmth and satisfaction. She knew that the drive to West Lyme would be a happy one, with herself and Stephen back to the companionship they had always enjoyed, and with the promise of better times to come.

The atmosphere in the Land Rover was less comfortable. Although the two younger children were excited and chattering, Marianne barely spoke and Rob was subdued, perhaps realising for the first time that he was leaving Burracombe behind for several months. Hilary and Travis made conversation about the estate, more to ease the strain than because they needed to, and as they all prepared to board the train at Tavistock, Rob said in a voice that seemed choked with tears: 'You will give Tavy a hug from me, won't you, Mr Kellaway? I shall miss her so much.'

'I will,' the estate manager said, smiling down at him. 'And it won't be so very long before you see her again. You'll be back at Easter, and you know you're always welcome at Wood Cottage.'

'Come along, Robert,' Marianne said sharply. 'Help me with this luggage.' She held out her hand to Travis and smiled prettily at him. 'Thank you so ver' much, Mr Kellaway. You have been very kind to my Robert. And thank you to your wife, too.'

She just can't help flirting with any man she meets, Hilary thought, but from the amused twitch of Travis's lips, it seemed unlikely that she was making much impression on him. Hilary helped gather the suitcases and bags together, and shepherded the children on to the train, then turned to Travis herself.

'I'll see you tomorrow,' she said quietly. 'Thanks, Travis.'

'It's no trouble at all,' he replied. 'I'll meet your train. And ... take care, Hilary.'

Their eyes met and she felt a small shock, as if something unexpected had passed between them. It's almost as if he knows, she thought in astonishment – yet how could he? Nobody knew about herself and David. Nobody knew that they might meet today.

Unless... Her mind went back to that day in Hyde Park, when they had run into Joe and Russ Tozer. And the night in Piccadilly, when she and David had stood looking up at Eros. Could the Americans have mentioned it to anyone? Was it already all round Burracombe?

No. It couldn't be. She shook herself and smiled back at Travis. It was just a figure of speech, that was all. It meant nothing. He knew nothing. David was still a secret – her secret.

'I will,' she answered, and climbed aboard the train as the guard blew his whistle. The engine let off steam and she slammed the door just as the wheels began to turn. She sat down in the seat Rob had been saving for her and watched as Tavistock receded into the distance.

In a few hours, the visitors would be boarding the Dover train and she would be free. Free, if only for a short time, to follow her own heart.

Chapter Twenty-Four

Felix returned his hire car that morning, knowing that from now on he'd be using trains and buses again to visit Stella. He walked softly into the ward that afternoon, sorry that she was no longer in a room on her own, but glad that it meant the doctors thought there was an improvement in her condition. He found her bed near the door, where the nurses could keep a closer eye on her, and bent to kiss her lips.

'You're looking better, darling. How do you feel?'

'Not too bad. My shoulder aches rather a lot, but the bruises are dying down a bit. I wish I could feel my legs, though.'

'You will do, soon enough,' he said. 'And at least you don't have any pain from them.'

'I'd rather feel the pain,' she said restlessly. 'At least I'd know there was a chance they'd get better and I could walk again.'

He stared at her. 'Of course you'll walk again!'

'You don't know that. The doctors themselves don't know that, so how can you?'

It was the first time he'd ever heard her speak to him so irritably. He paused, aware that it came from her pain and anxiety, and laid his hand gently over hers.

'No, I can't know it,' he said quietly. 'But I can hope, and I can believe. I can have faith, and as you know, faith can move mountains.'

'So they say,' she muttered, and pulled her hand away from under his. 'Oh, I'm sorry, Felix. I'm just feeling out of sorts and fed up. I didn't mean to snap.'

'Darling Stella,' he said, 'you can snap all you want to. It won't stop me loving you. I know you're still my dear Stella underneath it all. I just wish I could take your suffering away. If only it was possible, I'd willingly be in your place, and do the suffering for you.'

'Well, you can't.' She heaved a deep sigh, then said, 'I'm not very good company this afternoon, Felix. You'd better go home.'

'I'll do no such thing. Not unless you ask me to.'

'I just have.'

'Yes, but not because you really want me to go. That was just because you feel grumpy. You know you'd be even grumpier if I actually went.' He found her hand again and stroked her fingers gently. 'Shall I tell you what's happening in Burracombe?'

'You can if you like,' she said ungraciously. 'I can pretty well guess, though. Everyone's had a lovely Christmas, they've all been to church and all had presents and sat up half the night singing old songs, and that's about it. Maddy told me anyway. And now she's gone back to West Lyme, so I shan't see her again for a while.'

'She's coming back at the weekend. You'll see her then.' He racked his brain for something else to say. 'The Frenchwoman – Madame Aucoin – was going back to France today, too. And young

Rob's going with her. With the other two children, of course.'

Stella gave a small nod, as if she wasn't much interested, and Felix gazed at her in despair. He said, 'Would you rather we didn't talk for a while? If I just sit here, holding your hand?'

'I don't mind,' she said drearily. 'It's up to you.'

'I want to do what you want,' he said anxiously, and she shrugged.

'I told you, I don't mind.'

Felix felt helpless. It was quite clear that Stella did mind, but he couldn't be sure what she minded most. He thought that in her present mood, whatever he suggested would probably be the very thing she didn't want. He wanted to do the right thing, he wanted to please her, but for this afternoon anyway, that seemed to be impossible.

'All right,' he said. 'I'll just sit here with you and not talk unless you want to. Go to sleep if you like. It's enough for me just to be with you.'

Stella said nothing. She turned her head away and let her hand lie limply in his. He watched her face, trying to battle down the feelings of hurt that rose in him, telling himself that she was in pain, feeling miserable and frightened, and that her reactions were perfectly normal. He knew it was true and that he shouldn't be feeling hurt, but he couldn't help it. Eventually he decided that all he could do was accept it as a part of the pain that he could share, and the tenderness he felt for her flooded through him so that the hurt was washed away.

After a little while, he saw that she was asleep.

Felix was so intent upon watching Stella's face that he was not aware at first of the doctor standing beside his chair. He turned with a start, and at the same moment Stella opened her eyes and smiled at him. He felt a swift relief that her bad temper seemed to have gone, and gave her hand a small squeeze before standing up.

'Mr Copley,' the doctor said. 'I'm glad you're here. I want to have a little talk with you both.'

Felix stared at him, gripped by sudden anxiety, which increased when the doctor began to draw the curtains around the bed. He glanced quickly down at Stella and saw an answering fear in her eyes. He said, 'What is it? What's happened?'

'Nothing's happened – nothing new, at any rate.' He indicated the chair Felix had been sitting in. 'Please, sit down again. I just thought it best for us all to have a talk – to clear up any questions you may have.'

'Will you know the answers to them?' Felix asked, knowing which question was uppermost in both his and Stella's minds. 'Has there been a change in her condition?'

'Not a major change,' the doctor replied, and Felix thought there was a wry note in his voice, as if he wished there had been. He smiled at Stella. 'We can all see that you're getting better – you're improving every day. There's no brain injury, and the broken bones will heal. You'll have to stay here for a while yet, but as things are I see no reason why you shouldn't go home again when we're satisfied with your progress in that direction.' He hesitated, and Stella spoke, quickly

313

and abruptly.

'When you're satisfied?' she repeated. 'But when will that be?' The doctor didn't answer immediately, and she went on, panic beginning to infuse her voice. 'There's something more, isn't there?' She looked from one to the other. 'It's my legs. I still can't feel them. You keep asking me if I can – every day you ask me, and it's never any different.' Her eyes turned wildly to Felix. 'I'm paralysed – that's what it is. I'm paralysed, and I'm never going to be able to walk again!'

There was a brief, shocked silence. Felix drew in a sharp breath, but before he could find words to speak, he felt the doctor's hand on his shoulder and heard the quiet voice above his head.

'That's still not certain, Miss Simmons. Sometimes these things take longer to heal than we would wish, but they usually *do* heal. We know there was a good deal of bruising to your spine, and until that clears, we won't really know the outcome. But–'

'But you think I *might* be paralysed,' she said flatly. 'That's what you want to tell us, isn't it?'

'There's a possibility,' he said. 'Yes.'

Felix found his voice at last. 'We've always known that might be the case. Why are you telling us now, if you're still not certain?'

'He *is* certain,' Stella said. 'It's gone on too long. I ought to have been able to feel something by now.' She turned her face away. 'He's trying to break it gently. He knew I would realise it soon. I think I already had.'

Felix stared at her in dismay. He turned to the doctor.

'Is this true? *Are* you certain?'

'No, we're not. Not entirely.' The man sighed and rubbed his hand over his face. 'But Miss Simmons is right to say that it's gone on rather longer than we like, and the possibility does seem rather strong. I'm sorry.'

'Never walk again?' Felix repeated numbly. 'My Stella, never walk again?'

'It's still only a possibility,' the doctor said again. 'There's still hope. People have recovered from much worse injuries.'

'But you want us to be prepared,' Felix said. 'You want us to be prepared for Stella to spend her life in a wheelchair.'

'Yes,' the doctor said quietly. 'I do believe there is still hope, but I think you should be prepared.'

Felix looked down at Stella's face. It was paper white, her eyes like two huge dark holes cut out of a waxen mask. He bent quickly, tightening his hand on her fingers, and laying his face against her cheek.

'Darling, it won't make any difference. We'll still be together. I shall always love you and look after you, whatever happens. And you heard what the doctor said. It's only a possibility, we can still have hope. We *must* still have hope...'

But Stella turned her face away from him, and he felt only the salt of her tears against his lips; and only her long, shuddering sigh gave him answer.

Hilary saw the family safely on to the Dover train and turned back towards the station entrance. She felt a mixture of sadness and relief. Sadness

315

because she had grown fond of Rob, and relief that Marianne was once again safely out of Burracombe and out of Stephen's way. She didn't think there was any chance of the Frenchwoman seducing him for a second time, but the atmosphere over Christmas had been distinctly uncomfortable, and Hilary was thankful to be able to go back home and return to her normal life.

But first, there was David.

He was waiting at the turnstile as she came through, handing her ticket to the collector. Her heart thudded almost into her throat as she caught sight of him, and her knees trembled. She stumbled forward into his arms, and he caught her and held her close, his lips against her hair.

'David ... David...'

'Hilary, darling.' He lifted her face with his fingertips and they kissed. 'Oh, I've waited so long for this... Let's go somewhere quiet. I want to look at you. I want to know you're really here.'

'I'm here all right,' she said with a shaky laugh as they hurried through the crowds. 'I just wish it were for a bit longer. You really can't stay tonight?'

He looked down at her soberly. 'I wish I could. I really wish I could. But...'

'Sybil?'

His lips tightened. 'Let's wait until we can talk properly. I've a lot to tell you.'

Suddenly afraid, she let him sweep her along to the taxi rank. They got into a cab, and he asked the driver to take them to Marble Arch. The Lyons Corner House was there, a huge white building with restaurants on several floors, where you could be anonymous. It was better than a hotel, where someone you knew might see you, and the food, although simple, was always good. There was even one restaurant where there were still Nippies, the bright young waitresses who had made such a name for themselves for their good, quick service, before the war had swept them all into the services and left diners to queue up with trays as if they were in a canteen.

David found a corner table, behind a potted palm. There was a gipsy band playing, and it was almost like the old days. They ordered their lunch and then looked at each other.

'How have you been?' he asked at last, folding both his hands around hers.

'Missing you,' she said. 'Missing you terribly. Oh David, I think it was the worst Christmas I've ever had.'

'For me too.' He paused. 'Your father – how is he?'

'Better, I think. But each time he has one of these attacks, I'm afraid it will be the last. It will be one day, won't it? You're a doctor. You know.'

'Yes, it very probably will,' he agreed. 'But it needn't be for a long while yet. With care...'

'That's just it. He doesn't want to take care. And there are the things he can't control anyway – Rob, and Marianne. And Stephen. Even me, I suppose,' she finished a little despondently. 'Though I think he does more than he realises.'

'He always has. He's a manipulator, Hilary. He knows just how to control you, by appealing to your sense of obligation and your feeling for him as your father.'

'Perhaps. But I can't just abandon him. If I did

317

and he had another attack – or even died – I'd never forgive myself.'

'I know, darling. It would haunt you all your life. And don't worry – I won't ask you to do that. I'll never ask you to do anything you might regret.' He paused again, and Hilary looked more closely at his face, noticing the new lines that had been etched there in the short time since she had last seen him. There was a tautness in his jaw too, and she felt a sudden pang of fear.

'And what about you?' she asked. 'You said you had things to tell me. What are they, David?'

Their food arrived and they sat back, watching it being placed in front of them, thanking the waitress, longing for her to leave them. Finally, she did, and Hilary repeated her question. 'What do you have to tell me, David?'

He picked up his knife and fork, then laid them down again. He looked into her eyes and she saw the shadows there. Her fear increased and she clasped her hands together, waiting in agony for him to speak. 'Is it Sybil?' she asked at last, and he nodded.

'Yes. It's...' He stumbled, then started again. 'Hilary ... Sybil has asked me for a divorce.'

Stella slept for the rest of the visiting hour and at last Felix had to go without being able to speak to her again. He bent and kissed her cheek very softly, without disturbing her, and left the ward with the rest of the visitors. Feeling rather depressed, he walked to the station and caught the branch line train, travelling through darkness along the valley to the Little Burracombe halt, where he got off and walked through the lanes to the vicarage.

To his surprise, there were lights on in the house and the front door was on the latch. He pushed it open and went indoors, expecting to find one of his parishioners there, but it was Tessa Latimer who emerged from the kitchen, her dark hair tumbling loose around her shoulders and her face flushed. She smiled at him and said, 'Surprise! I thought you might be pleased to find a hot supper waiting for you when you got home.'

'Well ... yes. That's very nice,' he said, non-plussed. 'But how did you know when I'd be back? And how did you get in?'

'Oh, the verger let me in. And I knew you must have gone to visit Stella, so I guessed when you'd be here. I've got a casserole in the oven, and jacket potatoes, so we can eat whenever you're ready.' She smiled at him again. 'But I expect you want to freshen up first, and maybe you'd like a drink. It's not a nice journey from Plymouth in the middle of winter.'

'A cup of tea would be welcome,' he said, but she shook her head.

'I was thinking of something stronger! A gin and tonic, perhaps, or maybe a whisky. You've got both in your cupboard – I had a peep.' Her dimples showed. 'There's sherry and port as well – you're very well stocked for a vicar!'

'I've just had my family staying for Christmas,' he said, still bemused. 'Well – maybe a sherry, then.' He remembered his manners. 'And you'll have one too, won't you?'

'But of course. I'll fetch it.' She flicked out of

the room, her dark red skirt swirling about her legs. Felix made his way into the kitchen, which was filled with the enticing aroma of simmering beef and vegetables, and sat down at the end of the table. He did not feel equal to inviting Tessa into the drawing room. He rested his head on one hand and tried to think what to do next. The young woman evidently expected to stay and eat with him, and then there would be the question of taking her home. I'll have to walk her across the Clam, he thought, and envisaged a trudge down through the lanes, across the river and up the other side to Burracombe and then back again.

He felt almost overwhelmingly tired.

Tess came dancing in with the sherry bottle and two glasses. She poured generous shots and sat down at the side of the table, close to him. She lifted her glass and twinkled her dark blue eyes.

'Happy New Year, Felix. It's not too soon to wish you that, is it?'

'I don't think so. And I hope it will be a happy year.' He realised that his voice lacked conviction, and added with a somewhat forced enthusiasm, 'Happy New Year to you too, Tessa.'

'How is Stella now?' she asked in a sympathetic voice. 'Is she getting any better?'

'Oh yes. A lot better.' Felix was determined to put a brave face on in public. 'She goes through bad patches, of course. Nobody knows quite how long it's all going to take, and I think that gets her down a little, but on the whole she's doing very well.'

'Dad says she has some paralysis.'

'Yes, she has.' Felix felt a flash of anger towards

Dr Latimer, before realising that most people probably knew this by now. 'It's not going to last, though.' He quashed his own worries as he spoke the words.

'Oh, is that true? I'm so pleased. Only he thought it might be permanent. Such a shame, if she could never walk again – and so difficult for you. I mean, a vicar's wife has to be such a help to him, doesn't she?'

'Stella will be a help to me whether she can walk or not,' Felix said shortly. 'But I feel quite certain that she will walk again.' He finished his sherry. 'That casserole smells very good. Did you make it yourself?'

'I did!' Tessa drained her glass too and jumped up. 'It's ready now, if you are. And the potatoes too. I'll dish it up, shall I?'

'I'll just go and wash first.' Felix escaped to the little cloakroom at the end of the hall and locked himself in. He leaned against the wall for a moment, trying to calm himself. The casserole did indeed smell good, and he knew he would enjoy it, for he was very hungry, but just then he felt that he would rather have a crust of dry bread and a glass of water on his own than share a meal, however delicious, with Tessa Latimer. He knew perfectly well what she was trying to do, with her tumbling hair, her tight white blouse and flaring red skirt, and her sherry and casserole, and he knew that he was quite immune to her overt charms, but it was still a difficult situation for him. She could not be left to walk home alone, she certainly could not stay at the vicarage, and he had no wish to find himself walking the dark lanes with her clinging to his arm. Over and above it all, he was desperately tired and still very anxious about Stella and the mood she'd been in this afternoon. He'd put it down to pain and depression over the accident, but a small voice was telling him that it might not be entirely due to that. It might be something else...

'It's ready!' Tessa trilled from the kitchen, and he roused himself, washed his hands and went back.

The food was on the table, a rich beef stew glowing with golden carrots, and hearty jacket potatoes as an accompaniment. Felix looked at it and decided to put his worries aside until he had eaten. Things always looked better after food. And maybe some other solution would occur to him. Perhaps he was exaggerating the situation anyway.

'I've poured you another sherry,' Tessa said, smiling and dimpling as she sat down. 'I looked for wine but you don't seem to have any. Cheers!'

'Cheers,' Felix said, raising his glass, and began to attack his dinner.

Chapter Twenty-Five

'A *divorce?*' Hilary stared at David. 'But ... why?'

He shrugged and lifted his hands. 'Because she's Sybil. Because she always likes to deal out surprises, especially around Christmas.' He paused. 'And because she knows about us. Or thinks she does.'

322

Hilary felt her heart plummet. '*Knows* about us? But how?'

'Your father wrote to me,' he said heavily. 'To thank me for collecting Rob at Paddington when he ran away. Presumably you gave him my address.'

'Well, yes, I did,' Hilary said miserably. 'I couldn't see any way of refusing when he asked for it. But how could that make Sybil know about us? Father doesn't suspect a thing, I'm sure he doesn't. David, I'm so sorry.'

David squeezed her hand. 'It's not your fault. And it was a perfectly ordinary letter. There was nothing in it to make anyone suspicious. It's just that Sybil saw it – she must have been going through my post – and jumped to conclusions. He mentioned you, of course, and the fact that we were friends, and that was enough. She accused me of having an affair and – well, I couldn't deny it. Even if I had, she wouldn't have believed me.'

Hilary was silent for a moment, trying to assimilate his story. At last she said, 'But you told me that you and Sybil were living more or less separate lives anyway. She has her own lovers. Why should it matter to her what you do?'

'Because Sybil having her lovers is a very different matter from me having mine. Not that I've ever had any before,' he added quickly. 'I never wanted to. And I don't consider you an "affair", anyway – what we have is far deeper than that. But other people might not see it that way.' He paused again. 'Apart from that, it's not just to do with us. It's far more to do with Sybil.'

'What do you mean?'

'Her latest lover,' he said a little grimly, 'is rather more serious than the rest. He's also a good deal richer – a businessman in Derby, driving a Daimler and living in a big house. And Sybil wants to marry him.'

The waitress appeared beside them, casting an anxious glance at their untouched plates. 'Is everything all right, sir? Would you rather choose something else?'

'No, it's quite all right, thank you,' David assured her, and Hilary shook her head. The girl smiled doubtfully and left, and David picked up his knife and fork. 'We'd better make an effort, I suppose. Maybe this wasn't the best place to come after all.'

'We had to go somewhere.' Hilary poked about with her fork. 'But surely, if Sybil wants to marry this man, it should be you divorcing her.'

'She doesn't see it that way. She has no intention of being the guilty party – that's why your father's letter came as such a godsend to her. No, she wants to hold me up as the errant husband, with herself as the long-suffering angel of a wife, which will also mean a good divorce settlement awarded to her and leave me penniless and with my career in ruins.'

Hilary put down her fork and stared at him. 'David, that's terrible. Could she really do that?'

'Of course she could. And she will, too. Sybil is nothing if not vindictive. But there's one thing I won't allow.' His voice tightened. 'And that's for her to drag your name through the mud too. I won't have her naming you.'

Hilary lifted a hand to her forehead. 'David, can we go? I can't take this in – not here, with all this noise.' The chatter of other diners and the strains of the gipsy band, which had given them a measure of privacy, had turned into something very like torture.

David lifted his hand and the waitress hurried over. 'My friend isn't feeling well,' he said. 'Could I have the bill, please?'

'Of course, sir.' She hurried away and Hilary stood up, shakily enough to convince the girl that David's explanation was true. She did indeed feel nauseous, and her head was spinning. David helped her with her coat and she waited, trembling slightly, while he paid the bill and took her arm to lead her out. Once on the pavement, they looked at each other.

'It's too cold for the park,' he said. 'Can we go to your hotel?'

'But that could be the worst thing we could do. Suppose Sybil's having you followed? She'd have evidence straight away.'

He rubbed his face distractedly. 'This is crazy. We've got to find somewhere to talk. I can't leave you without having made some decision.'

'Let's just walk,' she said dispiritedly, and he nodded and took her hand. But even that felt dangerous, and she slid her fingers away, tears pouring down her cheeks. They took a few steps and then he glanced at her, saw the tears and stopped, grabbing roughly at her hand again.

'I'm not going to let her stop me doing this. I don't care if we are being followed – she's made her threats anyway.' For a moment, she thought he was going to pull her into his arms, but he hesitated, then drew back, still keeping hold of her hand. 'We'll walk down to the Embankment and along the river.'

The Thames was cold and grey, moving sluggishly between its banks, with a thin wind skittering across the water to sting their faces with an icy spatter of rain. They turned left to pass Cleopatra's Needle, and Hilary pulled her scarf over her chin. She glanced up at David. His face was cold, his expression remote, and fear twisted her heart. Was this the end?

'What are you going to do?' she asked. 'If she really wants to marry this man...'

'Oh, she does. There's no doubt about that. I told you, he's rich. A far better catch than a mere family doctor. But I think she'd allow me a little leeway in how it's done.'

'What do you mean?'

He sighed. 'She wants her divorce and she doesn't care who's hurt while she gets it. But she might not insist on involving you. It could be done quietly – the usual way.'

Hilary stopped and looked at him. 'You mean a hotel. Some woman who'd want payment and a chambermaid finding you in bed together in the morning. David, you can't do that!'

'I don't see what else I can do.'

'But it's horrible. It's sleazy and disgusting. And what sort of woman would do it anyway? I can't bear to think of it.'

'I wouldn't spend the night with her,' he said. 'I'd sit in a chair all night. We'd only be in bed for a few minutes.'

'No!' She covered her ears with her hands. 'No, you can't! Not even for a few minutes. David, *please...*'

'If I don't,' he said, 'she'll cite you.'

'But she doesn't know anything about me!'

'She knows you exist. She knows you know me, well enough to know I was in London that day, well enough to help you with Rob.'

'That's not proof.'

They stopped and leaned on the Embankment wall, looking across the river towards the Festival Hall, which had been built just three years earlier. David wrapped his arm around her shoulders and spoke quietly.

'Darling, she doesn't need proof. She can simply threaten to cite you. You'd receive a summons and your name would be made public. You'd have to prove your innocence.' He paused, and she knew they were both thinking that this was impossible. 'She'll drag you through the courts and through the newspapers,' he said. 'Can't you imagine it? A doctor and the daughter of an army colonel and landowner? They'd have a field day.'

Hilary was silent. She knew that it was true. Divorce in such circumstances always made the newspapers. 'And you'd be struck off,' she said.

'Yes, probably. The BMA doesn't take kindly to scandal in the medical profession.'

'But it's so unfair!' she cried. 'You and Sybil haven't been properly married for years. Why does she have to be so spiteful?'

'Because she's Sybil.' He sighed again. 'It's my own fault. I've been so much happier since we met again, and she can't have failed to notice it,

327

or to guess why. Your father's letter simply confirmed suspicions she already had. If she hadn't met this man, she'd have simply turned a blind eye. But she'd have stored up the information, just in case she ever needed to use it. This was always on the cards, you know – that she'd leave me as soon as she met someone who was able to give her more, and serious about doing it. I always knew I was living on thin ice.'

'But to ruin your career...'

'It would have ruined my career whenever it happened,' he said. 'Fairness doesn't come into it.'

There was another long silence. The wind blew a sudden gust, and Hilary shivered. They walked on and crossed Waterloo Bridge, making their way vaguely through the streets towards Lambeth.

'You can still see so much of the bombing here,' Hilary remarked as they passed a wasteland that had once been houses, shops and offices. 'It'll take years and years to rebuild everything.' Her own words sounded meaningless in her ears; she hardly knew what she was saying. 'They've done a lot in Plymouth, though. Was there much bombing in Derby? I don't really know much about that part of the country, I'm afraid. I know about Coventry, of course, but–'

'Hilary, stop it!' He gripped her arm so tightly that she winced. They stopped and this time he did pull her into his arms, holding her tightly against him. 'Darling, I can't bear it.'

'Neither can I,' she whispered, burying her face against his coat. 'David, what are we going to do?'

'What we can't do,' he said, 'what I won't *let* her do, is drag you through this. It would ruin both our lives. It would destroy your reputation for a start, you'd have to leave Burracombe and it would kill your father. Neither of us could live with that on our consciences.'

'But if you don't,' she said, 'you'll have to do it the other way. And I can't live with that, either.' She raised her head and looked at him hopelessly. 'I just don't know what we *can* do.'

They stood for a few moments in the cold, empty street, a bleak wind cutting across the waste ground from the river and chilling their bones. Above them, the sky was the same muddy grey as the water, with clouds like bruises scudding close to the tops of the tall buildings of Westminster which could be glimpsed past the bridge. Hilary felt as if the desolation of it all were settling into her heart, and her whole body ached with the tears she longed to shed.

'It's going to destroy your career anyway, isn't it?' she said at last. 'You won't be able to practise any more whatever happens.'

'There are other things I could do. Laboratory work – research, perhaps. I could still earn a living.'

'But your reputation will have gone too. Oh David, it's so cruel.'

'Divorce is a cruel thing,' he said. 'It's such a hard law. The only grounds apart from adultery are cruelty or insanity. Even Sybil can't accuse me of either of those, so it has to be adultery, and even if I were to divorce her – and God knows, I've plenty of cause – my own situation wouldn't be any better. And she'd cite you anyway, so we'd still be dragged through it all – the courts, the newspapers. It would be even worse than it is now.'

'Could we go abroad? I've heard of people doing that, living quietly somewhere. We wouldn't need much money – I don't need expensive clothes or jewellery.'

'And how would your father feel about that?' he asked, and she sighed.

'I know. Whichever way we turn, we come up against another brick wall. I don't know what to suggest.'

They walked on again, slowly, still hand in hand, as they tried to find a solution. By the time they reached Westminster Bridge, they were no further forward, and as they stopped and looked up at Big Ben, Hilary said, 'We're going to have to call her bluff.'

David looked at her. 'What do you mean?'

She shrugged slightly. 'Refuse her. Tell her she can't have a divorce. She hasn't any real proof – a letter from my father thanking you for meeting Rob will never stand up in court as evidence of adultery. We met innocently at the reunion, where we also met a lot of other people, and nobody but us knows any more than that. She's just trying to frighten you, David, and you're not going to let her do it. *We're* not going to let her do it.' She lifted her chin and met his gaze. 'If Sybil wants to marry this other man, she'll have to find some other way to do it, some way that doesn't ruin your life.'

'And if there isn't any other way?'

'Then she'll just have to stay where she is.'

'But that's not what we want!' he burst out. 'If she stays with me, we can never be together.'

'I know,' Hilary said quietly. 'But I think in our hearts we always knew that.'

David looked at her intently. He took both her hands in his, and his eyes narrowed as he said, 'Are you saying we must never meet again? Because from now on, I'm quite sure Sybil will never take her eyes off me. She'll have me followed wherever I go in her attempts to get proof that she can use against me.'

Hilary's gaze faltered, but she lifted her chin again and replied, 'Yes, I think that must be what I'm saying.' Her voice strengthened a little. 'I *won't* have your life and career and all you've worked for ruined for this, David. You're a fine doctor – I know that from what I knew of you during the war – and it would be criminal to put an end to that, for you and for the people you help. I won't let it happen.' Her fingers tightened around his. 'I love you and I always will, but I can't allow all that to happen to you, simply because we met at the wrong time. It would spoil all that we have.'

'And all that we thought we could have in the future,' he said. 'That's spoiled too. Can we really throw it all away?'

'It's not being thrown away. It's being set aside.' She met his eyes once more. 'Nothing stays the same for ever, David. Things change. In five years, ten years, even one year, it might all be different again. We just have to wait.'

'It may be too long to wait,' he said. 'The change

331

may come too late. Hilary, please don't say this is the end.'

'It's not the end,' she said. 'It's never going to be the end, because we'll always love each other, whatever happens.' And then she broke into a storm of weeping and he took her into his arms and held her close, in the middle of Westminster Bridge, with the majesty of London all about them and the grey waters of the Thames flowing beneath, and Big Ben striking the hour high above their heads; a sonorous, ringing tone that neither of them would ever forget.

Chapter Twenty-Six

The doorbell rang just as Felix had decided, reluctantly, that there was nothing for it but to walk Tessa home through the cold, dark lanes. He had strung the meal out as long as possible, answering all her questions about Stella and what might be done about the wedding, refused her suggestion that they go into the drawing room – 'we'd be more comfortable there, and I lit the fire before you came home, so it'll be nice and warm' – and offered her tea or coffee at the kitchen table. There was nothing else he could think of to keep her at arm's length, and he was on the point of going for their coats when the jangling sound in the hall announced the arrival of another visitor.

Felix's heart sank. He prayed that it would not

be Olivia Lydiard, or some other parishioner who might put an unfortunate construction on Tessa's presence, and went to answer it.

Charles Latimer stood on the doorstep, the shoulders of his dark winter coat lightly sprinkled with sleet. Looking past him, Felix saw that his car stood in the drive, and his heart soared.

'Hello, Felix,' the doctor said. 'I've come to take my daughter home. I assume she's still here.'

'Yes, she is,' Felix said with relief. 'Come in. I was just about to suggest we walk home, since I've not got a car now.'

'Were you?' Charles asked in surprise, wiping his feet on the doormat. 'Didn't she tell you I was coming for her? I told her I would – knew you wouldn't feel like that long walk at this time of night. How are things at the hospital?' He un-wound his scarf.

'Oh – getting better, slowly.' Felix remembered his manners. 'Would you like a drink? Something hot? Or maybe a whisky?'

The doctor shook his head. 'We'll get straight off, if you don't mind. I'm sure you're too tired to entertain any more this evening. By the way, Mary said you're to keep the casserole – there should be enough for you to have another decent meal out of it tomorrow. You won't need to be disturbed a second time.' He gave Felix a glance which spoke volumes, and Felix realised that Charles Latimer was under no illusions about his daughter. He grinned back, trying to appear non-committal but afraid that he was failing miserably.

At that moment the kitchen door opened and

Tessa emerged, looking none too pleased to see her father, who was already taking her coat from the hallstand. He held it for her to slip her arms into, and she smiled and dimpled at Felix.

'It was lovely to have supper with you,' she said, as if she'd been invited specially. 'I'll come again, shall I?'

'That probably won't be necessary,' her father said. 'Felix must have an army of parishioners only too happy to provide him with hot meals, and I expect he wants to have some time to himself when he comes back from the hospital. Apart from which, he's a busy vicar and no doubt has all manner of parish affairs to occupy his time.'

'Oh, but he must want *some* time off,' she began, and then fell silent as she caught a look from her father. 'I'll see you again soon, anyway,' she added. 'I really do want to know how Stella gets on.'

'Go and wait for me in the car for a minute,' Charles said, and watched her go. He turned back to Felix. 'I probably need to apologise for my daughter. She still has some growing up to do, I'm afraid.'

'It's perfectly all right. She's been good company. I just don't think she quite realises how some of what she says and does could be construed.'

'Mm. Perhaps.' The doctor didn't sound convinced. 'Anyway, tell me about Stella. You said "slowly". Is there some further concern about her?'

'I don't know. Physically I think she's doing quite well, apart from the lack of feeling in her legs, which the doctor does seem to think will come back in time. But...' He hesitated.

'Mentally?' Charles offered, and Felix sighed.

'I'm worried about her,' he confessed. 'She seems depressed, and irritable. Not like her usual self at all.'

'That's quite normal, you know. She's bound to have these ups and downs. She's been through an enormous shock.'

'I know. It's just – well, I've got a nasty feeling there's more to it than that.' He looked at the doctor apologetically. 'I can't put my finger on it, and I may even be imagining it. But I'm terribly afraid that there's more wrong than anyone knows at the moment. And there doesn't seem to be a thing I can do to help her.'

Dottie, serving in the bar of the Bell Inn, was also worried about Stella.

'I know it's early days,' she said to Rose and Bernie as they opened up and waited for customers to arrive, 'but I slipped in to see her this afternoon, just before young Felix arrived, and her was proper quiet. She've got something on her mind, it's plain to see.'

'She's been through a bad time, though,' Rose pointed out, unknowingly echoing the doctor's words. 'It's bound to take its toll. There's always some reaction.'

Bernie came back from unbolting the side door and nodded his head. 'Stella's a fine young woman. Her'll pull through all right, you'll see. You must know that, Dottie – you know her better than almost anyone here, except for the young vicar, of course.'

335

Dottie nodded, but she still looked pensive. 'You'm right, but nobody knows even now just how bad those injuries of hers were.'

'Still, us got to look on the bright side,' he insisted. 'And here come our first customers, so don't let's show 'em a long face. Evening, Jacob, and what'll yours be? Usual?'

Jacob Prout carried his tankard to the inglenook by the fire and took out his pipe. His daytime smoking was Woodbines from a crumpled green packet, but in the evenings he liked to get his pipe going. It was more relaxing, he claimed. Wreathed in a cloud of smoke, he said: 'Weather be brewing up again. Bit more snow on its way, if you asks me.'

'Gawd, I hope not,' Ted Tozer said, coming in just in time to hear Jacob's forecast. 'It's been trouble enough getting out to the stock up on the moor as it is, these past two weeks. Us can do with a bit of dry weather now to stiffen up the ground.'

Joe and Russell followed him in, stamping and blowing on their fingers. They asked for the local brew, and Dottie poured out the glasses and handed them over the bar. Joe paid, and as he gave her the money their eyes met and she felt herself colour. Since their long talk by her fireside, soon after Stella's accident, they'd had little time alone together, but she knew that he would want to see her again before he and Russ said goodbye to Burracombe. She was fairly certain that she'd convinced him that she wasn't likely to go to America herself – unless perhaps for a short visit – but she wasn't quite so certain that she'd convinced herself.

Since that talk, Dottie had found herself un-accountably restless. Part of it, she was sure, was due to her anxiety over Stella, but she'd also caught herself more than once thinking more about the town that Joe had made his home, and wondering about it. A small town like Tavistock, yet with a department store three storeys high – what could that be like? And the big glass factory too – how could it be in the least like Tavistock? And yet the country all around Tavistock had been a busy industrial area once, with copper and tin mines everywhere, and the canal that had been built over a hundred years ago, specially to carry the ore to the ships on the River Tamar at Morwellham. It hadn't always been just a peace-ful market town.

Dottie knew that her heart lay in Burracombe and the moors and fields and woods all around it. As a girl, she had walked them all, often with Joe Tozer, and although she had gone willingly to London to work in the theatres there, she had often thought wistfully of the amethyst glow of the heather and the burning gold of the gorse, and longed to return. She could never settle anywhere else – and never in another land altogether.

Yet she couldn't help being curious about Corn-ing. It would be nice to go there – just for a visit – and see where Joe lived. See where he'd built his life, worked and brought up a family. See his home, so that she could picture it when she was home again, sitting by her own fire and dreaming of what might have been.

It might help settle a ghost or two, she thought,

because as sure as God made little apples, she would know for certain then that she would never have been happy there. She would know she'd made the right decision, all those years ago.

'Be you going to hypnotise that old beer-pump into giving me another drink?' Jacob's voice demanded in her ear. 'Or be you practising for when they puts your waxwork in Madame Two-Swords? Whichever it is, I'll have another pint, if you don't mind me interrupting.'

Dottie jumped and laughed. 'Sorry, Jacob. I was miles away.' Her eyes met Joe's again, and she flicked her glance away and turned to attend to the other customers who had just come in. 'Now, gentlemen, what can I do for you?'

Joe grinned at his son and indicated a table towards the back of the room. 'Let's take our drinks over there, and me and Ted can have a game of dominoes. We shan't get that many more chances.'

Russ followed his father and uncle to the table, but his mind wasn't on the game. He was thinking of Maddy and wondering how she was getting on back in West Lyme. He was still feeling the disappointment that she had gone back without saying goodbye to him; their last meeting had been at church on Sunday morning, when she had given his hand a warm squeeze and smiled into his eyes before being whisked off by Stephen Napier, and Russ had felt a chill finger touch his heart, as if that had been their real goodbye.

Aunt Alice had told him not to count his chickens, but he'd been reluctant to take her advice. He and Maddy had – he thought – become

338

close during those night-time drives to and from the hospital and those long waits in the bare corridors. She had almost promised to come over to Corning for a visit, and he'd believed that once he got her away from Burracombe, she would be his. Now he was less sure, and he didn't like the feeling.

Until now, Russell Tozer's life had run smoothly. He'd grown up in a loving household with happy, hard-working parents and two sisters who had idolised their brother. At school he had shone both academically and in the sports he loved, and he'd had his pick of the high-school girls. He'd had two quite serious relationships that had ended amicably, and he had felt himself ready to settle down. When he met Maddy, he'd thought he'd found the girl he wanted to settle down with.

And now she was slipping through his grasp. That final handshake had been more like a wave from a ship that was disappearing over the horizon, and his chances of bringing her back were slim.

But not entirely gone, he told himself, staring into his ale. He was still here, in Burracombe, and Maddy was only a couple of hours' drive away. Napier was further than that, tied to his RAF station and unable to leave it for at least a fortnight. Russ wouldn't be much of a man if he didn't take the chance that was still there, offered to him on a plate.

'My stars, what's got into everyone tonight?' Jacob grumbled. 'Move something, boy, for pity's sake, unless you been frozen to the spot just like Dottie. I'd be better off playing with snails than you lot.'

'Sorry, Jacob,' Russ said, returning his attention to the game. 'I was just thinking, that's all... It seems hardly any time since we arrived in Burracombe, yet it's like a second home now. I'm not sure I want to go back just yet.'

'That's you and me both,' Joe replied, his glance drifting towards the bar where Dottie was still pulling pints and laughing at a joke Bert Foster had just made. 'I'm not sure I want to go back at all.'

Jackie Tozer had no doubts at all about going to America. She was at the farm now, going through her cupboards with Alice, trying to decide what she should take with her.

'It's not as if you'm going for the duration,' Alice said, frowning as she saw the pile of clothes on Jackie's bed. ''Tis only a bit of a holiday.'

'It's a bit more than that, Mum. I'll be there at least a couple of months. I'm going to get a job and work for a while, remember.'

'You won't be staying too long, though, will you, maid?' Alice begged her. 'You know I'll worry about you the whole time.'

Jackie sighed. 'You don't need to do that. I'll be with Uncle Joe and the family, and Corning's not like New York.'

'It's in New York State.'

'Yes, but that's a huge place, about the size of – of Wales,' Jackie said, with no real idea of the size of an American state. 'And it's mostly countryside, just like here. The city's a long way off.'

Alice looked unconvinced. 'I dunno. The nearer

it gets, the more I don't like it. I wish now us'd never said yes.'

'Well, you did and that's all there is to it.' Jackie slapped a pile of jumpers on the bed impatiently. 'Look, it's not fair to send me off knowing that you're worrying about me. It makes me feel guilty. How am I going to enjoy it, thinking of you being upset all the time? Why can't you just let me go with a smile on your face? I bet that's what Granny did when Uncle Joe went.'

'Her didn't smile much that I can remember,' Alice said, but privately she knew that Minnie hadn't grumbled much either. She'd been too relieved that her son had survived the First World War and the 'flu epidemic that followed it to complain that he was going to live on the other side of the world. Maybe Jackie was right; maybe she should be pleased that her daughter was happy, doing what she wanted to do with her life, even though it didn't seem to involve staying at home, getting married and having children as Alice herself had done.

'All right,' she said. 'I'll stop worrying, if I can. And if I can't, I'll stop telling you about it. I can't do no more than that. And I hope you enjoy yourself – I do, really.'

Jackie turned and gave her mother a quick kiss. 'Thanks, Mum.' She paused, then spoke more quietly. 'I know it's not easy for you, and I know you can't help worrying. But I promise I'll be careful. I won't do anything you and Dad wouldn't like, and I'll write to you every week and tell you how I'm getting on. And I *will* come back. I promise I will.'

341

Alice gazed at her and hoped this was true. But she knew in her heart that this was a promise nobody could give. Life changed, people changed, and travel seemed to change them both, more quickly and in different ways than anyone could predict. She knew that her fears could easily come true – Jackie might go to America and find her own heart and home there, just as Joe had done, and never return. And there would be nothing that Alice, Ted or anyone else could do about it.

Chapter Twenty-Seven

Hilary spent a lonely, sleepless night in her hotel and caught the train home next morning feeling heavy-eyed and lacklustre. Her world seemed to have crumbled around her; everything that she had dreamed of and hoped for in the past few months had come to nothing. Even though she had known that a life with David was almost certainly impossible, she had clung to the hope that it might somehow happen. Now that hope had been destroyed, and she felt cold and empty, no more than a shell.

After hours of walking and talking together, their conclusion had been inescapable. Hilary would not allow David's life and career to be ruined, and David could not contemplate the damage to Hilary's reputation, not to mention her father's health, that a scandal would bring. And scandal there would certainly be: a divorce following an affair between a doctor and the daughter of a prominent army officer and landowner would be juicy meat for the newspapers, who would descend on both Derby and Burracombe as they reported the court proceedings. The thought of their probing questions asked throughout the village, in the Bell Inn, the village shops, even the lanes as Norman Tozer drove the cows to the milking sheds and Jacob Prout went about his work, brought hot and cold waves of dread to Hilary, and she knew that she could never inflict this on the village she loved.

'Why does it have to be like this?' she asked David miserably, as they stood together at Euston station, waiting for his train. 'Just because we love each other, we turn into criminals.'

'Well, not quite,' he said. 'We can't be put in prison for it.'

'We might as well be. You're in prison, trapped with Sybil, and I'm in prison in Burracombe.' She listened to her own words with a sense of amazement. Burracombe, a prison? And yet, in a way, it always had been – ever since she had come home to look after her mother and then stayed for her father's sake. 'Every time I try to get away, something happens to stop me,' she said. 'Until now, because I love the estate and the village, I've let it. But this time... David, I don't know how I'm going to bear it. I *can't* let you go!'

'Don't let's go through it all again,' he said. 'We've decided what we must do. If I go home now, and try to make Sybil see sense, there might be some way out. If she'd only give up this idea of marrying again... She can see this man whenever she likes, so long as she's discreet about it.

343

It's what she's always done up to now, after all.'

'But now there's money involved,' Hilary observed. 'He's wealthy. That's the difference, isn't it?'

'I'm afraid it is. I can't believe she wants a scandal, though, any more than we do. I'm sure that what she said is just bluff – and fury that I've found someone else. She always thought she had me just where she wanted me, and suddenly she's found she hasn't. That's a large part of the trouble.'

'So you'll go home and be the dutiful husband again.'

He looked at her in sudden pain. 'Don't say it like that, darling! If it were just me, I'd say to hell with her – tell her to do her worst. But I can't drag you through all that. I can't.'

'And I can't let her destroy all you've built up,' she said sadly. 'So there we are. Back in the same cleft stick. And no chance of ever being together.'

'I won't say that. I've got to have some hope, even if it's only a shred.'

'But we're not going to see each other again, are we?' she said quietly. 'We're not even going to talk on the phone – or write. It's over. Sybil's won.'

Their eyes met and then they were in each other's arms, clinging tightly as Hilary's tears broke out and she sobbed against his coat. Regardless of the people swirling about them, they kissed, knowing that this must be the last time, that this was goodbye. Meeting again would be far too dangerous – if Sybil weren't already having David followed, she would certainly do so on any future trips to London. At the thought, Hilary pulled away, suddenly afraid that even now they were being watched, perhaps even photographed.

'Go now, please, David,' she said breathlessly. 'Please...' And then they heard the whistle of the train and knew that in a few minutes it would be pulling away from the platform. For a long moment they stared at each other, then they reached out their hands to touch one last time, and then with anguish in his eyes he turned away and vanished in the crowd.

Hilary stood quite still, watching as the throng swept through the gates and along the platforms to their various trains. David was lost to sight; she thought she caught a glimpse of his head as he boarded the train, but it could as easily have been another man. The next second, he disappeared in a cloud of steam and she started forward, as if to call him back, but the train was already moving and she knew it was too late.

It was always too late for us, she thought, turning away. From the moment we first met, in Egypt, when he was engaged to Sybil and I was engaged to Henry, it was already too late. We should have known it from the start.

It was late evening. David had caught the last train to Derby and there was nothing for her to do but make her way back to her hotel. He had wanted to see her back there after they had eaten dinner in a tiny Greek restaurant, but she had insisted on going to Euston with him, to eke out their last moments together. Now she took a taxi back and went straight to her room, to lie sleepless and aching with tears, until at last morning slumped grey and chilly through the window and she could catch her own train home.

Travis met her at Tavistock station and cast a concerned look at her face. 'You look worn out, Hilary. Is everything all right? Did Madame Aucoin and the children have problems with their tickets or something?'

'No, everything went fine,' she assured him, realising that she'd almost forgotten the official reason for her journey to London. 'Rob seemed a bit upset to be leaving, but I think he was looking forward to going home and seeing all his old friends there. It's a pity it didn't work out for him here.'

'It was all too sudden for him, and he's really too young to be uprooted like that. I'm sure he'll value his time here as he gets older.' Travis dropped her small travelling bag into the back of the Land Rover. 'I think it was right that he should go back. Not that it's any of my business,' he added with an apologetic grin, 'but Jen and I saw quite a lot of him, and we're fond of him. I think you did the right thing in letting him go.'

'I do too,' she said, and smiled back. 'Rob was very unhappy at that school. I know the school itself is good and the masters fair, but some of those rituals the boys carried out were nothing short of torture. Boys brought up in this country, knowing others who have already been through it, know what to expect, but it came as a shock to Rob and he couldn't take it, on top of all the other changes we'd forced upon him.'

'They'd have come as a shock to me too,' Travis

said as they drove down Kilworthy Hill into the town, 'but then I didn't grow up in such rarefied circles. I was just a simple country boy who went to the local grammar school.'

'And I think Rob would have been better off to have done the same,' Hilary said. 'What my father can't see is that Rob's home in France is very different from ours here. His family is more like Micky Coker's, and he gets on well with boys from that background. But to Father, that's something that should be severely discouraged.'

There was a short silence, then Travis glanced at her and said, 'So if that's not what's made you look so tired, I wonder what is? You don't have to tell me if you don't want to – I'm only the estate manager. But I like to think we're friends as well.'

'We are,' she said, and leaned her head back, closing her eyes. 'But there's nothing – nothing I can talk about now, at any rate. Maybe one day...'

He nodded. 'If you ever feel like it, just say. Whatever it is, it won't go any further. You know that.' He shot her another quick look. 'Sometimes it helps to talk things over.'

Hilary smiled faintly but didn't reply. They drove in silence for a few minutes, and then Travis began to talk casually about the estate and their plans for the coming year. Things were changing in farming, and they needed to keep up with the changes, whether good or bad. The effects of the war were still being felt, in the country as in the cities, and nobody could afford to cling to the old ways any more.

Hilary listened and responded, but her mind was still half with David, back in Derby now, and won-

347

dering how he was dealing with the situation Sybil was forcing upon him. She still could not believe that they had parted, agreeing not to communicate again, not knowing if or when they would ever meet again. It would have been better if we'd never met, she thought, better if neither of us had gone to that reunion. So short a time ago, yet so much had happened since. It was as if a long-delayed time bomb had finally had its ignition struck and had exploded, with dramatic results.

They arrived at the Barton and Travis drove straight round to the yard. He handed her her travelling bag and turned to climb back into the Land Rover, but paused first, his eyes on her face.

'Remember what I said,' he told her quietly. 'If you need to talk, Jen and I are here. And – take care of yourself.'

Hilary smiled and nodded. 'Thanks, Travis. I will.'

She turned to go into the house, through the back door and boot room and into the kitchen, where Mrs Ellis was preparing lunch. After a few words of greeting and an enquiry about her father, she went straight upstairs to her room, closed the door, and lay down on the bed, her arms crossed above her head.

Travis was right. She needed to talk to somebody, somebody who would listen to her story and not be shocked. But it wasn't Travis, or even Jennifer, that she would talk to. She knew just who would be sympathetic, who would listen and not judge, who might not be able to advise her – who could? – but who would stand by her and support her.

At the first opportunity, she would go and see her friend Val Ferris.

Val, however, was not available just then. Over Christmas she had caught a cold, and it had developed into bronchitis. She was in bed, with red eyes and nose, and a grating cough, when Hilary called at Jed's Cottage the next day.

Luke answered the door, with baby Christopher in his arms. He looked tired, as if he'd been up all night, but he invited Hilary in and gave her the news about Val before returning to his task of feeding the baby with a bowl of what looked like porridge.

'It's Farex,' he explained. 'We put him on it just before Christmas. Just as well, too, as Val daren't feed him or even see him at present in case he catches her cold.'

'Oh, poor Val!' Hilary exclaimed, her own troubles momentarily forgotten. 'How are you managing? D'you need any help?'

'Thanks, but we're all right. Val's mother's having him in the afternoon, and of course I'm on holiday now. Dr Latimer says she should be over the worst by the time I go back to school next week – not infectious, anyway – so we should get through OK.'

'But you try to get your own painting done during the holidays. If I can do anything... Why not let me take him now, once you've finished his feed? I'll take him for a walk and then leave him up at the farm, if that would be any help.'

Luke thought for a moment, then shook his

head. 'Thanks all the same, but we don't want him to feel like a parcel being handed around. We'll get by.'

'Well, the offer's there if you need it.' Hilary hesitated. 'I suppose Val doesn't feel like seeing anyone at all just now.'

'Not really. She's feeling pretty ropy and she doesn't want to pass the infection on anyway. Was there anything special you wanted to talk to her about?'

Hilary shook her head. 'No. Nothing at all. I just called in for a chat. It's always an odd sort of time, these few days between Christmas and the New Year. She won't be fit to come out and join hands round the oak tree either, will she? It'll seem funny without her there.'

'There are plenty of Tozers to make up for her,' he said with a grin. 'In any case, we probably wouldn't have gone – couldn't take this young man out in the cold at midnight.' He finished feeding the baby and wiped his porridgy cheeks. Christopher laughed and grabbed at the flannel, and Luke pretended to rub it on his nose. For a moment his attention was focused on his son, and he didn't see Hilary's expression as she watched them.

I'll never have a son of my own, she thought sadly, nor a daughter. All that's over for me now. If I can't have David, I don't want anyone, and having David would mean ruining so many lives, hurting so many people. There'll be no children for either of us.

She said goodbye to Luke, asked him to give her love to Val, then stroked the baby's peach-like

350

cheeks and kissed the top of his fuzzy head before letting herself out of the cottage. Outside, it was grey and raw, with a spiteful little wind sending the last leaves of the winter scudding along the road. There were few people about in the village, and those that were out were too intent on getting home again to stop for conversation.

Hilary took a long route back. Alone, she could let her mind drift, allow herself to think about David and all they had given up. At home, she would be subject to her father's demands and forced to set all her own longings aside.

She looked into the future and saw it as cold and as bleak and as colourless as the day itself, and wondered what else it could possibly hold for her now.

'Who was that?' Val asked when Luke went up to the bedroom to see her after he'd settled Christopher in his cot. He'd brought it downstairs when Val's cold had started, and was sleeping down there himself, on the narrow camp bed he'd used when he lived in the charcoal burner's hut. 'I heard voices.'

'It was Hilary. She dropped in for a chat but I told her you weren't receiving visitors just at the moment. She offered to help with Chris if we need her.'

'That's kind of her.' Val was lying propped up against three pillows, her face almost as pale as the white cotton, her nose and eyes red. Luke noticed with anxiety that the red seemed to have seeped into her eyes themselves and her lashes were fringed with matter. Her voice was hoarse and her chest rasped as she breathed.

'I think I ought to ask the doctor to look in again,' he said. 'You don't look at all well.'

'It's just a chest cold,' she wheezed. 'I'll be all right in a day or two.'

'I'll ask him just the same. Are your eyes sore?'

'A bit. They feel a bit weepy.'

More than a bit, he thought. They look like pools of blood. He said: 'I don't think you'd better have Chris up here with you for a while. In fact, it might be better for him to go to your mother for a couple of days. It'll give me time to look after you properly.'

She stared at him. 'You don't think it's serious, do you? Honestly, I don't feel all that bad.'

'Liar,' he said equably. 'No, of course I don't think it's serious. But we don't want to take any risks with Christopher, and I do think we need the doctor to have another look at you. I'll drop in while I'm out this afternoon and see if he can pop in later. He might be able to give you something to soothe your eyes.'

Val nodded, evidently too weak to argue. She asked, 'What did Hilary want?'

'Nothing in particular, as far as I know. Just a chat.' He frowned. 'Although, come to think of it, she did look a bit odd. As if something was bothering her. I guess she wanted to chew it over with you, whatever it is, but she didn't seem too worried when she realised she couldn't. I don't suppose it was anything much.' He straightened her bedclothes and held her forward while he plumped up her pillows. 'Now, I'm making some soup for dinner. You'll be able to manage that, won't you? You need to keep your strength up to feed Christopher.'

'I know.' She flopped back and sighed, her eyes closed, and he saw a tear slide from under her lashes and down her cheek. 'I'm sorry, Luke. I'm a complete failure. A simple cold and I can't even feed my own baby. Is he taking his food all right? Does he mind the bottle?'

'Not as long as it's got your milk in it.' Luke didn't mention the struggle he'd had to get Christopher to accept a rubber teat instead of his mother's nipple. 'And he's gobbling up his Farex, so you needn't worry about that.' He leaned over her and kissed her cheek gently. 'Get some sleep now, and I'll bring the soup up when it's ready.'

'You shouldn't be kissing me,' she said fretfully. 'You'll catch it yourself and then where will my poor baby be? Oh Luke, I miss him so much! I just want to *hold* him.'

'I know. And you will soon, I promise. That's why I want the doctor to come and see you again, so that he can give you something to get you well as quickly as possible.'

He went downstairs, hoping that she had not guessed how anxious he really was. The baby was asleep now, making small bubbling sounds, and the soup, made from turkey stock Alice had given him the day before, was simmering very gently on the stove. He stirred it slowly, his mind going back to the weeks before Christopher's birth, when Val had been so ill and they had all been so frightened for her.

A twinge of the same fear uncurled, like a slow-moving worm, in his stomach.

Chapter Twenty-Eight

New Year's Eve was always a festive time in Burracombe. As many of the villagers who could would gather round the great oak tree in the middle of the green, holding hands in a big circle – often making three or four circles – and waiting for the church bells to strike the hour. Ted and the other ringers had arrived early and rung for twenty minutes or so, the clappers fitted with leather muffles so that they sounded one clear note and one soft, to denote the passing of the old year. Just before midnight, they would lower the bells into their safe position, mouths downwards, and stop ringing while Ted and Travis climbed hastily to the bell chamber to remove the muffles. Then the tenor bell would chime the twelve notes of midnight and on the thirteenth stroke all the other bells would join in, to ring the clear and happy notes of welcome to a new year as they were raised once more, rung in peal and then lowered for the last time.

The people of Burracombe, waiting breathlessly in their circles, cheered at the sound and began to dance around the tree. It was lit with lanterns, hung there earlier by Bob Pettifer and Reggie Dodd, and together with the coloured lights they had strung around the door of the inn and the lights of every cottage window and door, flung open to allow them to stream out into the night, the village seemed to sparkle with colour and warmth. For a few brief moments, all troubles were forgotten in the optimism of a new year, a new beginning, and hearts were lifted by the sounds of the bells in their changes and the glow on the faces of those who danced and kissed and shook each other's hands with the warmth of people who live close together and share in the sorrows and joys of each year as it comes and goes.

'What a year it have been,' Jacob Prout said as the dance came to an end and they broke away from the circles into little groups. 'Starting off with they terrible floods over the east of the country – my stars, that were a storm and a half, all they poor souls stranded on their rooftops and some of 'em killed too. And then the old queen dying, though she were a good age, mind you... And the Coronation in June. And us getting to the top of Everest just before Coronation Day. Seems like years ago, don't it, instead of just six months.'

Alice Tozer, standing with Minnie (who had insisted on coming out, and was so well wrapped up she looked more like a mound of scarves and blankets than a person), nodded. 'It's been a year to remember, all right. Winston Churchill knighted – and that weren't before time, neither, after all he done for us during the war. Sweets coming off ration at last, back in February, and sugar in September – always seemed a bit queer to me, that, since sweets are made mostly of sugar! And the Queen launching that new royal yacht, the *Britannia*. I heard that on the wireless –

nobody knew what 'twas to be called till she broke the bottle of champagne over it. I dare say they'll get a lot of use out of that on their world trips.'

Everyone remembered different things. Basil Harvey, who passionately disapproved of capital punishment, still mourned the controversial hanging of eighteen-year-old Derek Bentley, executed even though he did not fire the shot that killed the policeman that night, nor even handle the gun. Nobody knew, Basil argued, when he shouted 'Let him have it, Chris!', whether he had meant to tell the younger boy to hand over his weapon rather than shoot, but he had never been given the benefit of the doubt and had lost his life for it. Nor had any allowance been made for the fact that he undoubtedly had problems with his mental development and might not even have understood the seriousness of what was happening. Basil still grieved over these facts and prayed that one day the practice of hanging would cease.

Joyce Warren and her husband Henry remembered the deaths of opera singer Kathleen Ferrier and poet Dylan Thomas. Tom Tozer remembered that England had won the Ashes for the first time in nineteen years. Micky Coker and Henry Bennetts, who had been allowed to ring the new year in for the first time, were still smarting over England's football team's defeat by Hungary, their first defeat on their home ground by a foreign team for ninety years.

The old year meant many different things to different people, but their hopes for the new year were very much the same. A year of promise and fulfilment. Of good health and good fortune. Of the warmth of village life, the caring of one for another, the sense that although they lived in different homes, with their own ways, they were part of a larger family, that met together in friendship and would always turn to offer help in times of need.

It was inevitable that after the first flurry of excitement and good wishes had died down, the villagers should remember that such times were always present, and that there were friends who were already in need. Val Ferris, who was still in bed with bronchitis, although Charles Latimer said she was over the worst and could have her baby with her again; and Jean and Jessie Friend, whose brother Billy was ill with the same complaint and giving his sisters and the doctor much more concern, for gentle, simple Billy suffered a good deal with his chest.

There was most concern, however, over Stella Simmons and her fiancé Felix. Stella's recovery after the accident that had happened in early December had been slow, and although visitors were now permitted, she had seemed tired and dispirited to those who had been to the hospital.

'It do seem queer without they two,' Minnie Tozer said as she and the family walked back to the farm. 'But there, the young vicar got to be with his own parishioners now. I feel real sorry for all he'm going through. Let's hope the new year treats 'em both a bit more kindly.'

'It's funny how a date can make everyone feel different,' Alice mused, keeping her mother-in-law's arm firmly clasped within the crook of her own. 'I mean, why should we all make such a to-do about January? 'Tisn't as if it's anything special as a month – the coldest and darkest of the year, with weeks of winter still to come. I've never properly understood why the year starts then anyway. Seems to me spring's the right time, when everything's starting to grow and blossom and all the young animals and birds are getting born.'

They arrived at the farmhouse door, where they were met in the kitchen by Joanna and the warm smell of cocoa and freshly made toast. They stamped their feet on the mat, pulled off their boots and gloves, and gathered round the big table for an annual ritual that had become their own.

'I've got to say,' Joe said, looking round at the faces still glowing from the cold, 'this is one of the best New Year's Eves I can ever remember. Russ and me are going to be real sorry to be going away in a coupla weeks' time.'

'And we're going to be sorry to see you go,' Alice told him. 'It's been a pleasure to have you both around.'

'Shame Jackie couldn't be here tonight,' Joe observed. 'But I guess she had to work, since she had time off on Boxing Day.'

'She was on duty till ten tonight,' Alice nodded. 'And again at seven tomorrow morning – *this* morning, I should say. And so are the rest of us – Ted and Tom even earlier, to get the cows milked – so it seems to me us should all be off to bed.' She rose from the table and touched Minnie's shoulder. 'Come on, Mother, 'tis well past your bedtime.'

The family dispersed, leaving Ted and Joe on

either side of the range, their feet on the fender and their pipes wreathing smoke around their heads. The visit was drawing to a close, and both felt a desire to make the most of these few moments at the beginning of a new year. The presence of the two Americans had brought changes to the family – pleasure most of all to Minnie, who had thought never to see her younger son again and had never met her grandson at all, and both pleasure and dismay to Ted himself, who was still having difficulty in reconciling himself to Jackie's determination to leave England. Like Alice, he had grave doubts that she would ever come back on a permanent basis. America was the land of opportunity and, once gone, Jackie would grasp her opportunities with both hands.

'You'll look after the maid, won't you, Joe?' he said at last, staring into the glowing coals. 'Her's still only young, and if 'tweren't for you being there, I'd never have said yes to her going.'

'Don't you worry, Ted. I'll treat her like my own daughter. And the girls will be there, too. She'll be as welcome in their homes as she is in mine. We'll take good care of her.'

'Well, us'll just have to hope. I know us can trust you to keep your eye on her.' Ted knocked out his pipe and rose, padding across the kitchen in his socks. 'I'm off to bed now, Joe. See you in the morning.'

Joe nodded. 'I'll be going pretty soon myself. I'll just finish this smoke first.' He shook hands with his brother. 'Happy New Year, Ted.'

After Ted had gone, Joe went to the back door and opened it, standing on the threshold and breathing in the cold, frosty night air. The stars were thick in the black velvet of the sky and there were no lights to be seen anywhere. The festivities and rejoicing of both Christmas and the new year were over, and Burracombe was asleep.

Joe stayed for a few minutes, thinking back to the days when he and Ted had been boys on this very farm, sharing in the chores, scrapping and squabbling as brothers will, but always good friends at the heart of it. Growing up together, until the war parted them; falling in and out of love a dozen times with village girls, until Ted found his Alice and Joe found – and lost – Dottie.

He made up his mind that he would see Dottie again before the year was very much older, and make one last attempt to persuade her to go back to America with him.

Val was up for the first time on New Year's Day, and Hilary found her sitting in an armchair by the fire, still rather pale and with red-rimmed eyes, but, as Luke said when he let her in, well on the road to recovery.

'It'll brighten her up to have a good old chin-wag, but she does get tired rather quickly,' he warned her. 'I'll make you some coffee and then I'll take Chris for his morning outing.'

'I won't stay too long,' Hilary promised him, and went in to greet her old friend. 'Well, you're looking better than I expected. What do you mean by scaring us all like that?'

'Go on, I didn't scare you.' Val pointed to the other armchair. 'Move that ironing and sit down. It's good to see you, Hil. What sort of Christmas did you have?'

Hilary made a face. 'What sort do you think we had, with dear Marianne running us all ragged? Look, why don't I do this ironing for you while we talk? I'm sure Luke's got enough to do, looking after you and the baby.'

'Well, I have to admit his domestic skills do rather come to a halt when faced with an ironing board. If you're sure you don't mind, it's in the cupboard under the stairs.' Val watched as Hilary fetched out the board and plugged in the iron. 'D'you know, that was one of our best wedding presents. Mum still swears by her flat irons, three of them on the go at a time, heated on the range, but give me an electric one any day.'

'Me too. I don't know why people want to go on using the old sad irons. They say it gives a better finish, but I don't believe it.' Hilary reached for the first garment from the pile and laid it on the board. It was one of the baby's flannelette night-dresses, and she stared at it, feeling an unexpected lump in her throat.

'What's the matter?' Val asked. 'You look as if you've seen a ghost.'

The ghost of children who will never be born, Hilary thought, and shook her head quickly. 'Nothing. Just admiring the smocking. Is it one Dottie made?'

'No, I did it myself, as a matter of fact.' Val frowned. 'There *is* something wrong, Hil, isn't there? You're looking so sad – as if something's happened. Luke noticed it too. Is it to do with Marianne and Rob? Or is it your father?'

'No, it's none of those.' Hilary realised she had

more or less admitted that there was something. 'Well, I came here the other day to tell you, so I may as well. But stop me if you're getting tired.'

'I won't get tired. And we're on our own now – Luke will be out for nearly an hour. He believes Christopher needs lots of fresh air. Tell me, Hil.'

Hilary set the iron on its end and looked across the board at her friend. 'I hardly know how to start. Well, at the beginning, I suppose – at the reunion.'

'The reunion? The one you went to in London – when was it? In November?'

'Yes. You know what these things are like. You meet all kinds of people you'd forgotten ... and some you never forget.' Her voice dropped on the last phrase. 'I met someone I thought I'd managed to put out of my mind ever since we came back from Egypt. Apparently, I hadn't.'

There was a silence. Val watched her friend's face, waiting for her to go on. After a minute or two, Hilary said, 'He hadn't forgotten me, either.'

'Am I to take it,' Val said, choosing her words with care, 'that there was a bit of a thing between you, out in Egypt?'

Hilary sighed and nodded. 'You could say that. You were too wrapped up in Luke to notice, and I don't think anyone else realised it either. We just – well, we fell for each other, hook, line and sinker. But I was engaged and so was he, and we decided that nothing could come of it. We said goodbye and came home, and I thought that was that. But apparently not.'

'You hadn't been in touch since then, though? Until the reunion?'

'No, not a word. That was our agreement. I didn't even think he'd be there. But he was, and the minute we saw each other...' Hilary set down the iron again and dropped into a chair, her head in her hands. 'Oh Val, I don't know what to do. I just don't know what to do.'

'Oh, Hilary!' Val exclaimed in distress. She rose from her chair and went over to drop on her knees beside Hilary, putting her arms around the other woman's shoulders. 'Come over here and tell me all about it. Leave the ironing.' She switched off the light the flex was plugged into and drew Hilary out of her chair. 'Come on, we'll sit on the settee.'

It was several minutes before Hilary could compose herself enough to speak. Since watching David walk away from her at Euston, she had not allowed herself to cry properly, and now the tears refused to be held back any longer. She rested her head against Val's shoulder, sobbing, while Val held her close and stroked the chestnut-brown hair, murmuring words of comfort.

At last Hilary drew away a little, sat up and felt for a hanky. She blew her nose, wiped her eyes and cheeks and gave a wavering smile.

'Sorry. I didn't mean to cry all over you. Only I've been keeping it all to myself for so long ... there was nobody else to tell...' Tears threatened again, and she drew in a deep breath and held it for a moment. 'It's all right. I'm not going to collapse again.'

'Collapse if you want to. That's what I'm here for. You don't even have to talk about it if you don't want to.'

'I do. I feel I'll go mad if I don't talk to some-body.' She took in another deep breath. 'Do you remember David Hunter?'

'Vaguely. He was a doctor, wasn't he? Tall, and rather good-looking.' Val searched her memory. 'Actually, yes, I do remember that you were quite friendly with him.'

'*Quite* friendly!' Hilary echoed with a short laugh. 'It was a bit more than that, I'm afraid. Oh, we didn't have a full-blown affair, but I have to admit we got pretty close to it. It was only the fact that we were both engaged...' She paused, then said rather bitterly, 'Neither of us wanted to hurt the other people, but as things turned out, we might just as well have done. It would have saved a lot of misery now.'

Val made a little murmur and waited. Hilary wiped her eyes again and went on.

'Henry was killed, of course, and would never have known, and David went back to marry Sybil. Who never really loved him but just wanted the kudos of being a doctor's wife and has taken a series of lovers ever since. He's been miserable all those years and I've been on my own, and...' Her eyes filled once again and her voice trembled, then she broke out: 'It's so *unfair,* Val! We could have been so happy all this time, and now it looks as if we'll never be able to be together. It's so *unfair.*'

'Oh, Hilary.' Val stroked her hand. 'Isn't there any chance at all?'

Hilary shook her head miserably. 'None. Oh, she wants a divorce – now, of all times – but only on her terms. Which are that *he* has to be the guilty party. She's been unfaithful to him over and over again, for years, but he's not to mention any of that. It's got to be him. And you know what that means.'

Vat gazed at her in consternation. 'You don't mean she'll involve you? But surely she has no grounds.'

'Oh, she has grounds all right,' Hilary said, and looked at her friend's face. 'Well, what d'you think I've been doing when I've been to London since the reunion? I suppose you're shocked – well, maybe you shouldn't be, because I'm human too, you know. I'm not the buttoned-up old spinster people think. I've got feelings – and this time I've just let them go. And I'm *glad*. Because it might be all I ever have to remember.'

'Hilary, don't talk like that. Of course I'm not shocked. How could I be, after what happened between me and Luke? I'm just – well, surprised, I suppose. And I'm sorry, because I shouldn't be. Of course you've got feelings, just like everyone else. But how does Sybil know?'

'She doesn't, not really. She just suspects. Father wrote David a letter, you see, thanking him for helping out with Rob, and she put two and two together and found they came nicely to four. Anyway, the point is that she wants to marry the latest fancy-man – he's got pots of money, apparently – and she doesn't intend to be the guilty one. So either David's got to provide evidence – and I hate the thought of that, it's so sleazy – or she'll cite me. And that will be bad enough – even if she can't prove it, we'll be dragged all through the courts *and* the newspapers.'

'But that's awful,' Val said. 'Oh Hilary, you poor thing. And you've been keeping all this to yourself, all over Christmas?'

'Well, not quite. I only knew about the divorce when we met after I'd seen Marianne and the children off on the Dover train.' Hilary gazed at her hopelessly. 'I don't know what's going to happen next.'

'Has David decided what to do?'

Hilary lifted her shoulders and let them drop. 'There's nothing he can do. Whatever happens, he'll probably be struck off – the BMA takes a very dim view of doctors committing adultery – and I really don't want that to happen. I can't bear the thought of him being "discovered" in some sleazy hotel room with a prostitute, and he won't contemplate me being involved. He says it would ruin my reputation and my life here and probably kill Dad into the bargain, and the worst of it is, I know he's right.' She screwed her handkerchief into a sodden ball and thumped her fist on her knee. 'Not that I care tuppence for my reputation, or even my life in Burracombe, but I can't be responsible for giving Dad another heart attack.'

'So what's going to happen?'

'I don't know. He's gone back to try to persuade Sybil to change her mind – she's threatened to leave him before and it's never actually happened – and I've come back to Burracombe to try to remember what it was I liked so much about living here.' Again, the hopeless shrug. 'It's not going to be much fun for either of us.'

'You mean ... you're going to give in? You're

366

going to let her win?'

'What else can we do? The divorce laws are so harsh, Val – so cruel. We're in a cleft stick, both of us.' She lifted her head and gave Val a look filled with anguish. 'We found each other only to lose each other again, and this time it's so much harder. I just don't know how I'm going to go on living this time, Val. I just don't know...'

Chapter Twenty-Nine

On Monday, the village school opened again and Miss Kemp introduced the new teacher to the children. Miss Watkins was a plain woman, a few years older than Stella, with straight black hair that hung down on each side of her face and a rather abrupt manner that worried Miss Kemp and clearly disconcerted the children, who were accustomed to Stella's gentle, friendly young ways. But she was here for just one term, the headmistress explained, since they had not yet been able to find a permanent teacher. And Mrs Warren had offered to come in and help for two afternoons a week. At this, to her surprise, the children seemed to brighten.

'Will us be able to do a new play?' Betty Culliford asked. 'Mrs Warren said something about Easter.'

'I think it's a little early for that,' Miss Kemp began, but the new teacher broke in firmly.

'No, we shall be concentrating on our reading

and our writing.' She turned to the headmistress. 'I'm a great believer in the three Rs. A little bead work for the babies, and perhaps one afternoon a week spent in activities like drawing and painting to encourage coordination, is quite acceptable, and it sounds as though this Mrs Warren – not an experienced teacher, I believe? – could be quite helpful in that direction, but apart from that I believe in sensible, structured work. And discipline,' she added, looking round the room with a gimlet eye and catching sight of Edward and George Crocker. 'I see you have twins,' she added disapprovingly.

Miss Kemp's heart sank a little. 'Yes, those are George and Edward Crocker. They're nice enough little boys but inclined to take advantage of their likeness. They wear different-coloured jerseys each day.'

The new teacher stared at them as if they had been an unfortunate mistake on the part of the school, and they gazed back unwinkingly. They looked particularly innocent this morning, their hair brushed smoothly back, their faces clean and shining and their eyes bright with what Miss Kemp knew to be mischief. They were wearing new jerseys, probably Christmas presents, one with a large G knitted into the front, the other with E. It was a good idea, but Miss Kemp knew that there was no guarantee that they would actually be wearing the right ones.

'I've dealt with twins before,' Miss Watkins said grimly. 'They'll be no trouble to me.'

Miss Kemp hardly knew whether to feel respect or anxiety at this announcement. She said uneasily, 'Well, I'll leave you all to get to know each other. I'll be just the other side of the partition, so call through if there's anything you need.' This was addressed to Miss Watkins, but she had the feeling that the children might well find reasons to call through as well.

She went back to her own class, wondering why the school governors had chosen the hatchet-faced teacher but knowing that it was because there simply hadn't been anyone else. She'd been at the meetings herself, when Basil Harvey had reported that there had been no replies to their advertisements for a new infant teacher and they'd agreed to ask for a locum. No doubt a new teacher would come along when the current teacher training college year ended, but all the new young teachers were settling into their first posts during the Christmas term and unlikely to apply for new posts.

Still, Amelia Watkins hadn't been the only applicant. There had been two others, both male, which neither Basil nor Miss Kemp had felt appropriate for the youngest children, and Miss Watkins had the added advantage of having moved recently to live in Tavistock, which meant that she could travel in quite easily by bus each day. The other two would both have required lodgings, which Dottie Friend was unable to supply at least until Stella was married. And Aggie Madge, who also let rooms, had developed a bad leg ulcer in November.

So Miss Watkins had been the only possibility. Somewhat to her surprise, Miss Kemp found herself looking forward to Joyce Warren's help on two afternoons a week. She wondered how the two women would get along together.

Monday was Felix's day off, and he spent it going to Plymouth to see Stella. He was surprised to find the little branch line train packed with women, but soon discovered that it was the first day of the January sales and they were all hoping to get bargains in the big new stores.

'Sheets, that's what we need,' Billy Madge's mother declared, settling herself beside him with an armful of shopping bags and pressing him into his corner. 'I've sides-to-middled our bedsheets so often I've forgotten where the middle is.'

'It's new shirts for my Jack I be looking for,' Hilda Dodd said. 'I can't turn the collars no more. I've used the tails to make new ones as it is.'

The others nodded in agreement. Shirts had been mended, trousers and jackets patched and socks darned until there was almost nothing left of the original garment, and they were all planning to stock up in the sales. Ivy Sweet said she was looking for a new frock, and Jessie Friend wanted warm vests for her brother Billy, who was still suffering with his chest. The younger women wanted children's clothes, and Alice Tozer was planning to get material for new curtains for the spare room.

'We've had those rolls of wallpaper standing in the corner of our bedroom ever since Joe and Russell arrived,' she told Jessie. 'Ted and Tom were supposed to put it up before they got here, but they caught us out, coming before they was expected, and it never got done. Now Joe says they'll do it themselves, before they go back to America, so I thought I'd strike while the iron's hot and do the curtains at the same time.'

'Where will they sleep, if they'm decorating the room?' Jessie asked.

'Oh, they reckon they'll do it in a day. Get the furniture out on the landing early in the morning and work straight through. With two of 'em at it, it won't take long, and they can paint the skirting boards the next day.'

'Don't know as I'd like to sleep in a room that's only just been decorated,' Ivy Sweet remarked with a sniff. 'Doesn't seem healthy to me.'

Alice took no notice. She and Ivy never had got on, and whatever she said, the other woman would have some cutting reply. She looked across at Felix, wedged beside Betsy Madge, and said, 'And how's Stella, then? You'm going in to see her, I dare say.'

'That's right. I can't go in until this afternoon, so I'm going to see a friend of mine first – the curate at St Andrew's. We're having lunch together and then I'll go to the hospital.'

'Poor maid,' Jessie Friend said. 'What a Christmas you've had. Not like what you were expecting, was it?'

'Not a bit,' he agreed with feeling. 'But we all have our crosses to bear, and Stella's a lot better now. I think she's turned the corner.'

'Terrible thing to happen,' Hilda said. 'Terrible.'

'I suppose she'll be in a wheelchair once her does come home,' Ivy Sweet observed. 'Still, at least being a vicar you'm at home a lot. It's not like as if you were a working man.'

Felix blinked at this, and Alice interposed at once, saying in an annoyed tone, 'Felix works as hard as any man, as you'd know if you ever went to church, Ivy Sweet, and as far as being in a wheelchair goes, this is the first I've heard of it. There's no question of it, is there, Felix?'

'Not as far as I know,' he said, wishing he'd got into a compartment with people he didn't know – he couldn't face their questions or the real answers to them. 'As I say, she's a little better every time I go in. And how was your Christmas, Mrs Tozer? Busy, I imagine, with your American visitors to entertain.'

'Bless you, we don't hardly count Joe and Russ as visitors – family, they are, and slotted into place just like they've always been around. Us'll miss 'em when they goes. Taking our Jackie with them too, as I expect you've heard.'

'What, a young maid like that off to America?' Ivy Sweet exclaimed, eager to get her own back. 'I'd be worried sick if it were my girl.'

'No doubt you would,' Alice retorted smartly, 'but then us have brought our Jackie up to be trusted. And it's not like she won't be with family. Joe'll look after her, and he've got two married daughters to take her under their wings.'

To Felix's relief, the talk then turned to other village matters and he was able to gaze out of the window and think about Stella. He was more worried about her than he wanted other people to think. She seemed so depressed and so remote, at times, as if her thoughts were far away. He understood what Charles Latimer had told him, that this depression was normal after such a shock and

372

that she would recover in her own time, but he had a niggling, uneasy feeling that it was more than that. He needed to be with her, to hold her hand, stroke her cheek and hair, to comfort her. It was a wrench to leave her at the end of each visiting hour, and he was no sooner outside the ward door than he was looking forward anxiously to the moment when he would enter it again.

At last the train puffed into the station in Plymouth and he leaped out, remembering to help the women down to the platform before he hurried away towards St Andrew's church, where his friend from theological college. was waiting for him. It would be good to talk to someone from his own world, he thought, but he wasn't sure that even his friend would really understand his feelings now. Who could, who had not been through the same grinding anxiety? Who could ever really understand?

He found Stella propped up in bed, her leg still stuck out in front of her in its plaster cast, but with some of her bandages removed. He kissed her and sat down beside the bed, his eyes searching her face.

'You're looking better, darling. A bit less like an Egyptian mummy.'

To his surprise, instead of smiling at the small joke, her eyes filled with tears and she turned her head away. He leaned forward, taking her hand.

'Sorry, sweetheart. It wasn't very funny, I know. But it's so good to see you with some of those bandages off.'

She nodded and flinched a little. His worry grew.

'Does your head hurt?'

'It always hurts,' she said wearily. 'I hurt all over. Except for my legs. I wish they *would* hurt. At least I'd know then I was going to be normal again.'

'Darling! Of course you're normal. What a thing to say.'

'I won't be normal if I have to spend the rest of my life in a wheelchair. I'll be a cripple.'

'Stella, don't use that word.'

'It's the right word, though, isn't it? People use it all the time, about people like me. Cripples. People who can't walk, who have to use crutches or be wheeled about like babies. People who are no use to themselves or anyone else.'

There was a short silence. Then Felix said carefully, 'It's not like you to be sorry for yourself.'

'Oh, is that what I am? Sorry for myself? And why shouldn't I be? I'd be sorry for anyone else in this position, so why shouldn't I be sorry for myself.'

'Because,' he replied, choosing his words with care, 'it won't help you to get better. Being sorry for yourself takes up a lot of energy, and you need that energy to help yourself heal. Truly, darling, I've seen it before. People who decide they'll get better, people who decide to make themselves better, usually do. Whereas people who – who...'

'Who are sorry for themselves,' she supplied bitterly, 'don't.'

There was another small silence. Then he said, 'Not always, no.'

'Well, there you are, then,' Stella said. 'I shan't get better.'

'Stella! Darling, please don't talk like that,' he begged. 'I can't bear to hear you. I didn't mean you're really sorry for yourself. You're not that sort of person. You're just feeling a bit low at present, that's all. It's perfectly natural. Charles says–'

'So you've been discussing me with Charles.'

He stared at her. 'Well, he is a doctor, darling. Our doctor. Why shouldn't I discuss you with him? I'm worried about you. I want you to get better and I don't like seeing you so miserable.'

'But you've just said it's natural for me to be miserable.'

Felix ran his free hand through his hair. 'It is. Of course it is. But it would be so easy to slide into real depression, and if that happens–'

'This isn't real depression, then? It's some sort of fake depression? I'm putting it on?'

'*No!* No, of course not... Look, Stella, you're twisting everything I say to mean something different. Why don't we talk about something else? About Burracombe – about the school, if you like.'

'I suppose so,' she said moodily. 'They'll have opened again this morning, won't they? The new teacher will be there. What's she like?'

'I haven't seen her yet. Basil did, of course, when they interviewed her. He says she's rather plain – quite a lot older than you. Rather a disciplinarian, he thinks.'

Stella stared at him. 'A disciplinarian? What does that mean? She won't hit them, will she? My babies?'

'No, of course she won't hit them. I suppose he

meant she'll just keep them in order.'

'And I didn't.' Clearly, she was going to put the wrong interpretation on everything he said today. He sighed.

'You kept them in very good order. Everyone knows that. The whole village is sorry to lose you as a teacher.'

'I won't even be able to go back to that,' she said. 'I can't be a teacher again if I'm in a wheelchair.'

'But of course you won't be going back,' Felix said. 'As soon as you're well again, we'll be getting married. You'll be my wife.'

There was a long silence. Stella looked away, and he watched her face, feeling suddenly afraid, his heart thudding. At last she turned and looked at him, and for a moment he could see the old Stella again.

'I'm sorry, Felix,' she said, her voice quieter now. 'I've been foul to you. It's not because you've done anything wrong, and it's not because I'm suffering from some sort of depression. It's because there's something I've got to say to you, and you're not going to like it.'

'Do you have to say it?' he asked in a low, fearful voice. 'Can't you just not say it at all?'

'No, I can't.' She was silent again, and when she spoke next it was in a different tone, as if she had changed the subject, yet at her words his heart sank even further.

'It would have been our wedding day in less than a fortnight.' She looked down again and her fingers picked restlessly at the sheets that covered her legs. 'I suppose I'll have to decide what to do with my dress. Dottie had almost finished it before the accident.'

'Well, when you're on your feet again, she'll put the finishing touches to it and it will be all ready for when we do get married,' he said, wondering why she had introduced this subject, yet feeling a worm of fear nibbling at his mind. 'As soon as you feel up to it, we'll set a new date and–'

'No,' she said.

Felix stared at her. 'What do you mean, no?'

'No, we won't set a date. We won't be getting married, Felix.' She lifted her head and looked at him, and he saw with a shock that her eyes were clear and determined. 'I've been thinking about it, all the time I've been lying here, and I've made up my mind. I can't marry you. I can't ever be a proper wife to you. You'd better just go away and forget me.'

'*Forget* you? Of course I can't forget you!' He gripped both her hands. His whole body was trembling, his heart thumping. 'You're talking nonsense.'

'It's not nonsense. We both know that I might never get completely better. I might have to spend my life in a wheelchair. Don't say no again, Felix, please. We know it's true. Don't we?'

Her gaze held his and he pushed his lips together and gave a little sigh. He knew that at this moment he had to be totally honest with her. 'Yes, we do. I still think there's a lot of hope, but ... yes, there's a chance. But I've *told* you, over and over again, *it doesn't make any difference*. I still want you to be my wife.'

'But that's just it, Felix. If I stay like this – if this paralysis doesn't go away – I can't *be* a wife to

377

you. I can't be a wife and ... and I can't be a mother.' Her voice dropped to so faint a whisper that he had to bend close to hear her. 'Felix, if I don't get better, I won't ever be able to have children. *You* won't be able to have children. I can't do that to you. I can't deprive you of what you ought to have – a family.' She looked at him again and her eyes were filled with tears. 'That's why I can't marry you.'

Chapter Thirty

Maddy was walking on the beach at West Lyme with the Archdeacon's dog when Stephen found her. It was a bleak, cold day. The sea was as grey as the sky, a sour wind whipping the tops of the waves into a thin foam of white, and the sands were left wet and cold by the outgoing tide. Archie ran in and out of the water a couple of times, but even he was discouraged and contented himself with snuffling amongst the rocks, nosing into piles of seaweed and picking up odds and ends of jetsam that had been deposited by the water. The air was filled with the sound of the wind and the waves and the harsh cries of seagulls as they were thrown to and fro in the sky, swooping and diving and cackling as if at some unpleasant joke.

Maddy walked with her hands thrust deep into the pockets of her big coat, a soft woollen scarf swathed around her neck and a fur beret pulled close around her ears. She didn't see Stephen until he was beside her. He touched her arm and she jumped and stopped.

'Stephen! Where on earth did you spring from? You nearly frightened the life out of me.'

'Sorry. I didn't mean to startle you.' He laid his hand tentatively against her sleeve. 'How are you, Maddy?'

'I'm all right.' She could see that he wanted to kiss her, and she felt a sudden warmth and tenderness towards him. She lifted her face and he bent to touch her lips briefly with his. 'Oh, it *is* good to see you, Stephen.'

He blinked, startled by the sudden feeling in her words. 'It's good to see you too, Maddy. I've missed you since Christmas.'

Maddy laughed a little. 'It's only a few days.'

'It seems more like years,' he said quietly, and they looked at each other for a moment before she turned away and began to walk again. 'How did you get leave to come here so soon?'

'It's just a twelve-hour pass. I've got to be back by midnight.'

'But you can stay for supper?'

'If I'm invited,' he said, and she smiled at him.

'Oh, I think you're invited.' She hesitated, then said in a very low voice, 'I've missed you, too.'

Stephen took her hand in his and for a few minutes they walked without speaking. Then he said, 'What's the latest news of Stella?'

Maddy's face clouded. 'I don't really know. Oh, Felix rings me every evening to tell me how she's getting on, of course he does, but – I don't know what it is, but in the past few days he's seemed a bit odd. There's something he's not telling me,

I'm sure.'

Stephen frowned. 'You mean she's not getting better?'

'No, I don't think it's that. There's a lot they still can't tell, but on the whole she seems to be doing really well. The broken bones are healing and the bruises have gone, and she's much stronger. There's no damage to her brain' – her voice shook a little – 'which was what they were scared of when she was unconscious. I don't know what it is, Stephen, but I've got this feeling there's something bad going on. I can tell by his voice – and more by what he doesn't say than by what he does say.'

'Have you asked him outright?'

Maddy was silent for a moment; then she said, 'I think I'm afraid to, Stephen. I'm afraid of what he might say.'

There was another pause. Stephen said gently, 'You'll have to ask him in the end, if he doesn't tell you. But it may not be anything to do with Stella. Perhaps there's something else worrying him.'

'No, it's to do with Stella, I'm sure. And he *ought* to tell me!' she burst out. 'She's my sister! I've a right to know.'

'Perhaps it's something between them,' he suggested.

'Like what? What could it possibly be?' She bit her lip, then went on more quietly, 'I suppose you're right. The only way to find out is to ask him, and if he won't tell me, I'll find out at the weekend anyway. I'm going to Burracombe on Friday evening and I'll see her on Saturday.'

'Well, that's not so far away.' He tucked her hand into the crook of his arm. 'It's probably something quite unimportant that he doesn't want to worry you with. Let's try to forget it for an hour or two, shall we, and just enjoy being together.' He glanced sideways at her face, trying to gauge her mood. 'I meant it when I said I'd missed you.'

'Yes, I know. I meant it too.' She sighed and then turned to him, stopping again as she put her free hand on his other arm. 'Sorry to be a grouch.'

'You're not a grouch. You're worried about your sister. It's perfectly natural.'

'Yes, but you didn't come all this way to hear me worrying, did you?'

'I came to share with you whatever you want to share,' he said. 'You don't have to hide anything from me, Maddy.'

Maddy looked up into his face. She searched his eyes, finding there a gravity that she had never really seen before. Stephen had always been so full of light and laughter – sometimes a little too much so. He had never seemed to take anything seriously, making a joke of life as he flitted through it, and for a long time she had thought him shallow and facetious. Lately, she had begun to recognise a deeper side to him, and she wondered if his flippancy had been a way of hiding his true self.

'Nor do you have to hide from me,' she said quietly. 'You said the other day that there had to be truth between us, and that means being our real selves with each other. If we can't be that, we can't go on at all.'

Stephen returned her look. He understood what

she meant, for, as he had watched Maddy grow up in the past year from a spoiled girl, who had been cherished a little too much, to a young woman able to set her own feelings aside and put others first, so he had grown himself to a man who knew that a glamorous sports car and money to splash out on smart restaurants were not the most important things in life. Not important at all, in fact.

'There is truth between us,' he said. 'I've hidden nothing from you, Maddy.'

'I know. I've been thinking about what you told me – about Marianne.'

'And?' he said, his heart beating fast.

'It doesn't matter,' she said. 'What you did – it was nothing to do with me. I'd turned you away – I couldn't expect you to wait for ever. Anyway, it's over and done with, and it's not half as bad as what I did.'

'What do you mean?'

'Being so horrible to Ruth and Dan Hodges because they're having a baby,' she said. 'That was much worse.'

Stephen looked at her. It was barely a year since Sammy's death. She had been through so much in that time, grown so much more thoughtful, even wiser, and he knew that the changes in himself had been equally profound. He was still afraid that it was too soon, yet he dared not leave it any longer, for he still didn't know where Russ Tozer stood with her.

'So now there's truth between us,' he said at last, 'can you tell me if there'll ever be any hope for me, Maddy? Or will we always be just friends?'

'If we are, we'll be very good friends.' She took his hands and clasped them tightly between hers. 'But I think ... Stephen, I really, really think that we'll be more than friends. Because over the past few days or weeks – or maybe even longer than that, I don't know – I've begun to realise that I love you. It's taken me a long time, and I don't want to rush things even now, but I think – no, I'm *sure* – that if you ask me the right question, I'll probably say yes.'

Stephen's heart was hammering so hard that he thought it would burst his throat. He brought their clasped hands to his lips and said shakily, 'Do you want me to ask it?'

Maddy met his gaze. Her face was pale; the wind whipped her hair from under her beret and around her cold cheeks. But her eyes were warm and shining as she whispered her reply.

The wind snatched the word from her lips, but he could see the shape of it and he tore his hands from hers, wrapped his arms about her and drew her hard against him. In a frenzy of kisses, he covered her mouth, her cheeks, her eyes and her ears and finally, his mouth almost lost in her hair as her beret was pushed to one side, he said, 'Maddy ... Maddy ... will you marry me? Will you ... *will* you?'

Maddy's arms were as tight around him as his around her. Half laughing, half weeping, she cried, 'Yes! Yes, I will! But – oh, my *hat!* Stephen, my hat!'

The fur beret had been seized by the wind and was now flying along the beach, hotly pursued by Archie, who was racing along the wet sands,

383

barking madly. Laughing, Stephen and Maddy ran hand in hand after him, until the beret finally came to rest against a rock and the dog plunged into the pool beside it and rescued it. He emerged, soaking wet and grinning, with the bedraggled hat in his mouth, came straight to Maddy and, as she took it, shook himself vigorously all over them both. Maddy burst out laughing.

'For goodness' sake!' Stephen exclaimed. 'Maddy, you're soaked.'

'I know. I don't care. But what about your uniform?' She tried to brush the salt water from his tunic, giggling almost uncontrollably, and he put his arms around her again to hold her up.

'That doesn't matter. But you must be frozen. We'd better go back to the house, before you catch cold.'

'I won't,' she said, recovering herself. 'I'm tougher than you think. Oh, Stephen, I'm so happy!'

'So am I,' he said, drawing her close again regardless of their sodden clothes. 'So am I. Happier than I ever thought I'd be in my life. Maddy, I love you with all my heart. I'll always look after you. You're all I want – all I've ever wanted.'

They stood close for a while, each thinking of the past – Stephen of the other girl he had once loved, a long time ago, and lost; Maddy of Sammy; both knowing that those loves would never be forgotten, but were now a part of the past. The love they shared was their present and their future, and they were wise enough now to know that it must be cherished and nurtured, to keep it shining as it shone at this moment in both their hearts.

In Burracombe, other hearts were occupied with love. As Joe Tozer made his way to Dottie Friend's cottage, he too was thinking of the past, and he could see by Dottie's face as she opened the door that it had been in her mind too.

'Joe,' she said. 'I thought you might call by. You'd better come in out of the cold.'

He followed her into the warm kitchen, where her cat lay curled up on the old armchair in front of the range. Dottie had been making scones, and the kitchen table was floury. She indicated that Joe should sit in the chair on the other side of the fire, and went on cutting out rounds with a glass tumbler.

'I'll make a cup of tea when I've got these in the oven,' she said. 'Don't do 'em no good to keep them waiting.'

'That's all right,' he said. 'I didn't come to be fed.'

'All the same, you'll take a cup of tea. Or coffee if you'd rather, but I've only got Camp and I know you don't go a lot on that.'

'Well, it's not coffee, is it?' he said with a grin. 'You come over to America, Dottie, and I'll show you what real coffee is.'

Dottie cut out the last two rounds and put the scones on a baking tray. She opened the door of the range and slid the tray into the hot oven, closing the door with a snap.

'Didn't take you long to get around to that,' she remarked, moving the kettle over to the hot plate, where it immediately began to sing. She poured

385

a drop of hot water into the teapot, swilled it out in the sink, then spooned in tea. By then, the kettle was boiling and she made the tea, putting the red knitted cosy on the pot while she went to the cupboard for cups and saucers. 'But then you always were a fast worker, Joe.'

'I hope you didn't think that of me when I asked you the first time to go to America,' he said. 'You knew I was sweet on you. We'd been walking out for months before that came up.'

'That's true enough,' she acknowledged. 'But you got to admit, once you got an idea in your head, you want to get hold of it straight away. You'm a bit like a terrier catching a rabbit.'

'And are you the rabbit?' he asked with a grin, and she flapped a hand at him.

'You know what I mean. Anyway, I suppose you've come round this morning to try to get me to change my mind.'

'I have,' he admitted. 'You don't mind, do you?'

'I don't mind you trying,' she said, 'but you ought to know by now you'm wasting your time.'

Joe sighed. 'I'd like to think I'm not, Dottie.'

'I dare say you would,' she retorted, pouring milk into two cups, 'but you are, all the same.'

'Why not come just for a visit, like I suggested? You'd enjoy it, and I'd enjoy showing you where I live, and introducing you to my girls and their families. Why not, Dottie?'

'Well, for a start,' she informed him, passing his tea, 'it's too expensive. Where d'you think I'd get the money to go jaunting across the world in one of they big liners? And don't say you'd pay the fare, Joe, because I won't have it. I've never been a kept woman in my life and I'm not going to start now. Besides, I'm too old.'

'Too old to be a kept woman?' he asked, and she snorted with exasperation.

'You know what I mean! I'm too old to go travelling. Burracombe's my place and it's where I'm going to stop.'

'You're not too old to travel,' he said, stirring sugar into his tea. 'It's comfortable on those liners, Dottie. You get a nice little cabin with everything you could want, there's dining rooms and places to walk and see the sights–'

'Sights? What sights d'you get at sea?'

'All sorts of things. Whales and porpoises and birds – there's no end to it all. And the sea changes all the time. I can watch it for hours.'

Dottie sniffed. 'Maybe so, but what if it gets rough? I don't fancy being seasick for five days.'

'If you did, I'd look after you. But I don't reckon you would.' He gazed at her. 'Say yes, Dottie. Let me pay your fare – I can afford it and there's no one else to spend it on. The girls and Russ are all doing well, they don't need my money, and there'll still be plenty for 'em when I go. It would be a real pleasure to have you come and stay.'

She sighed and sipped her own tea. 'I dunno, Joe. It's such a long way.'

He sensed a wavering in her. 'It's only a few days away. Less than a week. You could come and stay for a month and be back here six weeks after you left. Six weeks, Dottie – that's not so very long, is it?'

'I wouldn't fit in. I'd be like a fish out of water.'

'No, you wouldn't. Look, Dottie, America's full

387

of new people arriving all the time. All sorts of people, looking to make their homes there. We're used to it. We don't see them as strangers like you do here – we just take 'em as they are and make 'em welcome. And you'd be more than welcome. I've got a lot of friends in Corning, Dottie, all ready to make you welcome.'

She gazed at him, chewing her bottom lip. He could see that she was tempted. She said, 'But what about all the folk in Burracombe? What about Stella? How can I go away, leaving her as she is, and poor young Felix too? They've spent a lot of time here in this cottage with me. They'm like my own. I can't go off just when they might need me most.'

'You don't have to. It's nearly another two weeks before we go. Stella will be well on the mend by then.'

'And then there'll be the wedding...' she worried.

'That's not going to be before Easter now, is it? Maybe not even then. You'll be back in plenty of time for that.' He leaned forward and took her hands. 'Say yes, Dottie. Say you'll come and visit with me for a month. I won't ask you to stay longer than that. I won't ask you anything more. Just come and see how you like it.'

'I haven't got a passport.'

'That's soon sorted out. We'll get the application forms as soon as possible. Please, Dottie.'

There was a long silence. Then Dottie leaped up with a cry of dismay.

'My scones! They'll be burning!'

She pulled open the oven door and snatched out the tray. The scones weren't burning at all;

they were a rich golden-brown, perfect for splitting and buttering to go with the tea. But Dottie continued to tut as she slipped them on to a wire rack and then put two on separate plates. She passed one to Joe and put the butter dish between them, and as she handed him a knife, their eyes met.

Joe smiled. In the sudden flash of excitement in her eyes, he could see the Dottie he had known and loved as a girl, the Dottie he had wanted so badly to take to America with him all those years ago. This time, he thought, he might be going to get his way...

Chapter Thirty-One

Hilary was in the kitchen, making pastry, when Felix walked in. He came through the back door, through the boot room, and she paused in surprise when she saw him.

'Felix! I didn't hear you arrive. Did you ring the front doorbell?'

'No, Travis brought me. He met me coming up from the Clam. I hope you don't mind me barging in.'

'Of course not. Sit down in Mrs Ellis's rocking chair and I'll make some tea. It's her day off today, so I'm on kitchen duty.'

She spoke cheerfully but there was a brittle note to her voice that Felix registered even through his own misery. He looked at her carefully.

'Are you all right, Hilary?'

'Yes, fine, thanks. Just a bit tired after the past couple of weeks. Quite glad to start a new year, really.' She spoke casually, her back turned to him as she got out cups and saucers, but Felix frowned a little. He wanted to ask her again, but kept silent, knowing that they were good enough friends for her to tell him anything she wanted him to know, and aware that he was too immersed in his own unhappiness to be of much use anyway.

'What about you?' she enquired, setting the cups on the table. 'How's Stella today?'

To her astonishment, his face seemed to fold in on itself, almost as if he were about to cry. Swiftly she left the teacups and crossed over to him, dropping to her knees beside his chair. 'Felix, whatever's the matter? Is she worse?'

'No,' he replied in a hoarse, unsteady voice. 'No, she's getting on well. At least, I think she is. She says the doctors are pleased with her. It's just that...' His face crumpled completely and he shook his head. 'Hilary... She says – she says she won't marry me.'

'Won't *marry* you? But why on earth not?'

'Because she thinks she's going to be in a wheelchair. She thinks she's always going to be paralysed. She thinks she can't be what she calls a proper wife, and she'll never be able to have children. Hilary, I don't know what to do. I don't know how long I spent with her, trying to persuade her that none of that matters, that I want her as my wife whatever her condition is. I want *her* – the Stella I know and love. Oh, of course it *matters* if she can't walk or have children – I'm not that stupid. But it won't stop me loving her. It won't stop me wanting to be with her.'

'It would make things more difficult,' Hilary said slowly. 'She obviously realises that.'

'What does *difficult* matter? Life often *is* difficult. Lots of people have difficulties – worse difficulties. And suppose it had happened after we were married?' he demanded. 'Would she want to leave me then? Would she want me to leave her? In any case, how does she think she's going to manage? Who's going to look after her? Dottie? Maddy? She's not thinking clearly at all, Hilary. She's just got this obsession with having to be a proper wife and mother, and she's not thinking about anything else at all. And nothing I say makes any difference. I can't seem to get through to her.'

'It must be just an idea,' Hilary said. 'It's got itself into her head – maybe someone's said something and she's got the wrong end of the stick. It'll probably go as soon as it came and she'll have forgotten she ever had it.'

'I don't think so,' he said miserably. 'I think she meant it.'

They stayed still for a while and then Hilary got up. 'I'll make the tea.' She busied herself for a few minutes, then asked, 'How does she seem otherwise? Is she particularly down?'

'Depressed, you mean? Well, she was to start with – but irritable, more than depressed. And when she told me, she was upset, I could see she was. But then she seemed – well, she seemed almost, in a strange way, to cheer up. As if coming to a decision had made her feel better.' His face folded again. 'Almost as if she's *glad* of an excuse to end our engagement,' he blurted out. 'Hilary, do you think that's it? D'you think she's been re-gretting it all this time and not had the courage to tell me? Maybe she never really wanted to marry me at all.'

'No! Of course that's not it. You mustn't think that way. Stella loves you as much as you love her, I'm sure of it. I know you both, I've seen you together and I've seen Stella in hospital. This is just some idea that's hooked itself into her. She'll get over it, I'm sure she will.'

'I wish I were,' he sighed. 'I wish I were as sure.'

Hilary glanced at him. She poured out the tea and took a cup over to him. Gently, she said, 'Would it help if I were to talk to her, do you think?'

'I don't know. It might make matters worse if she thinks I've been talking to anyone else.' Gloomily, he sipped his tea. 'On the other hand, why *shouldn't* I talk to someone else about it? It's my whole life that's been turned upside down. But as for you talking to her – I just don't know.' He sipped again, then burst out: 'Damn and blast those bloody ponies! Why did they have to be all over the road that night? Why? *Why?*'

'It's the way life works,' she said soothingly. 'It does some very nasty things to us at times.' She thought fleetingly of herself and David. She had not heard from him since their parting at Euston, and did not expect to. He was gone, swept out of her life as suddenly as he had been swept in. She looked down at Felix's fair head, bent over as he rested his face in his hands, and thought of the day when he had proposed to her. They'd both known at once that it had been a mistake, but suppose she'd accepted him, suppose they'd actually married? They'd have made as good a fist of it as they could, she imagined, and none of this heartache would ever have come about.

Or would their own heartache have been even worse?

'Don't bother with the washing-up,' Gilbert ordered his daughter when they had finished dinner that evening. 'Leave it for the morning. We'll have coffee in the drawing room.'

Hilary hesitated. 'I don't like leaving it for Mrs Ellis. It's not really fair, when she has her own work to do.'

'Won't hurt, just for once. I don't like you doing that sort of thing anyway. I want to talk to you.'

Hilary opened her mouth to protest again, then closed it. Her father's tone was serious, and anyway she could do the washing-up after he'd gone to bed. She only did these domestic chores two days a week and she knew that the housekeeper, tolerant as she was, would not be pleased to find a mountain of dishes awaiting her in the morning.

She made the coffee and took it in, wondering what her father wanted to talk about. Her mind was still occupied with Felix's disclosures. He hadn't been keen on her going to see Stella, yet to Hilary's mind it could hardly make matters worse. And with her own unhappiness weighing heavily on her heart, she couldn't bear to see even more sadness in her friends. Stella must be equally miserable, she thought. She loved Felix and had been looking forward eagerly to their marriage. Wheelchair or no wheelchair – children or no children – this terrible accident couldn't be allowed to destroy their lives completely.

Her father was in his favourite armchair before the fire, with the high back and the wings to shelter his head from any draught. She put the tray down on a low table, poured his coffee, and went to her own chair, opposite. He was gazing into the fire and didn't seem inclined to speak immediately, so she waited.

'It's the matter of my will,' he said abruptly after a while. 'I want you to get Wolstencroft down here again.'

'John Wolstencroft? But he was here only a few weeks ago. You've just made your will, Father.' For a moment, she wondered if he might be losing his mind.

'I know that! What d'you take me for – a fool? But I'm beginning to think I might have been a bit hasty. Might make a few changes.'

Hilary stared at him. 'Changes?'

'Yes, changes, and don't start behaving like a parrot.' He was always at his most testy when he felt at a disadvantage. 'Have to admit, I was taken by surprise when young Rob turned up out of the blue. Wanted to do my best for him – don't think I can be blamed for that...'

'Of course you can't.'

'...but I might not have given myself time to think properly. And then that blasted heart attack or whatever that old woman of a doctor wants to call it... And there's you and Stephen. Don't want to be unfair to you... Well, it's all made me think a bit, that's all.'

Hilary waited again, hardly daring to move. Her father was still staring into the fire, talking almost as if to himself.

'Young Rob... He's a good boy, image of his father, of course, but what's he like inside? What's he thinking? You tell me he wants to be an engineer. That's no use to a place like Burracombe. Seems to be more like his uncle than his father. Never did understand where Stephen got it from, and now there's this boy talking the same way. Well, you can't fit a round peg into a square hole, I've learned that over my life. Tried it a few times, and it's never worked, never will.'

'He could change his mind,' Hilary ventured. 'He's only twelve. He could grow to love Burracombe as we do.'

Gilbert sighed and shook his big head. 'I don't think so, Hilary. He's enough of a Napier to know his own mind. I knew mine at that age, and so did his father. So did Stephen, when you come to think of it, though I didn't want to see it at the time.'

Hilary looked at him. She had never heard her father talk like this, never heard him admit that he might be wrong. She hoped it didn't mean anything sinister. Didn't they say that people started to put their houses in order when death was approaching, even if they weren't fully aware of it?

'You're not planning to disinherit Rob, are you?' she asked.

Her father sighed again. 'No, not that. But I'm going to shift things around a little. Leave him enough to see him into the career he wants, whatever that turns out to be, and look after his mother. I've already made her an allowance, as you know, but I'll increase his. But the estate... I'll leave that to you and Stephen equally.'

Hilary's mouth dropped open.

'To me and Steve? Equal shares?'

'That's what I said,' he retorted, his testiness returning. 'Sort it out between you.'

'But ... Steve's not interested in running the estate.'

'He doesn't have to, does he? He can leave things to you and Travis, if you continue to employ him. It'll be up to you.' He turned his head suddenly, fixing her with his bright, narrowed stare. 'That's what you want, isn't it?'

'Dad,' she said, struggling to find the right words. 'You're talking as if – as if all this is going to happen soon. You've got years ahead of you. Things might change again. Don't you think you should wait?'

'No, I don't. I think I should sort it out now, before we go any further. Look, my girl, I've had two of these attacks now. Charles thinks if I have another one, it'll be the last. I'm not such a fool as to disbelieve him. I want the estate left in safe hands when I go, and yours are the safest. Stephen offered a few weeks ago to stay and take it on, run it with you, and I snapped his head off, but I knew he meant it and I knew he meant well. That's why he's getting an equal share. As far as I can see, all it'll mean is that you'll have it to yourself, as long as you pay Robert and Marianne their allowances and give Stephen whatever's due to him. It's the fairest way, the right way, and I want Wolstencroft here as soon as possible so that it can all be put into his hands. Ring him first thing in the morning, will you, and tell him.'

'Yes, all right. If that's what you want.' She hesitated again, knowing that what she was about to say next might ruin everything, yet knowing that she had to say it. 'But ... suppose I don't stay here after all.'

'Don't stay here? You? Why in God's name shouldn't you stay here?'

'I might not,' she said desperately. 'I might – I might go away. Get married.'

'*Get married?*' He stared at her as if she had suddenly sprouted an extra head. 'After all this time? Is there a chance of that?'

'No,' she admitted forlornly. 'I don't think there is. But just supposing...'

'Then,' he said firmly and uncompromisingly, 'I would hope that you would consider the estate as well. Leaving here needn't mean you need lose interest in it. With someone like Kellaway to help you, it could still go on. But unless you absolutely have to, I'd hope you wouldn't leave it. Bring your husband here, if you ever find one. Bring up your children here too. Because they'll be the next generation to inherit Burracombe.' He gave her another narrow glance. 'I'd like to think of my other grandchildren – *your* children – growing up here as you and Baden and Stephen did. I'd like to think of them with Burracombe in their blood and their bones, as it is in mine and yours.' He turned away and looked back into the fire. 'Get Wolstencroft down here as soon as you can,' he said, and never saw the tears on Hilary's cheeks.

Chapter Thirty-Two

The news that Dottie Friend was going to America spread round the village like wildfire. In the post office, there was talk of nothing else.

'You mean to tell us she never even hinted at it?' Ivy Sweet demanded. 'I call that downright deceitful.'

'I don't see why,' Jessie Friend said defensively. 'And there's no call to use that sort of language, Ivy. Dottie's business is her own business and she came round here and told me the minute she made up her mind. Which wasn't until three days ago, if you want to know the exact date.'

Ivy coloured up and tossed her ginger head. 'Well, it all seems a bit queer to me, her deciding so sudden. And wasn't there talk about her and Joe Tozer backalong, when he first went off to America? There was one or two of us watching her shape for a few months after that, I can tell you.'

'More shame to you then, and for bringing it up now,' Jessie retorted. 'Our Dottie's always been a respectable woman, and never a hint of anything else, which is more than I could say of some people around here.' She stared pointedly at Ivy's hair, which everyone knew had only gone ginger at the time her red-headed baby had been born towards the end of the war. 'She's worked hard all her life and if anyone deserves a bit of a holiday now, it's her. Not that she won't be missed in the village, by your George as much as anyone, I'd say.'

'And just what do you mean by that?' Ivy demanded dangerously.

'Why, only that he'll miss those pies and cakes she bakes for him to sell in the shop,' Jessie said innocently. 'Whatever else could I mean? You'll have to turn to and give him a hand yourself now, won't you?'

Ivy sniffed and flounced out, forgetting that she had come in to buy stamps. The other customers laughed, and Jacob Prout said, 'That told her, Jessie, and serve her right. That sort don't mind dishing it out, but they never likes it when someone gives it back. But how can Dottie just go off to America at a minute's notice? Don't her need a passport and such?'

'Joe's seeing to all that for her. It don't take long. He come in for the application form the minute she said she'd go. Luckily I'd got some in, when young Jackie Tozer decided she was going. Seems like half Burracombe's off to America.'

'Those Tozers got a lot to answer for,' said Mabel Purdy, the school cleaner. 'I knew as soon as I saw that big car they come in that there'd be trouble.'

'I don't call Dottie having a holiday "trouble",' Jessie said, on the defence again.

'No, but I don't reckon Ted and Alice Tozer are all that happy about their Jackie, and I don't blame 'em either. The maid's not twenty yet – letting a girl that age go jaunting off halfway round the world's bound to lead to trouble. Get all sorts of ideas in her head, she will.'

'Well, that's not our business,' Jessie said. 'And she'll have plenty of family to look after her, not to mention Dottie. What a party, eh!'

Jacob, who had come in to collect his pension, went next door to Edie's shop to spend part of it on cigarettes. Ivy had got there before him and was holding forth once again on the subject of Dottie's travels. He cut her off short in the middle of a flight of fancy which had Dottie taking it into her head to go to Hollywood, expecting her experience of London theatres to get her work in films, and said bluntly, 'You'm talking a pack of nonsense, Ivy Sweet, and everyone here knows it. Why don't you get off home and do something useful for once, instead of making an exhibition of yourself all round the village?'

Ivy stared at him, an ugly flush of red flooding into her cheeks and down her neck. He returned her look steadily, and at the contempt in his eyes she turned away, addressing her next remark to Edie.

'I'll not bother about they groceries now, Edie. I'll do my shopping in Tavi instead, in future. I don't like the class of customer you get here.'

She stalked out, and Jacob laughed. 'Good riddance to bad rubbish,' he said loudly. 'I'll have a packet of Woodbines, Edie, if you please.'

'You'll wait until it's your turn to be served,' she said sharply. 'And I'm not sure I'll serve you at all. You just lost me a good customer.'

'Go on,' he said. 'Her's not going to traipse into Tavi on the bus three times a week to do her shopping. Her'll be back like a bad penny. You don't get rid of rubbish like that so easy.'

'It's not rubbish I'm thinking of,' Edie said. 'It's customers. I'm trying to make a living here, Jacob.'

'I'm sorry,' he said, taken aback. 'I didn't mean nothing against you, Edie.'

'It don't matter what you meant. That's what's happened. I dare say you'm right and after a week or two her'll be back, but that's a week or two of her business lost, so just you remember that before you starts laying into any of my other customers.'

Jacob flushed but said nothing. He waited until the other customers had been served and the shop was empty, then said, 'I really am sorry, Edie. I never meant her to take the huff like that. It just riled me, hearing her say those things about Dottie. She'd already been at it in the post office, making insinuations. Why should Dottie Friend have that sort o' remark made about her? Someone had to say summat.'

'It's all right, Jacob,' Edie said in a mollified tone. 'I know what Ivy's like and so does everyone else. Nobody was taking any real notice.'

'Maybe not, but her still shouldn't be allowed to go round passing remarks. I'm sorry it's lost you business, though. And I'll have twenty Woodbine, if you'm still willing to serve me.'

'Oh, I'll serve you. The rate I'm losing custom this morning, I can't afford to pick and choose my customers!' But the words were spoken with a smile and Jacob knew he'd been forgiven. They both also knew that he normally only bought his cigarettes in packets of ten, and that this had been his olive branch. He took the packet, handed over

401

his money and gave Edie a nod.

Walking back along the lane to where he was clearing out ditches filled with debris after a recent heavy rainstorm, he encountered Joanna Tozer coming back from the bus stop with a load of shopping. They stopped to say good morning, and he said: 'I hope Edie Pettifer don't see you and blame me for losing her another customer. She just had Ivy Sweet flouncing out because of summat I said.'

Joanna looked at him in surprise, and laughed. 'No, these are things Edie doesn't stock. But whatever did you say to upset Mrs Sweet? Not that it's hard to do,' she added. 'Tom's mother's always crossing swords with her one way or another.'

'Oh, it was just over Dottie Friend going to America. I dare say you know all about that.'

She nodded. 'Caused quite a stir in the family, it has. Dad's never stopped chi-iking Uncle Joe about catching her at last. Apparently they were walking out before he went over as a young chap, and Mother reckons Dottie never really got over him. I don't think it's anything like that really, though. She's just going for a holiday.'

'It's still quite a journey, for a holiday,' he remarked. 'Mind you, Ted's right about Joe being sweet on her all those years ago. I can't see Dottie leaving Burracombe for good, though.'

'Nor can I. But it's eased Mother's mind about Jackie, to know Dottie's going to be there too. It's not that she wants Dottie to be in charge of her or anything – Jackie'd never stand for that – but it's a help to know there'll be someone from home around if she does get a bit homesick.'

'I don't reckon that young maid's likely to be homesick. More likely to go a bit wild, if she's given her head. That's what Ted's afeared of, anyway – he's said as much in the pub. I'm not sure Dottie's going to be much help there.'

'No, but she'll be a reminder of home. That might be all Jackie needs to keep her steady. She's a sensible girl really – I don't think they give her enough credit for it.' She picked up her basket. 'Anyway, I must get on, Mother wants some of this for dinner. Fish on Friday!'

She walked on along the lane and turned up the farm track. It was true that Dottie's sudden decision had taken them all by surprise, but on the whole it was approved. Dottie Friend was a steady woman who was not likely to let her head be turned by American ways, and her presence was bound to be a good influence on Jackie.

Joanna, who had come to Devon as a Land Girl during the war, didn't really understand the younger girl's desire to travel. She herself had settled into farm life as if she'd been born to it, had married Tom when he returned after the war was over, and wanted nothing more than to stay in Burracombe for the rest of her life, bringing up her children and eventually taking over the farm, as Ted and Alice had done. But this wanderlust seemed to run like a thread through the family – first Joe, then Jackie. And even Tom's brother, who had stayed in the army and was now in Germany, didn't seem to have any desire to settle back at home.

She hoped the same desire to travel didn't appear in her own children. The thought of Robin or Heather wanting to leave home the minute they were grown up, and go to live on the other side of the world, filled her with horror. How did any mother bear it, she wondered, when her children suddenly announced that they were leaving home to go so far away you might never see them again? How had Minnie borne it? Wasn't it a rejection of all you had done for them?

'You can't own your children,' Minnie had told her, when she'd asked these questions. 'You must just look on their time with you as a sort of loan. You take care of them, teach them how to behave, to be kind and decent and all that, and then you have to let them go. Otherwise you'd go mad with worrying about them.'

But Joanna thought her eyes looked sad, all the same, and she knew Minnie was dreading the coming parting from her son and grandson, knowing that this time almost certainly would be the last. She'd gone upstairs after that conversation to look at her own son, Robin, asleep in his bed with his hair tangled into curls on cheeks that still had the roundness of a baby's, and at her daughter Heather, whose twin sister had slipped away from life so tragically on Easter Day. And she had felt her heart clench with love for them. I'll never be able to let them go, she'd thought. I'll never, ever be able to let them go.

Stella was lying listlessly in her bed when Hilary walked into the ward on Friday afternoon. Her pale face brightened a little as she saw her friend, and she gave a small smile of thanks for the chocolates Hilary placed on her bedside table, but her brown curls were lank and dull, and her eyes oddly blank. She showed little interest in village news, and after a while Hilary said, 'What's the matter, Stella? Felix says you seem really down at the moment. It's understandable, seeing what you've been through, but don't you feel at all better?'

Stella shrugged. 'I don't see how anyone can expect me to. I'm stuck here in this bed and it doesn't look as if I'll ever get out of it. There's no point in feeling better.'

Hilary felt a sudden exasperation. She said, 'I'm sure there is. You don't want to go on feeling the way you were a week or two ago.'

'I don't want to go on feeling anything,' Stella said grumpily. 'I'd have been better off...' She stopped and her eyes met Hilary's. 'Well, you know what I mean.'

Hilary stared at her, appalled. 'Stella! You mustn't say such things.'

'Mustn't I? Why mustn't I? Because it upsets you? Because it might upset Felix? He knows what I feel. He knows I'm no use any more. So why have I got to pretend I feel better? Why?'

'Because you do,' Hilary said firmly. 'Because you *are* better, and you're going to get better still. You're going to get up out of that bed and one of these days you're going to walk down the ward and out of the door. And what's more, you're going to walk down the aisle to marry Felix.'

'Who says?' Stella challenged her. 'Has one of the doctors told you that? Because they haven't told *me,* and I'd have thought I'd be the first to know.'

'I believe it,' Hilary said steadily. 'And Felix believes it too. All that's needed is for you to believe it.'

'Oh, and I can make it happen, just like that, can I? I can throw off this plaster and those crutches they said they'd give me, and I can walk again, just because I believe it? Don't be a fool, Hilary. It doesn't happen like that. My leg's been broken and my back's been hurt and nobody knows if I'll ever be able to walk again. *Nobody.* It's not a matter of believing, or not believing. It's a matter of *fact.*'

Hilary felt helpless. Stella's words were true, yet she still felt that if she could only rouse some self-belief, it might help the healing process. She gazed at her friend and said gently, 'Wouldn't you like to think you were going to get better, Stella?'

Stella stared at her and turned her head away. 'Well, of *course* I would! What a stupid question! Do you think I like being stuck here in this horrible bed with all these horrible people around me being ill and these horrible nurses and doctors making me do things I don't want to do, and people like you who are supposed to be my friends coming in and asking stupid, horrible questions? Of *course* I want to get better! But I'm not going to. And that's all there is to it. So just go away and *leave me alone!*'

There was a long silence. Hilary was conscious of other patients and their visitors glancing in their direction. She sat still, not sure what to say. Stella was staring at the wall, only her restless fingers moving as they picked at her sheets. Eventually, Hilary said quietly, 'I'll go if you really want me to go, Stella, of course I will. But are you sure it's what you want?'

There was another silence. At last, Stella turned back slowly and Hilary saw that her eyes were full of tears.

'Oh, Hilary, I'm sorry,' she said miserably. 'No, please don't go. I know I'm being a selfish pig and you would rather be anywhere than here – but please stay a bit longer. I just don't know what's the matter with me. I want to hit out at everyone. Even poor Felix...' And her voice broke as she began to cry.

Hilary moved closer and put her arms around the shaking shoulders. 'It's no wonder you feel so bad,' she said. 'Look at what's happened to you. You're right, nobody knows if you're going to get better. It *is* stupid of us to try to pretend you are. What we ought to be doing is thinking of the future – what you're going to do if you can't ever walk again. How you're going to manage then.'

At this, Stella seemed to fire up again. 'Don't you think that's what I think about all the time?' she demanded. 'And I just don't know, because nobody will tell me. Nobody will talk to me about it. They just brush the question aside, as if I'm a fool and wouldn't understand. It's not my *brain* that's been hurt. I know I was unconscious for a long time, but that was just a bit of concussion – that's better now. And I'm *not* a fool. I'm an intelligent woman and I don't like being treated as if I were an idiot.'

'Neither would I.' Hilary began to feel some indignation on Stella's behalf. 'But maybe the reason why they won't discuss it is because they don't think there's anything to discuss. They know you're getting married. You'll have a husband to look after you. There's no reason for them to wonder how you'll manage because they know you won't have to.'

Stella looked at her. 'But it's not true,' she said. 'I'm not going to marry Felix. And you know that, don't you, Hilary? That's why you're here today – because he's asked you to come and persuade me.'

'Stella–'

'I've already told you. I'm not a fool. Please don't you treat me like one, as well.'

Hilary sighed. 'All right – yes, it is why I'm here today. I told Felix I'd come. Stella, he's in a dreadful state. He doesn't know what to do. He loves you so much and he can't think of anything else but the fact that you were going to be married and now you say you're not. Why? Why won't you marry him? It doesn't make sense.'

'Of course it makes sense. I've told him why, and I'm sure he's told you too.' Stella's voice was steady now, with a determination that frightened Hilary more than her anger or bitterness had ever done. 'I can't marry him because I can't be a proper wife to him and I can't give him children. I would have thought that was all the reason he needed.'

'Well, it isn't. And you don't even know it for certain. The doctors keep saying it's early days and you could get all your feeling back. You can't destroy everything you have with Felix. It's like killing something good and valuable.'

'Valuable? When I'm useless?'

'Useless? I don't agree that a person who can't walk is useless. You'll still be yourself, Stella, even if you're in a wheelchair. You'll still have your lovely personality that warms everyone you meet, you'll still be the thoughtful, intelligent person you've always been, you'll still be able to give Felix the love and support he needs to do his job. All right, you might not be able to arrange the church flowers – although I can't see why not – and you might not be able to go to church meetings or services – though I can't see why you shouldn't do that either – and you might not be able to visit sick parishioners, although quite frankly I can't see why you shouldn't do *that*. In fact, the more I think about it, the more I think you'll be able to do pretty well anything you could do if you *could* walk. And I'm still not at all convinced you're not going to be able to walk, anyway. Nobody's told you that for certain.'

Stella didn't answer for a minute. Then she said, 'So I could do anything – except be a proper wife or mother.'

'And has Felix complained about that?' Hilary asked, quick as a flash.

'No, of course not. He's too kind. But he must have thought about it.'

'And, having thought about it, does he agree that that's a good reason for letting you go?' Hilary leaned forward. 'Stella, if this had happened a few weeks after you were married instead of a few weeks before, you wouldn't be having any of these doubts. It would be part of your life together and you'd both just get on with it. So why can't you do that now?'

'Because it *didn't* happen after we were married, and it gives him the chance to find a woman who *can* be a proper wife, a proper vicar's wife, and have a lot of children to fill that rambling great vicarage.'

'But he doesn't *want* another woman!'

'He doesn't now,' Stella said stubbornly. 'He will in the end, though, and then he'll thank me.'

'All right,' Hilary said, trying another argument. 'Suppose it had been Felix who was hurt instead of you? Wouldn't you still want to marry him – even if he had to spend the rest of his life in a wheelchair?'

'Of *course* I would!' There was a note of real indignation in Stella's voice, as if Hilary had insulted her. 'But that's different!'

'How? How is it different?'

'Because Felix is a *man*,' Stella said, as if explaining to one of her infants in the school. 'He would have to be looked after. And he wouldn't be able to be a vicar. He'd *need* me.'

'And don't you think he needs you now?'

'Not in a wheelchair, no. I'd be nothing but a burden to him.'

'But if *you'd* be prepared to look after *him*, why can't you–'

'It's different. That's all.' She lifted her chin and looked Hilary straight in the eye. 'It's no use, Hilary. I've made up my mind. You might as well give up.'

Hilary sat back, feeling drained. She seemed to have exhausted all her arguments and got nowhere. For a moment or two, neither of them spoke. Then she rose to her feet.

'I'll have to go now. All I can ask is that you think again. Think about how upset he is. He's *distraught*, Stella. And he doesn't have to be – all he wants is to take you home and look after you. All he wants is to have you with him, walking or not. Don't you think you're being rather unkind to him? Don't you think you're being rather cruel?'

She walked away, already furious with herself. Those last remarks had been unkind and cruel on her part and she wanted immediately to go back and apologise. But when she turned at the door, she saw that Stella was staring at the wall again, her face set and stubborn.

Even that didn't get through to her, Hilary thought despondently. It's like talking to a glass wall; nothing is getting through to her just now.

Chapter Thirty-Three

By the time she reached home, Hilary was almost in despair. She had done no good by going to see Stella and might even have made matters worse. She was missing David more bitterly than ever before, and even her father's change of heart concerning the estate and its inheritance failed to cheer her. Much as she loved her home, much as she had thrown herself into it, an estate and great house without the love and warmth of family life would be no more than an empty shell. That was what Burracombe had always stood for, that was why it was so big; so that it could support a family, all the families of the village and the surrounding farmland. It wasn't made to be the home of just one person.

It was a surprise to find Stephen's car standing in the yard, and she pulled in beside it and went through the back door, wondering what had brought him home so soon. Mrs Ellis was in the kitchen, peeling potatoes.

'I see Stephen's home,' Hilary said, dumping her bag on the kitchen table. 'I didn't think he'd be getting leave again so soon.'

'He said he'd "wangled" a pass,' the housekeeper told her, smiling and raising her eyebrows at the same time. 'There's a deal of wangling goes on at that RAF station, if you ask me.'

'I don't know how he does it. So you're having to stretch supper to an extra one again.'

'An extra two, as it happens. Maddy's with him.'

'Maddy?' Hilary echoed. 'Why ever...?' Her heartbeat quickening, she hurried along the corridor to the old baize door which used to separate the main house from the working areas and these days was kept open. She took off her thick coat, gloves and scarf and hung them on one of the hooks, then slipped into the little cloakroom to wash her hands and brush her hair. She could hear voices coming from the drawing room, and she opened the door to find her father in there, with Maddy and Stephen, all drinking tea round the blazing fire.

'Well, this looks cosy,' she said, trying to keep her voice casual. 'Hello, Maddy. How nice to see you. We weren't expecting you this weekend, Steve.'

'Maddy wanted to come and see Stella,' he said casually, 'so I thought it would be a good chance to pop in. I'm only staying tonight. Then I'll slip back on Sunday afternoon to take her home.'

Hilary's brows rose higher than Mrs Ellis's had done. 'That's very helpful of you.' She poured herself a cup of tea and turned to Maddy. 'I've just been to see Stella myself, as it happens.'

'How is she?' Maddy's voice was anxious, but there was a suppressed excitement about her that Hilary couldn't fail to notice. She glanced at her brother and saw the glitter in his eyes. So that's how the land lies, she thought, and felt a flicker of warmth. It'll be good if someone's happy around here.

She said, 'I'm afraid Stella's a bit low at present. She's got this idea in her head that she's never going to be able to walk again.'

Maddy stared at her. 'But surely that's not true! The doctors said it was too early to tell.'

'I know. But Stella thinks she knows best.' Hilary stirred her tea, trying to decide whether to tell Maddy the rest or not. Finally, she said, 'You may as well know all of it. She says she won't marry Felix after all.'

'But that's ridiculous!' Maddy burst out. 'How can she say such a thing?'

'She says she can't be a proper wife to him, or give him children,' Hilary said wearily, and sank into a chair. 'I'm sorry, Maddy, I shouldn't have sprung it on you like that. It's just been rather a fraught afternoon.' She put her cup down, leaned her elbow on the arm of the chair and rested her head against her hand.

'Oh, Hilary,' Maddy said in a voice filled with concern. 'You look exhausted. And poor Felix. Whatever must he be going through?' She glanced at Stephen. 'We ought to go and see him.'

'We will. We'll go over this evening.' They exchanged a look, and then he said, 'But there's something we want to tell you first.'

Gilbert, who had said nothing until now, stirred in his armchair. He gave them both a sharp glance from beneath his shaggy brows and said, 'Thought something must have brought you both down here on a Friday afternoon. Well? What is it?'

Hilary saw the colour rise in Maddy's cheeks. She lifted her head from her hand, aware that this was an important moment that nothing else must be allowed to blight. 'Yes, come on,' she said. 'Tell us.'

Stephen reached across and took Maddy's hand. He looked self-conscious, but there was a grin of delight playing at the corners of his mouth as he said, 'Maddy and I are engaged.'

Even though Hilary had been half expecting it, the words still came as a surprise. To her father, she could see that they came as a complete shock. He stared at the pair of them, his eyebrows almost lost in his mane of silver hair, and for a second or two, Hilary feared he might be going to have another heart attack from sheer astonishment. For a moment he stuttered, then he said, *'Engaged? To be married,* you mean?'

'Well, I don't know any other sort of engagement,' Stephen said, his grin breaking out.

'But – but I thought...' The old man's gaze rested on Maddy's face. 'It's barely a year since...'

'Since Sammy died,' she said quietly. 'I know. But it doesn't make any difference, Colonel Napier. I love Stephen and I know he loves me. It doesn't stop me loving Sammy – or the memory of him. I thought myself it was too soon – but it doesn't seem to be, after all. That's all I can say.'

'I hope you'll give us your blessing, Dad,' Stephen said, and Gilbert seemed to shake himself.

'Blessing? Of course I do! Always fond of the little girl, ever since she used to come here as a scrap with Fenella, to stay with your mother. Only too pleased to welcome her into the family. Come here, my dear, and give your future father-in-law a kiss.' Maddy did so, blushing, and he leaned over to shake his son's hand. 'Hilary! What in the devil's name are you thinking of? Why aren't you doing something about champagne?'

'Well, give me a chance,' she protested, laughing, and got up to take Maddy into her arms. 'I'm really, really pleased for you both. And Stella will be too. It might almost bring her out of this awful depression she's got into.' She smiled at her brother. 'Well done, Steve. It's time we had a bit of good news around here. And I'll go and see about the champagne straight away.'

'No – wait.' Her father called her back as she set off toward the door. 'There's something I want to say first.' She went back to her chair a little slowly, wondering if he was going to tell Stephen now about the change to his will.

As she half expected, he began, 'I've been thinking about the estate. Lot of money tied up in it, money it seems to me you youngsters could do with. I know you don't want the estate, Stephen, and I've come to terms with that. I know there's a chance young Rob will never want to run it either. Hilary's making a good fist of that, and she's drawing the proper rate of pay for doing it. But I don't want her thinking she's just an employee – a sort of glorified manager.' He glanced at her, and she tried hastily to mask the astonishment she knew must be on her face. 'I've had a talk with Travis and we agree that the estate could manage pretty well without one of the farms. Abe Endacott, over to Sampford, has been asking for a while now if he could buy, and I've decided to let him have it. The money will be shared between the pair of you.'

If anyone had dropped a pin then, even on the thick Turkish carpet in front of the fire, Hilary thought, it would have deafened them. She stared at her father, then at her brother and Maddy. Gilbert watched them, smiling to himself, taking some amusement from their reaction to the bombshell he had just dropped. At last, Hilary found her voice.

'But when did you decide all this? When did you and Travis have these talks?'

'While you were in London, of course,' he replied, and she felt her face colour, realising that she was not the only one to have had secrets during those clandestine visits. 'I've had a bit of time to think since I've been laid up,' he went on, 'and it seems to me I've not always been entirely fair to either of you. Want to make amends a bit, that's all.' He waved a dismissive hand, but

416

Hilary was not to be so easily deflected.

'But can we really afford it? A whole farm?'

'It's only the rent we'll be losing,' he reminded her. 'And the maintenance – Abe can take it over himself now. He's a good man, he'll look after it.'

'But the estate – you've always been so against splitting it up.'

'And I'm not splitting it up now. It's one farm, that's all, the furthest one away – probably ought never to have been part of Burracombe in the first place. You're not saying no to the money, are you, Hilary? Stephen?'

'Well – no,' she said uncertainly, not fully realising yet what this could mean to her. 'But–'

Stephen broke in. 'I'm certainly not saying no! It's very generous of you, Dad, and I appreciate it. We both do,' he added, turning to Maddy. 'It'll help us set up our own business when I leave the RAF.'

Gilbert shrugged. 'Call it a wedding present, then.'

'Wedding!' Hilary remembered why she was standing at the door, on her way to fetch champagne. 'We need to talk about that, too. When is it going to be?'

'Probably not until I'm out of the Service,' Stephen said. 'And that's another thing – we don't want our engagement talked about yet. We don't want it official at all. It's just between us – and Stella and Felix, of course. We need time to get used to it ourselves before we tell anyone else.'

'Of course.' Hilary glanced at Maddy's face, understanding that the girl felt she ought to let at

417

least a few more months go by until she was sure she had recovered from Sammy's death. 'But we can still have champagne now?'

'Oh yes!' Stephen said with a laugh. 'We can certainly have champagne now! I never pass up a chance for a celebration.'

Hilary laughed and went out, closing the door behind her and feeling lighter of heart than she had felt for months. Some things do go right, after all, she thought, and turned towards the cellar door.

A celebration would do them all good.

Chapter Thirty-Four

Maddy and Stephen went to see Stella the next morning, having managed to 'wangle' (Stephen's word) special permission to visit before he had to return to the airbase. They were there by nine thirty, causing some consternation amongst the nursing staff, who were busy with their morning tasks, but the ward sister allowed them in, her mouth tight with disapproval, and pulled the curtains around Stella's bed, more to give the other patients privacy than for their own benefit.

'We've got some news for you,' Maddy said, smiling, and Stella nodded.

'I can see what it is. I'm really pleased.' She sounded it too, although her face was still wan. 'It's good to know you're finally settled. Give me a kiss.'

Maddy bent over her and for a few minutes they chatted about their plans. 'Well, we haven't really got any yet. We don't want to announce it for a while – not until you're out of here, anyway. We want a proper celebration, with you and Felix both there.' Maddy glanced at her sister when she said this, but Stella's face gave nothing away. 'And it's happened so suddenly – we want time to get used to it ourselves before we make it official. So it's just between the family for a while.'

Stella nodded, and Maddy waited for a moment, then continued, 'We've told Felix, of course. We went over to see him yesterday evening.'

'Felix? Why did you tell him?'

'Because he's family, of course,' Maddy said with a little frown. 'Of course we told him.'

Stella looked at her. 'Oh, come on, Maddy. I'm sure he told you that our engagement's off.'

There was a brief silence. Then Maddy said, 'He told us you wanted to call it off, yes. But *he* doesn't consider it's off.'

'Then he should,' Stella said sharply. 'I made it perfectly clear. Maddy, please don't you start trying to persuade me as well. I had Hilary in here yesterday afternoon, telling me I was being unkind and cruel to him. Unkind and cruel – to *Felix*. As if I could ever be that.' Her voice shook. 'I love him. That's why I'm letting him go. I can't tie him down to the sort of wreck I'm going to be for the rest of my life. And nothing, nobody, is going to change my mind about that.' She took in a deep, jagged breath. 'So please stop talking about it. Talk about yourselves. Where are you

419

going to live? What are you going to do?'

Maddy looked at her in distress. 'Stella...'

'*Please,*' Stella said. 'Otherwise I shall call Sister and tell her you're upsetting me.'

'Stella!'

'I mean it. Tell me about yourselves. Please, Maddy, give me something nice to think about. You don't know how awful it is to be in here, not knowing what's going to happen to me.'

Maddy looked at her for a moment, then said quietly, 'I think I do, actually. I was in hospital myself for a while, not all that long ago, after Sammy's accident. I didn't know what was going to happen to me, either.'

'I'm sorry,' Stella said. 'I shouldn't have said that. But please tell me what you're planning to do. You must have some idea.'

'Well...' Maddy glanced at Stephen. 'You know Stephen's always wanted to go to Canada and start up an air freight business...'

'You're not going to emigrate!'

'It's one idea, yes. Why shouldn't we?'

Stella didn't answer. She bit her lip and lowered her eyes. Maddy gazed at her uncertainly, and Stephen said, 'It is just one idea, Stella. We might do something in this country. I'm going to look into the possibilities of starting up something here.'

'Something to do with flying?'

'Yes. I love it and I'm a good pilot. Can't let it go to waste.'

'Round here?'

'Well, I don't know,' he said. 'It all depends on where it would be needed. Anyway, there's plenty of time to think about all that.'

Stella looked up and gripped Maddy's hand. 'I don't want you to go too far away. You're all I've got.'

'No, I'm not,' Maddy said. 'You've got Felix. You've got a life ahead of you, as his wife. You know you have.'

Stella dropped her hand as if it had burned her. 'Don't start that again – please.'

'I'm sorry,' Maddy said tightly, 'but I *am* going to start it again. You've got to think again about this, Stella. You can't throw away everything you had with Felix because of something that may not happen anyway. You don't *know* you're not going to be able to walk again. You don't *know* you'll never be able to have children. Nobody's said so. It's something you've thought of yourself and brooded over so much you think it's true. And you'll *make* it come true, because you've given up trying. You're just going to lie there and let your life waste away because you won't even *try*.'

'That's not true! You don't know what it's like!'

'Maybe not,' Maddy said. 'But I know what it's like to feel sorry for myself.'

'What do you mean?'

'Have you forgotten what I've been like this past year?' Maddy asked. 'How selfish I was, thinking only about myself and what I'd lost? Have you forgotten all that?'

'You'd lost Sammy. It was natural.'

'It was natural to grieve for him, yes, and maybe it was natural to feel sorry for myself – a bit. But I went on and on with it, didn't I? I started to think

421

I was the only one something awful had happened to. I used to go and see Ruth and Dan, who had also lost Sammy, but I wasn't going to comfort them, I wanted *them* to comfort *me*. I got so selfish in the end that I even hated them for having another baby.'

'I don't think you could be blamed for–'

'Well I do, and so did Felix. If you remember, Stella, it was Felix who got me out of it. He told me a few home truths, and they made me think at last. I saw what I was doing, to myself and to everyone else, and I realised what a nasty, selfish little bitch I was turning into.'

'*Maddy!*'

'I was,' she said, ignoring Stella's shock and Stephen's glance of astonishment. 'Nasty and selfish. That's what feeling sorry for yourself can do, if you let it go on too long.'

'Is that what you think I'm doing?' Stella asked, her voice mutinous.

'Partly, yes.' Maddy's voice softened and she leaned towards her sister and took her hand again. 'Darling, I'm not saying you haven't been through an awful time and I'm not saying it's going to be easy now. But you do have a good man who loves you and wants you, whether you can walk or not. It's going to break his heart if you send him away. I saw him last night, Stella. His heart's breaking already.'

There was a long silence. Stella turned her head away. Maddy and Stephen gripped each other's hands tightly as they saw a damp patch forming on her pillow. She drew in a deep, shuddering sigh.

'I don't know, Maddy,' she whispered at last. 'I

don't know what to do...'

'Then don't do anything,' Maddy advised. 'Don't make any huge decisions until you're a lot, lot stronger and the doctors know more about what's likely to happen. Let Felix come back. Remember what he did for me – what you both did – and let him help you as well. And there's another thing.' She paused, and Stella turned her head at last to look up at her. 'I thought you were going to give me a brother. Stephen hasn't got one now, so if you don't marry Felix I shall never have one, and if you ask me that's *just not fair!*' Her voice rose in a parody of a little girl's petulance, and Stella laughed in spite of herself.

'You sound just like you used to when you couldn't get your way as a child, Maddy.' She turned her eyes to Stephen. 'I hope you know what you're taking on.'

'I think I do,' he said, folding his hand more closely around Maddy's. 'But I hope she'll continue to surprise me, as well. That's what makes life fun.'

'Fun?' Stella said. 'I've almost forgotten what fun is.' Then she caught herself up and gave them both a wry glance. 'There I go again – being sorry for myself.' Her voice shook. 'I'm not sure I'm going to be able to do this, Maddy.'

'You will. I know you will. You're a strong person, Stella. You always have been. My big sister, looking after me in the air raids over Portsmouth – remember? Taking care of me in that tiny little Anderson shelter, when Mummy was having Thomas and there was nobody but that nice man from April Grove to help her. What was his name?'

'Mr Vickers. Tommy Vickers. That's why we called the baby Thomas.' They were both quiet for a while, thinking of those terrible months when Portsmouth was bombed over and over again, and that last dreadful night when both their mother and baby Thomas were killed. 'We've been through a lot together, when you come to think about it,' Stella said quietly. 'Even losing each other for all those years when we were sent to different orphanages. I shall never understand that.'

'Nor me. But we found each other again, in Burracombe. That's our home now. Even if Steve and I do go to Canada, we'll always come back to Burracombe. And you'll be there too, Stella – married to Felix. Won't you?'

She looked intently into her sister's eyes, but Stella turned away again and Maddy's heart sank a little. That was too soon, she thought. I've gone too quickly for her.

'I don't know,' Stella said at last. 'I really don't know, Maddy. All I can say is – perhaps.' She looked up into their anxious faces. 'I'll think about what you've said. I'll try to stop feeling sorry for myself. I know there are people here worse off than myself, so I'll try to think about them instead. And I'll think about Felix, too. I do love him, you know. I really do love him.' And her voice wobbled as the tears came again, quiet, healing tears that were without self-pity but were a release from the torment that had been building inside her for so long.

Maddy glanced at Stephen and said, 'I think we ought to go now.' She bent and kissed Stella's wet cheek. 'I'll come again tomorrow, darling. I'll ask Felix to bring me, shall I?'

'If you like.' And then, more positively, 'Yes, please. Ask Felix to bring you. I – I might want to talk to him.'

They left the ward and walked back through the corridors without speaking. As they reached the main door, Stephen said, 'What do you think?'

'I don't know,' Maddy said. 'It's hard to tell. She seemed as if she might be coming round, but – I don't know. Stella can be very strong-minded and hard to shift once she's made up her mind.' She turned to look at him. 'I suppose we'll just have to wait and see.'

Maddy returned to the Barton at lunchtime. Stephen had dropped her at the railway station in Plymouth and she'd come back by train, walking up from the little halt. She told Hilary about her talk with Stella, drank the soup Mrs Ellis had prepared, and chatted to the Colonel. But Hilary had a feeling that they were doing little more than going through the motions, and when lunch was over, she caught Maddy in the hall and asked if there were anything more to tell.

'Not really,' Maddy said, putting on her coat. 'To be honest, Hilary, I don't know whether I had any effect at all. There were moments when she seemed to take it in, and others when she seemed just as determined as ever to give Felix up. All I can say is, she's willing to see him tomorrow – but

I wouldn't hold out any hope that it's going to be good news.'

'Are you going over to see him now?'

'I will, later on. He asked me to come to supper this evening – you don't mind, do you? But I'm going to the Tozers now, to see Russ. I have to tell him about me and Stephen.'

Hilary looked at her. 'Yes, I suppose you do. But that means more people knowing, and you wanted to keep it quiet for a while.'

Maddy gave a rueful shrug. 'In a village like Burracombe, that's like asking for the moon! I ought to tell Dottie as well – she was the only family I had for a long time, and if she's going to America soon, it will probably come out while she's away, and she'd be terribly hurt if she hadn't been told. I don't suppose any of them will deliberately let it out, but you know what the village grapevine's like – nobody has to say a word, yet everyone knows your business even before you do yourself. Look at what happened to Travis and Jennifer.'

Hilary smiled. Travis Kellaway had taken Jennifer into Tavistock to buy an engagement ring one Saturday morning, and by the time they arrived home, the village not only knew all about it but had decided on the date of the wedding – which just happened to be the date Travis and Jennifer had agreed upon anyway. Jacob Prout, who ought to have been the first to be told, had been bitterly hurt to find it out in the village shop, and it had taken Jennifer all her best efforts at persuasion to convince him that he hadn't been deliberately left out.

'Well, let them wonder for a while,' she said. 'But I agree you've got to tell Dottie.'

Maddy walked down the drive and along the lane to the farm track. She could see Luke Ferris going through the gate that led through the woods to the old charcoal burner's hut where he had lived for some time, working at his paintings, and Norman Tozer getting the cows in for afternoon milking. The Standing Stones looked grey and forbidding on the horizon and the moors were bleak and colourless under the dull, leaden sky. The air had turned cold, a biting wind nipping at her cheeks, and she wondered if more snow might be on the way. I hope it doesn't stop Stephen getting here tomorrow, she thought anxiously. She could always go back to West Lyme by train, of course, but she wanted to see him. It was curious how, now that she had finally admitted her feelings for him, she was missing him all the time they were apart. Or maybe she always had missed him, and had never been able to admit it before.

Russ Tozer was in the yard when she arrived at the gate. He turned and looked at her, surprise mingling with pleasure on his face. 'Well, you're a sight for sore eyes! Come on in.'

'Not just yet,' she said. 'I want to talk to you first, on our own.'

His glance sharpened and he took her arm. 'Shall we go for a walk? It's a little muddy.'

'I don't mind. Let's go through the copse.' They crossed a field and went into the little wood where willow trees had once been pollarded for basket-making. Ted still harvested some each year, for Aggie Madge and one or two other women who kept the old tradition alive and sold their baskets in Tavistock market now and then, but in the main, the trees had sprouted long twigs from their stumps and the copse was turning into a thicket, with just one or two clear paths through.

Russ and Maddy walked a little way in silence, then he said, 'Have you thought any more about coming over to the States with me and Dad? Only it's getting a little late to arrange tickets.'

Maddy stopped and faced him. 'Yes, I have thought about it. I'm sorry, Russ – I won't be coming. It was a lovely idea and I'm grateful to you for asking me, but I can't.'

He looked down at her gravely. 'Any particular reason?'

'Yes.' She looked up into his eyes. 'It's a secret at the moment – I don't want everyone to know – but I'm going to marry Stephen Napier.'

His expression flickered, but for a moment or two he didn't speak. Then he said, 'I thought that might be it. We didn't see much of you over Christmas, so I thought you were probably too tied up with him.'

'Not just him. There was Stella, too. Russ, I really am grateful for all you've done for me – for us all. It's been a dreadful time and I don't know what we'd have done without you and your father. You've been really kind to us.'

'We did what we could,' he said. 'And I've got to admit, I hoped it might bring you and me closer together.'

'It did.' She looked at him seriously. 'I'm very

fond of you, Russ. I really am. But Stephen's waited for me for a long time, and I know now that I do love him.'

Russ nodded. 'Then there's nothing more to say. Except to wish you the best luck in the world, Maddy.' He took her gently in his arms. 'Have you got a kiss for a friend?'

'Yes. Of course I have.' She lifted her face to his and they kissed. Then she said, 'You may see us over there sometime anyway, if Stephen starts his air freight business in Canada. You're not far from the border, are you?'

Russ laughed. 'No, but Canada's a mighty big place. I'll look forward to it all the same. But wherever you go, I guess we'll meet up again sometime. And we'll keep in touch. This isn't goodbye, is it, Maddy?'

'No,' she said, 'I don't think it is.'

They linked arms and walked on through the little wood and across the fields, coming out at the top of the village, where they wandered back towards Dottie's cottage. A wreath of smoke curled up from the chimney and Maddy stopped at the gate.

'Are you coming in too?'

Russ shook his head. 'No, you go on your own and have a good old chinwag. We'll be away by the end of next week and you might not get another chance. Have to say, I'm rather looking forward to seeing Dottie in America!'

He laughed and swung away up the darkening village street. Maddy watched him go, feeling a little sad. She knew that she had done the right thing in not going to America with him, but there was nevertheless a small pang at giving up what could have been a whole new life. She would never know, now, just what might have been...

Russ disappeared in the twilight and she turned to open the gate and go up the familiar path to the cottage that had once been her home.

'Marrying Stephen?' Dottie exclaimed. 'My stars! You do spring some surprises, don't you!'

'It surprised me a bit too,' Maddy admitted, laughing. 'And I don't think Stephen quite believes it yet.'

'Well, I *am* pleased. The two of you are made for each other. Mind you, I did think you and young Russell...'

'I know. I feel rather bad about Russ. He was so good to me when Stella had her accident. But I've just told him, and he doesn't seem too heartbroken.'

'He'd have made you a good husband,' Dottie said, 'but there, if it's not to be, it's not to be. You must go where your own heart takes you, and young Stephen Napier's improved a lot in the last year or so. I'd not have given you a ha'penny for him a while ago!'

'And what about you?' Maddy asked, sipping the tea Dottie had put in front of her. 'Off to America with your own fancy man!'

Dottie turned a little pink. 'Now, there's no call for that sort of language. Joe and me are good friends, that's all.'

'Just good friends?' Maddy asked wickedly. 'That's not what I've been hearing.'

430

'Then you'm listening to the wrong sort of talk. Not that we weren't a little bit more than friends, years ago,' she admitted with a sidelong glance. 'But that was all over before he went off to America, and it's not likely to start up again at our age. This is just a holiday, that's all, so that I can meet his girls and their families. A bit of a swansong.'

Maddy reached over and patted her hand. 'I don't mind what it is, Dottie. You don't have to justify it to me, nor to anyone else. I'm just pleased you're going, and I hope you have a lovely time.'

'I'm not sure I ought to be going, though,' Dottie worried. 'Not with poor Stella still lying in hospital and not knowing what's to happen. And Felix breaking his heart because she's saying she won't marry him.'

'I know,' Maddy said soberly. 'But I had a talk with her this morning, and I'm hoping she'll change her mind. I think she's just depressed. I don't think she really means it.'

'I hope not. It would be good to be able to go off next weekend knowing that her'd come round and they were making plans for the wedding again. Though dear knows when that'll be now. It should have been today – January the ninth – did you realise that?'

'Yes, I did. It's very sad, Dottie, but you can't let it spoil your plans too. You go off and have a lovely holiday in America, and I'm sure that by the time you come back, the wedding will be on again and you'll be working like a madwoman trying to get the dresses finished in time. You've

431

nearly done Stella's, haven't you?'

'I have, but I haven't touched it since the accident – didn't have the heart for it. It won't take me long to put the last touches to it. I hope you'm right, Maddy, and that's what I'll come home to. And now tell me about your own wedding. A proper smart affair that'll be, won't it? You'll get married from the Barton, I suppose?'

Maddy stared at her. 'No, I won't, Dottie. Of course not. I'll get married from here. This was my home after Fenella adopted me, and I still think of it as home. I always will. And you've been like a second mother to me. So just remember – when the time comes, you're going to need a lovely new outfit for yourself, with a really beautiful hat!'

Chapter Thirty-Five

Felix was trembling when he entered the ward the next afternoon. He'd taken his services that morning almost as if he were in a trance, giving his sermon and leading the prayers with only half his attention. Ashamed, he had prayed for forgiveness, but his prayers for Stella's recovery and for her change of heart had been more intense. He knew, as he walked into the hospital at Maddy's side, that this afternoon would bring Stella's decision, and he was still deeply afraid of what it would be.

432

'You mustn't think that,' Maddy urged him when he told her this as they waited in the corridor for visiting time to start. 'How can she make up her mind so soon? She could change it half a dozen times in as many weeks – as many days.'

He looked at her gloomily. 'That doesn't really help.'

'I know. I'm sorry.' She patted his hand. 'But honestly, isn't it a good sign that she's agreed to see you at all? It's only a few days since she told you to stay away.'

'Perhaps that's what I should have done. Perhaps I should stay away. Maybe I won't go to see her this afternoon, after all.'

'You will,' Maddy said sternly. 'You'll go in and you'll make her see sense, if she's not already seeing it, and I'm going to make sure you do. Honestly, the two of you! Anyone can see you're crazy about each other. It's just silly, if you ask me.'

Felix cast her a bitter glance. 'It's all very well for you to talk. You're happy.'

'And I want you to be happy too.' The ward door opened and the bell rang. 'There. It's time to go in.' She gave him a little push.

'Aren't you coming too?'

'Certainly not. You and Stella have got to do this alone.'

He gave her one last agonised glance, which she returned with a cheerful smile, and walked away like a man going to his doom. Maddy watched, her smile fading, feeling more anxious than she had let him see. Suppose Stella hadn't changed

433

her mind. Suppose he came out feeling worse than when he went in. How would he be able to bear it, and what could she possibly do to help him?

A touch on her shoulder made her turn quickly. 'Stephen! Oh, thank goodness you're here.'

'Has he gone in?'

'Yes, a few minutes ago.' She turned back to watch the door. Other visitors were filing in, some carrying flowers or magazines, others with boxes of chocolates or bags of fruit. Felix had taken nothing. Neither of them had thought of it; they had been too taken up with their anxiety.

'I can't stay long,' Stephen said. 'If I've got to get you to West Lyme and then back to the airfield before my pass runs out. It's only till midnight.'

'I know. Felix knows.'

'How will he get home? Are there any trains this afternoon?'

'I think the last one goes at four, but Hilary said she'd come for him. She's hoping to get here in time to pop in and see Stella for a few minutes too. She would have brought us, but the phone rang just as we were leaving so we said we'd catch the train and see her later.'

Stephen nodded. 'I hope it's good news.'

'What do you mean?'

'Well, she's been rather strange just lately. As if she had something on her mind – not just the estate and Rob and Stella, though they're quite enough, but something different – something she hasn't talked about. Anyway' – he grinned – 'I was too excited about us to worry too much. But

I've thought about it a bit since, and felt a bit guilty at not having taken more interest.'

'I hadn't noticed anything,' Maddy said. 'But I don't really know Hilary all that well.' She looked at the door again. 'I almost wish I'd gone in with Felix!'

'You were right to wait. It's something they've got to sort out for themselves.' He pulled her hand into the crook of his arm and held it there, stroking her fingers. 'Not having any regrets, are you?'

'As if I could!' After a moment, she said, 'I saw Russ yesterday and told him.'

'Oh? And how did he take it?'

'How could he take it? No, he was very nice about it. Said he thought that was the way things would go. I told him we might see him sometime, when we're in Canada.'

Stephen gave a yelp of laughter. 'We're not likely to be on his doorstep!'

'Nearer than here, anyway,' she said. 'And we'll have holidays, won't we? I'd like to see them again, Stephen. They've been such good friends these past weeks.'

'I know.' He stroked her fingers again and she leaned her head on his shoulder as they waited for Felix to emerge.

Hilary got into the car. She was shaking all over and had to press the starter three times before the engine fired. She sat for a moment trying to regain control, knowing that she could not drive until she felt more steady. At last her shaking subsided, and she let in the clutch.

She tried to focus her mind on the drive, through a silent Burracombe and into the cold, leafless lanes. There was nobody about. Probably most people had finished their Sunday roast dinner, done the washing-up, looked out of the window and decided that an afternoon by the fire was preferable to a chilly walk. The nipping breeze of yesterday had increased to a biting wind, and dead leaves were whirling over the road and huddling against the foot of the stone walls. Overhead, the sky was low and threatening, and once or twice she thought she heard hard little pellets of snow strike against the windscreen.

Out on the moor, a few ponies were clustered against the lee of the wall, their rumps turned to the wind, their heads lowered. She thought of the night when Felix had run into the ponies just outside Princetown and Stella had been injured. The moor was a dangerous place at night, its narrow, twisting roads icy and treacherous. If Rob had not run away that weekend and been put on the train by David, if she had not been compelled by her father's heart attack to stay at home so that Felix and Stella had gone to meet him at Exeter, the accident would never have happened.

David…

She forced her mind away from him. You could as easily say that if Rob had not been bullied at school … if her father had not sent him there in the first place … if Marianne hadn't brought her son to England … if Baden had never fallen in love with Marianne and married her before losing his life on the way to Dunkirk...

And if Hitler had never invaded Poland, she told herself impatiently. You could go all the way back to Adam and Eve at this rate. If God had never made serpents... It was ridiculous.

If she could only stop thinking about David.

Determinedly, Hilary stared through the windscreen. There was simply too much to think about at present. Stella and Felix. Maddy and Stephen. Her father, his health a little more worrying with every new setback. The news that he was going to change his will again. John Wolstencroft was coming tomorrow to discuss it, and that meant meals she hadn't considered, maybe even a bed for the night if the weather got worse. Or maybe he wouldn't be able to come at all. And then this latest idea, about the sale of one of the farms. Both Hilary and Stephen had been completely taken aback. Splitting up the estate...

It was only one farm, it was true, but could it be the beginning? What else was in his mind, that he hadn't yet seen fit to mention?

David...

I can't not think about him, she thought desperately. I've spent all my life thinking of other people, and now I can't keep my mind on them any more. He keeps breaking in. And yet I can't *let* myself think of him. It's too much. Everything is just too much...

As Felix approached the bed, he felt as if his legs would give way at any moment. He could see Stella's face turned towards him, her expression giving little away. Yet there was a kind of tremor there, an emotion he couldn't identify, lurking behind her eyes. If it were not for her words the last time he'd seen her, he might have said it was excitement, but that was hardly likely now.

'Hello, darling.' He felt awkward, not knowing whether to kiss her or not. He decided that he would, and bent to touch her lips with his. He felt their softness tremble and a wild desire rose in him, to snatch her up against him, crush her to his chest, pull her from the bed and take her away from this place, where she seemed to have become a different person, where she was no longer his Stella. He fought it down and straightened up again, seeking some reassurance in her eyes.

'Hello, Felix.'

He sat down and took her hand. 'You didn't mind me coming?'

'No. Of course not.'

'I didn't know what to do,' he said desperately. 'I didn't know if you ever wanted to see me again. But I couldn't leave things like that. Stella, darling–'

'Have you seen Maddy?' she asked, cutting across his words.

'Yes. Yes, she and Stephen came over last night. They're here now – at least, Maddy is, Stephen's supposed to be arriving any minute. He's taking her back to West Lyme after she's seen you again.' He was babbling now, saying anything just for the sake of talking, to keep her from saying the words he dreaded most. He faltered to silence, his eyes fixed on hers.

'They're engaged,' she murmured. 'It's good, isn't it? I'm so pleased for them.'

'Yes. I am, too.'

'Maddy wanted a brother,' she said, apparently inconsequentially. 'I never really knew that, did you?'

'No,' he said, bewildered. 'But didn't you have one? The baby brother who died in the air raid?'

'Yes. Thomas. I didn't realise how much she missed him.'

Felix looked at her, wondering what she was thinking, why she had suddenly begun to think about her lost baby brother. He waited, gently stroking her fingers.

'She was reminding me of the things you said to her when she was so upset over Sammy,' Stella went on. 'How you and I both said she was spoiled and selfish.'

'Did I say that?' he asked in astonishment. 'Surely not.'

'As good as, yes. Oh, you were very kind and wise about it, but that's what it boiled down to. I certainly said it, anyway.'

'But why was she talking about that now?'

'She was showing me how selfish I've been,' Stella said calmly. 'And she was right.'

'No!' This time, he did take her in his arms, though very gently. 'Darling, you wouldn't know *how* to be selfish.'

'Anyone can be selfish at times,' she said. 'And I have been. But I didn't mean to be, Felix.' Her voice, so unnaturally calm, broke and sounded more like the Stella he knew. 'I was thinking of you. I didn't want you tied to a crippled wife. I didn't want to spoil your life.'

'You wouldn't be!'

'That's all it was really.' She was clinging to him now, crying. 'The thought of not being with you – not being married to you – it was breaking my heart. That's why I asked you to go away. I just couldn't bear it any longer.'

'Oh, Stella ... Stella...'

She withdrew a little. 'Felix...'

'Don't say any more, darling. Just let me hold you. Just let's be together, quietly by ourselves.'

'No. I must say this.' She leaned back on her pillows and he loosened his hold, keeping his arms about her but looking into her face. 'Two things, really. One is – that I'm sorry I've been so unkind to you. Really sorry. And if you still want me, I'll marry you. But you've got to be really sure, because I was right, you know – nobody knows yet whether I'll ever be able to walk properly.'

'I'm really sure,' he said steadily. 'If you like, I'll propose to you again.' He went down on one knee and held both her hands in his, looking up into her eyes. 'Darling Stella – will you marry me?'

'Before I answer that,' she said, tears already beginning to slide from her eyes, 'I have to tell you something else.' She took a deep breath. 'I was awake all night, thinking about this, and it was early this morning when I realised that Maddy, Hilary, Stephen – all of them – were right. I knew then that I could marry you. And then – it was like a miracle, Felix – it happened.'

'What?' he asked. 'What happened?'

'I felt a tiny twinge of pain,' she said. 'In my toe. My big toe, on my right foot. *I felt it, Felix.* I felt my toe throb...'

His heart leaped. 'You felt your toe? But that means – it means there's no paralysis. You'll get your feeling back. You'll be able to walk again!'

'No. It doesn't mean that – not quite. I told the doctor, and he said it's a good sign but we've still got to be patient. I might never be able to walk well, but with care and perhaps more treatment and a lot of hard work, I might learn again.' She sank back on the pillows and now, at last, she was smiling at him, the sweet, open smile that he loved, that began at her mouth and spread over her whole face, wrinkling her nose and then crinkling the corners of her eyes. 'So the answer is – yes please, Felix, I will marry you. And I'll do my best, my very, *very* best, to walk up the aisle to do it!'

There was just time for Maddy, Stephen and Hilary to gather round Stella's bed to hear the good news, kiss them both and congratulate them before visiting time was over and the ward sister rang the bell and ushered them sternly out. Felix lingered for one last kiss, and the others waited in the corridor, laughing with relief.

'How about you, sis?' Stephen asked Hilary. 'Are you OK? Your phone call wasn't bad news, was it?'

Hilary looked at him. For a few moments, unbelievable though it seemed, she had almost forgotten David's call. Now it came pushing its way back into her mind and she remembered every detail with perfect clarity. His voice – his dear, familiar voice – sounding so strange, as if he were being strangled. The words that he'd had to repeat several times, before she could take them in.

'Darling,' he'd said. 'Is that you?'

'David!' Her shock had been so great that her legs trembled and her knees almost gave way. She sank quickly on to the telephone seat. 'David, why are you ringing? What's happened?'

'It's Sybil,' he said abruptly. 'Hilary, she – she's...'

'What?' Her voice was sharp with anxiety. 'What's she done? What has Sybil done?'

'She hasn't done anything.' His voice was unbelieving. 'She's had a stroke. Hilary – *Sybil's had a stroke...*'

A stroke, she thought now, still struggling to take in the meaning of the word, and what it meant to herself and David. A serious one, surely, or David would not have telephoned. But just how serious?

'We won't know how bad it is yet,' he'd told her, his voice shaking. 'We don't know just what it will mean. But I had to tell you. I thought you had to know.'

And now, with the anxiety over Stella eased at last, the full impact rushed upon her. Sybil had had a stroke. She might even die – perhaps, she thought with a shock, she had died already, since David's phone call.

Or she could herself be paralysed. Helpless. Bedridden – perhaps for years. And utterly dependent upon her husband.

Whatever happened, Hilary knew that the coming months were going to bring decisions and, perhaps, heartbreak such as she had never been compelled to face before.

443

The publishers hope that this book has given you enjoyable reading. Large Print Books are especially designed to be as easy to see and hold as possible. If you wish a complete list of our books please ask at your local library or write directly to:

Magna Large Print Books
Magna House, Long Preston,
Skipton, North Yorkshire.
BD23 4ND

This Large Print Book for the partially sighted, who cannot read normal print, is published under the auspices of

THE ULVERSCROFT FOUNDATION

THE ULVERSCROFT FOUNDATION

... we hope that you have enjoyed this Large Print Book. Please think for a moment about those people who have worse eyesight problems than you ... and are unable to even read or enjoy Large Print, without great difficulty.

You can help them by sending a donation, large or small to:

**The Ulverscroft Foundation,
1, The Green, Bradgate Road,
Anstey, Leicestershire, LE7 7FU,
England.**
or request a copy of our brochure for more details.

The Foundation will use all your help to assist those people who are handicapped by various sight problems and need special attention.

Thank you very much for your help.